EMPOWERED

Ignite God's Vision for Your Life with a Kingdom Mindset

Natalie Masucci

Dedication

To my beloved family, my rock and constant support: Nino, my husband, whose unwavering belief in me and support has propelled me to soar higher than I ever thought possible; Thomas, my son, whose presence adds strength to my wings and emboldens me to embrace the unknown: and Monica, my daughter, whose encouragement fuels my ambition and inspires me to break new boundaries. You are the foundation of my success.

May you all embrace the Kingdom Mindset, unlocking the limitless possibilities God has in store for you, and may His success strategies guide you to victory in every aspect of your lives.

I would also like to express my heartfelt appreciation to those who have played influential roles in my journey. To my mother, Maria Stefanutti, your continuous prayers and support have been an invaluable source of motivation. And to Principal Franco Troiani, your encouragement and embodiment of a growth mindset empowered me to follow my passion of helping people and become an author.

Thank you all for touching my life in such positive ways. This book is a testament to the transformative power of God's love.

Contents

Introduction

On my way home from work in 2019, I had an encounter with God unlike any I have ever had before or since. I remember singing along with the radio as I drove home from school. As I parked the car in the garage, the presence of the Lord engulfed the garage and my car, almost as if a warm blanket had been placed on me. I became frozen, unable to move. The Holy Spirit began speaking to me and downloading new revelations about His kingdom mindset at lightning speed. He connected the dots to things I had never heard or thought of before. Although it felt like I was there for a long time, I believe it was only about half an hour of receiving divine impartation and revelation. It was truly amazing!

When the encounter ended, and I entered the house, my husband immediately noticed something different about me and asked, "What happened?" I was still in the Lord's presence, still feeling the anointing. My face must have been glowing, much like Moses's after his burning bush encounter with God.

I believe the Holy Spirit prompted me to share these new revelations about God's mindset with the Church, which is why I wrote this book. Understanding how God thinks and operates, and actively cooperating with Him, has the potential to completely revolutionize your life. God desires His children to thrive and excel in the specific areas where they have been positioned. He longs for us to experience victory, fulfil our life assignments, and reclaim territory for His kingdom. This book aims to inform and equip the body of Christ with God's kingdom mindset and success strategies.

<u>If the world can achieve success in life through positive thinking, the law of attraction, and the power of manifestation,</u> how much more should the children of God be successful by embracing His Kingdom mindset? God's Kingdom mindset is not limited to education but applicable in business, finance, law, medicine, entertainment, and every other sphere. His success strategies are effective for everyone, regardless of age, gender, or socio-economic status. Success is not a coincidence; it is a deliberate choice. Fulfilling your life assignment is of utmost importance. To achieve maximum impact and success, you need to adopt God's mindset.

Now, the question is: Do you know how to walk alongside God? Are you presently walking with God? In other words, are you embracing His kingdom mindset and implementing His success strategies in your life? Perhaps, like many individuals, you find yourself walking away from God. Many of us spend our lives avoiding God due to the belief that He is angry with us or because He appears distant. We run away from our purpose because we feel unqualified and fearful. We create distance between ourselves and God by embracing falsehoods and adopting the wrong mindset.

But what does it mean to run with God? How can we run alongside Him? Running with God involves embracing His kingdom mindset and using His criteria for success to live the victorious life that God has planned for us. <u>You see, you were created for a purpose. You have a race to run or an assignment to fulfil during your lifetime.</u> God is relying on you. He wants you to run with Him not only to reach the finish line but also to emerge as a winner. Running with God means pursuing your race in a manner that leads to victory. This book will guide you in rewiring your mind to align with God's perspective and activate the switch for success and victory in your life. You were created not just to survive but to thrive. You were designed to overcome and make a difference until Jesus returns.

Did you know that you have the ability to train yourself to think differently? You can change the internal dialogue in your mind and shift your perspective. In fact, God expects you to do so. He wants you to transform the way you think and alter certain habitual behaviours to experience greater success and victory in life. You can train your mind to adopt God's kingdom mindset. As Romans 12:2 says, *"Do not conform any longer to the pattern of this world, but be transformed by the renewing of your mind."* This book will teach you how to renew your mind and adopt God's kingdom mindset.

Allow God to be the editor of your life's story by embracing His mindset. With the help of the Holy Spirit, you will be able to turn the page and embark on the next chapter of your life's journey. Are you feeling stuck? Have you experienced setbacks or felt like a train wreck? Are you running low on fuel? Perhaps you're unsure of how to transition to the next chapter in your life. Do you understand the season you're currently in? Recognizing when a season or chapter is ending is crucial so that we can embrace the new things that God wants to do in our lives.

I will share my story of redemption and restoration with you and provide you with a step-by-step strategy to align your thinking with God's way of thinking.

Chapter One

The Untapped Power of our Thoughts

Our brains are remarkable computers capable of extraordinary feats. Our thinking is a powerful force that shapes our mindset. Therefore, it is crucial to consider what we think about. The way we think, whether positively or negatively, ultimately determines our life outcomes. Our behaviour is rooted in unspoken beliefs, which are derived from dominant thoughts and attitudes. **What we focus on the most, we can manifest. Our prominent thoughts shape our reality.** This concept is known as the Law of Attraction. <u>God is the creator of the Law of Attraction found in Proverbs 23:7.</u> It is one of the many laws that have been established in the world. God's Law of Attraction goes beyond using your thoughts to attract the things you desire, shaping your ideal future. It is not merely a New Age approach to manifesting dreams, but rather a timeless law of God, inherent in His very mindset, that brings about success in all aspects of life and empowers you to fulfil your life's purpose.

Do you desire success? To achieve success in life, it is essential to understand and align with God's laws and His way of thinking. **This book will provide you with insights into God's ultimate success strategy: His Kingdom mindset.** You will gain knowledge of how God operates and how He desires you to operate as well. Our minds are fashioned after God (1 Corinthians 2:16). Our brains possess the remarkable capacity to accomplish extraordinary feats. Mindsets serve as mental frameworks consisting of ideas and belief systems that aid us in adapting and functioning in the world. Mindsets assist us in navigating life, particularly during complex and challenging circumstances, and they can even provide us with a broader perspective. **God's mindset serves as an empowering tool for His children.**

Erroneous thinking and negative mindsets hinder us from fulfilling our purpose and experiencing victory in life. Our beliefs play a crucial role in determining our outcomes; therefore, it is important to evaluate them, as they may be holding us back. Your thoughts and mindset could potentially undermine your future. Consider the origins of your beliefs:

are they influenced by your culture, upbringing, and society, past experiences, traditions, or social media?

"Thoughts are real, physical things that occupy mental real estate. Moment by moment, every day, you are changing the structure of your brain through your thinking."

— Dr. C. Leaf

Jesus is our role model. He came to Earth with a specific purpose, and everything he did and said was aligned with fulfilling that purpose. *John 5:19 Jesus replied, "Truly truly, I tell you, the Son can do nothing of his own accord, but only what he sees the Father doing, because whatever the Father does, the Son also does."* Jesus embodied God's mindset. He was focused and intentional about completing his purpose.

Jesus came so that you and I could experience an abundant life (John 10:10). He desires for us to be blessed and be a blessing to others. He wants us to reach the highest level of influence in the seven mountains of this world, enabling us to bring about positive change in our respective spheres of influence. These areas include family, religion, education, media, entertainment, business, and government. Jesus desires our success and encourages us to adopt His mindset and employ His strategies for victorious living in this life.

That's why the devil opposes you in the realm of mindset, self-improvement, and change. Why? Because the devil understands that if you're not actively pursuing change, you're essentially choosing to remain stagnant. He wants you to settle for mediocrity, to embrace the status quo, and to cling to what is safe, convenient, and comfortable. The devil employs two major lies to deceive you. First, he convinces you that you are incapable of change, and second, he convinces you that you don't need to change. These two falsehoods keep you trapped in a wrong mindset, hindering your progress in fulfilling your purpose. It is essential for us to learn to recognize and identify these lies.

Lie #1 you cannot change.
"I can't help it; it's the way I am!"
"I am who I am; I cannot change."
"It's not me; it's just the situation I'm in.
"It is what it is."
"I don't have enough time or strength."
"I'm too old."
"I'm not smart enough."

Lie #2 you don't have to change.
"I'm fine; I'm happy the way I am."
"I have enough; I don't need anything more".
"This is my lot in life."

The statements above exemplify limiting beliefs, often referred to as lies from the devil, which you may have embraced as truths. They stem from a fixed mindset, whether consciously or unconsciously, and our brains perceive them as absolute truths. However, they are not. These beliefs can be overcome and replaced. By engaging in the process of renewing your mind, which involves resisting, eliminating, and replacing such beliefs, you can become a version of yourself that you never thought possible. You have the potential to become the person that God intended you to be. You have the ability to transform yourself and your life. God desires for us to experience continual change, growth, and maturation throughout our journey in life. To develop into the individuals God created us to be, we must transition from a fixed mindset to a growth mindset. God wants us to embrace a mindset of growth.

Change is a constant reality with God. He is always bringing forth something new (Isaiah 43:19), and He anticipates that we will undergo ongoing transformation and growth, becoming the individuals He designed us to be.

Through this book, I aim to assist you in recognizing the presence of limiting beliefs that may have gone unnoticed. By identifying and replacing these beliefs, you will be empowered to pursue your purpose, dreams, and goals. This process will bring clarity to your vision, enabling you to understand your purpose more clearly. Often, people struggle to see clearly due to the influence of the world's lies that cloud their perception. Satan's lies can obstruct our vision. To effectively pursue your purpose, it is crucial to eliminate limiting beliefs, which are lies from the enemy presented in the form of a fixed mindset. These beliefs are designed to hinder your progress, distract you, and derail you from your path.

A growth mindset acknowledges that your abilities can develop to align with your dreams. Your abilities have the potential to grow. <u>God's mindset goes even further by recognizing that He has planted seeds of greatness within you.</u> These seeds, which represent your talents and abilities, are intended to flourish and not remain dormant. **With God, everything has the capacity to grow.** The entirety of the gospel is built upon the principle of seedtime and harvest. Your dreams and goals are not too big; rather, it is your faith that may be too small. God does not want you to diminish your dreams but rather to expand your faith. He desires for you to grow into the fulfilment of your dreams.

To transition to God's mindset, it is necessary to recognize our past errors and engage in repentance. Repentance entails more than simply feeling remorse for our actions or mistakes. It involves making a commitment to personal transformation and embracing a new perspective. God desires for us to acknowledge that we have unintentionally adopted a wrong mindset and to then shift our mindset to align with His.

Mindset holds great significance because what we believe about ourselves shapes our actions. If we have a belief that we are capable of achieving something, we are more likely to pursue it. Conversely, if we believe we cannot succeed, we may not even attempt it. God understands the workings of our minds and desires the best for us. Embracing a growth mindset enables us to dream big, cultivate our faith, and ultimately fulfil our divine destiny.

"If you aim at nothing, you will hit it every time."
—Zig Ziglar

"It's better to aim high and miss than to aim low and hit."
—Les Brown

How do we free ourselves from limiting beliefs and wrong mindsets? Follow the 5 R's:
1. Recognize
2. Repent
3. Resist
4. Replace
5. Repeat

Recognize limiting beliefs and thoughts.
Repent means to feel remorse or regret for past actions and to make a sincere decision to change one's ways, turning away from those actions and committing to live according to a higher moral or spiritual standard.
Resist means refusing to accept limiting thoughts any longer.
Replace means finding a promise or truth from the word of God to think about instead.
You will need to **repeat** this sequence many times to retrain your brain and renew your mind.

Our thoughts, attitudes, and beliefs shape our mindset, which in turn greatly influences our life's outcomes. Our brains have limited capacity, and what occupies the majority of that mental real estate plays a crucial role in determining our trajectory. Therefore, **our mindset determines our success. God is the author of the kingdom mindset. God's kingdom mindset is different in many ways from the growth mindset referred to in education, religious and leadership circles. We will examine these differences in this book. God's kingdom mindset is superior, and His success rate is 100%.**

I desire victory and success in my life. I long to embrace the fullness of everything that God has in store for me. I am determined to fulfil my life assignment, to make a significant impact on the world, and to leave a positive legacy behind. I refuse to allow the enemy to continue stealing from me, and I hope you share the same sentiment. The enemy robs us when he persuades us to adopt a fixed or counterfeit mindset. God desires to liberate us from any incorrect mindsets and limiting thoughts, even those we may not be aware of.

How can we attain this freedom? Firstly, it requires the realization that we have unintentionally embraced counterfeit mindsets. Secondly, it entails genuine <u>repentance</u>. Repentance extends beyond mere remorse for our actions or errors; it entails a commitment to personal transformation. True repentance involves a complete turnaround and a shift in our perspective. God urges us to acknowledge that we have embraced incorrect mindsets and then actively strive to align our mindset with His.

As children of God, we are not bound to be victims of our biology. Our mindset plays a significant role in shaping the quality of our lives, surpassing the influence of our DNA. It is our mind that is intricately designed in the likeness of God. The Bible says that we have the mind of Christ (1 Corinthians 2:16). If we possess the mind of Christ, we have the ability to align our thinking with His. By thinking like God, we gain the capacity to influence and regulate our biology and brain. In this book, you will discover the thought patterns of God and His kingdom mindset—how He thinks and operates. Understanding God's ways enables us to collaborate with Him and attract success in every aspect of our lives.

"What you are is a gift from God bestowed upon you, and what you become is your gift back to God."

The mindset you embrace profoundly influences your personal growth: Speaking for myself, I aspire to leave a lasting legacy for my children, grandchildren, and future generations of my family. How about you? How would you like to be remembered? Personally, I am committed to leaving behind a legacy rooted in utilizing God's kingdom mindset to fulfil my purpose and contribute to the betterment of the world. This book will guide you in understanding that you possess the essence of heaven within you, manifested through God's mindset, which ultimately determines the quality and success of your life.

Just as nothing can destroy iron itself, but only its own rust, similarly, nothing has the power to destroy you; it is solely your mindset that can lead to destruction.

In our exploration, we will delve into the various kinds of thoughts we entertain and the mindsets we have cultivated throughout our lives. It is important to recognize that our mindset can be influenced by factors such as our cultural background, environment, upbringing, socio-economic status, personal experiences, gender, and even the impact of social media. It is through our minds that we make the conscious choice to either reject or embrace the lies propagated by the enemy, as mentioned in James 1:21. [1]

The experiences we have encountered since childhood, along with the perceptions absorbed from our environment, shape the complex programs recorded in our minds, ultimately forming our reality. These mental programs and perceptions are then expressed through our verbal and non-verbal communication, serving as a reflection of our self-perception.

How to check if you have developed a fixed mindset unknowingly

Think of the saying "Good guys finish last" do you agree with this statement? What about "Beggars can't be choosers"? Or "No good deed goes unpunished" Or "Don't get your hopes up." These statements represent incorrect mindsets or beliefs that we have developed and unconsciously adopted. **They are incorrect because they are not in line with the truth of the Word of God.**

Incorrect mindsets act as obstacles that impede our progress in fulfilling our life assignments. The enemy seeks to persuade both you and me that good-hearted individuals are destined to finish last, thereby discouraging us from applying the success strategies outlined in the Bible by God. However, these strategies assure us of victory in our endeavours. By accepting these false assertions, we have fallen prey to

---

[1] *Switch on your brain*- p.22

deception. Deception involves believing falsehoods without recognizing their true nature.

For most of us, the statements above ring true. We have heard these words throughout our entire lives. However, as a child of God, you are not a beggar. Instead, you are a joint heir with Jesus, blessed with a rich inheritance. "Now if we are children, then we are heirs—heirs of God and co-heirs with Christ, if indeed we share in his sufferings in order that we may also share in his glory." Romans 8:17 The enemy seeks to deceive us into believing that acts of kindness will result in punishment rather than blessings. This is a lie. Engaging in good deeds brings blessings, not punishment. According to the law of sowing and reaping established by God, whatever we sow will return to us, both good and evil (Galatians 6:7-10). Therefore, when we perform a good deed, something good is bound to come our way. Some people refer to it as **Karma**. When you do good, it is natural to expect good in return. Believing otherwise is misguided. Just like a farmer who sows seeds and anticipates a harvest, when we sow seeds of goodness by helping others and obeying God, we can expect a bountiful harvest of goodness to come our way.

The enemy wants to deceive us into thinking that we are devoid of choice, but this is unequivocally false. **God has granted us free will**. You possess free will, and it is a constant part of your being. You hold the power to choose, always. "You, my brothers and sisters, were called to be free. But do not use your freedom to indulge the flesh[a]; rather, serve one another humbly in love." Galatians 5:13 Limited thinking leads to a restricted life and limited success. God desires for you to broaden your perspective to encompass His boundless possibilities. God's mindset replaces impossibilities with possibilities. Open your mind to embrace the mindset of God's kingdom and experience limitless potential.

"Impossible is God's starting point."

—Toby Mac

When you possess a God's kingdom mindset, **you can confidently embrace hope** because you recognize that the God of hope resides within you. You have the expectation to learn, grow, evolve, and achieve success. In this book, I will demonstrate that you indeed have a choice. Each day, and multiple times throughout the day, you make choices that influence the trajectory of your life. How we respond to life's events and circumstances carries a tremendous influence on our mental and physical well-being, as well as our overall life outcomes.[2]

***

Reading this book marks a pivotal moment in your life. It is a moment of destiny. Your thoughts, words, and actions following this moment will shape your future success. God desires our prosperity and wants you to discover His kingdom mindset, utilizing it to fulfil your life's purpose. God hopes that you embrace His mindset as you run the race of life, enabling you to emerge victorious. Today, make a decision that sets your destiny in motion.

Every time you make a choice, you are turning the central part of you, the part of you that chooses, into something a little different from what it was before. And taking your life as a whole, with all your innumerable choices, all your life long, you are slowly turning this central thing either into a heavenly creature or into a hellish creature: either into a creature that is in harmony with God, and with other creatures, and with itself, or else into one that is in a state of war and hatred with God, and with its fellow-creatures, and with itself... Each of us, at each moment, is progressing to one state or the other. ~ C. S. Lewis, Mere Christianity

By learning about and embracing God's mindset, you align your life with your heavenly calling and purpose. Following God's will and purpose brings you into harmony with Him. Your choices hold great significance. The small changes you make today will have a profound impact on the future, creating transformative shifts in your life.

Within each of us lies an <u>internal image</u> of who we are and what we are capable of. This image is shaped by the experiences we have encountered since childhood, as well as the perceptions we have absorbed from our environment. Our minds store these intricate programs, ultimately shaping our reality. Our thoughts, words, and actions are influenced by these mental programs and perceptions, serving as a reflection of our self-perception (mindset).

Regrettably, life's challenges and the influence of negative forces have often succeeded in extinguishing the hopes and dreams within us.

---

[2] *Switch on your Brain*- P.20

10

It is not only ourselves who suffer when this happens, but others as well. Each of us possesses unique gifts and blessings from God that are meant to positively impact others. When we fail to reach our full potential, those individuals are deprived of their answered prayers and miracles. The internal image we hold acts as a glass ceiling, limiting what we can accomplish. If we view ourselves as ordinary or insignificant, we will not rise above that perception. However, it is important to remember that God never creates failures or rejects. He does not settle for mediocrity; instead, He instills excellence in His creations. He has plans for each of us that surpass our current circumstances. We were designed for greatness. Why settle for being ordinary when we were meant to be extraordinary? God's mindset shatters the glass ceiling within our minds and propels us to surpass expectations. God desires more for us than we even desire for ourselves. "Now unto him that is able to do exceeding abundantly above all that we ask or think, according to the power that worketh in us" Ephesians 3:20

Whether we are aware of it or not, many of us struggle with a form of **Identity Dysmorphia.** This occurs when the image we hold of ourselves on the inside does not align with the reality of who God created us to be. To heal from this, it is essential to discern what is based on evidence or truth, particularly God's Word, and what is merely perceived. Through introspection, we will learn to scrutinize our thoughts, distinguishing between those rooted in truth and those rooted in deception. This book will guide us in delving deep into the origins of our perceptions and identifying the underlying causes. In many cases, it will require unearthing long-held deceptions that we have mistakenly accepted as truths throughout our lives.

"What thoughts are you allowing to play in the movie theatre of your mind?"
—Natalie Masucci

Due to **Identity Dysmorphia, we tend to underestimate ourselves and fail to see ourselves as God sees us.** In Jeremiah 29:11, it is proclaimed that God has a magnificent plan for our lives, that He has called and appointed us. His plan is not average but extraordinary, with the intention to prosper us. The belief that "old habits die hard" is an example of a misperception or limiting thought, as this book will demonstrate how you can successfully change your habits. Jesus assures us that His yoke is easy and His burden is light (Matthew 11:28-30), indicating that changing our mindset to align with God's will be an achievable and manageable task. It's time to stop underestimating yourself and embrace the truth of who you are in God's eyes.

How we perceive ourselves is indeed of utmost importance. The internal image we hold has a significant impact on our lives. The remarkable aspect is that when we view ourselves as already successful, that perception continues to expand and grow. However, if we believe that we won't achieve much, it becomes a self-fulfilling prophecy.

Whose voice do you value? Whose voice are you listening to?

In Genesis 3:11, God posed a question to Adam and Eve, asking, **"Who told you that you were naked**?" Prior to their sin of consuming the forbidden fruit, they were unaware of their nakedness. God had not informed them, as they were enveloped in His presence and covered by His provision. It was the enemy who deceived them, causing them to recognize their nakedness and subsequently feel shame, leading them to fashion coverings from fig leaves.

What thoughts are you struggling with right now? Who told you them?

I want you to reflect on the earliest occurrence of a thought or idea in your mind. When did that thought first come to you? Can you recall the initial time you felt unworthy, unloved, unqualified, ugly, useless, scared, different, dirty, fat, or any similar emotion? It may be necessary to trace this thought back to your childhood.

I want you to ask yourself some questions.

Questioning is a powerful strategy: God asks questions, and He wants us to do the same. I want you to be mindful of your thoughts. First, consider whether the thought empowers or disables you. A simple rule I follow is that good thoughts originate from God, while bad thoughts come from the enemy. Determine if the thought or belief is aligned with goodness. If it is, then it stems from God.

Next, ask yourself about the sender of the thought. Examine the packaging and manufacturer to identify the source. Can it be found in the Word of God? If not, reject it. Resist it! Remember, you have the power to decide whether to accept or dismiss these thoughts. "Submit yourselves therefore to God. Resist the devil, and he will flee from you." James 4:7 Take control over your thoughts. While you may not control the thoughts that arise, you can choose which ones to entertain.

Lastly, question whether it is worth allowing yourself to think about the thought. Will dwelling on it produce positive or negative outcomes? What will indulging in this thought yield? Consider the potential results before continuing to entertain it.

Learning to control our thoughts is part of God's kingdom mindset: In His Word, God provides guidance on the types of thoughts we should cultivate. He encourages us to immerse ourselves in His empowering teachings and feast on His Word.

"Finally, brothers and sisters, whatsoever things are true, whatsoever things are honest, whatsoever things are just, whatsoever things are pure, whatsoever things are lovely, whatsoever things are of good report; if there be any virtue, and if there be any praise, think on these things." Philippians 4:8

God emphasizes the importance of monitoring our spiritual diet and being selective about the input we allow into our minds. The adage "garbage in, garbage out" holds true here. The quality of our thoughts and subsequent actions is influenced by the quality of the information and influences we absorb.

Our spiritual well-being and success in life are indeed influenced by our **"diet,"** encompassing everything we consume. It is essential to consider **what we have been ingesting**, both in terms of thoughts and influences. Are we consuming junk or healthy food for our minds? **Are toxic thoughts or edifying thoughts dominating our thinking?** Do we possess a fixed or growth mindset? Furthermore, it is crucial to evaluate the habits, conversations, and overall lifestyle we have been embracing. It is not possible to partake of both mindsets simultaneously and expect success. As James 1:8 states, *"A double-minded man is unstable in all his ways."*

This life is often referred to as a battle of faith. We are called to engage in the good fight of faith. When we find ourselves in a fight, it is crucial to prepare adequately in order to emerge victorious. So, how does one prepare for a fight? One important aspect is maintaining the right diet. It is essential to commit to a healthy diet, as it equips us with strength and enhances our chances of winning the battle. The same applies to your mindset. You need to make a conscious decision to adopt a healthy diet based on the truths from the Word of God that will uplift and strengthen you. Remember, what you put in is what you get out.

There are certain foods or thoughts associated with a fixed mindset that you must reject. Allowing these thoughts to enter your mind will hinder your progress. In Daniel 1:8, we witness Daniel taking this exact approach. He firmly decided not to consume the rich royal food and wine. Instead, he requested a diet consisting solely of vegetables and water, which is a much healthier option for an athlete. Even today, many people follow the 'Daniel Fast' to promote healthy eating habits and strengthen their faith. The food we choose to consume has a significant impact on our mindset. You cannot consume junk food and expect to maintain good health or achieve positive results. Similarly, indulging in excessive news consumption, excessive television watching, spending excessive time on social media, and constantly focusing on symptoms or circumstances can be likened to ingesting harmful junk that hinders your spiritual faith life. God has the power to transform your thought patterns, desires, and temptations with His divine mindset.

Voices become viewpoints; what you hear gets in your heart. What you scroll gets in your spirit.

The voices you listen to are like the foods that you eat, which determine your mindset. You can learn to stop the spiral of toxic/junk thoughts in your head by running with God and using God's mindset.

Heaven's DNA resides within you, which means that you can develop a mindset aligned with God's kingdom. "13 For you created my inmost being; you knit me together in my mother's womb. 14 I praise you because I am fearfully and wonderfully made; your works are wonderful, I know that full well." Psalm 139:13-14

With God's mindset, you can learn to identify, capture, and reject negative thoughts. Remember, it is your decision what kind of "food" you consume. You are not a victim of what Satan or the world throws at you. You have the power to make small lifestyle changes now that will benefit you in the future. Choose to eliminate junk from your diet and remove toxic thoughts from your mind. Begin incorporating more healthy foods and habits in accordance with the Word of God today. Taking the step of reading this book is a move in the right direction.

When a negative thought arises, how will you respond? Those with God's kingdom mindset respond by firmly stating, 'No, I do not accept that thought,' 'You have made a mistake. You have come to the wrong address. No one by that name resides here!' 'I am a new creation in Christ Jesus.' You may not be able to prevent thoughts from entering your mind, but you have the power to decide which thoughts you will entertain. You have control over your emotions. You can choose to feel sad or mad, to see yourself as a victim or a victor, to be overwhelmed or to overcome. **God's desire is to restore us back to His original intent on the earth.** Restore us to the state of Adam and Eve before the fall, where they had unwavering trust in God's love for them and never entertained the lies of the enemy. They walked in an intimate relationship with God. It is important to remember that God granted

Adam and Eve authority over all the earth (Genesis 1:28). **God is restoring us back to our original position of authority through His kingdom mindset.** <u>With God's kingdom mindset, you can assume your position of authority, take back what belongs to you and live the abundant and successful life Jesus died to give you.</u>

God's voice stills you, leads you, reassures you, enlightens you, encourages you, comforts you, calms you and convicts you. God is a God of love and order. If the voices or thoughts you are hearing don't sound like the things above, then they are not from Him. Satan's voice rushes you, pushes you, frightens you, confuses you, discourages you, worries you, obsesses you and condemns you.

Make sure you're not the weapon formed against yourself that's causing you not to prosper.

Personal Example of overcoming negative thoughts: I recall driving home one day with a myriad of thoughts racing through my mind. Thoughts telling me that I would never be able to overcome this trauma, when suddenly I heard a voice within me ask, "Who told you that?" The question caught me off guard. I was alone in the car. I glanced around to ensure no one else was present. Until that moment, I had never questioned the origin of my thoughts. As I pondered on the source of thoughts suggesting disability, inadequacy, and addiction, I realized that they did not come from God. They were lies from the enemy, attempting to hold me back. **This was a major breakthrough on my road to recovery and healing. Determining the sender of our thoughts is critical. Once you realize that the thought isn't from God, then you will begin to resist it.**

God has brought about healing from within me, addressing my mind, restoring my soul, and making me whole. I am sharing my personal struggles in order to help you because there is no need for you to endure another day of suffering. Once I realized that it was the enemy who was responsible for those worthless, helpless, and hopeless thoughts plaguing my mind, a glimmer of hope emerged. "I can overcome this," I thought. "God loves me; He is not disappointed in me. God is not against me, but rather for me and with me." I began to believe that I could conquer those debilitating thoughts, and indeed, I did. You have the ability to do the same. God's love for you remains unwavering. What He has done for me, He will also do for you. You have the capacity to break free from toxic thought patterns resulting from past traumas and mistakes. Remember, you are precious and valuable in the eyes of God. "Since you are precious and honored in my sight, and because I love you, I will give people in exchange for you, nations in exchange for your life." Isaiah 43:4

Thieves don't break into empty houses: You hold great importance and value in the eyes of God. The enemy seeks to assail you with negative thoughts precisely because of your immense purpose and potential.

Satan is an expert deceiver! The Bible affirms that he is the father of lies and has deceived the entire world (John 8:44). He is a compulsive liar, and everything he utters is falsehood. Every word he has spoken to you is a lie. Satan prowls around like a raging lion, projecting a menacing facade. Similar to how a lion roars to instill fear and immobilize its prey, Satan seeks to paralyze us through fear. However, we must understand and firmly believe that Satan has been rendered powerless. His fangs were removed, and his claws were declawed over 2,000 years ago. [3] **Those with God's Kingdom mindset know that the enemy is "all bark and no bite!" He's like a little dog with a loud bark but completely harmless.**

According to 1 Peter 5:8-9, our adversary prowls around like a roaring lion, seeking whom he may devour. However, he can only devour those who heed his roars and succumb to fear. He should not have the power to devour a child of God. Especially a child of God who embraces and follows the kingdom mindset. We have the Lion of the Tribe of Judah dwelling within us. He is currently roaring over all the lies and disabling thoughts of the enemy through His kingdom mindset.

We no longer need to entertain the lies of the devil in our minds. Instead, we can choose to believe in the completed work of Christ at Calvary. Thoughts may arise, but we should not allow them to linger. Satan will try to flood your mind with thoughts in an effort to paralyze you. The overwhelming influx of thoughts can be daunting, with messages such as, "You can't do this" or "You lack what it takes." "This will ruin you." **We can learn to think about what we are thinking about and intentionally decide what stays and what goes. You will learn how to verify the sender by checking the packaging and manufacturer of your thoughts before allowing or rejecting them.**

"To hear God's voice, you must turn down the world's volume."
—700 club

In James 4:7, it states that if we resist the devil, he will flee from us. We resist the devil by refusing to entertain his toxic and negative thoughts.

---

[3] *Bondage Breaker*- P.94

When we resist him, the Bible assures us that he will flee from us. "Flee" means to run away as if in danger. It is an action that happens swiftly, so we should expect those thoughts to vanish immediately when we resist them. Just imagine Satan running away in terror. It brings me great joy to envision the devil, who has tormented me with his thoughts, fleeing in terror. When we resist thoughts, it clearly states that they will flee from us, not just possibly flee from us. If we do our part to resist them, they must flee. Resisting the devil means rejecting his lies, toxic thoughts, and fixed mindset. Perhaps he has been telling you that you will never overcome addiction, never get married, never have a child, never forgive, never recover from an illness, never get out of debt, or never restore your marriage. Resist his lies, and he will flee. God's mindset will empower you to be licensed and formidable against the enemy's lies!

"We need to learn to be more conscious of our thoughts and take captive the ones not of God."
—Dr. Caroline Leaf

"Some people are self-conscious, some people are people-conscious, some people are sin-conscious, some people are unconscious, but faith is God–conscious!"
—Mark Hankins

In 2 Corinthians 10:5, we are instructed to demolish arguments and every lofty opinion raised against the knowledge of God. We are to take every thought captive and make it obedient to Christ.

"To take captive" means to seize as a prisoner or exert control over. It implies a forceful action. In the context of our thoughts, we are instructed to take control over what we think about ourselves and our lives. With the assistance of the Holy Spirit, we have the ability to do so. We can apprehend and surrender disabling or toxic thoughts to God, making them His prisoners.

We are instructed to renew our minds with the Word of God: God expects us to change our thinking.

We have the ability to change both our thinking and our actions, and it is an expectation from God. Throughout the Bible, we receive guidance on what to think about, as evident in passages such as Philippians 4:8 and Romans 12:2. We are urged not to conform to the mindset of the world but to undergo transformation by renewing our minds. God's ways of thinking and doing things are distinct from the systems of the world. They are higher and beyond our full comprehension, as stated in Isaiah 55:8-9. From our human perspective, they may even appear foolish. As we currently utilize only a fraction of our brain's capacity (about 10%), our understanding of God's ways remains limited. However, as we grow in our knowledge of the Word and deepen our faith, we will gain a clearer insight into the workings of God and how everything aligns to fulfil His plans and purposes (1 Corinthians 13:12). Embracing God's kingdom mindset aids us in comprehending and aligning with His operational principles.

This life is temporary; heaven is our forever home. Are we living for heaven? Have we adopted God's kingdom mindset? Are we focused on accomplishing our divine purpose in life?

Here's how we can accomplish it: Begin with a <u>Thought Exchange:</u>
1. When a negative or toxic thought arises, promptly reject it.
2. Then intentionally shift your focus to something positive, such as a promise from the Word of God. Engage in a thought exchange, replacing negative thoughts with uplifting ones. We are encouraged to train ourselves to redirect our thoughts towards the right things, as mentioned in Philippians 4:8. *"Finally, brothers and sisters, whatever is true, whatever is honourable, whatever is right, whatever is pure, whatever is lovely, whatever is of good repute, if there is any excellence and if anything worthy of praise, dwell on these things."*
3. We are further instructed to meditate on good and positive things, focusing on what is pleasing to God. According to the Oxford Dictionary, to meditate means to deeply contemplate something and to concentrate one's mind either in silence or through chanting. In our case, we engage in this practice by using our mouths. Simply the act of meditating on God's wonderful promises itself serves as a method of relaxation, calming our minds. Speaking is an action that accompanies meditation, as we verbally declare those promises from the Word of God over ourselves. For example, we may affirm, "I have the mind of Christ" or "I think thoughts of life, not death." By deliberately thinking about positive things, we can experience personal victory in any situation.

Here are some examples of common negative thoughts and corresponding faith declarations that can be used to counter them:
1. <u>You should be afraid</u>-Don't be afraid, just believe (Mark 5:36).
2. <u>You're always going to be poor, and lack</u>-You serve a God of more than enough (2 Corinthians 9:8-11).

3. <u>You're not going to make it</u>-He didn't take you this far to leave, you know, He's the author and finisher of your faith (Hebrews 12:2).

4. <u>You're going to be defeated</u>-I made you more than a conqueror (Romans 8:37).

5. <u>Nobody loves you</u>-Neither depth nor height can separate us from the love of God (Romans 8:38-39).

6. <u>You're never going to beat this addiction</u>-greater is He that is in you (1 John 4:4).

7. <u>Something bad is going to happen to you</u>-I set my angels to charge over you to guard you in all your ways (Psalm 91).

8. <u>You're so tired</u>-I will give you rest (Matthew 11:28).

9. <u>You're so sick-</u> By the stripes of Jesus, you are healed (Isaiah 53:5).

10. <u>You're so lonely</u>-I will never leave you nor forsake you (Deuteronomy 31:6).

"The Bible is meant to be bread for daily use, not cake for special occasions."

#dailybiblereading (Instagram)

4. In order to embrace God's mindset, <u>it is necessary to make changes in the way you communicate</u>. You need to engage in **Word Replacement Therapy**, which involves speaking the Word of God regardless of your emotions. Remove the word **"never"** from your vocabulary and replace it with **"not yet."** By changing your words, you can transform your mindset. Remember that your feelings do not determine the truth; only the Word of God does. Choose to express what is true, and that is the Word of God. Replace any negative thoughts and words with the faith declarations mentioned above.[4]

"You can't control everything that comes into your life, but you can choose what you focus on and what you magnify."

—*Tiffany Layton*

***

In this book, you will discover how to cultivate a God-conscious mindset by embracing His thoughts about you and adopting His

---

[4] Claudette Walker-YouTube *"The Weapons of our Warfare"*

perspective. Being God-conscious involves recognizing His presence within us through the Holy Spirit and aligning our mindset with His. God desires to break the cycle of falling into the enemy's traps repeatedly, trapped in a destructive pattern. He wants you to overcome the downward spiral of sin and toxic thinking. Satan seeks to keep us fixated on our past mistakes, making us constantly aware of our sins and weakening us in the process. His plan is to confine us to a stagnant state, paralyzed by his toxic thoughts, preventing us from fulfilling our God-given purpose. Satan bombards us with thoughts that replay our past errors on the screen of our minds. However, the Word of God assures us that when God forgives us, He also forgets. If God no longer remembers our mistakes, then we, too, should release them from our memory. "No more shall every man teach his neighbor, and every man his brother, saying, 'Know the LORD,' for they all shall know Me, from the least of them to the greatest of them, says the LORD. For I will forgive their iniquity and their sin, I will remember no more.'" Jeremiah 31:34

The Bible states in Psalm 103 that God has removed our sins and past mistakes from us as far as the East is from the West. Your past mistakes have been forgotten. God desires to transform the way you think. The past is behind you and finished. Allow Him to be the author of your mindset. Start viewing each day as a fresh page brimming with possibilities. Every morning, you awaken with a fresh influx of baby neurons, and it is up to you to determine the quality of their growth based on how you employ your mind. Will they develop into positive or negative structures within your brain? This crucial decision rests upon your mindset. The growth of these neurons has the potential to influence not just your day, week, or month but your entire life, as they shape the structure of your brain. Thus, it becomes imperative to cultivate effective mind-management strategies and establish routines. One powerful method for achieving this is by cultivating a sense of God consciousness, which enables us to control our minds and foster the growth of positive structures within our mental realm.

> **"The past may influence you, but the past cannot define you. You are not your past."**
>
> **—*Eric Petree***

God has blessed us with the Holy Spirit, who serves as our guide, helping us identify dangerous and toxic thought patterns. When negative thoughts arise, the Holy Spirit prompts us to question their origin. We can choose to respond with statements such as, "No, I refuse to entertain that thought today!" or "No, I will not revisit that place!" The enemy attempts to trap us in a "sin consciousness" that fosters a fixed mindset, but we have the Holy Spirit as our internal compass. He always leads us towards the safety of God's Kingdom mindset. The Holy Spirit utilizes the truth found in God's Word to help us discern the enemy's thoughts. Since God is revealed through His Word, the more time we spend immersed in the Scriptures, the easier it becomes to hear the Holy Spirit's warnings and refute the voice of the enemy.

Research conducted by Dr. C. Leaf suggests that by identifying the underlying cause of mental distress, which often involves the lies and deceptions of the enemy that fuel toxic thinking, it is possible to replace them with new neural networks and healthy habits within a span of 63 days. Dr. Leaf has developed a helpful tool called the Brain Detox app called Switch, which can guide individuals through this transformative process. I highly recommend reading her books, "Switch on Your Brain" and "Cleaning Up the Mental Mess," as they provide valuable insights and practical techniques for implementing positive changes in your thought patterns.

We should embrace a straightforward principle for our lives: If it aligns with the truth, I'm on board; if it deviates from the truth, I'm not interested. When a thought arises in our minds that contradicts God's truth, which is revealed in His Word, the Bible, we should dismiss it. Similarly, if an opportunity presents itself to say or do something that compromises or conflicts with the truth, we should avoid it. [5]

Looking in the mirror of God's Word

God's Word serves as a revelation of your true identity and purpose. When you engage with the Word of God, it is akin to looking into a mirror and seeing your authentic reflection. The Word of God not only unveils the nature of God but also reveals who you truly are. It exposes your purpose, your worth, your authority, and more. The mindset we adopt acts as a lens through which we perceive ourselves. Embracing God's kingdom mindset enables us to see ourselves from His perspective, aligning our self-perception with His divine perspective.

The passage from James 1:23-24 emphasizes the importance of putting the Word of God into practice rather than merely listening to it. It compares someone who listens but doesn't act to a person who looks in a mirror but quickly forgets their reflection. The passage suggests that Satan actively works against recognizing one's true reflection and forgetting their genuine identity. Satan uses distractions, busyness, and even drowsiness to keep people away from the Word of God. He opposes exploring God's kingdom mindset and following God's

---

[5] *Bondage Breaker*- P. 106

standards for success. On the other hand, embracing the truth in God's Word can lead to a transformative experience, turning a person into a warrior. God's Word acts as mental armour, protecting the mind from harmful and paralyzing thoughts.

"God's kingdom mindset is like mental armour. Have you put on your armour today? Don't leave home without it!"
—*Natalie Masucci*

The passage from Romans 8:28 highlights that God is not a condemner like the enemy. While the enemy seeks to condemn and punish, God convicts us in a non-negative way. Condemnation often stems from religious teachings, but God's love for us is unconditional, and He is on our side. He understands our weaknesses and wants to work alongside us to help us overcome them. All God asks is for our trust in Him with our thoughts and lives. Trust is crucial in any relationship, and placing trust in God can lead to transformative changes in our thought processes. It may require stepping out of our comfort zones, but the rewards will outweigh any initial discomfort, as transformation takes time.

"Small hinges swing big doors."
—*W. Clement Stone*

God wants us to recognize our toxic thoughts and incorrect mindsets, similar to how the Prodigal Son realized his mistakes. God invites us to align our thinking with His kingdom mindset and leave behind our own ways and the ways of the world. In the story of the Prodigal Son, God the Father never gave up on his son and continually prayed for him, eagerly awaiting his return. The Father's expectation of his son's homecoming is evident in his watchful presence on the porch. When the prodigal son finally returned, God not only restored him to his original position but also blessed him abundantly. Despite already receiving his share, the son was reinstated as an heir. This story highlights the incredible goodness of God for us to reflect upon.[6]

God desires to bless you abundantly, just as He did with the Prodigal Son by adorning him with a ring and a new robe. His intention is not merely to restore you but to elevate you to a better state than before. God longs for us to place our trust in Him, specifically with regard to our mindset. Our mindset encompasses our thoughts, desires,

---

[6] *Luke* 15:11-32

and emotions. God's mindset represents a proven strategy for success that has the power to positively transform every aspect of our lives.

Having a kingdom mindset aligns with God's design for our brains, as well as our faith and love. It entails thinking positively and in accordance with the Word of God found in the Bible. It involves believing that abilities, intelligence, and talents can be cultivated and developed. As believers, we are encouraged to continuously learn, grow, and evolve throughout our lives, regardless of our age, socioeconomic status, gender, or race. God expects us to exert effort in nurturing the talents and dreams He has placed within us. The transformative power of putting forth effort can bring about changes in our abilities and shape us as individuals. [7]

God's mindset contains the belief that our faith can develop too.

Carol Dweck's book "Mindset: The New Psychology of Success" explores the concept of mindset as an individual's self-perception that influences their beliefs about themselves. Mindset refers to whether one sees their abilities and qualities as fixed or as qualities that can be developed. Mindsets can be applied to different areas of life, such as personal and professional spheres, determining how someone sees themselves as a teacher, parent, employee, or student. Importantly, individuals may or may not be aware of their own mindsets.

Mindsets can have a profound effect on learning achievement, skill acquisition, personal relationships, professional success and many other dimensions of life, including our purpose.[8]

Assumption versus Asking Questions

Assumptions stem from a fixed mindset, whereas asking questions aligns with God's mindset.

Your mind, influenced by your carnal nature, can sometimes lead you to make assumptions. Interestingly, your greatest adversary is not a person, situation, or thing but often the narrative created in your mind based on assumptions, projected fears, or insecurities.[9] The enemy capitalizes on assumptions as a tactic against us. He skillfully plays out scenarios in our minds, which usually prove to be incorrect. He incessantly replays worst-case

---

[7] *Dweck* p.42

[8] edglossary.org *Growth mindset* 08-29-13

[9] *Vex King*

scenarios, feeding our fears and anxieties. Why is it that we tend to instinctively focus on the worst-case scenario rather than the best? Refuse to let the enemy deceive you into assuming and expecting the worst. Instead, draw near to God's spirit through His Word, as our spiritual selves align with His growth mindset and purpose. The Holy Spirit always has a plan to protect, rescue, and restore us when our minds fall into assumption. God wants us to reflect on our victories and successes, not our failures. So, if you are going to assume anything, assume that the devil is a liar and that God is faithfully watching over you.

God's Kingdom mindset takes advantage of our propensity to make assumptions by teaching us to assume the best rather than the worst. As we assume the best of people and situations, it opens our lives to God's wonderful possibilities." God has a habit of using what the enemy means for our harm and turning it into something for our good (Romans 8:28)

> **"The assumptions we make often restrict our thinking and therefore restrict our possibilities."**
> —*John C Maxwell*

Avoid making assumptions altogether, as they can swiftly lead to problems and misunderstandings. Remember that every story has two sides, and there are multiple potential solutions to any problem. However, if you find yourself needing to assume something, assume that the devil is a liar and that God's word is true. <u>Train yourself to adopt a mindset of assuming the best rather than the worst.</u>

What if it's a setup for something better?

<u>How can you avoid making assumptions?</u>

Ask questions and gather more information about the situation. Find out the whole story.

Express what you really want or feel.

Do not take things personally.

Communicate clearly to avoid misunderstandings.
Be mindful of your words and actions.

Leave room for other scenarios/perceptions in your mind.

Check the usefulness of your assumption.

Try assuming the best rather than the worst.

Chapter Two

What is God's Mindset, you ask? How is it Different?

In this chapter, I will introduce you to the God's Kingdom mindset, which I believe is far superior to the growth mindset commonly discussed in educational and business circles. But what makes it superior? Allow me to elaborate.

God mindset is intentional and offensive-minded.

It is offensive because it equips us with strategies to counter the plots of the enemy who seeks to steal, kill, and destroy us. Additionally, it provides us with strategies to advance and take new ground for the Kingdom of God as evidenced by the following two scriptures.
"Sow with a view to righteousness, Reap in accordance with kindness; Break up your fallow ground, For it is time to seek the LORD Until He comes to rain righteousness on you." Hosea 10:12
Ephesians 6:10-18 "10 Finally, be strong in the Lord and in his mighty power. 11 Put on the full armour of God, so that you can take your stand against the devil's schemes. 12 For our struggle is not against flesh and blood, but against the rulers, against the authorities, against the powers of this dark world and against the spiritual forces of evil in the heavenly realms. 13 Therefore put on the full armour of God, so that when the day of evil comes, you may be able to stand your ground, and after you have done everything, to stand. 14 Stand firm then, with the belt of truth buckled around your waist, with the breastplate of righteousness in place, 15 and with your feet fitted with the readiness that comes from the gospel of peace. 16 In addition to all this, take up the shield of faith, with which you can extinguish all the flaming arrows of the evil one. 17 Take the helmet of salvation and the sword of the Spirit, which is the word of God. 18 And pray in the Spirit on all occasions with all kinds of prayers and requests. With this in mind, be alert and always keep on praying for all the Lord's people."

God mindset is intentional about our thoughts, words and purpose. The thoughts we have and choose to accept can profoundly influence the structure of our brains, leading them in either a positive or negative direction. Thoughts and feelings have a significant impact on the energy flow within our bodies, as well as on neurotransmitters and chemicals. For instance, emotions such as anger, fear, and anxiety can manifest physically through sweaty palms, queasy stomachs, and increased heart rates. Conversely, emotions like peace, joy, love, and happiness evoke feelings of calmness, safety, and relaxation. Experiencing joy can even bring about a smile and a profound sense of well-being.

In addition, God's mindset is offensive because it gives us the sword of the Spirit, which is the Word of God, with which we can proactively challenge every limiting thought and cast it down before it can adversely affect our lives. When we eliminate limiting thoughts, we take new ground in our minds and in our lives.

God's growth mindset encompasses the concept of "Multiple Perspective Advantage mode (MPA)."

As humans, we possess the incredible capacity to step outside of ourselves and observe our own thinking. With practice and intentional effort, we can develop this ability. Dr. Dharius Daniel refers to it as "The Principle of Perspective." God desires for us to engage in this MPA mode frequently, enabling us to objectively observe our thoughts as if viewing them from within a box and prompting us to ask ourselves important questions.

God's mindset employs a questioning strategy as a crucial component. God encourages us to cultivate the habit of questioning our thoughts and circumstances. But how do we go about doing this? By asking ourselves important questions, such as:
- Is this based on factual information or mere assumptions?
- Are these thoughts driven by emotions or supported by facts?
- Will embracing this thought be beneficial or detrimental?
- Does this thought hold validity and utility in my life?

By engaging in this process of inquiry and gathering information through questioning, we empower ourselves with knowledge. Armed with this information, we can then make informed decisions about whether to accept or reject the thoughts we encounter. Remember, information is a source of power and wisdom.

When you reject a thought, it loses energy and cannot develop into a physical structure within your brain. By actively rejecting negative thoughts, you prevent them from occupying valuable space in your mind. Once you have cleared out the negative, God will fill you with positivity, confidence, faith, and courage. We replace negative thoughts with God's affirming thoughts about us—thoughts of love, hope, and a promising future (Jeremiah 28:11).

God encourages us to prepare our minds by shifting our perspectives and expanding our mindsets. He wants us to envision a future that exceeds our expectations, where He can accomplish immeasurably more in our lives than we could ever ask or imagine (Ephesians 3:20-21).

The enemy relentlessly attempts to confine and limit your purpose and dreams by bombarding you with negative thoughts. He will employ any means necessary to derail you from your path. However, it is essential to remember that God did not create you and bring you this far to let you fail now. God does not want you to give up or quit. In Ephesians 6, God instructs us to stand firm and resist the deceptive schemes of the devil. God wants you to rise up and engage in the battle. The battlefield is in our minds (1 Peter 1:13).

God encourages you to use the enemy's box as a vantage point to observe, question, and analyze your incoming thoughts. By climbing up on the enemy's box, you gain a higher perspective, just like God. Use the enemy's weapon against him. God looks down from above to Earth, and He wants us to do the same. He wants us to observe our thoughts from a place of victory, from His throne room. In reality, we are seated with Christ in heavenly places (Ephesians 2:6-9), and we are royalty. What we need is a change of perspective, and MPA mode provides just that. The Bible teaches that we are seated in heavenly places; it's time we embrace our correct position and start looking down on our problems.

"Where you sit determines what you see, and what you see determines what you do."

—Dr. Dharius Daniels

MPA is God's vantage point and part of His mindset: When we look at thoughts and troubles from God's vantage point or perspective, it becomes much easier to take control because we are seated in the Victor's seat or on the throne. Troubles appear small when viewed from above, similar to how everything seems small when looking down at the earth from a plane. This is the perspective God desires us to have towards our problems. Those with God's Kingdom mindset understand that feelings do not hold the ultimate truth. "Feelings are temporary and transient."[10]

If you desire to transform toxic thoughts and overcome difficult situations, it is crucial to believe and speak only what God says about them. You must exercise control over your speech. Take authority over your human nature, express words of faith, and have an unwavering

---

[10] - Dr. C. Leaf

belief that what you speak will manifest. Your human nature tends to rely on seeing and feeling things before believing and speaking, but God's mindset operates in faith, speaking before seeing.

This task is often easier said than done because when we experience heightened emotions like fear, stress, anxiety, or anger, it becomes challenging to maintain objectivity. Just like it's difficult to see clearly in the midst of a snowstorm, when we're going through trials, and our emotions are running wild, it can be hard to stay focused. However, with practice, it becomes easier. The more you reject a thought, the weaker it becomes, and eventually, it loses its power to the point where it stops recurring altogether.

By regularly practicing the **"Multiple Perspective Advantage (MPA mode),"** you will enhance your ability to recognize the deceptive and limiting thoughts of the enemy and reject them before they can take root in your mind. Declare to the devil that he has no place in your mind. Remember, practice makes perfect.

Distraction helps, too: That's a positive distraction indeed. Engage in activities like dancing, stretching or singing praises that can help calm your emotions. Once you are in a state of calmness, you can revisit the thought and analyze it. Remember, you possess immense power within you - the power to choose your thoughts. MPA provides an opportunity to assess your current state - Who do you resemble and sound like in this moment? A victor or a victim? You no longer have to be a victim of your thoughts. In the name of Jesus, God wants you to take control.[11]

Science is increasingly validating the truths of God's ways. MPA mode enables us to operate from our spiritual essence rather than relying on our unreliable and deceitful emotions and feelings, which are inherent in our carnal nature. Our carnal nature pertains to the physical desires, pleasures, and cravings of the human body through the five senses. These aspects are transient and worldly, lacking in spiritual significance. God designed us to live from our spiritual essence rather than being driven solely by our flesh. MPA demonstrates the possibility of achieving this.

God calls us to develop a mature mindset aligned with His principles and overcome the impulses of our flesh. In the initial stages of our transformation, we resemble children, thinking with misconceptions and making numerous mistakes. Dr. Daniel emphasizes, **"We're not all seated in the same place, which is why our perspectives differ. Our levels of maturity vary."** As we evolve, we gain greater control over our thoughts.

---

[11] Dr. C. Leaf -*Instagram*

God invites you to change your seat today. You have been occupying an economy seat while God has reserved first-class seats for you. Shift your vantage point and view your life from a new perspective.

You will never surpass the need for warfare; instead, you must learn how to fight. The battleground resides within our minds, where the battle is fought against our thoughts. Joyce Meyer's book, "The Battlefield of the Mind," provides a comprehensive exploration of this concept if you wish to delve deeper through further study.

We are unable to perceive things as God does because He sees from His heavenly throne room. The Bible teaches us that His thoughts are beyond our comprehension, and His ways surpass our own (Isaiah 55:8-9). Thankfully, when we embrace His mindset and employ MPA, our vision becomes clearer, allowing us to see things as they truly are. MPA, or the principle of perspective, enables us to view our life circumstances from God's vantage point. From this elevated perspective, our problems appear smaller and more manageable.

Try using MPA this week.

Make a conscious effort to think about what you are thinking about. Write down your thoughts. What questions did you ask yourself? Did it work?

Start with a negative thought that you have been struggling with lately. Use MPA mode to analyze it. From your elevated vantage point, you can look down at your problems and notice the absurdity of some of your thoughts. Think "In the grand scheme of things"…
MPA helps us to determine the utility and validity of our thoughts. Not useful? Then reject it. Is it valid or true? If not, then reject it.

Questioning Strategy

Children have a natural curiosity and ask questions to explore the world. Their inquisitiveness helps them acquire knowledge. "Curiosity is considered linked to intelligence," as mentioned by Albert Einstein.

Adults often lose their curiosity, relying on assumptions and learning less as a result. Matthew 18:3 encourages us to become like children to embrace God's kingdom mindset. Children ask many questions, always seeking understanding. Curiosity keeps minds active and enhances mental strength. Just as muscles grow stronger with exercise, our minds benefit from curiosity and inquiry.

God encourages our curiosity and invites us to bring our questions to Him in prayer. He wants us to question our thoughts, circumstances, and purpose. Continuous learning and questioning are important to God. Asking questions helps us understand and solve problems, often revealing overlooked answers. <u>Effective questioning is a powerful strategy, so keep asking questions and avoid making assumptions.</u> Embrace the pursuit of truth and knowledge through inquiry.

The fear of failure stops us from asking more questions. Remember that fear is not from God but from the enemy. *{2 Timothy 1:7} "For God has not given us a spirit of fear but of power, love, and self-discipline."*

You might find yourself thinking, **"If I fail, it means I'm inadequate."** Such thoughts stem from a fixed mindset. It's crucial to recognize that failure is an inherent part of the journey. Not everything will go perfectly the first time, and there may be valuable lessons to be learned along the way.[12]

Mistakes happen to everyone. How you respond determines your growth. Learn from them and advance.

God uses the Questioning strategy in His mindset.
"We need people with experience and people who have the ability to ask stupid questions."

—Richard Gerver

<u>**Action Step:**</u> On a separate piece of paper, question your thoughts. How many of them are actually assumptions?

God Asks Questions. Satan Tells Lies.

Questions have the power to unlock new perspectives, facilitate learning, and bring about breakthroughs. Questioning is a fundamental strategy within God's mindset. When God poses questions to us or prompts us to engage in self-reflection, it is because He intends to reveal something significant. God encourages us to ask questions so that He can bestow wisdom upon us, guiding us in navigating life's circumstances. By asking questions, we expand our thinking beyond conventional boundaries and explore diverse scenarios and potential outcomes.

Satan is the father of lies, constantly deceiving and misleading. He manipulates us to assume the worst in every situation. Fear and assumption are not aligned with God's nature or His mindset. Instead, God encourages self-reflection and questioning.

---

[12] John Maxwell Team email, July 11, 21

God's mindset includes Word Replacement Therapy
God Expects Us to Mature: NEVER LIES

The world often communicates the message that we are inadequate and
fall short of expectations. It's noticeable how the news predominantly
focuses on negative events. This is because they tend to attract higher
ratings, and people have a tendency to be drawn to drama, Offence, and
tragedy. Feel-good stories, on the other hand, may not capture as much
attention.

I have learned the importance of limiting my exposure to the news
as I noticed its negative impact on my emotions, leading to feelings of
anxiety and hopelessness. The enemy, often referred to as the Prince of
the Air, [13] seeks to instill a fixed mindset within us by manipulating the
world systems, particularly the news, entertainment and social media.
He bombards us with negativity to reinforce negative perceptions.

The enemy wants us to believe in various lies, such as never getting
out of debt, never finding a life partner or having children, and not being
smart, thin, connected, or talented enough. He aims to create a sense of
hopelessness, failure, shame, and regret through deceptive thoughts
and spirits prevalent in the world. Satan utilizes the news and media to
spread these lies.

However, we must remember that most of the world operates with
a fixed mindset, while as believers, we are called to embrace a kingdom
mindset. Jesus Himself stated that although we live in this world, we are
not of it. "John 15:19"

It is crucial to recognize the contrast between the world's
perspective and the mindset God desires for us. God's promise to never
leave us or forsake us (Hebrews 13:5) is the only valid "never" we
should hold onto. <u>Whenever a thought starting with the word "never"
arises, we must immediately reject it, knowing that such lies stem from
the enemy.</u>

---

[13] *Ephesians* 2:2

A kingdom mindset involves believing God's Word about oneself and countering deceptive thoughts with **"but"** statements. For example, when thoughts of never getting out of debt arise, one responds with the assurance that God will provide according to His riches. "And my God will meet all your needs according to the riches of his glory in Christ Jesus." Philippians 4:19 Loneliness is addressed by acknowledging God's constant presence, even when feeling alone. "No one will be able to stand against you all the days of your life. As I was with Moses, so I will be with you; I will never leave you nor forsake you." Joshua 1:5

For example, when struggling with the toxic thought of loneliness, say, "I may feel alone, but God promises to never leave me; therefore, I am not alone". When struggling with thoughts of insufficiency, say, "I don't see how it's going to work out, but God promises to supply all my needs according to His riches in glory" <u>When we are tormented by toxic thoughts, learn to reframe them in our minds by using the word but. Say to yourself, "But God",</u> He can make way for me where there seems to be no way.

Reframing the way we speak to ourselves can help improve our self-talk: Reframe "I have to" to "I get to" When we have to do something it implies that we are doing it against our will and this causes stress. By choosing to say "I GET TO" instead, changes the feeling of burden to one of opportunity which reduces stress and improves mood.

Loneliness is often caused by accepting the lie that no one cares, leading to unhealthy coping mechanisms. The ultimate cure for loneliness is found in Jesus.

Those with God's kingdom mindset have more <u>buts</u> in their thought processes. They say things like: I was lost, But God found me. I was blind, but now I see. I was broke, but now I'm blessed. I was sick, but now I am healed.

They also use the word <u>"yet" instead of "never."</u>

"I may not be out of debt yet, but I'm working on it with God's help". "I may not have beaten this addiction yet, but I am getting stronger day by day".

During the Covid-19 pandemic, my school board implemented a hybrid teaching model combining in-person and online instruction, a new approach. Initially, I faced overwhelming negative thoughts, doubting my abilities and feeling too old and technologically inexperienced. I believed it would be challenging and only add to my workload. These thoughts increased my anxiety and stress levels.

<u>At that moment, I was faced with a choice: to accept these negative thoughts or resist them.</u> I could have easily succumbed to misery and spent my time complaining. However, I made a conscious decision to resist these thoughts. I did not want to become the person who feared

change, constantly complained, made excuses, and lived in misery. That was not the legacy I wanted to leave behind.

This was my thought process; this was a requirement for my job. If others could learn, then so could I. I resisted the thoughts with scriptures like *Philippians 4:13: "I can do all things through Christ who strengthens me".* "I said to myself, I may feel inadequate and think that I'm too old, but the Word of God says I can do all things through Christ who strengthens me. I can do this!"

Seeking guidance through prayer, I hoped for a clear sign to retire and avoid the challenges of remote learning. However, God's response surprised me. Instead of retirement, He wanted me to continue learning and improving my technological skills. He encouraged me to acquire new knowledge and face my fear of technology. Growing up without much exposure to technology, it felt intimidating and overwhelming. Looking back, I realized how much technology has advanced and how it reflects my own aging process.

I want to share that teaching hybrid during the pandemic has been a tremendous learning experience for me. I am truly grateful for the growth and knowledge it has brought into my life. Throughout this journey, I have felt the presence of God every step of the way, providing guidance and support. While we may not always understand why certain events unfold as they do, we can trust that God has our best interests at heart. He is constantly preparing and positioning us for the next level or season of our lives.

In order to navigate this challenging situation, I had to train my mind to find the silver linings and see the good in the circumstances. I realized that maintaining a positive mindset is a choice that greatly impacts the overall happiness and fulfilment in our lives. As the saying goes, **"The happiness of your life depends on the quality of your thoughts."**

"You have the veto power over your thoughts."
—*Dr. C. Leaf*

The more we practice resisting and replacing negative or toxic thoughts, the more confident we become. It's important to cultivate a kingdom mindset, just as God expects from us. Jesus serves as our example in this regard. He overcame "never thoughts," and it is our duty to overcome them as well. <u>Did you know that Satan tried to convince Jesus that He would never fulfil His purpose and redeem mankind?</u> Perhaps Satan is currently sending similar **"never thoughts"** your way.

It's important to fact-check your thoughts, as they often reflect insecurities and fears. Verify the accuracy of your thoughts, especially in emotionally charged situations. The enemy may try to convince you of things like never achieving your purpose or reconciling with your family. Remember that as a child of God, you have the power of Jesus within you. As Christians, we are inherently strong, with the essence of an overcomer (Revelation 3:21). With God's help, you can overcome the negative thoughts and beliefs that are troubling you.

You can overcome "never thoughts" with God's mindset:

1. <u>First, identify the sender of the thought.</u> Then, make a conscious decision to not accept it. Declare firmly, "I reject that 'never thought' in Jesus' name. That thought is not from God. It does not align with His truth." Remind yourself that such thoughts do not originate from your true self or from God, and affirm your refusal to entertain them.
2. <u>Next, replace the negative thought with a scripture or promise from the Word of God.</u> Find a relevant passage that brings encouragement, strength, and truth to counteract the negative thought.
3. <u>Fight back by consistently confessing God's Word over yourself.</u> Speak the positive promises out loud and declare them with faith. Remember, faith is a battle (1 Timothy 6:12). We are commanded to fight the good fight of faith. Our weapon in this battle is the Word of God, which acts as a powerful sword in the spiritual realm. The Word of God serves as an offensive weapon, capable of cutting away all the negative thoughts sent by the enemy. "For the word of God is alive and active. Sharper than any double-edged sword, it penetrates even to dividing soul and spirit, joints and marrow; it judges the thoughts and attitudes of the heart." Hebrews 4:12

Some examples of Limiting Beliefs:

1. <u>I Can't.</u> I can't do public speaking. I can't do this job.
2. <u>I Don't.</u> I don't know how to do that.
3. <u>I Shouldn't.</u> I shouldn't apply for the job because I won't get it.
4. <u>I'm Not.</u> I'm not a people person. I'm not athletic. I'm not a morning person.
5. <u>I've tried,</u> and I couldn't do it…
6. <u>It's too late</u> to pursue my dreams….I missed my chance.
7. <u>They're Better.</u> They will probably give her the promotion because she's more organized than me.
8. <u>I Don't Deserve</u> this raise as much as my colleague.

9. <u>I'm Not Worthy.</u> Oh, thank you, but I'm pretty sure I just got lucky.
10. <u>There's Someone Better.</u> My colleagues are far more knowledgeable on this subject.
11. <u>I've Been Told.</u> I've been told my experience doesn't align. My boss says I don't have enough experience to work anywhere else.
12. <u>My (Loved One) Says I'm.</u> My mother says that I've always been very shy and nervous. [14]

God's mindset focuses on the GOLD

To mature and change our mindset, we must examine our hearts and thoughts, choosing to stand on the Word of God and build up our faith and confidence. This transformation should be evident through our actions and attitude as others notice a positive change in us. Instead of focusing on faults and flaws, we should seek the silver lining and rejoice in small victories and improvements. God recognizes the value and potential He has placed within each of us, and He wants us to focus on these intrinsic qualities. We should direct our attention to the gold, the royalty, and the treasures within ourselves and others (2 Timothy 1:6). By adopting a kingdom mindset, we can shift our perspective to higher possibilities and embrace God's emphasis on the gold within us.

<u>Focusing on the gold is part of God's mindset. God chooses what He focuses on. He focuses on the positive, the growth, and the potential.</u>

The saying "She's got a heart of gold" refers to someone who is kind, generous, and compassionate, possessing rare and valuable qualities. God has placed a metaphorical "gold" within each of us, representing the gifts and abilities we need to fulfil our purpose. We carry a treasure and can draw on it in life. God deposits His spirit, faith, love, and strength within us, making us His golden children. With a kingdom mindset, we can transform negative and fixed mindset thoughts into positive ones, shining brightly like gold, by aligning them with the word of God. No magic is needed, but rather a deliberate shift in our thinking and perspective.

---

[14] "*13 Common Limiting Beliefs Holding Us Back.*" Career Contessa, www.careercontessa.com.

<u>**Example**</u>:

- I may not be where I want to be yet but thank God I'm not where I used to be.
- You've come a long way, baby!
- You're doing great.
- I'm a work in progress.
- I am getting better/stronger every day.

Eternal Perspective

We are created and destined for eternity. Our existence extends far beyond the time we spend here on Earth. Some believe that this life serves as a mere dress rehearsal for eternity (Hebrews 13:14-16). Our time on earth is merely a temporary residence.

Seeing the big picture means viewing our lives through an eternal perspective. It is the way God perceives our lives and how He desires us to see them as well.

<u>Seeing the big picture, or having an eternal perspective, entails understanding that God has a master plan for your life.</u> **Your life is intricately woven into a larger story.** Psalm 139:16 affirms that the blueprint or script of your life was penned in God's book even before you came into existence. As such, you were uniquely created for a special and specific purpose. Each of us has a distinct kingdom assignment. Before our birth, God inscribed the narrative of our lives in His book. We were brought into being for a unique purpose, something that only we can fulfil.

The world often emphasizes temporary matters, but God calls us to focus on eternity and fulfil our purpose. We should prioritize accumulating treasures in heaven rather than solely pursuing earthly desires (Matthew 6:19-21). Our time on Earth is limited, and it is important to make the most of it. We have the responsibility to choose and pursue what God has placed in our hearts, as our choices have lasting consequences. When our lives come to an end, God will evaluate how faithfully we fulfilled our assignments (Matthew 25:21). Our current way of thinking and living may impact our eternal rewards. Joel Osteen says, "If your thinking is limited, then your life is going to be limited." We should strive for both present success and treasures in heaven, which will bring everlasting joy.

Free Will; God gives us free will

We indeed possess the power of choice when it comes to our lives. We have the ability to decide how we think and the mindset we embrace. We can choose to align our thinking with God's perspective or opt for a different path. It is within our control to pursue and fulfil our divine purpose. God, respecting our free will, does not impose His will upon us. The choice to embrace and fulfil our purpose lies with us.

You might be saying, "I don't even know what my purpose is." But don't worry, even Jesus Himself was in a similar position. In John 5:30, He stated that He had to seek the will of the Father who sent Him. If Jesus had to seek God's will for His life assignment, then it is the same for us. We can do this by approaching God in prayer and immersing ourselves in His Word. Just as Jesus discovered His identity and purpose in the Scriptures, we too can find ours (Luke 4:21). When we uncover God's desires for us (His will) and act upon them, we are assured of success. Jesus serves as our guiding example.

God gave you a fingerprint that no one else has, so you can leave an imprint that no one else can. That's how valuable you really are. You are destined to leave your mark on the world.

Inner Image and Potential

Each one of us carries an inner image of who we are and what we are capable of. This image is shaped by our life experiences, culture, and the media we consume. Unfortunately, life's challenges and the influence of negative forces have often dampened our hopes and dreams. The consequences are not limited to ourselves but also impact others. <u>Within each of us, God has instilled unique gifts and qualities intended to bless those around us.</u> If we fail to realize our full potential, those individuals may miss out on the answered prayers and miracles that God intended through us.

The image within us often functions as a self-imposed glass ceiling, imposing limitations on what we believe we can achieve. If we perceive ourselves as unremarkable, we are likely to live up to that perception. However, it is crucial to recognize that God never designed anyone to be ordinary or insignificant. He creates with excellence, not mediocrity. His plans for each of us surpass our current experiences and circumstances. Andrew Wommack says that we were created for greatness. Why settle for being ordinary when we were meant to be extraordinary? By adopting God's Kingdom mindset, the glass ceiling in our minds will shatter, propelling us to exceed expectations and embrace the extraordinary life God has in store for us.

We all struggle with some form of **Identity Dysmorphia** because the image we have of ourselves on the inside often does not align with God's reality. To heal from this, it is essential to discern what is based on evidence or truth (God's Word) and what merely perception is. We will learn to examine our thoughts closely, differentiating between those grounded in truth and those influenced by deception or perception. In this book, we will delve deep into the roots of your perceptions and identify their underlying causes. Often, it will require a thorough exploration to uncover the deceptions we have accepted as truths throughout our lives.

"What thoughts are you allowing to play in the movie theatre of your mind?"

—Natalie Masucci

Due to Identity Dysmorphia, <u>we consistently underestimate ourselves</u> and fail to perceive ourselves as God does. However, Jeremiah 29:11 assures us that God has an extraordinary plan for our lives. He has called us and appointed us for greatness, not mediocrity. His plans are designed to prosper us. The belief that "old habits die hard" is a misconception that this book aims to dispel. You will discover that through adopting God's mindset and aligning with His ways, you can successfully transform your habits. Jesus assures us in Matthew 11:30 that His yoke is easy and His burden is light, making it easy to embrace His mindset and align our habits with His. It's time to reject the debilitating lies of the enemy and embrace the truth of God's perspective. Prove yourself wrong.

Expectation & Hope

What are your expectations? Our expectations are intertwined with hope and faith: Hope is the anticipation and desire for something to occur. In a biblical context, hope is a steadfast expectation and foundation that something good will manifest in your life or through your actions. What serves as the basis for your hope? Personally, my hope stems from the Word of God, which encompasses His promises and the principles for success. Where do you find your wellspring of hope? Are you preparing for more? Are you anticipating promotion and success? Are you anticipating a breakthrough or bankruptcy? Anticipating more trials or testimony and transformation? Expecting more problems or provision and protection?

God's mindset will cause you to expect certain things, like learning to control your thoughts, change your inner image, and develop into the person God created you to be.

Confidently lay hold of God's promises! They will flourish and yield abundant fruit. Maintain high expectations for these marvelous manifestations. The omnipotent God is actively working and advancing His purposes. 2 Corinthians 4:8, *"So we fix our eyes not on what is seen, but on what is unseen since what is seen is temporary, but what is unseen is eternal."*

Expectation is Key

<u>God desires you to embrace biblical hope for your life.</u> When we pray, it is crucial to have an unwavering belief in receiving the answer and to anticipate its manifestation in our lives. Initially, we receive the answer within our hearts in the unseen spiritual realm, and subsequently, it materializes in the natural physical realm through our faith. The visible aspects encompass the pressures, troubles, and circumstances prevalent in our world, which we seek to change. However, the Bible affirms that our circumstances can indeed undergo transformation. On the other hand, the unseen elements pertain to spiritual aspects, such as the truth found in God's word, God Himself, angels, and the Holy Spirit, which remain constant. <u>Hope serves as a precursor to faith, and through faith, our prayers are answered as it moves the hand of God.</u>

When we face difficulties or go through trials, our true nature is revealed. In such moments, the contents of our hearts become evident. If you were currently facing a problem, what would come out of you? Would your words reflect the mindset of the world, filled with fear and defeat, or would you speak in alignment with God's Word concerning the situation? **It is crucial to understand that what we say has a significant impact on how the situation unfolds.**

What are your anticipations? Are you anticipating a breakthrough or bankruptcy? Anticipating to overcome or be overtaken? Our words serve as indicators of our beliefs and mindset.

Do you tend to engage in fault-finding or good-finding? It is a challenge to be different and choose the path of focusing on the good. Will you make a conscious decision to prioritize the positive today? Rather than searching for what's wrong, direct your attention towards identifying the good aspects of people and situations. Do you celebrate success or constantly seek out failures?

Having a mindset aligned with God's teachings enables you to develop a perspective that actively seeks the good and anticipates positive change.

Expectation plays a significant role in our lives. What are you expecting? Do you anticipate defeat or victory? Are you merely holding on or barely getting by? Or do you anticipate a turnaround, breakthrough, or even bankruptcy? Those who possess God's kingdom mindset expect progress because they have made a conscious decision to combat negative thoughts and circumstances by confessing God's Word. "And my God will meet all your needs according to the riches of his glory in Christ Jesus." Philippians 4:19 They anticipate a favourable shift in their circumstances. They expect victory.

Remember, you are not running out; instead, you are running towards your destiny. You are running alongside God and embracing His mindset. By aligning yourself with God's mindset, you ensure that you will reach the finish line. You are not running out because God's supply is endless.

Personal Example:
I held the position of Public Relations Representative at my school for several years. In that role, I was responsible for communicating school events to the local media, the school board, and members of the community. However, I made a conscious decision to emphasize the positive aspects while celebrating the school's successes. It is important to acknowledge that failures were also part of the journey. Failures are inevitable on the path to success. With a mindset aligned with God's kingdom principles, we learn from our failures, anticipate progress, and maintain a focus on celebrating our successes.

During my tenure, the school's reputation experienced significant growth. Even now, parents express a strong desire for their children to attend our school due to our outstanding reputation and demonstrated history of success. It is true that what we focus on tends to become more visible. As I directed my attention towards celebrating the school's achievements, I developed a proactive mindset of seeking out and expecting more successes. Consequently, I discovered numerous positive activities and programs to share with the community, further enhancing our school's image.

<u>When you cultivate an attitude of anticipation and actively prepare for transformation and success, you are aligning your thinking with God's perspective.</u>

"Imagine the transformation that could occur in our students, employees, loved ones and children if we followed this strategy and focused on celebrating successes rather than fault-finding?"
—*Natalie Masucci*

If speaking kindly to plants helps them grow, imagine what speaking kindly to humans can do?

Vision and Purpose:

"I will share a revelation that will forever change the way you think of your life and purpose." In John 20:21, when Jesus is commissioning the apostles, He says, *"As the Father has sent me, so I send you."*

The Father sent Jesus and commissioned Him with the task of redeeming mankind and bringing them back to God. The Father's expectation was for Jesus to fulfil this life assignment, as there was no alternative plan or "Plan B" in place.

Jesus has commissioned and sent us into the world with a vision and purpose to fulfil. He has no other plan but the Church, represented by you and me. Jesus expects us to accomplish the goals and dreams He has placed on our hearts. There is no backup plan or "Plan B" because He is counting on us to fulfil our life assignments.

When Jesus commissioned His disciples, He equipped them with the Holy Spirit, who would guide and direct them. God does not expect us to accomplish everything on our own.

The gifts and calling of God on your life are irrevocable, as stated in Romans 11:29. It is important to reflect on the fact that Jesus has chosen and created us for a specific purpose in this particular moment in history. We are unique in our abilities and the tasks we are meant to accomplish. No one else can fulfil the specific role that we were created for during our time on Earth.

Since God is unchanging, He will never alter His mind regarding our assignment. He remains steadfast in His plans for us. You are more valuable than you think.

Allow this revelation to grow and intensify within you. This revelation will bring about a transformation in you, shaping you into the person you were destined to be. You will begin to comprehend your inherent value and power, empowering you to rise up, fulfil your purpose, and pursue your unique path. <u>Remember, your vision aligns with God's</u>

vision. It is not a selfish endeavour to pursue the destiny that God has ordained for you; such claims are lies fabricated by the enemy. By achieving financial prosperity and establishing a successful business, you will be equipped to fulfil God's plan of funding the spread of the Gospel and /or supporting various philanthropic endeavours. By going back to school to get that additional qualification, you will be positioned to help people and share the gospel in a new sphere of influence. **Biblical vision understands that the goals and dreams God placed in our hearts are part of God's story for His glory.** It's not about us. It's not our plan but God's plan that will prevail. He is the author. We are the characters. Many are the plans in a person's heart, but it is the Lord's purpose that prevails (Proverbs 19:21). Biblical vision is likened to an annual learning plan containing objectives, action plan and timelines. The objectives in our vision are our dreams, goals and expectations. My vision board acts as my annual learning plan. Biblical vision includes short term and long term goals which lead us to fulfilling our divine purpose.

May we be able to say to God at the end of our lives what Jesus said: **John 17:4-** *"I glorified you on earth by completing down to the last detail what you assigned me to do."* This is the power of biblical vision!

Action Step: On a separate piece of paper, write down the God-Given Dreams and Goals within Your Heart. They are in line with your purpose. In a perfect world, without any restrictions what would you want to do with your life? What are you passionate about?

Fight With Christ's Victory

We need to understand that we are not fighting FOR victory. We are fighting WITH victory! We're not striving to GAIN victory, but in Christ, we have already been given ACCESS to the victory He accomplished on the Cross. We must set our minds on this truth and meditate on it. Jesus, our role model, was sent ahead of us. He embodied everything necessary to fulfil His purpose, and indeed, He accomplished it. He overcame.

We are empowered to fulfil every purpose for which we have been sent, drawing inspiration from the victorious Jesus, the Author and Finisher of our faith. You have the strength to achieve the dreams and goals that God has instilled in your heart. They are an integral part of your PURPOSE. Seeds of greatness have been sown within you, waiting to be awakened. I am here to provide encouragement! You are capable! You will not falter! Failure is not an option. There is no plan B! Holding onto a grudge doesn't make you strong it makes you bitter.

(2 Peter 1:3) *"His divine power has given us everything we need for a godly life through our knowledge of Him who called us by His own glory and goodness."* You and I are EMPOWERED! You cannot and will not fail. God is counting on you and me. If God is for you, who can be against you (Romans 8:31)?

Offence

Offence is rampant in our society today. <u>In a world where everyone is constantly offended, God's mindset is offensive-minded.</u> Once again, we see how God takes a negative situation and turns it into a positive one. Offence is a burden that slows you down and hinders your progress. If you carry Offence, you won't be able to carry anything else. **People make so many mistakes on the assumption that a known past is safer than an unknown future.** Because of this assumption, they hang on to things that no longer serve them, like limiting thoughts and behaviours that keep them stuck. God desires for us to let go of any Offence we may be carrying in our lives. Those with a kingdom mindset possess a teachable spirit Proverbs 13:18 - *"Whoever heeds instruction is honoured"*. God wants us to be teachable and learn from our mistakes, which means being willing to change and grow. Don't hesitate to introspect and evaluate your thoughts, beliefs, actions, habits, and so on. Those with a teachable spirit accept correction without taking Offence or becoming upset. The Bible tells us that God corrects those He loves (Proverbs 3:12). He desires for us to be blessed and live a happy, victorious life, which is why He wants us to adopt His kingdom mindset and make positive changes in our lives.

Offence is a tactic employed by the enemy. If Satan can provoke you to be offended, he can hinder your growth, learning, and transformation. Satan does not want us to possess a teachable spirit, receive constructive criticism, or embrace change. His objective is to keep us defeated and incapacitated. God loves us too much to leave us where we are, He desires for us to go higher.

Growth and maturity come not just from knowledge of scripture but from its application. Merely knowing something without putting it into practice will not yield any benefits. It is only when you start applying what you have learned that you will witness changes in your life. Hearing is good, but action is necessary. It's not enough to simply talk the talk; you must also walk the walk. Unfortunately, many believers fail to follow the Lord's guidance, as outlined in His mindset and then wonder why they struggle to achieve success. <u>Application is an ongoing process.</u> The good news is that you have the ability to change your mindset. You have a choice, and you possess the power to apply the principles outlined in this book to transform your mindset starting today. Today can mark a new beginning for you. Today can be Day One of the rest of your life. Are you ready? I believe that you are! You can take the offensive today by dismantling negative thoughts and incorrect mindsets that have impacted your self-image and are restricting your full potential in life.

God can take something ordinary that no one wanted and turn it into something extraordinary many will celebrate. (whereheleadsillfollow)

***

Each one of us carries an <u>inner perception of ourselves,</u> shaped not necessarily by facts but by emotions and past experiences. A single negative encounter can distort a person's self-perception for a lifetime. For instance, someone who possesses beauty may perceive themselves as ugly or undesirable due to hurtful words spoken in childhood or a traumatic event. Similarly, individuals who achieve remarkable success may still view themselves as failures because of discouraging remarks claiming they would never amount to much. <u>Our inner self-image has the potential to become a self-fulfilling prophecy.</u> It is not secular wisdom or psychology but rather God's wisdom that can empower individuals to transform their inner self-image.[15]God's mindset emphasizes that our self-perception should be derived from His Word. You are who God says you are, you possess what His Word declares you have, and you can accomplish what His Word proclaims you can do!

Additionally, this journey of self-discovery will require us to cultivate self-compassion and extend grace to ourselves. It is essential to recognize that we are all imperfect beings and God's love for us is not based on our performance or perceived flaws. He sees us through a lens

---

[15] Andrew Wommack - *Instagram post*

of unconditional love and acceptance. By embracing this truth, we can begin to dismantle the negative self-image that has held us captive.

Moreover, as we gain a deeper understanding of our true identity in God, we will also uncover the unique gifts and talents that He has bestowed upon us. Each of us has been intricately designed with a purpose and a role to fulfil in this world. By embracing and nurturing our God-given abilities, we can make a positive impact on those around us and fulfil our part in God's grand plan.

Throughout this book, we will explore practical strategies and biblical principles to help us reframe our self-perception, align our thoughts with God's truth, and unleash our full potential. It is a journey of transformation, growth, and embracing the abundant life that God has intended for us.

Remember, you are fearfully and wonderfully made. The process of healing from Identity Dysmorphia and embracing our true selves may take time, but with God's guidance and the tools provided in this book, we can step into a future filled with purpose, confidence, and the joy of living out our God-given destiny.

"Your perception that you have of yourself dictates the reality that you live in."

—*Mark Mathys*

Those who embrace a Kingdom mindset comprehend that they are engaged in a continual journey of learning and personal development. They firmly believe that talents and abilities can be nurtured and developed, enabling individuals to fully realize their potential. [16]

This perspective fosters a genuine passion for learning and cultivates resilience, which are both essential for achieving great accomplishments. The global Covid-19 pandemic has undoubtedly tested our resilience as we were required to adapt to numerous changes.

God's mindset encompasses the belief that we are lifelong learners. He is likened to a potter, shaping and molding us as clay (Isaiah 64:8). We are in a constant state of transformation, growth, and development, becoming the individuals God intends us to be in order to fulfil our life's purpose.

God desires for us to recognize our inherent value and understand that each of us has a distinct purpose to fulfil. When we truly believe in something, we are willing to invest our efforts and go to great lengths to achieve success. Sweat becomes a visible demonstration of our

---

[16] *Dweck* p.45

commitment and hard work. It is through effort and diligent work that success is attained. Our beliefs about ourselves profoundly influence our actions and the choices we make.

Jesus serves as our ultimate example. He exerted immense effort in fulfilling His life assignment of redeeming humanity. He approached everything He did with intentionality. In Luke 22:44, during His prayer in the garden of Gethsemane, Jesus experienced such intensity that His sweat poured out like drops of blood. Why? He was contending against negative thoughts from the enemy. In that moment, Jesus carried the weight of our humanity and faced significant struggles. Despite his inner turmoil and the temptation to save Himself, Jesus pressed forward without giving up. I believe that as Jesus wrestled in prayer, He replaced those toxic thoughts with positive faith declarations from the Word, affirming, "I can and will accomplish what my Father asks of me." It was Jesus' immense love for us and His unwavering kingdom mindset that empowered Him with the strength and determination to endure all the way to the cross.[17]

"Every time you rehearse the truth, you negate a little more of the lie."

—Jesse Duplantis

In that pivotal moment on the cross, God allowed Jesus to experience abandonment so that we would never have to endure His forsakenness. By temporarily turning away from Jesus, God ensured that He would never turn away from us.

It is important to notice that as Jesus persisted in prayer, battling the never thoughts from the enemy that God sent angels to minister to Him and empower Him to persevere. Jesus' effort in prayer caused God to send angelic assistance and support (Luke 22:43). This is available to us as well.

God's mindset provides us with the strength and determination to persevere during challenging times. Through the Holy Spirit, God remains by our side, offering guidance and assistance. His presence is unwavering, and He never forsakes us. He faithfully accompanies us throughout our journey, offering His support and promising to aid us every step of the way (John 16:13-15).

Effort is essential in adopting God's mindset. Anything worth having requires effort, including the diligent work of identifying, rejecting, and replacing negative thoughts. Occasionally, the enemy tries to sow doubt, self-preservation, confusion, and fear, leading to

---

[17] Hagee Ministries *daily devotional* - 2020.

temporary struggles, just as Jesus experienced. I believe that Jesus wants us to exert effort as well, to put in the sweat and determination for what we believe in. We should strive to accomplish the goals and dreams that He has placed in our hearts. Nothing of true value comes without effort. Jesus was able to overcome thoughts of quitting and self-preservation, and so can we. He serves as our role model, and <u>God would not ask us to do anything He didn't expect His Son to do.</u> Fulfilling our life's purpose may not be easy, but it will be immensely worthwhile. Just as exercising can be painful yet necessary for good health, the benefits of fulfilling our purpose far outweigh the temporary pain or effort. It requires ongoing application of God's word and consistent effort to realize our destiny, but the rewards will be limitless: becoming the best version of ourselves, making a difference, spending eternity with God, and leaving a lasting legacy to make the world a better place. (2 Corinthians 4:17-18)

What thoughts are you struggling with right now?
<u>What program have you been running in your mind?</u>

Identify them and then replace them, just as Jesus did. Jesus refused to let those negative thoughts hinder him from fulfilling his purpose, and we should follow his example. He didn't allow pain and hardship to discourage him. Instead, let's substitute toxic thoughts with promises from the Word of God. Meditate on God's promises and affirm them over yourself in faith in order to renew your mind. <u>Remember, what you consistently hear, you will eventually believe</u>.

Demons speak lies into the minds of people. Don't run the devil's program in your mind. Jesus put forth effort to accomplish His purpose of redeeming mankind, and it will require effort for us to renew our minds and fulfil our life assignments too.

Didn't you know that the Messiah would have to suffer before he was given his glory? Luke 24:26

"Hardships often prepare ordinary people for an extraordinary destiny."

—C.S. Lewis

Throughout our lives, we go through a journey of change and growth. The Holy Spirit is actively transforming us to become more like Jesus, as stated in 2 Corinthians 3:18. This ongoing process is known as sanctification, which begins when we first become part of God's family and continues throughout our entire lives. As long as we're still breathing, God is continuously working on us and has a purpose for our lives.

Personal examples of a growth mindset:

I worked as an elementary teacher for 34 years, and throughout my career, I viewed teaching as more than just a job—it was a calling. As parents, guardians, grandparents, godparents, and educators, it is our responsibility, as stated in Ephesians 6:4, to prioritize ensuring that our children not only have knowledge of God and His Word but also develop a personal relationship with Him.

Throughout the years, I have had the privilege of meeting and collaborating with numerous incredible individuals who wholeheartedly love God and consistently demonstrate that love to their students, parents, and the wider community. One person who particularly stands out is my former principal, Franco Troiani. Despite being younger than most of the teachers on staff, he approached his role with a growth mindset, encouraging us to embrace new technology and curriculum initiatives. He prioritized building personal connections with the staff and focused on nurturing relationships. His signature phrase, "Stay well and pray often," clearly conveyed his reliance on God's providence and grace.

I vividly recall how our staff meetings would commence with a prayer, followed by our principal, Franco Troiani, offering words of praise and affirmation. He began each gathering with positive reinforcement and encouragement, expressing his pride in our work and his deep appreciation for our efforts. <u>He employed a gratitude-centred approach,</u> taking the time to acknowledge and celebrate the successes of both teachers and students from that month. Then, seamlessly, he would introduce new concepts or initiatives he wanted us to embrace. However, alongside his expectations for our growth, he genuinely believed in our ability not only to learn but to excel in those endeavours. He held us to high standards but was always there to provide assistance and support. Furthermore, he fostered an environment where our ideas and mistakes were welcomed, utilizing them as valuable opportunities for learning through constructive feedback.

> **"Know that when people in your life have certain expectations from you, it's not always a bad thing. They wouldn't have high expectations from you if they did not think highly of you."**
> *—Samreh Levi*

He skillfully divided mandates into manageable tasks, organizing them within a reasonable timeline. Collaborative learning was promoted, and input from all staff members was warmly welcomed. Additionally, he was understanding and accommodating, providing extra time whenever necessary. He consistently articulated the purpose and benefits of adopting these new initiatives, emphasizing how they would save us time and streamline our work. Phrases like **"We will get through this!"** and "Thank you for all you do!" were frequently spoken, reflecting his unwavering support and appreciation. His love for learning and unwavering faith were powerful influences on both my life and the lives of my colleagues. He really encouraged me personally to follow my dreams and write this book and pursue the calling on my life. For this, I am eternally grateful.

I am a living testament to the effectiveness of growth mindsets. At the age of 56, I embarked on a new career, wrote a book, and initiated a non-profit empowerment ministry. However, it's important to note that God's mindset surpasses mere positive thinking and adopting a growth mindset, as I will elaborate. It offers a far superior and transformative perspective that goes beyond our own understanding.

> **"Education kinda feels like we are stuck in a downtown core, surrounded by buildings, we can choose to focus on the buildings, but we immediately realize we can't move buildings, we can't get through them, but between every building, there are spaces, let's focus on those spaces, focus on what we can get through."**
> —*Richard Gerver*

My principal, Franco, guided our staff in recognizing and <u>directing our attention towards the spaces—the God-given opportunities—we encounter daily to make a positive impact on others.</u> By shifting our focus from limitations to possibilities, we were empowered. Such focus fosters a sense of purpose and fulfilment. For instance, it could be as simple as bringing a smile to a child's face or providing a colleague with a much-needed laugh to relieve their stress. It could also involve learning something new each day. We have the power to choose what we focus on, and every day presents us with that decision-making opportunity.

Recent research has provided valuable insights into how the brain learns most effectively, highlighting the significance of adopting a growth mindset for optimal learning. A few years ago, I began implementing growth mindset pedagogy in my Grade One class. First, I introduced the concept of a growth mindset, explaining how our brains function as muscles capable of growth. To instill confidence, I purposefully employed positive reinforcement and praise when presenting new tasks to my students. For instance, I would remind them of all the skills they had acquired since kindergarten, emphasizing that they were now "big kids" who had progressed to grade school. I would have them flex their muscles, metaphorically symbolizing the growth of their brain muscles through perseverance in tackling challenging tasks and activities. Encouraging them not to give up, I explained that their brain muscles were stretching. To add some lightheartedness, I would playfully joke that their heads were growing so big that they might not fit through the door anymore. Incorporating humour and laughter proved beneficial when introducing new concepts as it alleviated anxiety, fear, and tension, creating a more receptive learning environment.

Almost immediately, I observed a noticeable decrease in my students' anxiety towards new tasks. They exhibited less hesitation and procrastination, and their frequency of questions decreased. As the year progressed, my students began to anticipate and welcome new, challenging tasks. By ensuring they experienced early success, their self-confidence grew. I would continually attempt to "stump" them, but they continuously found ways to tackle the tasks. The element of challenge seemed to motivate them, particularly the boys. They were no longer afraid of the challenges and were determined not to let me win and do my celebratory happy dance! Whenever they succeeded, we would all join in dancing around the classroom to the song "Happy" by Pharrell Williams, ensuring that even if they didn't succeed, they still had fun. This further bolstered their self-confidence. I consistently praised their efforts and highlighted their problem-solving skills, often joking that they were becoming so smart that they might need to be promoted to the next grade or even skip a grade altogether. Implementing a growth mindset with my students helped them recognize their intelligence and talents. It nurtured their problem-solving abilities and equipped them with strategies that will serve them throughout their lives. Moreover, it empowered them to overcome fear and anxiety. I highly recommend adopting a growth mindset with your students and children for their personal development and success.

Our brain functions like a muscle, becoming stronger through exercise. Similarly, our mind strengthens when we consciously resist and replace negative and limiting thoughts associated with a fixed mindset. For instance, instead of thinking, "I don't understand math" or "I'm not good at math," we can reframe our thoughts by asking questions such as, "How can I approach this problem?" or "What prior knowledge can I apply?" or "Who can I work with to help me?" By engaging in this type of questioning, we invite more information and perspectives, effectively countering the negative thoughts.

Fortunately, circumstances aligned, and I had the opportunity to track the progress of several of my students over the course of a couple of years, coinciding with the challenging times of the Covid-19 pandemic. This allowed me to assess and quantify the advantages derived from cultivating a growth mindset.

On the first day back at school, I had my former students participate in an activity called "How I felt on the first day of school," where they completed a feelings graph. The options provided were "worried," "nervous," "scared," "excited," and "other." To my surprise, the majority of students expressed excitement about returning to school, particularly with me as their teacher. While I had concerns, they were genuinely excited. Despite the new class and grade level, which marked their return to in-person learning after the pandemic, they approached it with enthusiasm. They were not only excited about being back in a physical classroom setting, but also about having me as their teacher once again. There was a sense of comfort and familiarity because they either knew me personally, heard about me through their parents or the school community. They were aware of my reputation as a firm but fair teacher, and this knowledge contributed to their excitement. <u>Instead of being fearful of something new, my students embraced it with excitement</u>. This provided strong evidence in support of the benefits of fostering a growth mindset.

The enthusiasm my former students exhibited towards school changes, even during the challenging circumstances of a pandemic, demonstrated their strong growth mindset. While many children commonly experience anxiety and fear when faced with the start of a new school year, a different class, a higher-grade level, a new teacher, classmates, and routines, my former students were filled with excitement instead. I attribute this positive response to the groundwork we laid on developing a growth mindset in the previous year, as well as their familiarity with me as their teacher.

While praying, the Holy Spirit revealed to me the importance of reacting to changes as adults in the same way children do. <u>We should approach changes with excitement and anticipation, knowing that they come from God, who has an impeccable reputation!</u> Scripture reminds us that God is constantly doing new things (Isaiah 43:19). Just as children trust their parents and teachers, we are called to trust God wholeheartedly (Matthew 18:2-4). Instead of fearing change, we should embrace it with enthusiasm, saying, "Bring it on! I am eager to learn and grow!" Change signifies that God has something fresh and better in store for us. God desires us to have unwavering trust in Him and to transform our preconceived notions about change. Our perspective on change matters greatly. Let us choose to believe that when one door closes, it is because God is opening an even greater one.

Another effective strategy I implemented was pairing students who had grasped certain concepts with their classmates who needed assistance. Research demonstrates that when you teach something to someone else immediately after learning it, there is a remarkable 90% retention of information. By actively practicing what they had learned, students were able to retain approximately 75% of the material. These strategies are not only effective but also align with God's kingdom mindset. God, as the first and greatest Teacher, encourages us to share our knowledge and help others who are going through similar experiences. Through **deliberate practice**, God transforms our trials into testimonies and our messes into messages that can bless and inspire others. It is His desire for us to share our testimonies and learnings with others. This sharing process enhances lesson retention, reaching around 90%. Furthermore, while we are in the process of learning, God provides numerous opportunities to practice our newly acquired skills, ensuring a retention rate of 70% or more. <u>Deliberate practice is an integral part of God's mindset, aimed at preventing us from repeating the same mistakes.</u> God's intention is to elevate us with His kingdom mindset, continually guiding us toward higher levels of understanding and growth.

Ex: share your testimony with someone. Pray for someone who is going through what you did. Share a text, post, book, podcast or resource that helped you and teach someone else, a child, friend, co-worker something that you learned.

"Operating in God's kingdom mindset is like playing an instrument. You learn and get better with practice."

—Natalie Masucci

God's kingdom mindset goes beyond what has been taught about growth mindsets thus far. While it shares some similarities, it is not the same.

In God's kingdom mindset, we are not left alone to attempt to control our thought processes through our own strength. Willpower can only take us so far. God's mindset encompasses His Word (the Bible) and the assistance of the Holy Spirit. It also includes our WHY power, which is the driving force behind fulfilling our vision, goals, and purpose. Your WHY power always surpasses your WILL power. Adopting a kingdom mindset helps us pursue our life's purpose.

God's Word serves as the success criteria that guides our lives. The Holy Spirit provides ongoing descriptive feedback, enabling us to live by faith, make necessary corrections, learn from our mistakes, and consistently progress toward fulfilling the assignments God has given us. **God's mindset guarantees success because it is a partnership equipped with fail-safe mechanisms. As long as we remain in alignment with His ways and mindset, success is assured.**

"*{Proverbs 16:3 Commit your actions to the Lord, and your plans will succeed.} & {1 Kings 2:3-Observe the requirements of the Lord your God, and follow all His ways. Keep the decrees, commands, regulations, and laws written in the Law of Moses, and you will find success in all your endeavours and wherever you may go. }*

God's mindset is a partnership—a Holy Trinity consisting of you, the Holy Spirit, and the Word. You are not left to navigate on your own, relying solely on your own strength. God equips you with the Bible and the Holy Spirit dwelling within you, enabling you to always hear His voice, receive His guidance, and follow His directions.

What is your WHY power?

Your "Why" power is your rationale, your heart and the reason for what you're doing. Harnessing your why power is quite simple. In all situations in life, ask yourself why you are making this decision. Your why power includes your purpose. You persevere because you understand that this is part of your life assignment and that God is counting on you. For example, you take care of yourself because you know that your body is the temple of God. You understand that God wants you to be healthy and strong so you can enjoy life and fulfil your destiny.

Your willpower will get you through a 100-meter race, but your whypower will help you finish the marathon.

A Difference between God's Kingdom Mindset vs. Scientific Definition

In a scientific definition of a growth mindset, we acknowledge that our intelligence and talents can expand through practice, but we do not hold the belief that we can do all things. However, in God's kingdom mindset, we understand that through intentional practice, our intelligence, gifts, talents, and faith can all grow. We believe that we can do all things through Christ who strengthens us, as clearly stated in verses through the Bible. [18] Embracing this mindset removes all limits and barriers from our minds. If we can believe for it, then we can achieve it. The possibilities become boundless, and the sky is the limit!

Knowing that having a kingdom mindset is how God designed us to function is **empowering**. Having a kingdom mindset strengthens us and makes us not afraid to face new challenges and problems, just like it did with my students.

I believe that God has entrusted me with a mission to share His mindset, empowering His children worldwide with the necessary tools to effectively fulfil their God-given assignments. You have a significant purpose to fulfil, and your presence on planet Earth is essential. God's mindset provides you with the tools to strengthen your faith and navigate your journey. Walking by faith is a fundamental aspect of God's kingdom mindset.

Part of God's mindset involves understanding that we are not alone; we have a partner. God has graciously given us a helper, the Holy Spirit, who is constantly by our side to assist us on our journey of growth and navigating through life's challenges (John 14:26). The Holy Spirit is that gentle, inner voice within us. Some refer to it as intuition or gut instinct. Never underestimate the power of your gut instinct. It is not a sign of paranoia or craziness. The Holy Spirit within you can help discern potential dangers ahead. If something deep inside you tells you that something is wrong about a person or situation, pay attention to the warning. We will delve into the specifics of the Holy Spirit's role in later chapters. The Holy Spirit plays a vital role in God's mindset, providing ongoing descriptive feedback to ensure you always know how you are progressing and where you are heading. With God on your side, victory is your destiny!

"Holy Spirit's guidance in the form of descriptive feedback is a pillar of God's mindset."

—*Natalie Masucci*

Operating with God's mindset is like having your Father in the house: God is His word.

In the song "The Father's House" by Cory Asbury, the lyrics express that love breaks through when the Father is present. When our heavenly Father is in our midst, we find solace in laying down our burdens and

---

[18] *Philippians* 4:13, *Matthew* 19:26, *Luke* 1:37, *Matthew* 17:20, *Mark* 10:27, e.t.c

shame. With the Father's presence, we are immune to the enemy's lies. We can release our incorrect mindsets and limiting thoughts as He reminds us of our identity as His children. Having Father God in our lives, both through the Holy Spirit and our mindset, is a fundamental aspect of God's kingdom mindset. Who wouldn't desire a partnership with God? <u>When God is our partner, failure becomes impossible (Exodus 14:14).</u> Allow this truth to permeate your consciousness today and let it eradicate all self-doubt and fear within you.

Your partnership with God has good credit. That's why it's called SIGNIFICANT other. Sign/If/I/Can't

Consider your earthly father. Was he a man of integrity? Did he fulfil the role of a loving and supportive father? Did he create a sense of safety and security during your upbringing? Was he a provider who would go to great lengths to help you if you asked for assistance? If this wasn't your experience, I am deeply sorry. It should not have been so.

As a child, I always felt protected when my father was around. I knew he would defend me against any potential harm. Reflect on the trust that babies have in their parents. They instinctively rely on them to meet all their needs and care for them completely. Babies do not experience fear; it is a learned behaviour. <u>Fear is not natural,</u> meaning we are not born fearful. It is acquired through life experiences, words, warnings, thoughts, and observations.

Now, let's reflect on God the Father, the Creator of the Universe. God surpasses the faithfulness and goodness of any earthly father. He is a truly good Father who will move heaven and earth to reach you. The Bible assures us of God's faithfulness, stating in Joshua 21:45 that He keeps His word. God remains steadfast. As *Malachi 3:6 declares, He says, "I am the Lord, I do not change."* So, why do we worry? Why do we doubt? Our prayer should be, "Father, remind me that you are with me through the Holy Spirit." (You provide descriptive feedback to help me.) With our Father God in our lives, we can experience a sense of safety and security, regardless of what may be happening in our personal lives or in the world. Babies are born with trust, as it is an innate ability. Trusting is how God designed us. On the other hand, <u>fear is a learned behaviour</u>. **If something can be learned, it can also be unlearned**. Let us say no to fear and embrace faith and trust today. God desires to restore us to our original position—a place of complete trust in Him. Like babies instinctively trust their parents, God wants us to trust Him.

It is God the Father who defines us, not our circumstances or failures. **Failure** is merely an event, not a reflection of who we are as individuals. It is something that happens to us, not our identity.

Ultimately, it is God who has the final say in our lives and determines our success. His standards differ from those of the world. God does not expect us to be perfect; He simply desires our trust and obedience. He wants to collaborate with us and work through us. God encourages us to take action and persevere. Embracing God's kingdom mindset, which allows His presence to dwell in our lives, enables us to live without fear or worry and instead place complete trust in Him. Those who adopt God's mindset understand that He is good, He is on their side, He is within them, and He fights for them. God is faithful, and we can confidently place our trust in Him.

"God doesn't need our ability. Just our positive response to His ability."

—Andrew Wommack

FAITH

Faith is a spiritual muscle

Faith is an incredibly potent force. The Scriptures affirm that through faith, God brought forth the creation of the universe and its solar systems. With the declaration, **"Let there be light!"** (Genesis 1:3), <u>He unleashed His faith,</u> and not only did those words manifest into reality, but also, to this day, the universe continues to expand at the speed of light. God's words are still producing to this day!

"Faith is the force that gave birth to this natural world. So it can change or overcome anything in it."

—Kenneth Copeland

A key aspect of God's kingdom mindset is recognizing that faith is a spiritual muscle. The more we exercise our faith, the stronger it becomes. We activate our faith through both our words and corresponding actions.

This is how God's mindset operates: First, we discover what His Word says concerning the areas of our lives that require change or the things we desire. Then, we believe in it, speak it out, and take corresponding actions. It is through this process that faith springs into action, releasing its creative power to meet our needs.

When we actively exercise our faith, we place it under pressure, causing it to stretch and grow stronger, much like muscles in our bodies are formed. God expects us to nurture and develop our faith. Your faith has the capacity to grow. Romans 10:17 affirms that **"faith comes by**

hearing and hearing the word of God." Faith responds to the Word. Even as you read this book, your faith is expanding within you. It is not a sensation felt in the physical body, but rather a spiritual force that emanates from your spirit. God expects us to utilize our faith, following the example set by Jesus, to appropriate what rightfully belongs to us, bless others, and fulfil our life's purpose.

Our abilities have the potential to improve over time. God's primary concern is not our abilities but rather our availability to Him. Those who embrace God's mindset comprehend that their faith will ultimately grow and strengthen. As we navigate through diverse tests, trials, and life challenges, our faith, likened to a spiritual muscle, is exercised and fortified, resulting in increased strength.[19] Similar to the saying, **"What doesn't kill you makes you stronger,"** the majority of challenges, trials, and problems we encounter in life are not intended to annihilate us. Instead, they serve as catalysts to propel us forward, promoting personal growth and advancement to the next level in our relationship with God.

Those who possess a kingdom mindset firmly believe that their innate abilities are merely a starting point for their potential. They understand that the human brain has the remarkable capacity to change and adapt throughout life. Similarly, individuals with God's mindset grasp the concept that their faith, just like their abilities, has the potential to grow. God, being a faith-driven deity, would not design a life plan that does not require us to live by faith. Hebrews 11:6 reinforces this notion: *"And without faith, it is impossible to please God because anyone who comes to Him must believe that He exists and that He rewards those who earnestly seek Him."*

Faith is the currency of heaven—a spiritual equivalent to the money that can be utilized to obtain what we desire and need. <u>Thus, possessing great faith renders one rich.</u> It is through faith that we move the hand of God, relying on His Word and embracing His kingdom mindset as the operating system. Faith allows us to receive and experience the supernatural abilities of God in our lives. God expects us to walk by faith while finding solace in the knowledge that He is constantly present and working through us. Philippians 2:13 reassures us that God resides within us, working both to inspire and empower us to carry out His good will. We are not alone; God actively operates within us and through us. If God dwells within you, victory is inevitable! Our confidence does not stem from ourselves but from our partnership with God.

---

[19] *James 1:2, 1 Peter 1:6-9*

Next time someone tries to bring you down, remember this: Confidence is quiet, but insecurity is loud.

Faith is an actual and tangible substance in the spiritual realm, much like money holds value in the earthly realm. When we speak God's Word, the substance of faith is unleashed. As we believe in the spoken word, faith becomes a reality. Faith operates in the present moment; it is not constrained by time. While hope looks towards the future, faith exists in the present (Hebrews 11:1). Faith operates at an astounding speed, faster than the speed of light or even warp speed. The moment we believe, our desired outcome begins to materialize. <u>Faith bridges the gap between Jesus' past actions and our present reality</u>. Through His sacrifice on the cross over 2,000 years ago, Jesus has already provided what we are believing for. When we speak words of faith and truly believe in them, our miracles are set in motion. Faith enables us to walk in the blessings that God has predestined and prepared for us (Ephesians 2:10). God's faith-filled words have paved the way, and our own words of faith allow us to walk in His provision. Exercising our faith is an integral part of embracing God's kingdom mindset.

"When you hear no, I want you to say next. No means next with God."

—Steven Furtick

Scientific research has demonstrated that our brain undergoes growth and strengthening when we persist through challenging situations. In fact, new neural connections are formed within our brains. The brain operates on a principle where pathways that are frequently utilized become stronger, while those that are rarely used weaken and are eventually replaced. Interestingly, failure stimulates more neural activity than successfully completing a new task. As Dr. C. Leaf suggests, individuals with a growth mindset view failure as valuable data rather than a destructive force. Making mistakes and learning from them is an essential part of our maturation and personal growth.

When we comprehend that taking risks, making mistakes, or even experiencing failures or setbacks are inherent to the learning process, we become less disheartened when they occur. Instead, we embrace a mindset that allows us to move on to the next attempt when something doesn't work out. We persistently try different approaches until we find a solution. In my experience, my students became excited about the challenges I presented to them. In God's mindset, "no" simply means **"next."** God expects us to ask questions, engage in problem-solving, and persevere. With God, nothing is impossible.

Take a moment to reflect on a few questions: Why didn't it work? What can I learn from this? How can I approach it differently next time? By asking ourselves these questions, we engage in self-reflection and promote personal growth.

Those who possess God's mindset do not internalize failure; instead, they view it as a stepping stone towards their destined purpose. They adopt the perspective of **"I am one step closer"** rather than allowing failure to define them. Failure may happen to us, but it does not determine our identity. We are much more than the mistakes we make. These individuals grasp that our true identity is defined solely by God. In His Word, the Bible, we discover God's definition of us. The Bible declares that we are **"more than conquerors through Him"** (Romans 8:37). Conquerors do not succumb to failure; they emerge victorious. You have the ability to conquer your fear of failure. Moreover, you can alter your response to failure and redefine what it means to you. If God, who does not become upset or distraught by failure, sees it as a stepping stone to success, then we should adopt the same perspective.

If we don't risk failure, we don't risk success.
"If you live by people's applause, you'll die by their criticism.
You're living for an audience of one."

—Eric Petree

Having a kingdom mindset is empowering, as it offers a different perspective on failure. Instead of being discouraged by failure, it is seen as an opportunity for growth and learning. Failure becomes a valuable teacher, providing us with lessons and stories that we can share as testimonies. As the saying goes, **"Without a trial, there would be no testimony."**

For instance, consider students faced with challenging math problems at school. Those who possess a growth mindset are not deterred by failure. They actively seek out the learning experiences that failures offer. They intentionally surround themselves with individuals who are more skilled or knowledgeable, as they understand the value of learning from those who excel in their areas of expertise. <u>Rather than feeling intimidated, they are inspired by such individuals.</u> This practice of intentionally seeking out those who are better is a habit often observed in highly successful individuals.

The company you keep holds significance. Why? Because you tend to become like the top five individuals you spend the most time with. Reflect on the people you currently invest the most time with. It is not sufficient to simply have good friends around you; it is crucial to surround yourself with godly companions. Cultivate an environment of positivity. Godly friends will provide you with wise biblical perspectives, love, and encouragement during times of trial and temptation. They will assist you in staying on track towards your goals.

The individuals you choose to associate with today are actively shaping the person you will become tomorrow. Begin to evaluate and assess the time you spend with others. Prioritize spending more time with those who inspire and support your success while reducing the time spent with those who hinder your aspirations. Steer clear of negative individuals who bring you down or discourage you from pursuing your dreams. Instead, actively seek out positive role models and mentors who ignite your inspiration and can offer guidance along the way.

"Do not sabotage yourself by unwittingly adopting negative, unproductive attitudes through your associations with others."
—Epictetus

Individuals with God's mindset embrace **failure** as a stepping stone towards success, refusing to view it negatively. They understand that **failure** is an inherent part of the journey, one that fosters learning and growth. They recognize the principle that without taking risks, there can be no rewards. To gain something, one must be willing to venture into the unknown. Allow God to transform your mistakes into messages or miracles. God has the ability to turn your failures into fortunes and your troubles into a testimony. God is looking for a glory story. The more un-capable we feel, the more glory He gets!

"I have not failed. I've just found 10,000 ways that won't work."
—Thomas Edison

"By our very nature in Christ, we're created to excel."
—Kenneth Copeland

Mistakes are to be expected, but how should we respond when we make them? Our natural tendency is to be hard on ourselves and dwell on our shortcomings. However, instead of beating ourselves up, we should quickly repent for any wrongdoings and let go of them. Repentance allows us to receive God's forgiveness and move forward, leaving our past sins or mistakes behind. It is important to recognize that when we fail, it is our own fault and not God's. We must take responsibility for our actions and repent in order to receive His forgiveness. There is no need to continually punish ourselves when God has already forgiven and forgotten our mistakes (Isaiah 43:25).

Just like the Apostle Paul teaches in Philippians 3:13-14, we should forget the things that are behind us. We need to let go of our past failures and mistakes. Yesterday is gone, so we should not dwell on it. Instead, we should press forward towards the calling and the ultimate prize set before us by God. Let go of the regrets, the failures, and the mistakes, and focus on fulfilling our purpose and serving God. [20]

According to Lamentations 3:23, God chooses to remember our sins no more. If He does not hold onto them, we should follow His example and let go of our past mistakes as well. It is Satan who continually reminds us of our past errors, aiming to instill a fixed mindset within us. As Revelation 12:10 states, he is known as the accuser of the brothers and sisters. Satan's objective is to make us feel hopeless and powerless. However, it is essential to understand that our perspective plays a significant role in how we perceive difficulties, mistakes, and setbacks. Embracing a kingdom mindset means viewing these challenges as valuable experiences. By adopting this perspective, we align ourselves with God's way of thinking. <u>Mistakes serve as opportunities for growth, allowing us to remain humble, teachable, and dependent on God's guidance, provision, and ability.</u>

Scripture reminds us that God's mercies are new every morning (Lamentations 3:22-23). Each day brings a fresh start and countless opportunities. Take a moment each day to acknowledge God's presence in your life (Proverbs 3:6) and embrace His mindset. This reminder will give you the strength and joy to face whatever the day holds. God's mindset remains constant amidst life's uncertainties and changes. <u>Remember to recognize God's partnership with you every day. You are never alone; He is with you and ready to help you.</u>

When God places a dream or goal in your heart, keep pursuing it until you achieve it. He has already equipped you with everything you need to fulfil that dream. As 2 Peter 1:3 states, "His divine power has given us everything we need for a godly life." Notice that it is in the past tense, indicating that we already possess all the necessary resources within us. Once we grasp this truth, we will never let failure be a reason to give up again. You are not a quitter. Instead, view failure as an opportunity for growth and improvement.

When God gives you a dream, He also provides the provision for it. Let this truth sink in. God has already prepared everything you need, and it is up to us to utilize His kingdom mindset and access these provisions through faith. Believe in yourself, trust in God, and know that you have the capability to accomplish what He has placed in your heart. You've got this!

---

[20] George Couros p. -*Innovator's book.*

"God will never consult your past to determine your future."
—*Terri Savelle Foy*

The Bible

B.I.B.L.E. {Best Instructions Before Leaving Earth}

<u>The Bible serves as God's instruction manual for mankind.</u> Within its pages, we find God's kingdom mindset and His criteria for success. These guidelines provide us with the principles to live by, attracting victory and success in every area of our lives.

The Bible is an immense source of encouragement. It is filled with "I Am" and "In Him" statements that reveal our true identity. The Bible contains the gospel, often referred to as "the good news." It is good news because we have obtained victory through Jesus. Our success is not determined by our actions but by what Jesus has already accomplished. Jesus serves as the driving force behind our progress in life. He is the living embodiment of God's Word. Through His positive faith declarations, we are infused with His kingdom mindset, influencing our identity, perspective, and, ultimately, our success.

When we speak Positive self-messages or confessions about our capacity to learn and change, that encourages God's mindset. In God's kingdom mindset, He uses faith declarations in the form of "I Am" and "In Him" from His Word to encourage self-confidence, purpose, belonging, acceptance, and resilience in us.

I have personally witnessed how a lack of belief can hinder individuals and impede their ability to achieve their goals. By affirming powerful "I Am" statements about yourself, you can enhance your self-belief. Rather than waiting for others to believe in you, take action and believe in yourself, for God believes in you. Begin with small steps and make progress towards your goals each day. Your consistent actions will generate momentum, boost your confidence, and reinforce your self-belief.

The Word of God in the Bible is potent, anointed, and creative (Genesis 1:1). Therefore, when we speak God's Word (Jesus) over our lives, it has the ability to bring about actual change. Our spoken words, infused with the Word of God, have the capacity to reshape our circumstances. They serve as vessels carrying the supernatural power of God. Use your words to motivate yourself each morning. Speak to yourself in the mirror and say to yourself enthusiastically: You can and you will have a great day! Everyday is a good day because I'm a child of God! No crying, sulking or fretting. Fix your face. You can and you will be amazing today. You can and you will be successful today. You can and you will be phenomenal today. Now go out there and be great in their face. Fix your face and know that you are everything and everything is you. You will not let anyone ruin your day today. Now go be fabulous honey. And go have a great day on purpose. You're welcome!

"The Bible is like an Owner's Manuel for your mind. It tells us how to live our lives victoriously using God's kingdom mindset and His success criteria."
—*Natalie Masucci*

Hebrews 4:12 *"For the word of God is alive and powerful. It is sharper than the sharpest two-edged sword, cutting between soul and spirit, between joints and marrow; it judges the thoughts and attitudes of the heart."*

Hate has four letters, just like Love.
Enemies has seven letters, just like Friends.
Lying has five letters, just like Truth.
Negative has eight letters, just like Positive.
Under has five letters, just like Above.
Cry has three letters, just like Joy.
Anger has five letters, just like Happy.
Right has five letters, just like Wrong.
Hurt has four letters, just like Heal.

This poem illustrates how we can shape our mindset through our choice of words.

<u>God's Word is the only offensive weapon in the Bible.</u> All the other pieces of our armour are defensive in nature (Ephesians 6). God wants us to learn how to use His Word proactively to bring about change in our lives. We must be intentional with our words. The Word of God within us has the power to discern our motives and mindset. It is capable of breaking unhealthy thought patterns, negative habits, and limiting beliefs.

God exemplifies a kingdom mindset. This is His way of operating and functioning. It is characterized by positivity and power. It's interesting to note that God employed a kingdom mindset when dealing with Jesus. He demonstrated the use of positive faith declarations by speaking them over Jesus. God set the example for us to follow by His actions.

God spoke positive faith declarations over Jesus even before His birth. In the Old Testament, God proclaimed what Jesus would become and accomplish. God was declaring Jesus' identity and purpose. Similar to how expectant parents speak and sing to their unborn child in the womb, God spoke positive faith declarations over Jesus from the very beginning of time.

When I was pregnant with my son, Thomas, my due date was September 19th, so I would sing the song "See You in September" by The Happenings to him. Even though he was ten days late, he was still born in September, howbeit on the last day due to my words.

Let's look at Isaiah 9:6 *"For unto us a child is born, to us a son is given, and the government will be on his shoulders. And he will be called Wonderful Counsellor, Mighty God, Everlasting Father, Prince_of Peace."* (NIV) Through the prophet Isaiah, God prophesied the birth of the Messiah, Jesus. He declared things that did not yet exist as if they already did. Through positive faith declarations and prophecies, He spoke victory, identity, and purpose into His son Jesus long before His birth.

<u>I wonder what would happen if we followed our Father's example and did this with our children, students and loved ones.</u> Why don't you start speaking positive faith declarations over them from when they are born before they ever do anything? We can set the stage for their lives with our words.

Maybe your children are older, but why not start speaking faith declarations over them regardless of their current circumstances? When we speak positive faith declarations over ourselves and others in accordance with the Word of God, we unleash powerful spiritual truths that can transform circumstances and outcomes in our lives. For instance, you can declare each day, **"My son/daughter shall be a blessing to me all the days of my life. He/she is respectful and helpful."** Instead of withholding positive affirmations, why not express to your children statements like, **"You are such a blessing to me. Thank you for your kindness and consideration. I truly admire that about you. Your help means the world to me, and I sincerely appreciate it."**

In my own experience, I have always told my daughter Monica that she is "the expressed desire of my heart." This stems from my prayer during pregnancy, where I asked God to fulfil the secret desires of my heart according to Psalm 37:4. Such a declaration instills confidence and fosters self-belief. Monica has grown up to be a trailblazer, becoming the first doctor in our family. Achieving such a goal requires confidence and self-belief. By speaking positive faith declarations over your children, grandchildren, and students, you can instill a sense of pride in them. I truly believe that these words will shatter the barriers of unbelief and empower them to fulfil their true potential. Let your positive words shape the problem solvers, innovators, trailblazers, history makers, and world changers of the future.

Another example of God using positive faith declarations over Jesus is in the New Testament when Jesus was water baptized in Matthew 3:13-17. The Father speaks Jesus' identity over him. *"You are my beloved Son; with you I am well pleased."* Remember, this was the beginning of Jesus' ministry. He had not yet performed any healings, preached, taught, worked miracles, gone to the cross, or been resurrected. God's voice came first, declaring His love and approval for Jesus from the very beginning. Even before Jesus embarked on His ministry, before He performed any miracles or went to the cross, God had already approved and loved Him. This revelation, and more importantly, the realization of it, empowered Jesus to boldly enter the desert to face testing by the enemy. He walked towards the very place where His ancestors, the Israelites, had faltered and perished. God's voice gave Jesus the strength to confront his fears directly. He would no longer be afraid. Jesus overcame the enemy in the wilderness, and we, too, can triumph over our fears. The words spoken over us by God throughout the bible can empower us to face our own fears as well.

Jesus overcame the enemy's deceptions with His Words. During his temptation, Jesus replied, *"It is written"* to every limiting thought. Jesus used the Word of God to dispel the lying thoughts of the enemy. This is the strategy that Jesus modelled and wants us to employ also.

God wants us to be empowered by this truth, too, that He loves us right now. God chose to love you before you were even born (Ephesians 1:4). You hold immense worth and significance in His eyes. His love for you predates your adoption of His kingdom mindset and even before you embarked on fulfilling your life assignment. He loved you before you came to know Him. Just as Jesus conquered the poisonous thoughts of the enemy by relying on the Word of God, you, too, have the power to do the same. God's love empowered Jesus, and it continues to empower you today. You can follow His example. By emulating what Jesus did, you can experience the same victorious results. Victory is within your reach!

In the book **Prototype, Jonathan Martin** states that when God declared He was well pleased in Jesus and that He was His Beloved, Jesus believed Him. He goes on to say, *"And unlike every other person in human history...He never forgot."*

We should always strive to emulate Jesus and remember that God's love for us stems from His role as our Creator. God takes pleasure in us (Psalm 147:10). He is delighted that you are reading this book and seeking to understand His mindset, enabling you to live and operate as

Jesus did. Jesus lived in accordance with God's mindset. He utilized the positive faith declarations found in the Bible to empower Himself, face His fears, and continue moving forward in alignment with His purpose.

Just as God spoke positive faith declarations over Jesus, He also spoke them over you and me. Jeremiah 1:5 *"Before I formed you in the womb I knew you, before you were born I set you apart; I appointed you as a prophet to the nations."* You are God's beloved right at this moment, regardless of any actions or achievements. It is a truth that stands independent of your feelings. Can you accept and embrace this truth? Allow this profound reality, which is an integral part of God's mindset, to revolutionize your life. **God loves you exactly as you are because He intentionally created you in your unique form.**

We do not engage in actions to earn God's love; He assures us from the start that He already loves us. We engage in actions because God loves us. We engage in actions out of our love for Him, not out of obligation but out of genuine desire. We yearn to fulfil our divine purpose because we want to reciprocate His love.

No longer should we find ourselves constantly striving and hoping to hear the words "Well done, My Child" when our time on earth comes to an end. God declares His approval over us even before we step onto the treadmill of life, even before our birth, just as He did with Jesus. Before we were even conceived in our parents' thoughts, God spoke words of purpose and destiny over us. In the book of Jeremiah, God affirms that even before forming us in our mothers' wombs, He knew us, set us apart, and appointed us. Furthermore, God assures us of His great plans for us—plans for our prosperity, not harm, plans that offer hope and a promising future (Jeremiah 29:11). This realization sets us on an entirely new journey.[21] This realization grants us access to God's mindset. God's unwavering love for us forms a fundamental principle within His mindset. It is God's unconditional love for us that empowers us throughout our lives. Such is His love that He proclaims our victory, identity, and purpose even before anything else. He takes the lead, creating an environment charged with His positive faith declarations that shape our lives. When we align ourselves with God's will, we are essentially aligning ourselves with His spoken words over us.

---

[21] Excerpt from Prototype by Jonathan Martin- Faith Devotionals email

The Bible: God's Success Criteria: (Instructions for a victorious living)

The Word of God possesses a living nature due to the fact that Jesus Himself is alive. He is not only alive but also seated in a position of authority at the right hand of the Father.[22]   The Gospel of John commences with the statement, "In the beginning was the Word, and the Word was with God, and the Word was God." In this context, Jesus is referred to as the Word of God.

The Word of God, which is the Bible, originates from the very mouth of God as men were inspired by the Holy Spirit to write it. The Word is readily available and awaits those who choose to believe and apply it in faith. It is important to note that the Word of God is consistently effective in its impact. God's Word is the same yesterday, today and forever. [23]

God's Word is firmly established in heaven and holds eternal significance (Psalm 119:89). God, being unchangeable, remains steadfast in His Word (Malachi 3:6). In fact, He exalts His Word even above His own name (Psalm 138:2). The power of God's Word is enduring and unwavering. It was initially inscribed on stone tablets as the Ten Commandments in the Old Testament and is now engraved upon our hearts in the New Testament (Hebrews 10:16). We can confidently rely on God's Word because it is reliable and trustworthy. God faithfully upholds His Word. <u>Those who possess God's mindset firmly believe in His character and in the truth of His declarations concerning their identity.</u> Just as Jesus relied on God's Word when faced with temptation in the desert, we too can experience positive transformation in our lives as we align ourselves with God's standard, the Bible. If you desire change, embrace God's mindset as your own.

The most efficient path to transform your life is by shifting your thinking from a fixed or limited mindset to a growth mindset, which opens up a world of unlimited possibilities. Your attitude and perspective are the most influential tools at your disposal. However, it is essential to note that God's kingdom mindset surpasses even a growth mindset.

God's Word has the power to transform your present circumstances and amplify your dreams and abilities. It equips you with strength and fortitude, making you formidable and capable.

<u>By altering the words we use, we can effectively change our mindset</u>. When we incorporate God's Word into our speech, it has the

---

[22] *Mark* 16:19

[23] *Hebrews* 13:8

power to bring about transformative changes in our lives. Proverbs 18:21 reminds us that both death and life are influenced by the words we speak. Therefore, it is crucial to choose life by aligning our speech with God's Word and adopting His mindset. Speak words that are positive and edifying, words that leave room for growth, learning and other possibilities.

> **"Talk well to yourself and say, 'I will complete my destiny and reach my destination!"**
> —*Jesse Duplantis*

As believers, it is important for us to consider how we will engage with the Word of God. <u>Are we willing to learn from God's example and use it to speak positive faith declarations from the very beginning?</u> Can we follow Jesus' example in using the Word to counteract the lies of Satan? God desires for us to grasp the true purpose of His Word and utilize it accordingly. The spoken Word of God is active and accomplishes its intended purposes. Hebrews 4:12 *For the word of God is quick, and powerful, and sharper than any two-edged sword, piercing even to the dividing asunder of soul and spirit, and of the joints and marrow, and is a discerner of the thoughts and intents of the heart.* When we learn to speak faith declarations in alignment with God's Word, we will begin to anticipate changes in our circumstances and surroundings. The power of God is embedded within His Word. He employed His Word to bring about the creation of the universe and the world we inhabit. Consequently, He expects us to do likewise. Job 22:28 says, *"If we decree a thing, it shall be established in heaven."* God expects us to use His word to speak some things into existence in our lives, like provision, health, favour, strength, and peace. For example, say, "Today is going to be a great day! I will accomplish everything that I desire today. God is blessing all the work of my hands (Psalm 90:17) and redeeming my time (Ephesians 5:14,16-17)." By doing this, you are setting the stage or charging the atmosphere for your day.

The Word of God serves as the solution to every situation we may face in our lives. The words we speak possess the power to alter the trajectory of circumstances. Our spoken words are reflective of our mindset. When we firmly believe in the creative power of our words, we become formidable. We embody the warriors that God intended us to be. Zechariah 10:5 *Together, they will be like warriors in battle, trampling their enemy into the mud of the streets. They will fight because the Lord is with them, and they will put the enemy horsemen to shame.*

God desires for us to embrace His kingdom mindset. He anticipates our continual growth, transformation, and maturity. As we progress in our journey as believers, we are meant to transition from one level of glory to another.[24] God is always doing a new thing.[25] God desires to bring forth a fresh and innovative work within you. His plans for our lives surpass our own, offering something greater and more remarkable. Those who possess God's mindset willingly surrender their own desires and align themselves with His will (Proverbs 19:21).

Our thinking and prayers often tend to be limited and narrow in scope. We frequently seek to address and resolve our immediate problems and circumstances by praying and confessing the Word of God over our lives. However, <u>it is essential to recognize that God has far grander plans for us than simply fixing our present situations.</u> His desires for us transcend our own. God's plan is not just a regular-sized plan but a supersized one. He wants to enlarge and amplify your dreams and goals. To put it in familiar terms, think of the phrase, **"Do you want to supersize that?"** from McDonald's. <u>Yes, just as McDonald's offers to increase the size of your meal, God wants to supersize your dreams and goals</u>. The Bible assures us that God desires to do immeasurably more than we can ask or imagine (Ephesians 3:20 & Isaiah 54:2). **While it is indeed important to utilize God's Word and mindset to transform our current circumstances, His intention is for us to employ them for so much more.** He has given us His Word to empower us to live victoriously, bless others, and fulfil our unique purposes in life.

God desires to expand and magnify various aspects of our lives. He longs to supersize our dreams, faith, love, joy, peace, blessings, influence, and success. His intention is for the world to witness the abundant blessings bestowed upon His children. He desires us to be a living testament of His love and mindset to the world. God's ultimate wish is for us to utilize His Word to elevate ourselves to the highest possible level and fulfil the unique assignment He has for each of our lives.

Having a kingdom mindset involves transitioning from our limited and self-centred agenda to embracing God's expansive and open-minded agenda for our lives. It requires moving away from a fixed mindset and aligning ourselves with God's transformative mindset. God's agenda surpasses our own in every way. He desires to bring about significant shifts and transformations in our lives. When we align our thinking with His, we adopt a kingdom mindset. God invites us to let go of negative and restrictive thinking patterns and embrace His expansive and limitless perspective. Let us remain open to the possibilities that God presents before us. For instance, keeping our questions open-

---

[24] 2 *Corinthians* 3:18

[25] *Isaiah* 43:18

ended allows for diverse answers and perspectives. However, it is essential to note that God's kingdom mindset surpasses a growth mindset because it encompasses God's unconditional love and approval as well as identity and purpose through positive faith affirmations.

Reading this book and implementing the principles contained within it can serve as a transformative and defining moment in your life. It has the potential to be the most remarkable experience you will encounter. My prayer is that you approach this with a humble heart and surrender the agenda for your life to God. Release your own plans and embrace God's agenda. Let go of your old thought patterns and embrace those aligned with God's. By doing so, I firmly believe that your eyes will be opened, allowing you to perceive God as He truly is. You will gain insight into and comprehend God's mindset. His laws will begin to make sense to you. Your mind and spirit will undergo a profound shift. Are you prepared to initiate these transformative changes? It's time to move away from negative thinking and embrace the powerful and regal mindset of God. Remember, change is a constant aspect of our journey with God.

"When your focus on God's Word becomes 20/20 you stop all mental {guesswork}."
—Jesse Duplantis

FAITH:

We have been created in the image of God, who is a spiritual being and a God of communication (Genesis 1:27). Therefore, we, too, are spiritual beings who possess the ability to speak. While our spirits reside within physical bodies, it is within our spirit that God has bestowed upon each of us a measure of His faith (Romans 12:3). We are designed to walk in the same manner as God does, relying on faith rather than relying solely on what we can see. Just as God speaks things into existence, we are also called to speak and declare things that do not yet exist as though they already do (Romans 4:17). Additionally, we are meant to perceive and comprehend the unseen, focusing our attention not on the visible things but on the invisible things (2 Corinthians 4:18).

Our mindset, love and faith are the aspects of our being that reflect God's nature. Our faith serves as the channel through which we receive the supernatural abilities of God in our lives. It is important to recognize that our faith has the capacity to grow, and this understanding is a fundamental aspect of adopting God's mindset. Not only can our faith grow, but our abilities can also expand. Growth is intrinsic to everything connected to God. God is the ultimate cultivator, and His entire kingdom operates on the principle of seedtime and harvest. **Whatever we sow with our words will inevitably grow and bear fruit in our lives.**

God expects us to continue growing and evolving throughout our lives. There is no age limit when it comes to learning and embracing change. **The notion that "you can't teach an old dog new tricks" is a falsehood stemming from a fixed mindset.** As long as you are alive and breathing, God still has a divine plan and purpose for your life.

Faith is a dynamic force from God. He has given each of us a measure of His faith, the same kind of faith He possesses, so that we can access the blessings that already belong to us (Romans 12:3). According to Scripture, God has already prepared everything we will ever need. It is through our faith that we bring those blessings into manifestation. Through Jesus' sacrifice on the cross, we have been granted all that pertains to this life (2 Peter 1:3). There is no need for us to strive or struggle to make things happen because God has already accomplished it for us.

God doesn't want us to sweat to succeed but rest to receive.
—Natalie Masucci

Unfortunately, there are misconceptions about God's blessings. Some believe that if God wants them to have something, He will simply drop it into their laps, leading them to passively wait instead of taking active steps to pursue their blessings. However, this perspective contradicts Scripture. God has equipped us with the tools necessary to possess and fulfil our life assignments. <u>One of these tools is our faith, which is activated through speaking God's Word with corresponding actions.</u> Positive self-talk and faith declarations work in harmony to activate the blessings and promises of God in our lives. These powerful strategies are part of God's mindset.

Just as God gave the Promised Land to the Israelites, they still had to enter and possess it (Leviticus 20:24 and Numbers 14:8). Similarly, God has given us His kingdom mindset, but it is our responsibility to adopt it and operate according to it in order to enter into our Promised Land.

Entering our <u>Promised Land</u> is walking in our purpose. It will take faith to operate in God's mindset and appropriate all the blessings, help, provision that He preordained us to walk in so we can win our race in life. Be encouraged because the bible says *"And from the days of John the Baptist until now, the kingdom of heaven has been subjected to violence, and violent people have been raiding it."* (Matthew 11:12). We are meant to boldly claim what rightfully belongs to us. God desires for you to have it, and He is not the one holding back your blessings. The enemy is the one who tries to prevent you from entering your prophetic Goshen, sending obstacles and hindrances into your life. Utilize your God-given faith and seize what is rightfully yours today. The days of going without are over!

The Bible states that Abraham had strong faith, which implies that it's possible to have weak faith as well. What kind of faith do you possess? Is it strong or weak? The enemy desires for you to believe that you lack faith or that it is weak, but this is far from the truth.

Remember that God has bestowed upon each of us a measure of His own faith.[26] The faith that God has given us comes in the form of a seed, and He expects us to nurture and cultivate it. How do we accomplish this? The Bible tells us that faith grows as we hear the Word of God.[27] We can strengthen and develop our faith by actively engaging in uplifting and motivational teachings derived from the Word of God. Additionally, through prayer and faith confessions, such as "I Am" statements, we can declare God's Word over our lives. Building our faith requires dedicated effort and commitment. In James 2:7 it says, that *"faith by itself if it is not accompanied by action is dead."*

Our faith and mindset have a significant impact on our actions and words. Taking action is crucial! Here are some steps to consider:

1. Set aside a specific time in your schedule to immerse yourself in the Word of God. For example, you can listen to teachings while driving to work, cooking or cleaning, during your shower, workout sessions, or while taking a walk or walking the dog or while mowing the lawn or washing the car.
2. Make sure to schedule this time, as it helps ensure that it becomes a regular practice. Without scheduling it, it may easily be overlooked or neglected.

"What gets scheduled gets done." As you consistently expose yourself to the Word, your faith will grow stronger. Just like **Abraham**, you can possess strong faith. Abraham's faith grew stronger because he chose to focus on God's promise to him rather than his present circumstances (being too old to have a son) (Romans 4:19). <u>Our minds have a tendency to magnify whatever we focus on, whether positive or negative.</u> Our repeated thoughts shape our thinking patterns and occupy space in our minds. When **David** faced Goliath, he didn't dwell on the danger Goliath posed; instead, he emphasized the greatness of God.

---

[26] *Romans* 12:3

[27] *Romans* 10:17

By focusing his thoughts on the greatness of God, David built up his faith. His faith was evident in his words. *"Your servant has been keeping his father's sheep. When a lion or a bear came and carried off a sheep from the flock, I went after it, struck it and rescued the sheep from its mouth. When it turned on me, I seized it by its hair, struck and killed it. Your servant has killed both the lion and the bear; this uncircumcised Philistine will be like one of them, because he has defied the armies of the living God. The Lord who rescued me from the paw of the lion and the paw of the bear will rescue me from the hand of this Philistine."* And *"You come against me with sword and spear and javelin, but I come against you in the name of the Lord Almighty, the God of the armies of Israel, whom you have defied. This day the Lord will hand you over to me, and I'll strike you down and cut off your head."*(1 Samuel 17: 34 & 45-46) Instead of speaking fear, choose to speak faith. Shift your focus from your circumstances to God. Similar to David, our faith is revealed through our words. Take time to visualize yourself achieving success in your goals.

"We can get into a habit of always saying 'Someday... I'm going to do that, start that, quit that, and achieve that.' But remember, 'someday isn't a day of the week. It doesn't go 'someday, Monday, Tuesday...' When you start scheduling your days to take action, that's when you defeat procrastination. What gets scheduled gets done."

—*Terri Savelle Foy*

3. To cultivate strong faith, it is essential for the Word to dwell richly within us. John 15:7 "If you abide in me, and my words abide in you, ask for whatever you wish, and it will be done for you." <u>"Abide"</u> implies occupying the primary position, so when the Word abides in us, it takes precedence in our minds. The Word of God, in the form of His kingdom mindset, should dominate our thoughts. When we encounter challenges, if the Word dwells within us, it will naturally be the first thing that comes out of our mouths, just as it did for David.

   How can you possess God's mindset and speak the language of the enemy? Your words reflect your mindset. If God's mindset dwells within you, it will be His faith-filled words that flow from your mouth when faced with a problem. You may declare phrases such as, "My God will deliver me" or "My God will make a way for me." Your reactions to life's challenges will ultimately determine their outcomes.

4. "Faith without works is dead" (James 2:26). This implies that you must actively utilize your faith; otherwise, it remains dormant

within you. You activate and engage your faith through your words and corresponding actions. For instance, when you have faith or trust in something, you demonstrate it by taking action. Just like sitting on a chair, you exhibit faith because you trust that the chair will support you. If you lacked belief in the chair's ability to hold you, you would refrain from sitting on it.

The enemy seeks to convince us that our faith is insufficient to achieve our dreams. He deceives us into thinking that our efforts are in vain. He discourages us from even attempting, claiming that failure is inevitable. He wants us to believe that we are weak and that our faith cannot grow. However, it is important to recognize that the enemy is a master manipulator who speaks in half-truths. He selectively quotes the Word while leaving out crucial parts, often taking verses out of context to deceive us. The enemy is cunning and deceitful, which is why it is crucial to have a personal understanding of the Word of God. This empowers us to discern the enemy's subtle lies.

<u>With God's kingdom mindset, we develop the habit of consistently examining the accuracy of our thoughts in light of the truth found in the Bible.</u>

The Bible serves a greater purpose than mere motivation or pleasant quotes. It is the powerful and life-changing Word of God. God's Word acts as spiritual nourishment, fuelling and strengthening your faith and mindset, similar to how natural food nourishes your physical body. Regularly immersing yourself in it is vital to internalize its truths. When God's Word abides in your mind, it naturally manifests through your words and actions.

You can cultivate the ability to assess the validity and usefulness of your thoughts by aligning them with the truth found in God's Word.

Faith for Healing

Years ago, I received a devastating diagnosis of Lupus. Like anyone facing a challenging diagnosis, I was deeply affected. Although I was not yet familiar with the concept of God's mindset, I had enough knowledge of God's Word to understand that sickness was not His intention for me. I chose to believe in His promises of healing and put my trust in Him.

Immediately, the enemy bombarded me with limiting thoughts, suggesting that I lacked the necessary faith for my healing. He never denied that God is a Healer, but he targeted my own perceived lack of faith as a reason for me not to be healed. Initially, I fell into believing his lie, and it caused me significant distress. I began to question both my faith and my relationship with God. Satan made sure to remind me of every instance where I had faltered and failed to keep my word. I was burdened with guilt and condemnation. He deliberately brought up my past mistakes and failures to weaken my faith and prevent me from believing in my healing. The enemy had me convinced that I would never experience healing due to my past errors and perceived lack of faith. Maybe you find yourself facing a health crisis today? I pray that my testimony encourages you.

I am grateful to God for the presence of godly friends in my life who possessed a deeper understanding of His Word. Your inner circle is so important. They directed my attention to the scriptures that revealed how God had already imparted a measure of His own faith to me and that my faith could be nurtured and developed (Romans 4:20 & Romans 10:17). This news was incredibly uplifting and encouraging! In response, I embarked on a journey of voracious reading and avidly listening to anything related to divine healing and faith. The deeper I delved into studying God's Word, the more I discovered its transformative power. It brought me a profound sense of peace, strengthened my faith, and facilitated a shift in my mindset. I immersed myself in God's word until it was abiding in me. I even slept with my bible.

During that period, one practice I engaged in was reciting positive faith declarations aligned with the Word of God, specifically in the areas of faith and healing. Initially, I struggled to truly believe the declarations I spoke, but as I persisted, they transitioned from mere mental agreement to heartfelt conviction. You see, there is a concept known as <u>mental assent,</u> which occurs when we intellectually agree with something without truly believing it in our hearts. <u>Merely agreeing with God's Word in our minds will not bring any real benefit</u>. It becomes nothing more than information we possess. God's Word cannot bring about transformation if it remains unread and untouched in our Bibles. To experience the power of God's Word, we must take it as prescribed— read and meditate upon it regularly. Confessing it consistently is essential. God's Word serves as His prescription for healing and divine health.

Believing in the Word of God originates from the heart. Our belief is rooted in the depths of our hearts. Only when we genuinely embrace the Word of God within our hearts can it manifest its power in our lives.

I consistently declared God's Word over my life, affirming statements such as, "By His stripes, I was healed 2000 years ago; therefore, I am healed now," "I possess a measure of God's faith within me," and "My faith grows stronger each day." As time passed, my conviction in these declarations grew. I transitioned from mere mental agreement to a deep-rooted belief in my heart. When genuine belief takes root in the heart, faith is activated.

As this transformation occurred, my symptoms gradually diminished, and my test results began to show improvement. Then, after six months, all the symptoms vanished completely, and I experienced complete healing! My healing was gradual unfolding as my faith grew and I believed in the Word of God. The Word became my truth, a personal, intimate message from God to me.

The doctors couldn't comprehend it, but I could. The power of speaking God's Word is undeniable. It has been 29 years since my healing took place! When we speak God's Word, we align our thoughts with His. Uttering God's Word is akin to receiving His divine prescription for healing in our lives. Every ailment finds its remedy in the words we speak, guided by His truth.

This book will provide you with <u>foresight,</u> which holds immense significance. Vision is paramount in adopting God's mindset. The Bible emphasizes the crucial role of vision, stating that without it, we face destruction.[28]

With God's mindset, we are equipped to recognize toxic and restrictive thoughts. Intervening at the early stages of toxic thought patterns and issues can prevent heartache and even save lives. Drawing from my experience as a former educator, I understand the significance of **early intervention.** Taking action promptly requires less time and proves to be the most cost-effective approach. Providing intensive support early on, for a shorter duration, yields the best outcomes.

<u>God urges us to take action now to avert future losses. It is crucial to employ foresight and not wait until trouble, tragedy, or illness befalls us to transform our mindset</u>. Make the shift in your mindset without delay! Waiting another day is not an option you can afford.

DISCLAIMER

Please do not misunderstand me. I am not saying not to go to the doctor or not to take medicine, as I did both of those things. What I am saying is that regardless of the means, God is the healer. God wants you to be well. Jesus tells us in 3 John 2-5, 'Beloved, I wish above all things that you may prosper and be in health, even as your soul prospers.' As my soul prospered by meditating on the word of God in the area of healing, my faith grew. When I began to voice my faith through healing confessions, my symptoms improved until they were totally gone.

---

[28] *Proverbs* 29:18

Faith has a voice

Speaking to your circumstances is an action of your faith and mindset.

"Faith declarations serve as the expression of our mindset. Our words shape and construct our mindset." Speaking directly to our circumstances holds even greater power than prayer because it involves decreeing in alignment with God's Word. We are called to calm the storms ourselves by exercising our authority over them (Matthew 8:23-27). We are called to move mountains by speaking to them (Mark 11:23). Our faith is built through the words we speak, and our mindset is likewise shaped by them. Operating in faith is an integral part of embracing God's mindset, for He is a God of faith. Living by faith or living according to His Word is His desire for us. Faith is a continuous journey, not a destination. Walking by faith is a lifestyle that encompasses the decisions we make each day.

Use the foresight provided in this book to begin saying faith declarations over yourself about health and healing. If you wait until illness strikes, it may be too late. Some of the scriptures I used are; 1 Peter 2:24, James 5:15, 3 John 1:2 and Isaiah 53:5. God wants you to use this powerful success criterion and walk in healing and divine health all the days of your life. **"Faith has a voice"**

What have you been speaking over your life recently? In this book, we will discover how to conduct self-evaluation by examining our thoughts and words. Our mindset is shaped by the thoughts and words we entertain.

"We are the only creatures created by God with the remarkable ability to shape our future through the power of our words. Just as God formed the world through His spoken words, you have been bestowed with the authority to shape your own reality through the words you utter."
—*Bishop Keith Butler*

We are the pinnacle of God's creation. We are His masterpiece, destined for greatness. We are called to prophesy into our lives and future by boldly speaking God's Word over ourselves. Through our words, we actively shape our future. Our words reveal our dominant thoughts, beliefs and mindset.

I AM Statements: Positive Self-talk/Faith Declarations:

Jesus possessed a kingdom mindset, which is evident through His use of positive confessions and self-talk throughout His earthly ministry. Jesus consistently affirmed His identity by using powerful "I Am" statements, as recorded in the Gospel of John. The Apostle John beautifully captures the identity of Jesus through these declarations. The Gospel of John can be rightfully called the great "I Am" book. Jesus is described as:

1. The bread of life (John 6:35)
2. The light of the world (John 8:12)
3. The door (John 10:7)
4. The good shepherd (John 10:11 & 14)
5. The resurrection and the life (John 11:25)
6. The way, the truth, and the life (John 14:6)
7. The true vine (John 15:1)

These profound statements reveal the depth of Jesus' identity and emphasize the significance of positive self-affirmation in aligning ourselves with God's kingdom mindset.[29] Click on the link below to download powerful I Am statements from the Word of God that you can recite everyday.

"By adding in repetitive action, your brain will begin to relinquish any beliefs you have over what you can and cannot do."
—Dr. Clifford Saunders, Ph.D.

Jesus proclaimed numerous "I Am" statements in Scripture, which served to empower Him. As our ultimate role model, Jesus consistently spoke these "I Am" statements about Himself to inspire us to do the same. It is a powerful strategy for success within God's kingdom mindset. We are encouraged to continually affirm our identity and purpose, just as Jesus did.

Say, "I am well able to fulfil my destiny. I was born for such a time as this."

Jesus always affirmed His identity because that was the very area Satan attacked Him and continues to attack us. Satan's tactics have not changed; he relentlessly assaults our sense of identity. Satan is an

---

[29] https://empoweredwordministries.ca/wp-content/uploads/2022/12/I-AM-Statements.pdf

identity thief who seeks to make us doubt our true belonging, causing us to forfeit our mission. He cunningly plants thoughts like, "If you were truly blessed, why are you facing these challenges?" or "If God genuinely loves you, why would He allow this hardship?" or "If God truly called you, why is the path so difficult?"

If Jesus, while walking on Earth as a man, consistently affirmed His identity, then it follows that we should also continually affirm our own identity. The "I Am" statements found in John's Gospel serve as a means by which Jesus encouraged Himself and revealed some of His character traits to us. For instance, when Jesus declares, "I am the shepherd," He signifies His role as the one who leads, protects, and provides for us. Essentially, Jesus conveys that He is everything we will ever need Him to be. When we embrace God's kingdom mindset, Jesus becomes everything and everyone we require Him to be.

We can counteract the negative thoughts from the enemy by speaking the Word of God over our lives, just as Jesus did. Let us begin declaring affirmations such as: "I am blessed, I am forgiven, I am valuable, I am healed, I am focused on my purpose, I am equipped, I know who I am, I will fulfil my purpose, my latter years will surpass my former years, I will witness the goodness of God in my life, and more." In times of uncertainty, when we don't understand why things are happening, we can remember that if God allowed it, there must be a purpose in it. These challenges were not meant to destroy us but to promote us.

During seasons of life when we face uncertainty and don't know which way to turn, we are to rely on what we do know—the unchanging truths of God's Word—through the power of "I Am" statements. Click the link below to access powerful I AM statements that you can begin to declare over yourself.

"A silent tongue is a destiny robbed."

—Phil Pringle

"Outside of praying, your most important words are the words that you say to yourself."

—David Jeremiah

When we speak "I Am" statements, we are making powerful faith declarations that align with God's Word. These declarations serve to strengthen our confidence and faith, ultimately bringing into existence what we declare. Jesus stands as our ultimate example in this practice.

Even before going to the cross, He confessed profound "I am" statements about Himself, demonstrating the power of speaking truth over our lives. "I am" appears over 300 times in the bible, starting in **Genesis** 15:1 with *"I am your shield and your very great reward"* **then in Exodus** "I am who I am," and ending in **Revelation 22:16**. *"I am the Root and offspring of David and the Bright Morning Star."* [30]

When God declares "I am" statements about Himself, He is proclaiming absolute truths. These statements serve as reminders to Him and act as a source of motivation. Similarly, <u>when we recite the "I Am" statements presented in this book, we are not merely engaging in wishful thinking. Instead, we are declaring the facts about ourselves based on the Word of God.</u> These affirmations align us with the truth of who we are in God's eyes and empower us to walk confidently in His promises.

Some of the "I am" statements pertain to our identity, while others highlight the character of God. I strongly encourage you to set aside time to read and recite the "I am" statements provided in this book. Doing so will empower you, affirm your identity, and foster a kingdom mindset within you. Jesus serves as our ultimate example in this regard. He demonstrated the power of using God's Word and experiencing victory through it. Just as Jesus consistently employed positive self-talk during His earthly ministry, especially during challenging times like His journey to the cross, we too can follow His example.

For example, during the last supper, Jesus informed His disciples that He was the Bread of Life. At that moment, He had not yet gone to the cross, but Jesus was boldly declaring His purpose. His intention was to affirm His identity and assure His ability to fulfil His life's assignment by becoming the ultimate Bread of Life for all of us.

It is similar to when we speak affirmations to ourselves, such as saying, "I am a New York Times bestselling author," even before we have written our book. If our God-given vision is to become an author, we can begin to declare positive words that align with God's Word and His purpose for our lives. When we commit our work to the Lord, our plans will indeed succeed, as Proverbs 16:3 assures us.

We are called to imitate God, as stated in Ephesians 5:1. Following the example of Jesus, we are encouraged to counteract self-doubt, negative reports, adverse circumstances, or obstacles by choosing to challenge them with the confession of God's Word. When faced with such challenges, let us emulate Jesus and boldly declare the truths found in His Word.

---

[30] Hagee Ministries-*Instagram post*

For example, if you receive a negative doctor's report, instead of sharing and dwelling on its contents, choose to speak what the Word of God says about the situation. Take the time to discover what the Bible, God's criteria for success, says about your circumstances. <u>It is within your right and responsibility to reject any report or outcome that does not align with God's truth for your life.</u> Instead, pray and declare statements like, "I am healed by the stripes of Jesus" and "I believe in my healing." Refrain from identifying yourself with a specific illness or disease, such as cancer or any other deadly condition. By doing so, you avoid accepting it as a permanent part of your life. Instead, declare that you are fighting against it. When you are going through chemo treatments and you say to yourself that this is not the end, that's positive self-talk. The same principle applies to milder ailments like influenza. Rather than stating that you have a severe flu, declare that you are fighting a cold. Let go of statements like, "I think I'm coming down with something," "With my luck, this will turn into pneumonia again," or "I always get a sinus infection this time of year." Such negative self-talk stems from a fixed mindset. Remember, you have the power to reject and resist anything that comes against you by using your words effectively.

What have you been saying? Your words are incredibly important. The thoughts you entertain and the words you choose to express have the power to shape your reality. By verbalizing and affirming certain ideas, you allow them to take root in your mind and manifest in your life. Therefore, it is crucial to be mindful of what you confess and avoid expressing things you do not wish to see materialize.

Let me share an example about my cousin, Lisa. She received a diagnosis of advanced bladder cancer, and the oncologist informed her that it was an aggressive form of cancer. In response, my cousin confidently stated, "I have an aggressive form of faith!" She didn't reject the doctor's report, but she also didn't accept it. She recognized that she was facing a life-threatening battle, yet she firmly believed that her faith equipped her to overcome it. Her words established a powerful foundation for her healing journey. Today she is cancer-free.

You constantly have choices. It's up to you to decide which thoughts or reports you will embrace or dismiss. You have the power to choose how you respond to any situation or circumstance. You can either crumble under pressure or stand resiliently against it (Ephesians 6:13). Life revolves around the choices we make. We can choose to speak positively or negatively. We can speak life or death into existence. We can adopt a fixed mindset or a mindset aligned with the principles of a kingdom. Our choices have a profound impact on various aspects of our lives. They shape our outcomes and even have the potential to reshape our brains.

> **"Change your perspective; Things aren't falling apart; they're falling together."**
>
> —*Natalie Masucci*

When we look in the Word of God, it should be like **looking in a mirror.**[31] The mindset we possess serves as the lens through which we view the world. It shapes our perception of ourselves, our lives, and the world around us. To achieve success in life, it is crucial to align our self-perception with the teachings of the Book. It affirms that we are capable of everything it declares, and we possess all that it promises.

Scripture: James 1:23, someone with a kingdom mindset believes that we learn from our mistakes. We are in a process of growing; we are progressing day by day. **You are a work in progress**. We are on a learning curve. Some are quicker learners than others. Some, like myself, need remedial help, but we'll all get there. There is power in yet. We need to praise the effort and the perseverance that we see in others and ourselves. [32] Give yourself the credit you deserve for your hard work, and recognize the progress you have made. Keep up the great work!

***

God desires for us to have a teachable spirit (Proverbs 13:18). We should strive to be like coachable athletes who attentively listen to and follow their coach's guidance. In our case, the Holy Spirit is our coach, providing us with valuable feedback. Similar to how the apostle Paul likened his life to a race, we should approach our own journey with the aim of achieving victory (1 Corinthians 9:24).

Personally, I share your aspiration to strive for the first-place ribbon rather than settling for a participant sticker. If our goal is to win a race, we understand the importance of physical preparation— practicing to improve speed and strength, monitoring our diet, taking necessary supplements, and ensuring sufficient rest. We do whatever is within our knowledge and capability to gain an advantage. In this pursuit, having a kingdom mindset, aligned with God's principles, becomes our ultimate advantage. God desires for us to embrace this mindset and use it to live a victorious life.

---

[31] 1 *Corinthians* 13:12

[32] Dr. C. Leaf

We recognize the importance of mental preparation, much like **Mohamed Ali** did, through studying our opponents. With positive self-talk, we can undermine our opponent's or the enemy's confidence and bolster our own. Just as we consume the right diet to achieve physical victory, nourishing ourselves with a steady intake of the word of God and positive affirmations strengthens us spiritually. It is crucial to understand that whatever we feed on will grow and manifest in our lives.

When we persevere through challenging tasks or situations, we not only become smarter and stronger, but we also cultivate qualities of the Spirit such as patience, perseverance, faith, love, forgiveness, and more.[33] Perseverance stimulates significantly more brain activity compared to giving up. It is through perseverance that our brains undergo positive transformations. The challenges we face in life are not meant to merely be endured; they are meant to shape and develop us. **God desires for us to not only go through difficult times but to evolve through them, becoming better versions of ourselves.**

"God is faithfully putting a puzzle together in each life so that the final picture will resemble Christ."

—Beth Moore

Action Step

It is beneficial to confess the "I AM" statements from scripture over ourselves daily, following the example set by Jesus. These statements reflect our new names and identity in Christ. When we declare these affirmations over our lives, we speak life into our circumstances and strengthen our identity, faith, confidence, and resilience. When we boldly confess "I Am" statements, we are decreeing them into existence, emulating our Father God. (Job 22:28 & Romans 4:17)

This is not merely a positive confession, as that is associated with the New Age movement. Instead, what I am referring to is declaring our true identity and the blessings we already possess through Christ's sacrifice on the cross. It is not a simplistic "name it and claim it" approach. Rather, we are restating the promises of God as revealed in the Bible. We are declaring the truth. While positive thinking holds power, it is not the sole focus here. I am emphasizing the act of presenting the facts of our lives in the courtroom of heaven. We as members of God's kingdom, we are expected to utilize our kingdom

---

[33] *Romans* 5:3-4.

mindset and authority to appropriate what rightfully belongs to us and fulfil our assigned purpose in life.

When you accept Jesus as the Lord of your life, God assumes the role of author and editor of your life's narrative. You are no longer navigating life on your own; instead, you enter into a **partnership.** With God as your built-in helper, you become part of something greater than yourself. Understanding that God is the author and editor of your life, responsible for determining the final script, relieves the pressure from your shoulders. <u>Your role is to cooperate with Him through a kingdom mindset, striving to fulfil His plan for your life to the best of your ability.</u> Your job is to obey, while it is God's responsibility to bring about the desired outcomes. How do you accomplish this? Consistency is vital. Confess these "I Am" statements until you internalize and believe them. Once you truly believe them, they will initiate a transformation from the inside out. God specializes in bringing about transformation; His Word has the power to change our brains, mindsets, thoughts, hearts, circumstances, and lives.

God's Word has the power to bring about what He wills. God's mindset is His will. We understand through God's Word that His will is always our best-case scenario in life.

"I AM" Statements: Read these out loud every day.

Use these passages to renew your mind and embrace the truth of God's mindset. Personalize them and begin to see yourself through your new identity in Christ.

- ❖ I Am A Child Of God. Romans 8:16
- ❖ I Am A Son Of God. Romans 8:14
- ❖ I Am Forgiven. Colossians 1:14 & Psalm 103:12
- ❖ I Am Saved By Grace Through Faith. Ephesians 2:8
- ❖ I Am Justified. Romans 5:1
- ❖ I Am Sanctified. 1 Corinthians 6:11
- ❖ I Am The Righteousness Of God In Christ. 2 Corinthians 5:21
- ❖ I Am Redeemed From The Hand Of The Enemy. Psalm 107:2
- ❖ I Am Redeemed From The Curse Of The Law. Galatians 3:13
- ❖ I Am A New Creature. 2 Corinthians 5:17
- ❖ I Am An Heir Of God And a Joint Heir With Jesus. Romans 8:17
- ❖ I Am An Heir Of Eternal Life. 1 John 5:11
- ❖ I Am More Than A Conqueror. Romans 8:37
- ❖ I Am Healed By His Stripes. 1 Peter 2:24
- ❖ I Am Blessed. Psalm 1:1-3
- ❖ I Am A Partaker Of His Divine Nature. 2 Peter1:4

- ❖ I Am Kept In Safety Wherever I Go Psalm 91:11
- ❖ I Am Strong In The Lord And In The Power Of His Might. Ephesians 6:10
- ❖ I Am Blessed With All Spiritual Blessings. Ephesians 1:3
- ❖ I Am An Overcomer By The Blood Of The Lamb And The Word Of My Testimony. Revelation 12:11
- ❖ I Am The Light Of The World. Matthew 5:14
- ❖ I Am The Salt Of The Earth. Matthew 5: 13
- ❖ I Am Delivered From The Powers Of Darkness Colossians 1:13
- ❖ I Am Led By The Spirit Of God Romans 8:14
- ❖ I Am Getting All My Needs Met By Jesus Philippians 4:19
- ❖ I Am Casting All My Cares On Jesus 1 Peter 5:7
- ❖ I Am Doing All Things Through Christ Who Strengthens Me Philippians 4:13
- ❖ I Am An Heir To The Blessings Of Abraham Galatians 3:13-14
- ❖ I Am Observing And Doing The Lord's Commandments Deuteronomy 28:12
- ❖ I Am Blessed Coming In And Blessed Going Out Deuteronomy 28:6
- ❖ I Am Exercising My Authority Over The Enemy Luke 10:19
- ❖ I Am Above And Not Beneath Deuteronomy 28:13
- ❖ I Am Establishing God's Word Here On Earth Matthew 16:19
- ❖ I Am Daily Overcoming The Devil 1 John 4:4
- ❖ I Am Not Moved By What I See 2 Corinthians 4:18
- ❖ I Am Walking By Faith And Not By Sight 2 Corinthians 5:7
- ❖ I Am Casting Down Vain Imaginations 2 Corinthians 10:4-5
- ❖ I Am Bringing Every Thought Into Captivity 2 Corinthians 10:5
- ❖ I Am Being Transformed By Renewing My Mind Romans 12:1-2
- ❖ I Am A Labourer Together With God 1 Corinthians 3:9
- ❖ I Am An Imitator Of Jesus Ephesians 5:1
- ❖ I Am Blessing The Lord At All Times And Continually Praising The Lord With My Mouth Psalm 34:1[34]
- ❖ I Am Empowered Philippians 4:13
- ❖ I Am Complete-There Is Nothing Broken And Nothing Missing In Me! Isaiah 26:3-4
- ❖ I Have The Mind Of Christ. 1 Corinthians 2:16
- ❖ I Am Royalty. 2 Corinthians 5:21
- ❖ I Belong To God's Family. I Am A Resident Of The Kingdom.

<u>Confession:</u>

---

[34] Trinity Broadcasting Network P.O. Box A Santa Ana CA 92711 714-731-1000 GF435 Rev. Oct 94

- ❖ I Am God's Masterpiece!
- ❖ I Am The Apple Of His Eye.
- ❖ I Am A Precious Jewel In His Sight.
- ❖ I Reflect His Light. I Am His Beloved One.
- ❖ I Am Heard By God.
- ❖ I Am Seen By God.
- ❖ I Have The Mind Of Christ.
- ❖ I Have God's Kingdom Mindset.
- ❖ I Can Control My Thoughts.
- ❖ With Practice And Effort, My Abilities And Faith Grow.
- ❖ I Learn From My Mistakes.
- ❖ When I Fall Down Or Fail, I Get Back up with God's Help.
- ❖ I Will Keep Going and Growing and Improving.
- ❖ I Am Resilient.
- ❖ I Am Fulfilling God's Plans and Purposes in My Life.
- ❖ I Am Empowered.
- ❖ I Am An Overcomer!
- ❖ I Will Finish My God–Given Race!
- ❖ I Will Accomplish My Life Assignment.
- ❖ I Am A Winner!

"I Am" Declarations:

- ❖ I am **Known by God**. (Psalm 139:16)
- ❖ I am **Created with a Purpose**. (Jeremiah 29:11)
- ❖ I am **Important.** (1 Peter 2:9)
- ❖ I am **Valuable**. (1 Corinthians 6:20 & Matthew 10:29-31)
- ❖ I am **Saved** to the uttermost. Hebrews 7:25)
- ❖ I am a **New Person in Christ.** (2 Corinthians 5:17)
- ❖ I am **Washed by the blood** of the Lamb. (Revelation 1:5)
- ❖ I am **Seen**. (Psalm 56:8 & Genesis 16:13)
- ❖ I am **Chosen**. (Psalm 139:15-16 & Ephesians 1:4 & John 15:16)
- ❖ I am **Accepted by God.** (Ephesians 1:6)
- ❖ I am **Loved Unconditionally.** (John 3:16 & Jeremiah 31:3)
- ❖ I am the **Object of His attention**. (Psalm 8:4)
- ❖ I am a **Child** of God. (Romans 8:14)
- ❖ I am **part of God's family**. (Romans 8:14 & Ephesians2:19)
- ❖ I am the **Apple of God's Eye**. (Psalm 17:8)
- ❖ I am **Precious.** (1 Corinthians 6:20)
- ❖ I am **Special.** (Ephesians 2:10)
- ❖ I am **Heard.** (1 John 5:15)
- ❖ I am **Blessed beyond measure.** (Psalm 1:1-3& Deuteronomy 28:6)
- ❖ I am **Cared for.** (Ephesians 3:17-19)
- ❖ I am an **Heiress/Heir.** (Romans 8:17)
- ❖ I am **Favoured**. (Psalm 90:17)
- ❖ I am **Enough.** (2 Corinthians 3:5)

- ❖ I am **Carefree.** (1 Peter 5:7)
- ❖ I am **Beautiful.** (Psalm 139:14)
- ❖ I am **Unique.** (Psalms 139:13)
- ❖ I am **Protected**. (Psalm 91:11 & Psalm 121:3)
- ❖ I am **Resilient**. (Romans 8:37)
- ❖ I am **Strong.** (Psalms 18:35 & Philippians 4:13)
- ❖ I am **Driven.** (Like 10:19)
- ❖ I am **Worthy.** (Revelation 3:4)
- ❖ I am **Lovely.** (Daniel 12:3)
- ❖ I am an **Overcomer**. (Revelation 12:11)
- ❖ I am a **Warrior**. (1 Timothy 6:12)
- ❖ I am **Healed.** (1 Peter 2:24)
- ❖ I am **Forgiven**. (Psalm 103:12 & Colossians 1:14)
- ❖ I am **Complete**. (James 1:4)
- ❖ I am **Supernatural.** 1 Corinthians 3:16)
- ❖ I am **Empowered.** (Philippians 4:13)
- ❖ I am **Unstoppable**. (Ephesians 6:10)
- ❖ I am **Equipped.** (2 Peter 1:3)
- ❖ I am **Provided for**. (Philippians 4:19)
- ❖ I am **Rich.** (James 1:9-11)
- ❖ I am an **Ambassador.** (2 Corinthians 5:20)
- ❖ I am **Royalty**. (2 Corinthians 5:21)
- ❖ I am **His Bride.** (Revelation 21:2, 9-10)
- ❖ I am **Victorious!** (1 Corinthians 15:57)
- ❖ I am **God's Masterpiece!** (Ephesians 2:10)
- ❖ God's plans and purposes for my life will prevail!

"The names that God calls you are the only ones you should be answering to."

—Priscilla Shirer

Competition vs. Collaborative Learning

Mindset: The New Psychology of Success by Carol Dweck

Competition has received negative criticism lately. However, competition doesn't have to be inherently negative. It is crucial to strike a balance where we can cultivate a healthy competitive spirit while maintaining a strong self-image. In her book 'Mindset: The New Psychology of Success,' Dr. Carol Dweck explains that individuals with a fixed mindset, believe their traits are unchangeable and often feel the constant need to prove themselves through competition.

People with a growth mindset believe that they can improve their current abilities and acquire new skills through time and effort. Competition can be beneficial if it serves as motivation to become the best version of oneself. Those who possess God's mindset compete against their own limitations because they recognize that their race is not against others but is a personal journey assigned by God. They understand that each individual has a unique purpose to fulfil and that we all play a part in God's grand plan. Life is a race, but it is not a competition. We are all united as a team, participating in the same story and pursuing the same desired outcome. Hence, within the body of Christ, we should establish a 'No Competition Zone' because we are in this assignment together. Instead of competing, we should support and encourage one another, recognizing that our gifts and callings are bestowed upon each person for the collective good (1 Corinthians 12:4-7).

I believe that we need to repent and realize that we need each other. Their success is our success. Our victory is His (God's) victory. We could miss what God wants to do in our lives if we are competing with one another. If we are really going to change the world, to reach the lost, then we need to understand that there's room for diversity. We have different assignments with different gifts. We need to work together. It will take each and every one of us doing our part to bring in the great harvest of souls (Matthew 9:37). Let's help each other. For the sake of the Gospel of the Kingdom, let's declare a "No Competition Zone" where we are cheerleaders and not competitors. This is the only way we will achieve our mission.[35]

"My goal is not to be better than anyone else, but be better than I used to be."

This is why those with a kingdom mindset embrace teamwork and partnerships because they understand, through scripture, that we are stronger together. Deuteronomy 32:30 states that one man can chase a thousand, but two men can put ten thousand to flight. Our strength is multiplied when we work together. Each of us has a great purpose and valuable function. We all have our own assignments to complete. You cannot complete mine, and I cannot complete yours. No one can fulfil your part except you. God gave you a unique fingerprint so that you can leave an imprint that no one else can. We need to understand that we are all interconnected as part of the Body of Christ. We are one body with many parts (1 Corinthians 12:12-31). Therefore, we should help and encourage each other to reach our goals. Don't let competition lead you astray. God wants us to collaborate. Let's become each other's cheerleaders. Just as God and those who went before us are our

---

[35] James W. Goll. *"Declare a 'No Competition Zone'."* The Elijah List email, February 5, 2023.

cheerleaders, let's purpose to become each other's cheerleaders as well (Hebrews 12:1). Together, we will have a greater positive impact on the world.

There is a wealth of research available that substantiates the importance of working in collaboration with others. Venturing into something new can be intimidating, but by seeking support, you gain the wisdom, guidance, and mentorship of others to help you achieve your goals. A recent Stanford study demonstrated that people who collaborated were 48% more effective in working on assignments and goals. They worked longer, with increased focus, and reported feeling more empowered, supported, connected, and less overwhelmed. Collaborative work also contributed to a more positive self-identity and increased confidence. Working together inspires and motivates people.[36] Research is proving the truth of the bible more and more everyday.

I witnessed this in the classroom: projects were less overwhelming for students when they could work together. Even struggling students could contribute to the efforts of the group, which increased their self-confidence and sense of worth. I have also personally observed this in my adult work life. When faced with a new assignment, it is reassuring to know that you can collaborate with your colleagues. Group work or collaborative learning is empowering as it allows and encourages input from everyone.

Success isn't always about winning. God defines success differently than we do. Failure can even be considered a success by God, as He sees things from an eternal perspective. Failure is necessary in order to achieve success because it allows us to learn and grow. Unfortunately, those with a fixed mindset often view things as a competition. However, it's not about you or me; it's about God's plan. When you look in the mirror, your only competition is yourself. <u>You are competing against your own potential and striving to become the best version of yourself—the person God created you to be.</u>

"Success is stumbling from failure to failure with no loss of enthusiasm."

—Winston Churchill

---

[36] (tmaworld.com (http://tmaworld.com) (http://tmaworld.com/) "") - Stanford Study demonstrates how collaboration and teamwork can dramatically improve productivity - Aug 24, 2017).[1] (https://mail.google.com/mail/u/0/#m_2154614425875695238_ftn1) "") Accessed Instagram post Mon. Jan 2, 2023

When one part of the body hurts, the whole body suffers (Hebrews 12:1 and 1 Corinthians 9:24-27). It is disheartening to witness people, especially believers who should know better, competing against each other. When we undermine others, we hinder God's cause and become a liability rather than an asset. It's crucial to remember that it's not about you or me, my ministry versus yours, your business versus mine; it's about God's will and purposes in the world at this moment. God requires all of us to fulfil our assignments and desires for us to be successful. <u>He made it so that our confidence, strength, and effectiveness increase when we work together, which is why He encourages a collaborative learning model within His kingdom mindset.</u>

The collaborative learning model involves working together in groups of two or more to solve problems, complete tasks, or learn new concepts. Collaborative learning offers several benefits, including the development of self-management and leadership skills, the enhancement of skills and knowledge, the improvement of relationships, the promotion of learning from different viewpoints (empathy), the cultivation of critical thinking abilities, the encouragement of listening to criticism and advice (teachable spirit), the refinement of public speaking and active listening skills, and the fostering of cooperation.[37]

To accomplish God's plan in our lives, the church, and the world, we need to work collaboratively. **It is not the effort of a single soldier but the collective strength of an army that will lead us to victory in the battle. We as a society need to learn to work constructively with others.**

Satan operates by sowing <u>seeds of division</u> to hinder your spiritual growth and derail you from fulfilling your purpose. Do not yield to the spirit of division. Satan's strategy is to divide and conquer, while God's plan is to unite us and achieve victory. In Mark 3:24-26, Jesus emphasizes that a kingdom divided against itself cannot stand. Therefore, resist the spirit of division and safeguard your kingdom assignment. Instead, stand for cooperation and unity. Approach everything you do and say with a spirit of love. Choose to believe the best in others and actively pursue cooperation and unity with your fellow believers in Christ and in the world. Our unified power is something Satan fears, recognizing that we are stronger together. God commands us to work together. Romans 16:17-18 clearly advises us to avoid those who cause divisions, while 1 Corinthians 1:10 urges us to be united in mind, thought, and purpose. <u>Division often begins as a thought, and it is up to us to either accept or reject it. Similarly, unity</u>

---

starts as a thought. Embrace healthy competition as it empowers you to fulfil your own God-given purpose. When you look to others, let their lives encourage and inspire you. Avoid falling into the trap of unhealthy comparison. Remember that they have different assignments, possess distinct gifts and talents, and are on a unique journey. Comparing yourself to others only diminishes your confidence.

Each one of us is essential for the proper functioning of the body of Christ. The apostle Paul beautifully illustrates this in 1 Corinthians chapter 12, comparing the Body of Christ to a human body. Interestingly, some parts of the body that may appear weak and unimportant are actually the most necessary. Have you ever stubbed your big toe? It's excruciatingly painful! I once experienced an infected ingrown toenail, and it made me realize how frequently people step on our feet or how often we accidentally stub our toes in a day—far too many times! The pain made it difficult to walk. It's remarkable to consider that a seemingly insignificant toe, when injured, can cripple the entire body's ability to function properly. This serves as a powerful metaphor for the importance of each member in the Body of Christ.[38] We are all valuable and significant in the eyes of God. Each one of us has a vital role to fulfil. Instead of comparing ourselves to others, it is important to focus on our own journey and purpose.

The Apostle Paul illustrates the importance of everyone having a place within the body of Christ. Each part has a specific position and function, and when each part operates effectively, the entire body functions properly. When individuals are in their rightful places and work together, significant accomplishments are made for the kingdom of God. We truly need one another. In John 17:21, Jesus prays for our unity and oneness. Have you discovered your place? It is crucial that you identify your unique position and fulfil your kingdom assignment. Someone, somewhere, is relying on you to fulfil the purpose God has called you to. Discover your place and pursue your calling with determination. You are an indispensable part of God's plan. You are valuable and essential (Ephesians 4:16-32).

We must never allow ourselves to be trapped in the cycle of comparison. God has assigned each of us a unique purpose, and we should never compare our gifts to those of others. It is crucial to be comfortable and content with who we are and where God has placed us and then operate in the anointing He has given us. Our focus should be on embracing our true identity as God created us to be instead of attempting to imitate someone else. When we embrace our authentic selves, we bring glory to our Heavenly Father. **You were designed to**

---

[38] K. Hagin Jr. *Rhema Magazine.*

be an original, not a copy. Do not compromise or settle for being someone else. Be unapologetically you! It is important to concentrate on our own assignments and not be preoccupied with others. Comparing yourself to others is an insult to God, your Creator. God doesn't make mistakes; therefore, He didn't make a mistake when He created you. Resist any feelings of envy or jealousy regarding the accomplishments of others. God has anointed us to fulfil our own unique purpose, not someone else's.[39] **Find your place. Run your own race. Each purpose is needed, necessary, and valuable to God. If you don't know your place yet, then bloom where you're presently planted. Be the best that you can be.**

When we engage in comparison, we inadvertently invite the enemy into our lives. It leads to envy, jealousy, division, competition, and strife. Instead, let us direct our focus towards our own race. Comparison robs us of joy and diminishes our confidence. As children of God, we should avoid responding to comparisons with feelings of condemnation or pride. It is essential to recognize that God intentionally created us in a unique way. He does not make mistakes. You possess all the necessary qualities and abilities to successfully run your own race (2 Peter 1:3).

Every single one of us is significant. We can be likened to pieces of a jigsaw puzzle. Without one piece, the picture remains incomplete. Your presence, talents, and service are essential for completing the overall image of the body of Christ. You hold a vital role in God's plan, and there is a unique place that only you can fill. Discover your place and wholeheartedly pursue your own race. God eagerly awaits your participation. People are waiting for the impact of your purpose. No one else can fulfil the specific role that God created you for. You are the missing link.

"In the Christian race, we are not competing against each other; we're not trying to out-do one another. Rather, we are competing against our own potential and endeavouring to fulfil our particular callings effectively."

—Tony Cooke

God will never alter His perception of us, His love for us, or the names He has given us. He has anointed both you and me for a significant purpose. You are the individual specifically chosen for this task. God remains constant throughout time, unchanging from yesterday to today and forever (Hebrews 13:8-9). The names He bestows upon us are revealed in the "I Am" statements mentioned previously and will never

---

[39] Kenneth Hagin Jr. *Rhema Magazine- article*

change. As God's Word remains unwavering, we should likewise hold firm to the names and identities God has assigned to us.

Sometimes, we inadvertently label ourselves incorrectly due to the influence of negative thoughts. These thoughts, originating from a fixed mindset, can lead us to believe lies about our identity. However, it is crucial to remember that only God, the Almighty One, has the power to redefine our names. Fortunately, He is gracious enough to transform our mindset from a fixed perspective to His kingdom mindset. For instance, He can change our label from Defeat to Victory, from Broken to Whole, from Sick to Healed, from Addicted to Free, from Lost to Found, from Poor to Rich, and from Slave to Royalty.

The Bible tells us that God speaks over us daily. He declares His Word over our lives (Hebrews 3:15). Just think about that for a moment. The Creator of heaven and earth speaks directly to you today.

When we declare these powerful "I Am statements," we are aligning ourselves with God and emulating His ways. We are adopting God's best practices. God Himself utilizes positive self-talk, speaking His Word in the form of these "I Am" statements over us and over Himself. Therefore, when we speak these affirmations, we are partnering with God and following His example.

Example:
- ❖ No spoken word from God shall be without power or impossible of fulfilment (Luke 1:37).
- ❖ God, Himself stands over and watches over His own word, making sure it is fulfilled (Jeremiah 1:12).
- ❖ God's Word accomplishes that which He purposes, and it prospers in the thing for which He sent it (Isaiah 55:11).

God remains faithful to His Word, even when we fail to uphold our end of the bargain. His Word is unwavering and will be fulfilled regardless of human actions, words, or beliefs. If you choose to believe, God's Word will unquestionably manifest its power in your life.

Why not choose to believe what God says about you in His Word? God's Word is God's mindset. God is a man of His Word. He is the "Great I Am" and He speaks His Word. His "I Am" statements over Himself and over us. We are who He says we are because He speaks over us. God uses positive self-talk /faith declarations with us. His Word Is Positive. If God said it, then we can believe it. God keeps His promises. He never fails, and he won't start with you and me. [40]

What car are you driving? How's it running? Need a tune-up?

---

[40] Chandler Moore & KJ Scriven- *Man of your word-song*

You can compare the power of your words to that of driving a vehicle. If you consistently speak negative words filled with fear, doubt, and discouragement, you are steering your life towards defeat. It's like driving a beat-up jalopy in a race; there's no chance of winning. In fact, by engaging in negative speech, you're putting yourself at risk by even participating in the race. Our words serve as the steering wheel of our lives. If we continually focus on and talk about our problems, sickness, and debts, we will remain trapped in those circumstances. The words we speak can hinder us from experiencing God's promises and blessings, as well as fulfilling our purpose and assignment in life (Psalm 39:1).

Will you make the choice to speak words of hope and faith into your life? You have the power to change your words and embrace God's kingdom mindset. You can choose to believe the "I Am" statements found in the Bible and speak positive words of hope, empowerment, courage, and faith over yourself and your family. Remember, God has chosen a specific path for you to follow. He has placed you in this particular time and place for a reason. Instead of complaining about the journey, choose to appreciate the scenery. Don't get caught up in complaining about the mess and miss out on the miracles along the way. Allow Jesus to take control of your mindset. The route He takes you on may not align with your initial expectations, but with God's kingdom mindset, you can be assured that you will reach your final destination. God's path is rarely a straight line. It may involve ups and downs, bumps in the road, and even detours, but He will guide you to exactly where you need to be at the right time (Psalm 31:15).

"Change is one of the distinguishing characteristics of true believers."

Fixed Mindset

A fixed mindset involves adopting negative beliefs about ourselves and the world around us. It hinders our ability to embrace the blessings and achieve the success that God has in store for us. Individuals with a fixed mindset tend to believe that their talents and abilities are predetermined at birth and cannot be developed or changed. This kind of thinking plays into the enemy's agenda, as he seeks to hinder our progress and keep us stagnant, preventing us from reaching the promised land that awaits us. However, it is important to remember that the enemy's words are deceptive and untrue. In fact, the Bible explicitly states in John 8:44 that there is no truth in him, and he is the Father of lies.

Those with a fixed mindset believe that their intelligence is fixed from birth and cannot be altered. They also hold the notion that success is solely dependent on innate talent, disregarding the importance of effort. Consequently, if they believe that change is impossible, they see no reason to exert effort. This mindset leads them to believe that each individual has a predetermined limit on what they can achieve in life, analogous to a glass ceiling. For instance, statements such as "I'm not suited for academics," "I'll always be in debt," "My family has always relied on welfare," "Divorce is inevitable," "Cancer is prevalent in our family," or "No one in our family gets along" reflect a fixed mindset. These beliefs create a sense of hopelessness, as they are seen as immutable truths, leaving no room for change or improvement.

Heredity is a prime example of a common misconception stemming from a fixed mindset. Statements like "Heart disease runs in our family" "Cancer, dementia, and diabetes are prevalent in our family line" may align with scientific observations, but it is important to remember that God's Word surpasses scientific understanding. God is the creator of science, and His authority is final. His Word represents absolute truth. When you accept Christ as your Savior and Lord, you become a new creation and a part of the body of Christ. **Jesus' DNA now flows within you, and you are a member of the Royal family, not under the reign of King Charles, but under the kingship of Jesus (1 John 3:1-3).** Embracing your new identity as a child of the King and adopting a kingdom mindset, you can resist the enemy's lies and boldly declare that the curses of heart disease, cancer, dementia, and others are broken and cease to have power over you in Jesus' name (Galatians 3:13). You have the ability to draw a spiritual boundary and assert that the enemy will not advance any further (Matthew 16:19). It may have run in your family until it encountered you! You are the one who can break generational curses within your family line. As a child of God, the only hereditary traits you should accept are the blessings of Abraham (Genesis 12:1-3). So straighten your crown and walk confidently in your divine inheritance!

BELIEFS BECOME REALITY. Saying and thinking these types of limiting statements over and over create neural pathways that reach neurons and affect how we perceive the world and eventually reach to all parts of our lives, affecting our decisions. Ex. Self-fulfilling prophecy.

"Negative speaking is not in the vocabulary of heaven."
—Pastor Steve McCollin

A lack of confidence can cause us to behave in specific ways, just as fear can influence our actions. Our mindset plays a crucial role in how we present ourselves in life and also impacts how others perceive us. For instance, if we fear failure, we may shy away from opportunities, whereas confidence enables us to take risks and explore new avenues. <u>Our brains are wired to repeat patterns, so it is essential to be mindful of the programming we choose</u>. Are we reinforcing disappointment with negative thoughts and statements, or are we cultivating a mindset of success and fulfilment through positive thoughts and affirmations of faith? God desires His children to hold their heads high, shoulders back and walk confidently in life by adopting His mindset. He expects us to govern our minds with His perspective rather than allowing negative thoughts and low self-confidence to dominate us.

FEAR: "False Evidence Appearing Real." It is noteworthy that God emphasizes the command **"do not be afraid"** 365 times in the Bible, symbolically providing us with one "fear not" for each day of the year. This repetition highlights the significance of addressing fear in our lives. Fear serves as a primary strategy of the enemy, which is precisely why God repeatedly instructs us to resist its influence.

We are not to fear tomorrow because we know God holds our tomorrow. God is already in our future, so there is nothing to be afraid of (Jeremiah 29:4-14).

If you consistently affirm that you never receive favourable opportunities or experience success, it is likely that you will continue to attract such circumstances. The concept of "negative attracts negative and positive attracts positive" aligns with the Law of Attraction, which is believed to be a principle established by God in the functioning of the world.[41] Our words are powerful and creative. **We actually attract what we say.** Change what you say and stop attracting what you don't want. [42]

> **"Fear tolerated is faith contaminated."**
> —*Kenneth Copeland*

Fixed Mindset: A fixed mindset hinders your ability to make positive changes in your life as it convinces you that your intelligence, talents, weight, circumstances, or bad habits are unchangeable. Consequently, you may shy away from challenging situations and avoid taking risks due to the fear of failure. A fixed mindset essentially operates from a

---

[41] *Proverbs* 23:7

[42] Terri Savelle Foy-*vision boards*

place of fear. Do you find yourself afraid of failure? Does this fear prevent you from trying new things? Have you been expressing negative thoughts about yourself using some of these statements?

- I give up.
- I don't want to work harder.
- I'm tired.
- I'm never going to get this.
- I won't be able to do it.
- I'll never be as smart!
- I can't make this any better.
- This is too hard.
- I'm just not good at this.
- I haven't done it, I don't get it, I can't do this, I'm not good at this, It doesn't make sense, I don't understand.
- This is beyond me.
- I'm overwhelmed.
- I'm just functioning
- It's too heavy to carry

Fear frequently presents itself as fatigue. When you carry the weight of the world on your shoulders it wears you out. You were never meant to carry it but cast it upon the Lord (1 Peter 5:7). It's essential not to be too hard on yourself if you have made statements like these about yourself, as we all have at times. The crucial aspect is to acknowledge it and strive for improvements in the future. Recognizing the issue is the initial step towards change.

"F.E.A.R. has two meanings: Forget everything and run OR Face everything and Rise! The choice is yours."

—*Zig Ziglar*

<u>From the perspective of the fixed mindset, effort is perceived as something reserved for individuals with deficiencies.</u> If you firmly believe in fixed intelligence and see yourself as a genius, a highly talented individual without any shortcomings, then putting in effort becomes a risk. The notion of trying your best and still failing, leaving yourself without <u>excuses,</u> becomes the ultimate fear within the fixed mindset. It becomes paralyzing.[43] Those with a fixed mindset tend to have a more fragile sense of confidence, constantly seeking external validation. However, if our confidence and validation stem from our faith in God, it becomes unshakeable.

---

[43] *Dweck* p.42

Individuals with a fixed mindset often harbor a sense of superiority over others and exhibit a lack of tolerance towards mistakes, criticism, or setbacks. Unfortunately, this belief hinders their personal growth and impedes their ability to adapt and evolve.[44] The Bible teaches in Proverbs 16:18 that pride goes before destruction and a haughty spirit before a fall.

People with this mindset perceive constant <u>messages of judgement</u> from their parents, co-workers, employer and spouse.[45] As a result, <u>they are prone to taking Offence easily.</u> They tend to perceive constructive criticism as judgment, causing them to become offended instead of using it as an opportunity to grow and enhance themselves. Consequently, individuals with a fixed mindset often exhibit resistance to learning and are less receptive to new ideas and perspectives. God wants us to remain teachable, not be prideful. Pride is a negative emotion which should be avoided.

Mistakes are an inherent part of life. Everyone makes them, and everyone experiences regrets. Some people learn from their mistakes and grow, while others find themselves repeating them. The choice of whether to leverage your mistakes for personal growth lies within you. It ultimately depends on your mindset. You are not fated to continually fall into the same toxic patterns. Instead, you have the power to make different choices. One of the biggest mistakes people make is thinking they can change people by constantly criticizing them. It will only make things worse. But you can change people by praising them when you see them doing the things you like. You can be the catalyst for change in your own life and for future generations in your family. It's time to take your power back!

Someone once said, "He who is easily offended is easily manipulated." **Offence is a tool** used by the enemy, as he understands that by triggering offence, he can manipulate individuals. When you allow yourself to be offended, you tend to focus inward, which aligns with the

---

[44] *Dweck* p.48

[45] *Dweck* p.184-185

enemy's intentions. On the other hand, God desires us to shift our gaze towards Him, rather than solely on ourselves. There is no I in team.

Those with a fixed mindset tend to take offence at constructive criticism and resist change, while those with a mindset aligned with God accept it, embrace change, and continue moving forward. The Bible teaches us that God disciplines and chastens those He loves, as stated in Hebrews 12:6. **God's love for us is so profound that He refuses to let us remain stagnant.** I encourage you to approach constructive criticism with a fresh perspective. View it as an opportunity for improvement and growth, allowing it to shape you into the person that God intended you to be. Let it serve as a catalyst for transforming yourself into the best version of yourself.

Fear has the power to manipulate and compel individuals to act against their own desires. Manipulation, too, is a tool employed by the enemy. People with a fixed mindset often resort to manipulation, using it as a shield to mask their perceived inadequacies. They strive to exert control through their own strength rather than relying on God's guidance. It's time to cease striving and start placing your trust in God. He desires for us to surrender control and release our grip on it. Avoid becoming consumed by the need for control; manipulation is rooted in negative and deceitful control. You are capable of more than that. It does not define who you are. Instead of relying solely on your abilities to reach your destiny, learn to embrace God's kingdom mindset and rely on His guidance and His abilities.

> **"Insight doesn't create transformation. Application does. You have to practice new thoughts to create any change."**
> **—*Kara Loewentheil***

God expects us to embrace full responsibility for our lives, refusing to make excuses or place blame on others for the outcomes we experience. It's impossible to be both a victim and a victor simultaneously; a choice must be made. If you find solace in being a victim, seeking pity and attention from others, you will never attain true victory. Adopting a **victim mentality** is a characteristic of a fixed mindset. When you attribute everything wrong in your life solely to others, it communicates a sense of powerlessness, passivity, and surrendering control of your own destiny, relegating yourself to the passenger seat of your life.[46]
Adopting a victim mentality is a strategy employed by the enemy and is indicative of a fixed mindset. This mentality serves as nothing more than an excuse to justify certain behaviours. It is crucial to cease making

---

[46] Terri Savelle Foy

excuses that validate your actions and your resistance to change. Take responsibility for your life and take your power back.

"If you don't heal what hurts you, you'll end up bleeding on people who didn't cut you."
—Dr. C. Leaf

Part of taking responsibility for our lives involves actively seeking healing for past hurts, unforgiveness, and traumas. Unaddressed wounds become burdens that weigh us down, hindering our progress. Unhealed wounds often stem from fixed mindset thoughts and must be acknowledged, processed, and released. Thoughts like; I'm forever ruined. I'm damaged goods. I'll never recover from this. I don't have what it takes.

God doesn't consult your past to determine your future.
Learn to harness the pain from your past as fuel to propel you towards a brighter future instead of allowing it to hold you back. Remember, nothing is wasted in God's plan. If He allowed you to experience it, there is a purpose behind it. Seek to learn the lessons from your past, and then press onward with determination.

"Stress and pressure will make you say things you don't mean to people you really love."
—Dharius Daniels

A fixed mindset is a failure mindset: Making excuses rather than taking responsibility is a clear indication of a fixed mindset. Excuses have the power to rob us of our dreams and are often utilized as a tactic by the enemy. In Song of Solomon 2:15, it is mentioned that it's the little foxes that spoil the vineyards. These foxes symbolize excuses and potential distractions that pose a threat to our dreams and life's purpose. It's the seemingly insignificant distractions that can cause us to stumble. Have you ever caught yourself saying, "I'll do it later," only for later to never arrive? Or perhaps you've found yourself saying, "I don't feel like it," but that feeling never materializes. Maybe you've uttered the words "Someday," only to realize that day never comes. Satan ensures that there is always something else you should or could be doing, keeping you busy and exhausted, leaving little time for God. "Someday" is not a specific day of the week and, therefore, will never arrive. It is a subtle lie from the enemy intended to keep you bound and chained.[47] Instead of waiting for "Someday" or "One Day," I challenge you to declare "Day One." Today is the first day of the rest of your life! This is the day you stop making excuses and take ownership of your life.

How much time do you find yourself dwelling on thoughts of failure? It's likely more than you realize. Our society often promotes a fixed mindset or a mindset that associates with failure. We have been conditioned to adopt this fixed mindset throughout our lives. Many of us were taught not to get our hopes up and to simply accept the challenges that life throws our way without expecting much in return. Phrases like "Good guys finish last," "Only the good die young," and "Just roll with the punches" may sound familiar to you. These statements have been repeated to us countless times as we grew up, and unconsciously, we internalized them as truths. Your brain has formed these thought patterns as a result. However, this is not the way God intends for us to live. We must shed this mindset of failure and embrace a different perspective. [48] We must lose the fixed mindset and switch to God's kingdom mindset. Today is the day I adopt God's kingdom mindset!

The great men of the bible are not men who never failed, but men who didn't quit. They are not men who never fell but men who knew how to get up and keep going.[49]

We can impede the potential of God's work in our lives when we embrace a mindset of failure or fixed limitations. By making excuses, we inadvertently hinder God's desired accomplishments through us. Excuses work against God's will for our lives, and this is a matter of great significance with far-reaching consequences. <u>Our excuses place restrictions on what God can do in and through us.</u> When we shift blame onto others for our failures, we grant them control over us. If we do not proactively take charge of our lives, someone else will assume that role. According to Psalm 78:40-41, God wants us to take control over our lives, starting from the realm of our thoughts. God desires for us to exercise internal control that radiates outwardly. The state of our internal world, including our thoughts and mindset, significantly influences our external reality. Personally, I am committed to cooperating with God rather than limiting His work. How about you?

"Once you stop learning, you start dying."

---

[47] Terry Savelle Foy

[48] Jesse Duplantis Ministries-*Instagram post.*

[49] Tony Cooke. *Your Place on God's Dream Team: The Making of Champions-Instagram post*

—*Albert Einstein*

Fear sabotages our success. In sneaks in with fixed mindset thoughts like:

- I have insufficient education to apply for that job or promotion.
- I can't decide what I want to do.
- I can't learn now; it's too late. It's too hard.
- There's no point in trying, if I'm going to fail.
- I take feedback as a personal attack.
- I always struggle with…..
- I feel intimidated by the success of others.
- I can't make this any better, it is what it is.
- I've always been taught that I can't……[50]

Growth Mindset: Those who embody a growth mindset say things like:
- I'm on the right track.
- This may take some time and effort.
- Mistakes help me improve.
- Is this really my best work?
- I'll use some of the strategies I've learned.
- I can always improve.
- I'll keep trying.
- I need to figure out what I did wrong and get some help.
- What am I missing?
- What can I do differently?
- Holy Spirit help me figure this out.
- God what are you teaching me with this problem?
- I'm a work in progress.

<u>A kingdom mindset promotes a collaborative learning model that encourages seeking help. Asking questions and seeking assistance are not discouraged but rather encouraged in this mindset.</u>

Ask yourself these questions:
- How do you approach challenges?
- Do you tend to avoid them?
- How do you handle conflicts?
- Do you go to great lengths to avoid them?
- Are you someone who often prioritizes pleasing others?

---

[50] Crocket, L. *The Growth Mindset Choice: 10 Fixed Mindset examples we can change.* blog.futurefocusedlearning.net

❖   How do you handle obstacles?

Your response to these questions will provide insights into the areas where you may hold a fixed mindset. It's important to recognize that we all have aspects of a fixed mindset within us. By identifying these areas, we can begin the process of transformation. The ultimate objective is to align every aspect of our minds with God's kingdom mindset. This process is ongoing throughout our lives and may require time and effort.

If we genuinely possess a kingdom mindset, we hold the belief that our abilities can and will improve through effort and persistence. While we may not currently have all the answers on how to handle difficult people, challenging situations, or unruly children, we are actively seeking guidance and assistance from God. It is essential to recognize that Satan seeks to deceive us into believing the lie that change is impossible. However, we must resist the temptation to avoid new experiences and challenges, as they are not intended to destroy us but rather to propel us towards becoming the individuals God designed us to be.

At times, God allows unfavourable conditions to enter our lives for our own benefit. These circumstances serve as pruning tools, enabling us to bear more fruit in the future (John 15:2). Through these experiences, we are given opportunities to evolve. Similar to exercising a muscle, resistance is necessary to overcome challenges. It is impossible to grow stronger in any aspect of life without enduring obstacles that require us to adapt and respond effectively. It is during these trials that God is closest to us. As we persevere through hardships, our faith is strengthened. Our faith can be likened to a muscle that grows and becomes stronger through exercise. Interestingly, our brain undergoes significant growth and transformation during difficult times. **How we handle challenge and conflict wires our brains for success or failure.** [51] I encourage you to shift your perspective on challenges. Begin to see them as valuable learning opportunities intentionally designed by your Creator to foster your personal growth.

You see, God is constantly bringing forth new things (Isaiah 43:18-19), and so we should also be open to trying new things. When God presents a challenge before us, He expects us to rise up and face it. Instead of shying away from challenges, let us not be hindered by low self-confidence and fear. Instead, let us boldly declare, "Bring it on!" Once we grasp the understanding that challenges are not meant to destroy us but to empower us, our perspective towards them will shift,

---

[51] Dr. C. Leaf

and we will begin to embrace them. If we acknowledge that challenges are beneficial for our growth, why not actively seek them out? I challenge you to volunteer for a change in your workplace. Why not believe that it is a supernatural opportunity set up for you? A chance to demonstrate your problem-solving abilities, perseverance, wisdom, and more.

Change doesn't have to be viewed as something negative. Many of us fear change and the unknown, but it's important to recognize that change can actually be a positive thing. Start by changing your mindset. God is constantly evolving and bringing forth new things. He seldom repeats the same patterns because He has infinite ways to accomplish His will. Resist the anxious thoughts that stem from fear. Anxiety about the future and the unknown can lead to impulsive decisions that make the process of learning and changing more challenging. Instead, remain steadfast in your faith in God. Allow Him to work in His perfect timing.

Abraham and Sarah acted impulsively while waiting for the fulfilment of God's promise of a son. Growing weary of waiting, they attempted to bring about the promise on their own by having Ishmael. How many times have we found ourselves in similar situations? We desire God's blessings immediately and attempt to make things happen in our own strength and timing rather than relying on God. However, when we rush ahead of God, things often don't work out as expected. Throughout our lives, we will experience seasons of ambiguity and uncertainty. Instead of resisting or fearing these seasons, we should learn to embrace them, recognizing that God is leading us to a higher level in our relationship with Him. Seek discernment from God to determine if the change is from Him. If it is, then proceed without hesitation.

Change is not something to be feared by those who possess a God-centred mindset. They understand that amidst the shifting and uncertainty of life, they are securely anchored in God. God's mindset serves as their constant, their unwavering foundation, even in the face of change. When God is for you and resides within you through His kingdom mindset, the opinions or opposition of others hold no power. Regardless of the changes that may arise, we can trust that God works all things together for our good (Romans 8:28). Embracing change becomes an integral part of adopting God's kingdom mindset. When presented with an opportunity, take a moment to seek God's guidance. Ask if it aligns with His will and if He intends for you to pursue it. Instead of automatically succumbing to fear and hesitation, recognize that it may be a supernatural setup to propel you forward in your career or calling.

Accepting our righteousness through Christ enables us to walk in our kingdom authority and mindset. (Romans 3:22) **The kingdom of God is a recurring theme emphasized throughout the New Testament, mentioned 162 times.** God's deliberate repetition of this concept signifies its utmost importance. In Luke 17:20-21, it is stated that the kingdom of God resides within us, implying that we possess all that is necessary to fulfil our purpose. Those who possess God's mindset recognize that it is His grace that enables us to accomplish our calling. We do not rely solely on our own strength and abilities but on God's divine empowerment. His grace working in conjunction with our natural abilities, elevates us to the supernatural realm. **This is our superpower: God's grace empowering us to fulfil the purpose we were uniquely created and predestined for.** It is crucial to grasp the significance of God's all-sufficient grace, which encompasses our position as royalty in His kingdom and the transformative mindset it imparts.

"For we are God's handiwork, created in Christ Jesus to do good works, which God prepared for us to do" (Ephesians 2:10).

What is the kingdom of God? According to *Romans 14:17, "For the kingdom of God is not a matter of eating and drinking, but of righteousness, peace and joy in the Holy Spirit."* It encompasses both a spiritual position and a mindset. When we embrace God's mindset, we start to comprehend our rightful place within His kingdom. The Holy Spirit will guide us, teaching us that we are made righteous through Christ. The Prince of Peace will guard our minds and keep them at peace (Colossians 3:15). The joy of the Lord will become our source of strength (Nehemiah 8:10).

The kingdom of God is not defined by a physical location but rather by a position of authority. It is a regal position that we, as beloved children, are called to embrace. We belong to a kingdom, and as such, we are royalty. Our lives should reflect the principles and values of the kingdom. We have a destiny of greatness. Therefore, it is essential to confidently take up our position in the kingdom of God and to always remember our inherent royalty. So straighten your crown and embrace the privileges and responsibilities that come with being a part of God's kingdom (1 Peter 2:9).

"Grace is the ridiculously unwarranted and outrageously favourable posture of God that transforms wretched sinners into wretched saints and keeps at it until they look like Jesus."
—*Pastor Noell - Rive Church Michigan*

Fear is a powerful weapon used by the enemy to hinder and rob us. Those with fixed mindsets are often consumed by fear. It has the ability to keep us trapped in unhappiness, preventing us from pursuing fulfilling careers, experiencing healthy relationships, and embracing positive change. Fear is paralyzing and manipulative, causing us to act against our own desires and altering our thinking. It leads us to expect the worst and holds us back from growth. People with fixed mindsets tend to complain, make excuses, and resist change, ultimately keeping them stuck in unproductive cycles. A prime example of this is seen in the Israelites who, due to their constant complaining, wandered in circles for 40 years, unable to enter the Promised Land. What was meant to be a brief journey turned into a prolonged ordeal due to their mindset. In the process, they missed out on the miraculous provisions and blessings God had for them. Likewise, we must be mindful not to allow fear and a fixed mindset to prevent us from entering our own promised land. Let us choose faith over fear and embrace a mindset that leads us to our God-given destinies.

"Everything you've ever wanted is on the other side of fear."
—George Adair

We must prioritize guarding our words and replacing complaints with praise and gratitude. Individuals with a fixed mindset tend to be fearful, make excuses, and engage in murmuring and complaining. Conversely, those with a kingdom mindset are characterized by courage, gratitude, and a heart of praise towards God. Praise and gratitude are integral components of God's mindset, serving as powerful remedies to counteract toxic thoughts rooted in fear.

"Remember, in life, you will always be faced with a series of God-ordained opportunities brilliantly disguised as problems and challenges."
—Les Brown

One of our claims to fame will be that we survived a global pandemic. We are survivors! We have endured for a reason. You have a great purpose. The pandemic has provided an opportunity for you and me to refocus on our purpose and what truly matters in life. If you view it from this perspective, then you can find gratitude.

"This book is about changing our thought processes to God's. Progress is impossible without change. If we can't change our mindsets then we can't change anything."

The example of the Ten Spies is an illustration of both fixed and growth mindsets (Numbers 13:32+). We often find ourselves operating in both mindsets as well. The goal is to recognize these areas and make necessary changes. God doesn't have a Plan B; His plan is for us to operate from His kingdom mindset. According to the Bible, the ten spies brought back an evil report because they focused on the giants and circumstances in the land instead of the greatness of their God. This evil report stemmed from a fixed mindset. They magnified the size of the problems and made excuses. Fear gives rise to excuses. They saw the giants as too big and too strong, concluding that they couldn't succeed and suggesting a retreat to Plan B.

Only Joshua and Caleb had a good report. They saw the same obstacles as the others, but they chose to disregard them and decided to go and possess the land without hesitation, excuses, meetings, or discussions. Fear didn't hold them back. How did they do it? **They believed what God said and took action based on it. They demonstrated a kingdom mindset by trusting that God wouldn't ask them to do something they couldn't accomplish.** They believed they were empowered to fulfil it. They had faith that God was with them and for them. Joshua and Caleb refused to let obstacles deter or intimidate them. They didn't overthink the situation, as overthinking is often caused by fear. Instead, they kept moving forward, pursuing what God had instructed them to do: possess the land. Just like Joshua and Caleb, you and I have our own promised land. God wants us to enter into it. How? By following the example set by Joshua and Caleb—believing in and acting upon God's Word. So, go forth and possess your Promised Land! God has so much in store for you. Don't let fear rob you of God's best for your life. Joshua and Caleb were the only scouts who entered the Promised Land. The other eight did not.

When we believe in what God says about us in His Word, we will no longer be intimidated by obstacles. We won't hesitate when a new job offer, a move, a promotion, a new baby, or any other opportunity or change arises because we will be confident in our ability to handle it well. We can change the narrative of fear and affirm that we adapt to change effectively. We are fully equipped to navigate any change that comes our way. Instead of resisting, we will embrace change because we recognize it as a divine provision meant to promote and propel us forward into our destiny.

We have the power to change the world by changing ourselves. By transforming our mindsets, we can alter the trajectory of our lives. Just as seasons change, we are called to evolve into the individuals that God intended us to be. We can become courageous individuals, emulating the example of Joshua and Caleb, who boldly pursue the dreams and promises of God in their lives. As John Maxwell aptly states, "Change is inevitable. Growth is optional."

Say to yourself, **"I am actively growing and maturing into the best version of myself. I acknowledge that I am a work in progress, continuously evolving and improving. I embrace the changes taking place within me as I align with the person God created me to be."**

God desires our input. In prayer, we can discuss matters together. God wants us to state our case in the courtroom of heaven. Not only is God always doing a new thing, but God would never ask us to do anything that He would not do Himself. Did you know that God can and sometimes is willing to change? We see God's willingness to change in Psalm 6:4-5; Psalm 80:14; Psalm 90:13, Genesis 6:6, and Jeremiah 18:7-10. Therefore, when we embrace change, we are emulating our Father.

A growth mindset casts out fear and develops positive habits such as perseverance, determination, resilience, teamwork, positive self-talk and humility.[52]

<u>When we adopt an eternal perspective, we develop a kingdom mindset</u>. Setbacks and challenges no longer trouble us as much as they did in the past because we can see the bigger picture. The bigger picture is that life is a journey of discovering God and understanding ourselves, with Heaven as our ultimate destination. God is faithful. He will help us get to our final destination. Life is a continual process of self-discovery where we uncover our purpose, abilities, value, and authority. Jesus is depicted as the bridegroom, and the Church represents the Bride of Christ. Our lives can be seen as a wedding march towards the joyous marriage supper of the Lamb. As we press forward, we are walking towards Jesus. Similarly, as you continue to pursue your God-given dreams and goals, you are moving closer to Jesus! He eagerly awaits you at the end of the aisle. Let this truth uplift and inspire you today! With each act of obedience and faith we are getting closer to Jesus our Bridegroom.

2 Corinthians 4:17 says that our light affliction, which is but for a moment, works for us a far more exceeding and eternal weight of glory. Our light affliction is the battle in our minds. <u>The renewing of our minds is a continuous battle.</u> When we live a purpose-driven life, we have a kingdom mindset. Our purpose is to fulfil our divine assignment and bring glory to God. Our life's purpose is found in John 17:4, which reads,

---

[52] C. Dweck. *Mindset: The New Psychology of Success* p.13

"I have glorified you on earth by accomplishing the work you gave me to do." This is what Jesus said to His Father, and this is what we are to say too. Jesus wanted us to see that He loved His Father and would do exactly what His Father commanded Him to do, no matter the cost. Those with a kingdom mindset keep trying until they succeed. They have calculated the costs. They will do whatever it takes. Love is obedience. The rewards far outweigh the costs.

> **"Difficulty is what wakes up the genius."**
> **—*Nassim Nicholas Taleb***

If we want to win our race and excel in our God-given assignment, then we need to change and do more. The cost is total surrender to God's mindset, otherwise known as His way of doing things. The cost is total reliance on God. Everything we receive from God comes by trusting Him. As we depend on Him for all things, He provides everything we need and more. God is able to do exceedingly, abundantly above all that we ask or think (Ephesians 3:20-21).

<u>Our effort is the required cost.</u> In Luke 12:48, it says, *"For to those to whom much is given, much is required."* The greater the talents given to us by God, the greater our purpose is, and the more effort God expects from us. Having a kingdom mindset helps us understand that in order to fulfil our purpose, we must put forth effort. It takes effort to intentionally examine our thoughts. It takes effort to resist toxic thoughts and replace them. It takes effort to persevere through challenges. It takes effort to pick yourself back up and keep going.

But please don't be discouraged. Sometimes, a small change of mindset can help you stay in control of your thoughts and actions, leading to a more favourable outcome. Jesus promised that His yoke is easy and His burden is light (Matthew 11:28-30). You can do this!

<u>Having a kingdom mindset requires faith.</u> It takes faith to trust God's word. Faith stretches us. Sometimes, it takes us out of our comfort zones and brings us to a new level in our relationship with God. "A Comfort Zone is a beautiful place, but nothing grows there." The stretching process is known as sanctification, which is the work of the Holy Spirit within us, helping us change our mindsets and perspectives, learn, and grow.

Nowadays, everyone is addicted to comfort and convenience. Growing is uncomfortable. Obedience is often inconvenient. An effort is required to change your mindset. We need to be willing to submit to the process and determine to do it even when we don't feel like it because it is good for us. For example, it's like going to the gym to work out. You may not feel like going and have to talk yourself into it, but afterwards, you're so happy that you did. You feel great and enjoy the benefits that come from it, such as having more energy.

Our only comfort should come when we are in the master's arms. Our comfort zone should be in the secret place of God's presence. This body, this life is not our permanent address; therefore, we will never feel comfortable in it. (Psalm 91:1) <u>Change comes when we make a choice.</u> God sets high standards for us. He gives us all the tools needed, as well as Holy Spirit's coaching to help us reach them. When we submit to His will and the sanctification process (His kingdom mindset) it's a win-win situation. We are destined to win!

<u>"Keep on Faith Street"</u> is a story retold by Steve Harvey and Joel Osteen that goes like this: A man died and went to heaven. As he walked with Peter down a corridor lined with doors, he noticed that each door had a name on it. Peter told him, "Don't worry about those; just keep going." However, the man became curious when he saw a door with his own name on it. He asked Peter to see what was behind it. Peter replied, *"Don't worry about it; you're here now."* But the man insisted. Relenting, Peter opened the door, revealing numbered shelves filled with packages, each bearing the man's name. Curious, the man asked Peter what they were. Peter explained that they were all the blessings that God had intended for him during his life, but the man had never asked for them and never believed he could have them.

God has so much in store for us. He is the God of abundance, desiring for us to live a life filled with success and abundance (John 10:10). I don't want to leave behind a warehouse full of unopened gifts and blessings that God intended for me to enjoy during my lifetime. How tragic that would be! Instead, I will adopt God's kingdom mindset and believe in what His Word says about me. Then, I will use my faith to manifest all the blessings that God has prepared for me. These blessings are meant to help us fulfil our life assignments, and they are for you and your loved ones as well. You were created to be blessed and to be a blessing to the world.

"The voice of faith materializes the blessings of God in our lives."
—Natalie Masucci

They say that <u>cemeteries are the richest places in the world</u> because buried there are ideas never pursued, songs never sung, places never visited, books never written, businesses never started, medical advancements and cures never discovered, ministries never started, schools never opened, new products never created, new campaigns never launched, degrees never pursued, adventures never explored etc. Don't go to your grave with your dreams still in you. What dreams has God placed in your heart? We were created for a divine purpose and destiny. If God puts a dream in your heart, He expects you to fulfil it.[53] God wants you to use His kingdom mindset to fulfil all the goals and dreams in your heart.

"Talk is cheap. Don't just talk about what you want to do, but take action!" Actions speak louder than words. Actions reveal a person's true character, while words can often be mere pretense.

When we speak positive faith declarations, we must follow them up with corresponding actions. **Speaking God's Word activates our faith, and taking corresponding actions materializes our faith.**

You have been called to make a positive impact on the world! God is seeking to develop Christian leaders who will transform the world with His kingdom mindset and success criteria.

Sadly, the truth is that most people won't change the world. The majority will go through life in a defensive mode or with a fixed mindset, afraid to step outside their comfort zones, habits, and routines. Fear of failure and the unknown holds them back. They make excuses while secretly longing for a better life, a wider impact, and a deeper joy. Yet, they remain too afraid to seize those things. As a result of their fear, the victorious life they desire will pass them by like a ship in the night.[54]

Few people will go through life in <u>offensive mode by adopting God's kingdom mindset.</u> These are the courageous ones who will change the world. God wants His children to be these people. He created us to live a life of significance and be trailblazers, innovators, problem solvers, world changers, history makers and mountain movers. The reason why

---

[53] Terri Savelle Foy

[54] Terri Savelle Foy - *Dream It. Pin it. Live it.* pg.143

only a few people will achieve this mandate is that only a small amount of the population will <u>decide to do whatever it takes</u> to live a full, faith-filled life and to accomplish their purpose. Few will decide to go all out despite what the critics have to say. Despite their own doubts. Despite their having no idea where to start. Despite the inconvenience. Despite the gnawing fear inside of them that keeps on saying, "Stop, slow down, it's too hard, you'll never succeed". These are the ones that will <u>arrive at a life of maximum impact and influence.</u> They will taste a deeper joy and abundant life that God promises. **Which kind of life will you choose?** If you desire with all your heart to fulfil your purpose and be a world changer, then adopt God's kingdom mindset. It will transform you. You can change the world. Start by changing your mindset. Then live your life in <u>offensive mode</u> by going after everything that God has for you.[55]

Determine today that you will learn God's success strategy and mindset that will lead you to health, prosperity, peace, success and fulfilling your assignment.

I don't want to leave behind any of the gifts and blessings that God intended for me to have. I don't want to discover that I lived far below the life God designed for me when I reach the end, and what about you? Let's continue walking on Faith Street. Walking by faith means embracing a kingdom mindset. God has a perfect plan for your life, and He expects you to remain open to change and new possibilities. Make space in your mind for God's mindset and give it a place of prominence. God expects us to evolve into the person we need to be in order to fulfil our God-given goals.

"As we are working on our mindset, God's mindset is working on us, changing us one neuron at a time."

—Natalie Masucci

---

[55] Kingdom Builders- *Email*

Chapter Three

God's Success Criteria

Having a mindset aligned with God's kingdom develops positive habits. Following success criteria and having a personal development plan are strategies utilized by the most successful people in the world. God desires for His children to shine brightly and reach the highest levels of influence, which is why He provides us with His Success Criteria to follow. **God's personal development plan is known as Vision.** He intends for His children to excel and hold top positions in their respective fields. Occupying the top positions grants power and influence, enabling us to positively impact those around us and the world. Proverbs 29:2 *When the righteous thrive, the people rejoice; when the wicked rule, the people groan.* You were created to live a life of maximum impact and influence.

What are the success criteria? In the context of education, success criteria are created by the teacher and outline what successful learning entails. They are aligned with the learning goal and explicitly define the desired qualities and aspects to consider in a student's performance or work. In the grand scheme of life, our ultimate learning goal is our life assignment, designed by God. God purposefully created us to fulfil a need and solve problems (Ephesians 2:10).

God is the author of the Bible, which contains His success criteria. God's success criteria are guidelines for living our lives, found in both the Old and New Testaments of the Bible. The book of Proverbs serves as a manual for victorious living, providing answers to every problem we may encounter. At the core of God's ultimate success criteria is the Golden Rule: treating others as we would like to be treated, also known as walking in love (Matthew 7:12).

B.I.B.L.E.: Best investment before leaving earth.
The Bible is the Word of God. Through the Holy Spirit, over a period of 1,500 years, more than 35 men of old were divinely inspired to write it. Within the Bible, we find God's success criteria—the methods to follow in order to be successful in our life assignments. As mentioned in 2

Timothy 3:16, that all scripture is God-breathed and is useful for teaching and edifying the body of Christ.

The Bible is a vast source of encouragement. The Success criteria within it are both positive and empowering.

Jesus, during his earthly ministry, was referred to as the "Master Teacher." In the New Testament, he is mentioned as a teacher 60 times. He came to earth to impart knowledge about God's kingdom mindset and success principles, enabling us to continue the work of bringing heaven to Earth (the good news). (Matthew 7:21) Jesus served as our role model, embodying God's success criteria. Instead of leaving us to our own devices, he provided us with a comprehensive success manual in the Bible. When unsure about how to proceed, consulting the Bible is essential as it holds answers to all of life's questions.

The Bible was written to provide us with a manual on how to live a holy and successful life. It serves as an owner's manual for a victorious life. Knowing and following God's Word brings forth numerous blessings. Throughout history, many business leaders have utilized strategies from the Bible to build their success, with recent examples including John Maxwell and Tony Robbins. God's success criteria are effective for everyone, and they hold even greater significance for His children. Following God's way brings forth blessings, such as good health, provision, peace, and restful sleep. Through His success criteria, God's plan is to bless and empower us. Similar to a human parent finding joy in their child's obedience, God the Father rejoices when we follow His success criteria. For instance, just as obeying parents and doing chores often results in rewards like allowances or the fulfilment of desired activities, as we follow God's success criteria, He blesses us with invaluable gifts that money cannot buy, such as divine health, supernatural provision, favour, and a peace that surpasses human understanding.

These blessings serve as types of positive reinforcement that God bestows upon us. When we follow His success criteria, we are blessed abundantly. However, it goes beyond mere positive reinforcement because as we adhere to God's success criteria, we align ourselves with His divine plan and will for our lives. Within God's divine will, everything has already been prepared and provided for us; our role is simply to walk in it. Ephesians 2:10 states, *"For we are God's handiwork, created in Christ Jesus to do good works, which God prepared in advance for us to do."* This realization takes the pressure off us. We don't need to strive to make things happen; we just need to follow God's success criteria and walk in the path He has already prepared for us. This is truly good news! Our obedience in following God's success criteria unveils the pathway to walking in His divine will and experiencing success in every aspect of our lives.

As a fellow teacher, I understand the importance of providing students with success criteria or learning goals before assigning a task. Similarly, without the Bible, we would be left uncertain about how to successfully fulfil our life assignment. We would be in the dark, relying on guesswork and hoping for the best. However, God's success criteria eliminate all the guesswork and provide us with a clear plan to follow.

Following God's success criteria can save us from unnecessary pain and heartache. However, regrettably, many people are unfamiliar with the Bible. Some don't even own a copy, while others may doubt it's divine origin. Churches should encourage individuals not only to attend services but also to read the Bible on their own. After all, how can one lead a holy and successful life without knowledge of God's success criteria as outlined in the Bible? How can we fulfil our God-given assignments without following His guidelines for success? It simply isn't possible.

Invest in yourself. I wholeheartedly encourage you to purchase a Bible for yourself today. It will undoubtedly be the most valuable investment you ever make. Consider buying one for your children as well. Instead of treating it like any other book, regard it as the instructions from your loving Creator, who desires to see you thrive and succeed in life.

It is crucial to familiarize yourself with the success criteria BEFORE embarking on your purpose. They will guide you on what needs to be done to accomplish your task successfully. Success criteria serve as parameters to keep us on track and protect us from potential pitfalls. With various approaches available, success criteria provide boundaries to help us stay on the right path. To fulfil our life assignment, it is essential to align with God's way of doing things. Following God's success criteria guarantees proper task completion, and proper task completion leads to success.

"The best investment you'll ever make is in yourself."
—*Warren Buffet*

We have discovered that the Bible holds God's success criteria, and we can learn about them by engaging with the Word of God through reading and listening. It's important to note that when you read or hear God's Word, you must take action. **Merely hearing it will strengthen your faith, but true empowerment comes through putting it into practice.** Give God's Word the reverence and respect it deserves. A reverential fear of the Lord is healthy and appropriate (Proverbs 9:10).

Remember, these are not ordinary words; they are the words of Almighty God.

Let's examine Proverbs 4 closely and see what it teaches us as success criteria.

Proverbs 4:20-27- "My son, pay attention to what I say; listen closely to my words. <u>Do not let them out of your sight, keep them within your heart;</u> for they are life to those who find them and health to a man's whole body. Above all else, guard your heart, for it is the wellspring of life. Put away perversity from your mouth; keep corrupt talk far from you. Let your eyes look straight ahead, fix your gaze directly before you. Make level paths for your feet and take only ways that are firm. Do not swerve to the right or to the left; keep your foot from evil."

One of God's success criteria is to diligently guard your heart (Proverbs 4:23), which entails making it a daily habit in your life. Guarding your heart refers to protecting your thoughts and mindset. It involves shielding your mind from limiting thoughts and toxic thought patterns that aim to derail you. Purposefully examining and directing our thoughts aligns with God's mindset.

How can we achieve this? By keeping God's Word in our hearts, as stated in Proverbs 4. We should meditate on it and be mindful of it. When our focus is on God's Word, we won't give attention to negative thoughts.

Proverbs 4 further explains that the power of life emanates from the human heart. Death and life are influenced by the words we speak. When our words align with God's Word and His will, we can see them manifest in our lives. Corrupt talk refers to words of fear and doubt, making excuses, and complaining. By eliminating words of fear and doubt from our vocabulary, we rid ourselves of a fixed mindset. This action closes doors to the enemy, removes hindrances, and creates space for God to work in our lives.

This same strategy of meditating on the word of God is repeated in

Joshua 1:8 "Keep this Book of the Law always on your lips; <u>meditate on it day and night,</u> so that you may be careful to do everything written in it. Then you will be prosperous and successful." Keeping God's success criteria always on your lips involves consistently reciting what it says. For instance, you can say, "God's success criteria are leading me to prosperity and success" or "Everything I set my hands to prosper in Jesus' name!" There are abundant blessings promised to those who follow God's instructions. God guarantees prosperity and success, desiring His children to be blessed and become a blessing to others.

Following God's success criteria activates the success and victory switch in your mind.

Another success criteria found in the Bible is honouring your parents. This is not merely a suggestion; it is a commandment. Unfortunately, this value is not emphasized as much in today's culture. Many people tend to blame their parents for everything that goes wrong in their lives, resulting in a lack of honour and respect. Consequently, numerous individuals find themselves estranged from their parents, which is a deeply saddening situation. Perhaps you find yourself in this position, having not spoken to your parents for years. I encourage you to make a decision today to change that. Choose to follow God's success criteria and reach out to your parents. Seek reconciliation and forgive them, allowing God to heal your heart and answer your prayers.

God intentionally placed you in a specific family. Out of all the possibilities, He chose your parents for a reason. There is a purpose behind His decision. By not having your parents actively involved in your life, you may miss out on valuable learning opportunities designed to shape you into the person God intended you to be. You might also be lacking the support and encouragement you need to navigate through challenges more efficiently. There are numerous positive reasons why God placed you in your particular family. Being a part of a family is meant to be a blessing. <u>Have you ever considered that you were placed in your family as a blessing to them?</u>

The fifth commandment says *"Honour your father and your mother that your days may be long in the land" (Exodus 20:12).* The blessing of long life comes from honouring our parents. In the New Testament, this commandment is restated and expanded. *"Honour your father and mother, that it may be well with you and that you may live long on the earth" Ephesians 6:1-3.* The blessing of good health and well-being is also included. It is truly amazing! God is so good that He blesses us when we align ourselves with His ways. There are numerous benefits to following God's success criteria. Honouring and respecting our parents is an act of love and obedience to God's command. In return, He promises to bless us with a long and healthy life. What a wonderful benefit! Premature death is not our portion! We will not depart until we fulfil our life's purpose. When we have accomplished our mission and are satisfied, then we will go home to glory in our ripe old age. Gray hair is a crown of splendor; it is attained in the way of righteousness (Proverbs 16:31-33).

When we embrace God's success criteria for parenting, as illustrated in Proverbs 22:6 and Ephesians 6:4, we are entering into a partnership with Him in raising our children. God, being a loving and exceptional Father, will assist us in becoming the best parents we can be.

Speak this powerful confession by Bill Winston over yourself and your children.

Heavenly Father, in the name of Jesus, I pray and declare Your Word over my children. I surround them with my unwavering faith in Your promises, knowing that You are faithful to fulfil them. I confess and believe that my children are dedicated followers of Christ, taught by You and obedient to Your will. Your peace and calmness encompass my children, for You, O God, fight on their behalf against anything that opposes them. You provide them with safety and bring them comfort.[56]

I declare that my children willingly obey their parents in the Lord, recognizing them as representatives of God because it is right and just. They honour, respect, and value their parents, understanding the significance of this commandment which comes with a promise. As a result, all things go well with my children, and they enjoy a long and fulfilling life. I believe and affirm that my children choose life, love the Lord, listen to His voice, and hold fast to Him, for He is their source of life and the length of their days. Therefore, my children are positioned as leaders and not followers, above and not beneath. They experience blessings in their coming and going.

As parents, we commit not to provoke, irritate, or distress our children. We will not treat them harshly, burden them, or cause them to feel discouraged, gloomy, inferior, or frustrated. Our words and actions will not break or harm their spirits. Instead, we will lovingly raise them, providing guidance, discipline, counsel, and instruction rooted in the teachings of the Lord. We will train them according to their unique paths, and as they grow older, they will continue to walk in those ways.[57]

In the New Testament, the primary success criteria to follow is the commandment of love, as walking in love encompasses all other commandments and more. Recognizing the depth of God's love for us and living in accordance with love are essential elements of God's growth and kingdom mindset.[58] Walking in love means wishing no ill of another; it encompasses forgiveness and all the fruits of the Spirit, including patience, long-suffering, generosity, faithfulness, gentleness, kindness and self -control.

---

56 Bill Winston Ministries

57 bwm_africa. *Instagram post, part of The Children I am Confession*-Feb 13, 2023

58 *Proverb 22:6 &Ephesians 6:4*

***

God desires for us to adhere to the success criteria outlined in the Bible. He wants us to understand and apply the strategies for success in this life. It is important to note that God's definition of success may differ from the prevailing culture. His ways are distinct from the ways of the world. For instance, God considers honouring our parents as a significant aspect of success.

The Bible says that *"The Lord does not look at the things people look at. People look at the outward appearance, but the Lord looks at the heart." (1 Samuel 16:7).* When the prophet Samuel was tasked with anointing the next king of Israel, people naturally assumed that God would choose the tallest and strongest brother. However, God surprised everyone by selecting David, the youngest and smallest among them. Why did God make this choice? It's because God looks deep within us, examining our hearts, to determine our success. <u>True success begins with our thoughts, the beliefs we hold in our hearts, and our motivations.</u> In David, God saw the potential and the seeds of greatness to become the next king of Israel. God's measurement of success differs from the world's standards. Therefore, it is important not to evaluate the completion of our purpose solely based on society's definition of success. God makes it a habit of using the most unlikely people to accomplish extraordinary things. Abraham was old, Job went bankrupt, Noah was a drunkard, Jacob was a cheater, Joseph was abused, Elijah was suicidal, Naomi was a widow, Rahab was a prostitute, Gideon was afraid, Moses had a speech impediment, Martha worried about everything, Jeremiah was young, Samson was a womanizer, the Samaritan woman was divorced, Paul persecuted Christians, the list goes on and on. God looks at the heart. The world sees imperfect and flawed people however God sees us according to our potential.

<u>God is a master builder, but His approach to building is often unconventional.</u> Sometimes, He begins by deconstructing certain aspects of our lives—such as limiting thoughts, bad habits, and negative influences—before He can add new things. Preparation for success involves letting go of old baggage to create space for new opportunities.[59] Let's create space for the blessings that God has in store for us by eliminating the clutter of negative and toxic thought patterns, as well as our outdated methods of approaching life. By letting go of the old and making room for the new, we open ourselves up to the transformative work of God in our lives.

---

[59] Steven Furtick. *Sermon-* February 14, 2021.

What does following God's success criteria look like?

Taking risks, trying new things, perseverance, exerting effort, stumbling-falling-making mistakes- but then rising again. Learning from mistakes. Constantly evolving and growing. Embracing discomfort, living by faith, heeding descriptive feedback, making adaptations, forgiving oneself and others, praying, praising, and expressing gratitude. Daily introspection. Daily prayer. Being resilient. Rejecting the idea of giving up. Daily surrender and reliance on God.

<u>What does it sound like?</u>

Positive self-talk, Positive -Faith declarations, Praise, Gratitude, asking questions (challenging negative thoughts, making mistakes) and Prayer.

These are the qualities that God seeks from us. They serve as indicators that we are aligning with His standards of success. It is noteworthy that one of these qualities includes making mistakes. Yes, making mistakes is acceptable and even anticipated. The key is to learn from them and continue progressing.

Here is an example of a common misconception: Most people believe and even joke that when they become parents, they don't get any instructions or an owner's manual on how to be a good parent. This, however, is not true. <u>God tells us in the Bible how to be a good parent, but no one ever told us to read it.</u> For example, *Ephesians 6:4 "Fathers, do not provoke your children to anger, but bring them up in the discipline and instruction of the Lord."* <u>You cannot follow something that you don't know about.</u>

Perhaps you're feeling remorseful now for not being aware of what the Bible says about parenting. You are not a deficient parent. Don't berate yourself for the choices you made while raising your children when you were unaware of alternative options. You did the best you could with the knowledge available to you at that time. Through this book, I aim to educate you that the Bible encompasses success criteria for every aspect of life, ranging from parenting to business and everything in between. The Bible is a comprehensive compilation of success criteria. Jesus holds the solution to every challenge you will ever encounter.

"The Bible is the Owner's Manual for a successful life."
—*Natalie Masucci*

God's <u>Big Ideas:</u> Big Ideas Refer to Core Concepts, Principles, Theories and Processes That Serve as the Focal Point of Instruction and Assessment.

Learning goals serve as the intended objectives or desired accomplishments of a specific course. They typically outline the knowledge, skills, and competencies that students in that class are expected to attain.

Learning goals are written in student-friendly language.
The Bible is written in a language that is simple and user-friendly, ensuring that it can be understood by everyone. As you read the Bible Holy Spirit will help you understand it. He will give you revelation knowledge (1 Corinthians 2:11). It is written at a level accessible to elementary school students, ensuring widespread comprehension. With the wide range of available translations today, you can easily find one that suits your needs. It is crucial to familiarize yourself with the Word of God contained in the Bible. Without it, you cannot embrace a mindset aligned with His kingdom. God's Word serves as His criteria for success. Do not be deceived by the notion that you cannot comprehend the Bible. The enemy wants you to believe that falsehood so that you never read it and discover the truth. The Bible teaches that the truth will set you free (John 8:32)! Take a step today and purchase a Bible for yourself, or if you already have one, remove the dust and dive into its pages.

God's **success criteria encompasses numerous potent and affirmative learning strategies.** These strategies facilitate learning and the acquisition of skills. Let's begin by examining **purposeful practice.** The Holy Spirit serves as our guide on this life-long learning journey. It is His responsibility to lead us to God's intended destination. He initiates our progress gradually and assigns purposeful practice activities that we can independently engage in to deepen our understanding, boost our confidence, and strengthen our faith. For instance, <u>when we first begin to exercise our faith,</u> we start by believing in God for small things, such as a cup of coffee. As our prayers are answered, our faith expands. We can then move on to believing in God for bigger things, like being able to buy groceries and then meet our monthly financial obligations. Eventually, we reach a point where we can believe in God for anything, even the seemingly impossible. For God, the impossible is the norm. He desires for us to operate with His kingdom mindset, where the impossible becomes the starting point.

Another example of a purposeful practice is <u>prayer</u>. The Bible instructs us to pray at all times because prayer is a powerful tool that activates the power of God in our lives (Ephesians 6:18). Prayer serves as a success criterion. How do we incorporate it? Initially, we may feel uneasy praying independently because we are unsure of how to do it. In such cases, we can read books on prayer, utilize prayer prompts, or request others to pray for us. I have a valuable eBook on prayer titled **"Prayer 101"** available on my website,[60] which can assist you in learning how to pray effectively. Click on the link provided below. Gradually, with time, we start to learn from others, and their prayers serve as models for us. Eventually, we become capable of praying for ourselves and even for our family and friends. As our **prayers** are answered, our confidence and faith increase. Consequently, we gain the ability to pray confidently on our own. The **purposeful practice of prayer** has a threefold impact. Firstly, it enhances our understanding of prayer. Secondly, it enables us to practice prayer. And thirdly, it boosts our confidence in the effectiveness of our prayers.

Another example is setting boundaries. When we first attempt to do it, we have no idea how. With practice, you learn to clearly communicate your expectations and the reasons for them. After time you understand that boundaries are essential if you are going to fulfil your purpose, so you don't fret or hesitate to set them, and you enforce them without feeling bad about it.

With God, everything experiences growth. The principle of seed time and harvest forms the foundation of the gospel. Our faith flourishes as we actively utilize it, and our confidence expands in tandem. God is an expert cultivator. When He created us, He implanted seeds of greatness within us. He nurtures those seeds through His kingdom mindset. **Purposeful practice** <u>acts as the water that nourishes the seeds, causing them to sprout and flourish. God's success criteria provide us with the framework and learning goals for our lives.</u> His eternal perspective fosters resilience and perseverance within us. By speaking His Word in the form of positive self-talk and faith confessions, we construct our true identity and faith. With God's kingdom mindset, everything grows: our self-confidence, faith, courage, perseverance, resilience, love, gratitude, and success. The seeds planted within us (manifested as our thoughts) will yield a corresponding harvest in our lives. Do not leave this world with untapped talents. Do not depart without reaping the rewards of your harvest. The world is eagerly awaiting your contribution. God requires your presence.

---

[60] https://empoweredwordministries.ca/product/prayer-101-ebook/

"The thoughts we choose to think are the tools we use to paint the canvas of our lives."

—Louise Hay

As a master teacher, God uses the Think aloud strategy in the Bible to model learning for us. Thinking aloud is part of explicit instruction. God uses the **Think Aloud** strategy many times in Scripture. Think Aloud includes Modelling, which shows us exactly how to do something. An example of God giving us a Think Aloud lesson is found in John 11: 41-42, when Jesus spoke out loud for the benefit of the people standing there. He wanted them to hear him think and pray aloud so they would know how to pray too. Jesus thanked His Father for hearing him when He prayed. There are many references in the Bible, 1 Peter 3:12 and 1 John 5:15, that confirm that God hears us when we pray to Him. God hears us when we pray. This is so amazing. How many times do we pray and wonder if anyone hears? Just knowing that God has heard my prayers somehow makes me feel better. God wants us to know that we are loved, and we are heard. As the master teacher, Jesus teaches us by example. He confidently prayed out loud to His Father, and we should do the same. He modelled how to pray for us. It is important to know that God hears us when we pray to Him, and equally important to thank God for listening. Jesus said, *"Father, I thank you that you have heard me."* If we know that God hears us when we pray, then we should go ahead and thank Him for answering our prayer too.

In Isaiah 14:24, we see another example of a **Think Aloud.** *"The Lord of Hosts has sworn: As I have planned, so shall it be, and as I have purposed, so shall it stand."*

Here, God is vocalizing a prophecy for our understanding. He desires us to be aware of what He will accomplish, and He reveals the plan before it comes to fruition. Prophecy holds immense power. *God does nothing without revealing His plan to His servants, the prophets* (Amos 3:7). As we are made in the image of God, He also wants us to prophesy over our own lives. Let us prophesy goodness and not evil. Speak blessings over your life. Utter what you desire rather than focusing on the present circumstances.

What have you learned from this?

God provides us with purposeful, independent practice to enhance our learning and showcase it to Him. Examples of such practice include prayer, assignments/tasks, obedience and steps of faith. He desires us to rely on Him for every aspect of our lives. Each task is crafted to teach us that we require His assistance to achieve it. Similar to how the law was given in the Old Testament to emphasize the necessity of a saviour,

<u>purposeful practice is employed to underscore our need for God's grace in fulfilling our destiny.</u>

God desires us to engage in daily prayer, seeking Him for our needs. He longs to provide for us on a daily basis. Every day, we practice the act of praying to Him, seeking His assistance to accomplish the tasks set before us.

If we saturate our minds with God's mindset, His success criteria, attentively listen to the descriptive feedback of the Holy Spirit, and practice positive self-talk, there will be no space for Satan's deceptive lies. As believers, it is essential to live according to the Word of God, which serves as His success criteria revealed in the Bible. The Bible holds profound significance in cultivating God's kingdom mindset, akin to how the human heart sustains life. It represents the very heartbeat of God's mindset. In any situation or crisis we encounter, we are not powerless or without help, for we possess the heavenly power of the Bible behind us when we speak it forth.

The Bible resonates with the very heartbeat of God's mindset. God and His Word are inseparable; therefore, the Bible encapsulates His mindset.

Holy Spirit's Descriptive Feedback

If we look at our lives through an educational lens, Holy Spirit's leading is akin to descriptive feedback. Descriptive feedback is effective communication in its highest form. Holy Spirit's descriptive feedback not only builds our self-confidence but can also improve our effective communication skills when we emulate Him. Holy Spirit uses accommodations to promote our learning which can include changes in the environment, adjustments to curriculum formats, or specialized equipment. Jesus is the Master Teacher. He gave us Holy Spirit, who guides and protects us with his descriptive feedback throughout our lives. We are to be lifelong learners, always growing and maturing into the very image of Christ (2 Corinthians 3:18). You don't need to invest a significant amount of money in a life coach or success coach because you already have one. If you have accepted Christ as your Savior, God has bestowed upon you the Holy Spirit, the third person of the Godhead, to guide and coach you. <u>This incredible gift is available to every Christian, regardless of their denomination.</u> It is important to note that religions are man-made, but what I am referring to is having a personal relationship with Jesus. A genuine relationship entails continuous communication.

Holy Spirit is in you and always available. Holy Spirit serves as your inherent success coach. He constantly communicates with you, providing timely descriptive feedback to aid you in completing tasks and demonstrating your learning. Holy Spirit represents the voice of God within you. In *John 10:27, Jesus states, "My sheep listen to my voice. I know them, and they follow me."* To lead a successful life, it is crucial to follow the guidance of Holy Spirit's voice. His role is to steer you away from danger, navigate you through life's storms, and guide you towards the security of your purpose (John 16:13). Trusting His voice is paramount. Amidst the multitude of competing voices in our minds, God urges us not to heed the contrary thoughts that can lead to self-destruction. He instructs us to focus on Holy Spirit's voice rather than the storm. By obeying His voice, He will lead us through, ensuring our safe arrival at our intended destination.

"Holy Spirit is our built-in security system. He is always watching and trying to protect us from harm and danger. He sends out warning signals."

—Natalie Masucci

Descriptive Feedback

Descriptive feedback is a profoundly impactful tool for enhancing student learning. It highlights gaps in understanding and explicitly informs students on how to improve their learning rather than listing what they got wrong. **Did you know that God, the master teacher uses descriptive feedback with us?** It is an integral part of His kingdom mindset and is the operation of the Holy Spirit in our lives. This type of feedback provides specific information to the learner, enabling them to understand what they must do in order to make improvements. Descriptive feedback is conveyed through words, which hold tremendous power as they possess the capacity to either build up or destroy. The Bible declares that the power of life and death resides in the tongue (Proverbs 18:21). **Holy Spirit's descriptive feedback is rooted in God's Word and aligns with His success criteria and kingdom principles found in the Bible (John 14:26).** It is indispensable in aiding our growth and transformation into the individuals God requires all of us to be in order to fulfil our divine purpose.

Descriptive Feedback is an integral part of embracing a kingdom mindset and is the work of the Holy Spirit in our lives. The Holy Spirit, as the third person of the Trinity, resides within us when we accept Jesus as our Savior (Romans 8:11). He takes on the role of our mentor and coach, providing guidance and support. The Holy Spirit utilizes

Constructive Criticism that is genuinely helpful and edifying and never condemns us.

Descriptive feedback plays a vital role in fostering the belief that all students have the capacity to enhance their work and build upon their prior achievements. Effective feedback centres around the task at hand, offering specific insights into what the learner has done well and areas for improvement while being delivered within the relevant context. Timeliness and continuity are crucial aspects of feedback to ensure it can be applied to enhance performance. This approach allows for mistakes to be embraced as valuable learning opportunities, which is a fundamental aspect of God's operating system. When we make mistakes, God does not harbor anger towards us; instead, He perceives them as opportunities for growth.[61] God celebrates our attempts and learning.

Descriptive feedback guides the learner on the next skill or steps in the learning continuum that will bring them closer to their ultimate goal. It answers the question, "What should I work on next?" This conveys the notion of an ongoing journey of learning and growth. In His guidance, God employs words such as "next" to motivate us to persist in our pursuit.

Descriptive feedback includes your inner cheerleader, the Holy Spirit. It sounds like, "I appreciate how you… I saw how you… Your input to today's meeting was a game-changer for this project. Consistency is one of your biggest strengths." The Holy Spirit serves as our inner cheerleader, cheering us on as we grow and progress. He knows God's success criteria by heart and brings them back to our remembrance when we need them (John 14:26). **Another one of His roles is to protect us.** Have you ever heard a voice say, "Don't do that or don't go there warning you of danger? That is the voice of the Holy Spirit. Some refer to it as an intuition. Heed that voice.

Ever wonder… "how did I get here?" Holy Spirit can lead you back to God. Follow His directions. He's your built-in success coach and GPS system.

—*Natalie Masucci*

God wants us to have a lifelong learning mindset and assures us that making mistakes is okay. The Holy Spirit reminds us that everyone slips up at times and encourages us not to dwell in shame or guilt. Instead of a mindset focused on punishment, we should embrace the truth that God is love. While there may be moments of correction, it is

---

[61] *Purposefulfeedback.weebly.com*

never accompanied by condemnation. (Romans 8:1) We can be honest about our weaknesses, confront our fears, and approach God's throne of grace without fear (Hebrews 4:16). Rather than fearing punishment, we should see our mistakes as opportunities for growth and development. Mistakes are like stepping stones on the path of learning, and with the Holy Spirit's guidance, we can forgive ourselves and keep moving forward. God prefers mercy over punishment (Hosea 6:6).

Holy Spirit's Descriptive Feedback is constructive because it does not rely on comparisons, competition, or judgments of ability. It consists of constructive criticism that is positive and helpful. Instead of simply criticizing, it provides praise, next steps and suggestions for improvement.

In life, we often find ourselves repeating the same mistakes and facing similar setbacks. However, God desires for us to learn from these experiences and make necessary adjustments to achieve victory and success. By making small yet meaningful changes today, we pave the way for a brighter future. Your future self will undoubtedly appreciate the efforts and adjustments you make today.

The descriptive feedback provided by the Holy Spirit will never infringe upon our free will. He offers learning suggestions solely, leaving the choice to follow them entirely up to us. God has bestowed upon us the gift of free will, as He desires for us to willingly embrace and follow His ways (Luke 11:13).

The Holy Spirit understands the immense power of words and is, therefore, mindful of the way He uses them. His descriptive feedback is intentional and aligns with the Word of God. He communicates only what is necessary for our growth and edification. His approach is positive and direct. It is crucial for us to learn from the Holy Spirit's descriptive feedback and also be mindful of our own words. Our words and beliefs should be in harmony with the Word of God. It is important to keep our words concise, positive, and life-giving. The Bible instructs us to listen more and speak less (James 1:19). Let us heed the descriptive feedback of the Holy Spirit. It seems that God gave us two ears and only one mouth because we are meant to listen more than we speak.

The Holy Spirit reveals to us that there is a superior path to follow (Isaiah 55:8-9). He stirs our hearts, assisting us in making choices that align with God's plans and purposes for the specific position or situation we find ourselves in. It is crucial for us to be attuned to the promptings of the Holy Spirit. He will lead us into all truth, particularly when it comes to guidance and decision-making.[62]

---

[62] Keith Butler Ministries. *Daily Devotional*- December 29, 2020.

The Holy Spirit provides descriptive feedback to guide us and help us grow. Similar to the "2 Stars and a Wish" method used in education, Holy Spirit acknowledges our strengths and points out areas for improvement. It is important to include the next steps for continued learning and growth. By recognizing our weaknesses, we become aware of areas that require attention. John 16:13 *When the Spirit of truth comes, He will guide you into all the truth; for He will not speak on His own initiative, but whatever He hears, He will speak, and He will disclose to you what is to come.* The Holy Spirit's feedback helps us identify and address these areas, empowering us to overcome vulnerabilities and continue on our journey of growth and development.

God creates a safe learning environment in which mistakes are viewed as expected and valuable learning experiences that propel us to greater heights and improvements. When we make mistakes or encounter failures, there is never any condemnation (Romans 8:1). We learn the most from our mistakes. When providing feedback, the Holy Spirit emphasizes what could have been done better rather than dwelling on what was done wrong. His focus remains on the positive aspects. Restructuring simple sentences and utilizing different words has significant power in promoting compliance and enhancing mental well-being. [63]

Some examples are "I've noticed a significant improvement in your performance, behaviour and skills since your last review. I noticed there was an error in a couple of areas, and I need to discuss with you how we can avoid that happening in the future."

The Holy Spirit embodies gentleness (1 Kings 19:11-13), he speaks softly, he is not a bully. It is the enemy who employs guilt, regret, shame, and condemnation against us, aiming to undermine our self-confidence and lead us to surrender.

In contrast, the Holy Spirit consistently provides restorative descriptive feedback. His intention is always to restore us to a place of deep connection and relationship. He utilizes empathy, forgiveness, reconciliation, encouragement, and empowerment. The descriptive feedback from the Holy Spirit serves to uplift and strengthen our confidence and build our resilience.

In our roles as educators, parents, guardians, coaches, employers, pastors, and grandparents, it is important to adopt the Holy Spirit's approach to effective communication. Instead of using condemnation, we should focus on encouragement, following God's example. **Effective communication involves finding the balance between being truthful and considerate.** We must speak the truth in love, just as the

---

[63] Dr. C. Leaf-*Instagram*

Holy Spirit provides descriptive feedback to us. Our words should align with God's Word and promote restoration, relationship and life. By emulating the Holy Spirit's approach, we can positively impact the mental health and well-being of those around us. There is a right way and a wrong way to say things. Effective communication should come from a place of love and includes forgiveness. It should be always edifying and leave room for growth. Effective communication is kind and respectful. **Only people who are not happy with themselves are mean to others. Remember that**.

Our "<u>inside voice</u>" refers to our self-talk and mindset, originating from the guidance of the Holy Spirit within us (1 Corinthians 3:16). Just as we use our inside voices in a classroom for a calm environment, we are encouraged to use our inside voice when communicating with God, as He resides within us. This voice represents our internal authority and mindset, guided by the Holy Spirit's feedback. We should not let external voices or worldly influences dictate our lives. In contrast, our "<u>outside voice</u>" is used against the enemy. We employ it in prayer, boldly and loudly asserting our authority. By understanding and using both our inside and outside voices appropriately, we align ourselves with God's guidance and overcome challenges.

Your mind readily absorbs everything you silently communicate to it. It constantly listens in on your self-talk. Therefore, make a conscious decision to only speak positively. Let your words be filled with hope, love, truth, happiness, and success, and witness the remarkable transformation in your life.[64]

Negative self-talk and negative feedback are different concepts. <u>Negative feedback, as part of the Holy Spirit's descriptive feedback, is intended to help us identify areas for improvement.</u> It is important not to avoid or dismiss negative feedback or criticism because it can increase motivation and promote growth. Although it may be uncomfortable to receive negative feedback, it is an opportunity for development rather than destruction. God's Word aims to develop us into the individuals He created us to be, building our confidence, character, and self-esteem. Do not fall into the trap of taking criticism personally. Instead, embrace a teachable spirit and understand the purpose of negative feedback allows us to grow and fulfil our potential (Proverbs 15:5).

***

---

[64] Billiondollarappetite. *Instagram*- December 21, 2020

The Holy Spirit embodies a Kingdom mindset as a mentor in our lives. He serves as a guide rather than a judge. He convicts us only (John 16:8). During times when we find ourselves criticizing and belittling ourselves for errors, mistakes, or setbacks, the Holy Spirit is there to assist us. He teaches us to learn from our failures and mistakes, empowering us to take the necessary steps to succeed in the future. The Holy Spirit is fully aware of the plan for our lives (Jeremiah 29:11). His desire is for us to have clarity and understanding of what to do, which is why He provides us with the **next steps** (John 16:13 - "He will guide you into all truth"). All we need to do is ask, and the Holy Spirit will grant us clarity regarding the plan. He will give you the next step to take.

The Holy Spirit serves as a constant reminder that God is on our side, actively partnering with us on our journey of growth and transformation (Ephesians 1:13). We are sealed with the promised Holy Spirit until the day of redemption (Ephesians 4:30). While the Holy Spirit understands and empathizes with our disappointments, He doesn't provide false encouragement that could ultimately lead to more letdowns.[65] The Holy Spirit expresses truth in a loving manner. He respects and values our voices and perspectives. Moreover, He encourages us to examine issues and problems critically, considering them from an eternal perspective. For instance, He helps us recognize that in the grand scheme of things, certain mistakes may be insignificant.

The Holy Spirit's role is to cultivate a mindset aligned with God's kingdom within us, enabling us to fulfil our purpose, embrace our identity, and carry out our life's calling. He is known as the spirit of truth, and He never deceives or manipulates us in any way. The Holy Spirit communicates the truth to us in a loving manner. He assists us in growing into the individuals we need to become in order to achieve success. He actively works on shaping our character. The Holy Spirit meets each of us where we are and guides us to where God wants us to be. We are all at different points along the learning continuum.

"Be encouraged; it's ok if you're back at ground zero because you can only go up!"

— *Natalie Masucci*

When the Holy Spirit imparts the truth to us through His descriptive feedback, it can be likened to undergoing surgery. It may cause temporary pain, but it brings about a lasting cure. On the other hand,

---

[65] Dweck, Carol S. Mindset: The New Psychology of Success, p. 186.

when the enemy speaks lies, they act as painkillers. They may provide temporary relief, but they result in long-lasting negative side effects.[66]

The Holy Spirit is filled with compassion because He deeply loves us and desires the very best for us. God's will represents the optimal outcome for our lives. The Holy Spirit guides us and helps us understand that we are engaged in a lifelong journey of learning and growth.[67]

As members of God's family, we undergo a process of sanctification led by the Holy Spirit. This transformational journey involves the Holy Spirit providing descriptive feedback and success strategies and guiding our lifelong learning. We are compared to clay in the hands of a Potter, as the Holy Spirit molds and shapes us, leading us from one level of glory to another (2 Corinthians 3:18). Through this process, the Holy Spirit develops within us the fruits of the Spirit, including patience, perseverance, peace, kindness, joy, gentleness, and self-control (Galatians 5:22-23).

God's descriptive feedback is distinctive because it encompasses love, constructive criticism, truth, and encouragement all in one. Sometimes, He may provide negative feedback, but it is delivered in a positive manner. For example, He may ask, "What can you do better?" or suggest, "Next time, try this."

Due to the Holy Spirit's intimate knowledge of us, He orchestrates specific individuals and experiences that cater to our unique learning styles, needs, and interests along the journey of life. This personalized approach supports our growth and development (Romans 8:27).

The Holy Spirit provides personalized accommodations tailored to our individual learning styles, ensuring access to content and tasks for individuals with disabilities. These accommodations can include changes in the environment, adjustments to curriculum formats, or specialized equipment. The Holy Spirit, as a skilled teacher, personalizes our learning plans and incorporates necessary accommodations to facilitate our learning. Fairness in education means teaching individuals according to their specific needs, not treating everyone equally. Comparing our lives to others and feeling that things are unfair overlooks the nuances of fairness and equality. The Bible assures us that God is fair and just, and the Holy Spirit will provide the accommodations necessary for our success. We all learn differently, so Holy Spirit individualizes our learning plan. God's Descriptive feedback motivates us and empowers us to keep moving forward no matter what, with the understanding that we have a helper. "You will receive power when the Holy Spirit comes on you" (Acts 1:8).

---

[66] Big mama siciliana. *Instagram post-* Feb 3/21
[67] *Dweck* p.127-129

God can't make a way for you if you're following your own path.
—*Natalie Masucci*

Accommodations

As a master teacher, God implements accommodations in our individualized learning plan. Scaffolding is an accommodation strategy employed by the Holy Spirit to plan our learning and growth. Instructional scaffolding is a process where a teacher provides supports to students to enhance learning and facilitate the mastery of tasks. This is achieved by building upon students' existing experiences and prior knowledge as they acquire new skills. In the initial stages of learning, the teacher implements various supports or scaffolds to ensure students' success. As students gain proficiency in the required skills, these supports are gradually removed, allowing them to learn independently. According to **Vygotsky**, scaffolding is a **tool for fostering growth and enabling learners to attain greater independence.** By breaking down complex tasks into smaller, manageable steps, learners can progress towards their goals. Collaborating with skilled instructors or more knowledgeable peers aids in making connections between concepts and boosts confidence.[68]

The Holy Spirit is indeed a masterful teacher, providing continuous support throughout our lifelong learning journey. By scaffolding our learning experiences, the Holy Spirit helps us overcome fear and anxiety, fostering self-confidence, independence, resilience, and courage.

The Holy Spirit cares for us and consistently assists us in our growth and development. He faithfully guides us along a specific path that leads to the fulfilment of God's desired purpose for our lives and the completion of our unique life assignments.[69] An example of scaffolding can be seen when someone enters your life for a season to assist you with a problem or to assist in advancing in your faith journey.

---

[68] Aug. 18, 2020 https://educationaltechnology.net/vygotskys-zone-of-proximal-development-and-scaffolding/
[69] Proverbs 3:5-6 and Jeremiah 29:11.

This person could be anyone; a stranger, a friend, a mentor, a priest, a co-worker, a neighbor, or a pastor who supports and guides you in acquiring new skills or understanding.

Holy Spirit helps us to make wise decisions because He is wisdom and knowledge. Psalms 19:7 *"The law of the Lord is perfect, refreshing the soul. The statutes of the Lord are trustworthy, <u>making wise the simple</u>."* Following God's success criteria makes one wise! *1 Corinthians 3:18-19. Says, "that the wisdom of this world is folly with God."* God's wisdom is distinct from the wisdom of this world. While we have limited knowledge and understanding, God is all-knowing and sovereign. The Holy Spirit, as part of the Trinity, possesses knowledge of the future, enabling Him to guide and protect us from the various traps and schemes of the enemy. With His divine insight, the Holy Spirit can also save us significant amounts of time in our journey (John 16:13).

Wisdom surpasses mere knowledge as it encompasses the understanding of how to effectively apply knowledge. In the Bible, we see the example of Solomon, who sought wisdom from God and used it to acquire riches, wealth, and honour. Solomon's reign is described as a time of unprecedented prosperity for Israel, attributed to his wisdom (1 Kings 4:29-34). Similarly, the Holy Spirit desires to guide us in the same manner. Through His descriptive feedback, He offers us wise counsel. **We have the opportunity to possess the Wisdom of Solomon if we heed the Holy Spirit's warnings and follow His lead.** By doing so, we can avoid mistakes and save ourselves from unnecessary time, trouble, heartache, and sorrow. The Holy Spirit's guidance can make us appear wise, and His wisdom can lead us to success and prosperity in every aspect of our lives.

<u>In order to follow Holy Spirit's voice, you need to be able to hear Him.</u> If you don't hear from Holy Spirit, you can learn how. There are many ways that Holy Spirit speaks to us. He wants us to learn how to hear His voice. He can't protect us if we can't hear Him. **He cannot give us descriptive feedback to help us learn and grow if we don't recognize His voice**. If you are a child of God, then you can hear Holy Spirit's voice. Jesus tells us in John 10:27-28 that *"His sheep hear His voice."*

An example of the Holy Spirit speaking to me is when He brings a verse of scripture to my remembrance while I am praying or praising. It is a timely and encouraging word from Him. The Holy Spirit may also communicate with me through various channels, such as gut intuition, a friend, a song, a social media post, a phone call, a sign, a movie, or a text message. Trust yourself to hear. You were made to hear God's voice.

<u>Knowing God's Word will enhance your ability to hear from the Holy Spirit since God is His Word (John 1:1).</u> The more time you invest

in studying and immersing yourself in God's Word, the deeper your understanding of Him will grow, enabling you to recognize His voice more readily. It's important to note that the <u>Holy Spirit always speaks in alignment with the Word of God and will never contradict it (1 Corinthians 12:3)</u>. Therefore, by expanding your knowledge of Scripture, you provide the Holy Spirit with a broader vocabulary to communicate with you.

When we pray, God bends down and listens (Psalm 116:2). It's incredible to imagine that when we pray, God actually hears us. From your lips to God's ears, literally, your prayers are not in vain; they are heard by the Almighty. As stated in James 4:8, if you draw near to God, He will draw near to you. By engaging in prayer, we draw closer to God. When He draws near, His presence allows us to hear Him because He is near (Romans 10:8-9). Therefore, we should continue praying persistently until we hear His voice. Never cease in your prayers. If necessary, create a space of solitude free from distractions and external noise. Quiet your mind and block out all other thoughts. Instead, listen to your heart, as the Holy Spirit speaks to your heart, not your head. Pray until you receive a word or message, or revelation. Once you hear from the Holy Spirit, stand firm on that word or promise. <u>A word from the Holy Spirit holds more value than money in the bank because it is a certainty (2 Peter 1:21)</u>. Whatever He declares will come to pass in His perfect timing, bringing glory to Him and working for your ultimate good. Remember, God is the ultimate answer to every challenge we encounter in life.

Example: Years ago, my son Thomas broke his collarbone while playing hockey. We rushed him to the hospital, where an x-ray revealed a severe break. The medical staff scheduled an appointment for us to see an orthopedic surgeon in five days. I brought Thomas home, and at that moment, I prayed fervently for his healing. During my prayer, I distinctly heard the Holy Spirit whisper within me, "He's healed. He won't need surgery." I rejoiced upon receiving this message.

Five days later, as we arrived at the specialist's office, the report we received was completely different. The doctor examined the X-rays and informed me that Thomas required not just one but two surgeries. The first procedure involved screwing the bones in place, followed by a second surgery to remove the plate and screws. Uncertain of what to do, I sought a second opinion. I held onto the word I had received from the Holy Spirit, confident that the second specialist would validate that Thomas didn't need surgery.

However, the second specialist echoed almost word for word what the first doctor had said. I felt disappointed and faced a crucial decision.

Should I trust the doctors' reports or hold fast to the word I received during my prayer? Against all the evidence to the contrary, I chose to believe God's report. I requested a figure-eight brace for Thomas and brought him back home. The specialist expressed annoyance but agreed to schedule a follow-up appointment in a month's time.

At the one-month mark, Thomas's collarbone showed no signs of improvement. It remained broken and caused him ongoing pain. Even at the two-month appointment, the X-ray revealed no noticeable change. The specialist regarded me with disbelief, as if questioning my sanity. He delivered the disheartening news that Thomas's bones were too far apart and too jagged to ever fuse back together naturally. As I helped Thomas into the car to go home after that appointment, doubts began to creep into my mind. Thoughts like, "It's been two months, and nothing has changed," and "Thomas will need surgery, and now he'll miss his entire hockey season" plagued me. <u>Once again, I faced a critical decision: should I listen to the voices of doubt in my head or hold firm to the word I had received from God?</u>

I resolved that I had already come too far to waver in my belief. If the Holy Spirit had assured me that Thomas would not require surgery, then I would steadfastly believe it, regardless of the circumstances. Today, I share this message with you to encourage you: You, too, have journeyed too far to give up on God now. Stay committed to the path of faith, my friend, even when faced with evidence that seems contrary.

During our three-month follow-up visit, I approached the X-ray results with a mix of anticipation and anxiety. Deep down, I held onto a glimmer of hope, longing for positive news. And then, a miracle unfolded before our eyes. The specialist, brimming with excitement, pointed out the X-ray that displayed how Thomas's body had miraculously formed calcium around the fracture. At that moment, he delivered the incredible news that Thomas would heal naturally, without the need for surgery, and he would not experience any long-term complications from the break. I couldn't help but offer my gratitude to Jesus for this astounding outcome.

I am happy to report that Thomas' collarbone healed perfectly; he doesn't even have a bump where the break happened like most people do. Glory to God!

The Holy Spirit knew without a doubt that Thomas did not require surgery, and He made it clear to me during my prayer. His word is an unwavering truth. I had to hold onto that word and remain steadfast in faith until its complete manifestation. If I had doubted, Thomas would have undergone two surgeries and could potentially still be living with complications to this day. By heeding the advice of the Holy Spirit, my son Thomas was spared from unnecessary surgeries, pain, and suffering. <u>When you receive a word from the Holy Spirit, you can confidently stand upon it, knowing that it will undoubtedly come to pass. It will happen in God's perfect timing, for His glory and for our ultimate good.</u>

DISCLAIMER

I'm not suggesting that people should disregard their doctor's recommendations. What I am saying is that God knows all things, and having faith in God's Word has the power to change your circumstances. A word from Holy Spirit is a sure thing. You can trust Holy Spirit's descriptive feedback. Learning to hear the voice of Holy Spirit takes time. If you are unsure, seek confirmation from an elder and follow your doctor's advice

It is important to understand that God's word, when spoken through us, has the power to transform our circumstances. Did you realize that your current situation is not permanent? It can change. This realization is cause for great rejoicing! As stated in 2 Corinthians 4:18, *"So we fix our eyes not on what is seen, but on what is unseen. For what is seen is temporary, but what is unseen is eternal."* Thomas's broken collarbone was a temporary condition, but God's word to me holds eternal significance. My unwavering faith in God's word brought about supernatural healing for my son's collarbone, fundamentally altering his circumstances.

<u>You do not have to passively accept everything that life throws at you.</u> If God did it for me, He could certainly do it for you too. Remember that you are royalty, designed to reign on Earth with a mindset aligned with God's kingdom (1 Peter 2:9). It is time to reclaim dominion in various areas of your life. Take authority over the lies and deceit of the enemy. You have a choice to make. Decide to be fully convinced of your rights as a child of God, confidently embracing the privileges bestowed upon you.

<u>The Holy Spirit serves as our guide</u>. As stated in Romans 8:14, the Bible affirms that those who are led by the Spirit are recognized as children of God. <u>This implies that without being led by the Spirit, we cannot claim to be true children of God.</u> The act of being led by the Spirit is crucial. It is an integral part of fostering a relationship with God. <u>Being led by the Spirit entails attentively listening to the descriptive feedback provided by the Holy Spirit and willingly making the adjustments and changes that He suggests. If you are being led, that means you are following, not leading. We need to stop going ahead of Holy Spirit.</u>

As our guide, the Holy Spirit serves as our protector by warning us about danger zones (Psalm 23:4). God desires to prevent us from falling into repetitive traps and making the same mistakes. The Holy Spirit will gently prompt us from within, often referred to as a "check" in our spirit. He imparts a sense of uneasiness or unrest when danger lies ahead. It is crucial that we pay attention to these warnings and respond by saying, "I'm not going there" or "I'm not doing that," in order to avoid unnecessary heartache in our lives. By diligently following the descriptive feedback of the Holy Spirit, we can make wise decisions and steer clear of wrong paths. Ultimately, He will guide us towards a path that reflects positively upon us. **Holy Spirit leads us by peace** according to Isaiah 55:12 & Psalm 23:2-3. Peace is more of a feeling than a thought or word. If you feel an inward peace, then proceed; if not, then don't. If you sense any uneasiness in your spirit, this is the Holy Spirit's way of warning you to not proceed.

6 ways to hear the Voice of God or the Holy Spirit's voice:

1. Through Scripture - Psalm 119:105
2. The Inward witness - Romans 8:14-16 (prick, uneasiness or peace)
3. The Inward voice-Romans 9:1 (Intuition-gut feeling)
4. Led by the Voice of the Holy Spirit - Acts 10:19-20 & Acts 13:2
5. Visions and Dreams - Acts 2:14-18 & Acts 9:10
6. Angelic Visitations - Hebrews 13:2, Acts 8:26 & Acts 10:2 & Acts 12:7
7. The Lord speaks to followers directly – Acts 23:11 [70]

When we heed the Holy Spirit's descriptive feedback, we cease to waste our time, talents, and purpose. He will help us maintain focus and continue progressing towards fulfilling our life's purpose. As demonstrated, the Holy Spirit communicates with individuals in various ways, ensuring that everyone can hear His voice. You have the ability to hear His voice. You are being guided, and you will reach your intended destination, which is the fulfilment of your life assignment. I have faith in you!

The descriptive feedback from the Holy Spirit will align our thinking, speaking, and walking with God's ways. It enables us to adopt the mind of God, speak in alignment with His truth, and walk in His righteous paths. Through this guidance, the Holy Spirit will unveil hidden insights and revelations that propel us forward into the fulfilment of our purpose (John 16:13).

---

[70] Keith Butler-*Instagram post*

**"The greatest danger for most of us is not that our aim is too high
and we miss it, but that it is too low and we reach it."**

—*Michelangelo*

**"How do you know the difference between God's voice and your
feelings? The Word of God."**

— Natalie Masucci

Recap of all learning strategies used by God. (education model)

1. **Success Criteria** =found in the bible-rules to live by
2. **Learning Goals**: written is user friendly language in the Bible
3. **Annual Learning Plan**= vision
4. **Accommodations**-scaffolding
5. <u>**Purposeful practice-**</u>Select specific tasks to develop skills-prayer
6. **Explicit Instruction**; whole class (body) or small group (church) or individual
7. <u>**Think aloud**-model skills by verbalizing thought process</u>
8. <u>**Questioning strategy**</u>-Gather Evidence-<u>asking questions</u>
9. <u>**Safe learning environment** in which making mistakes are encouraged</u>
10. **Timely Descriptive Feedback**-2 stars & 1 wish
11. **Make changes**-Reflect and Re-evaluate success criteria & learning goals-re-adjust after a mistake or failure (introspection & prayer)
12. **Collaborative Learning Model**-I get by with a little help from my friends
13. **Demonstration of Learning**-successful completion of the task=victory or success /adopting God's kingdom mindset/obedience

What should I know or be able to do by the end of the period of learning?

- ❖ Be empowered to fulfil your God–given assignment.
- ❖ Making adjustments for further learning and growth.
- ❖ Work collaboratively.
- ❖ Successfully accomplish the task.
- ❖ Embody God's kingdom mindset.
- ❖ Staying positive and motivated.
- ❖ Asking questions.
- ❖ Focused on self- improvement.
- ❖ Accept constructive criticism/descriptive feedback
- ❖ Thinking outside of the box (MPA)

Encouragement (kingdom mindset) versus Condemnation (fixed mindset)

According to the Oxford Dictionary of English, encouragement is defined as the act of providing someone with support, confidence, or hope. It serves as a means of persuading others to persist in their endeavours. <u>Encouragement can manifest in various forms: a wink, a subtle nod, a warm smile, and words of affirmation, a pat on the back, a high five, a compliment, an approving glance, or even a thoughtful gift</u>.

Life can be challenging, which is why it is crucial for us to encourage one another. We all encounter moments of feeling stuck, getting hurt, experiencing failure, and carrying wounds. However, the individuals surrounding us during these times often play a significant role in helping us regain our strength and continue moving forward. When you find yourself paralyzed, who is there to lift you up? God intentionally places people in our lives for specific reasons and seasons. Take note of those who have supported you during your most difficult seasons, recognizing them as blessings from God and as divine assistance on your journey.[71] Knowing your people is crucial.

Barnabas, an apostle mentioned in the book of Acts, was a faithful companion of the apostle Paul during their travels. He earned the nickname "Son of Encouragement" because he consistently uplifted and motivated Paul to persevere (Acts 4:36). Barnabas played a significant role in supporting Paul. He believed in Paul's potential and saw the best in him. Barnabas served as both a supporter and encourager to Paul. As a result of this encouragement, Paul went on to become a prolific writer, contributing to the majority of the New Testament. This serves as a testament to the power of encouragement in our lives.

Likewise, God operates in a similar manner with us. He focuses on our strengths and potential (the "gold" within us) while gently and lovingly urging us to reach higher levels. Perhaps you, too, possess the gift of encouragement. It could be one of the purposes for which God created you. Who knows what things your encouragement may inspire others to do? Personally, God has called me to be an encourager to His people. My mission is to remind them of their true identity and their belonging to Him, so that they may continue to progress and move forward.

Sometimes, God needs to remove negative or toxic individuals from our lives to make space for new people to enter. It can be painful when people leave, and we may not always understand why it happens at the time. Who are the people in your life? You can ask God to bring the right

---

[71] John Gray. *who'sCarryingYou@myrelentlesschurch*

individuals into your life. Each person we encounter has a purpose in our journey. Some will test us, some will use us, some will love us, and some will teach us. People come into our lives for a reason, for a season, or for a lifetime. The ones who truly matter are those who bring out the best in us, encourage us to persevere, and help us fulfil our life's purpose, just as Barnabas did for the Apostle Paul. My desire is to be that kind of person for you. I am called to be an encourager, and through this book, I aim to uplift and empower you to pursue your God-given dreams and goals with a mindset aligned with God's kingdom, enabling you to fulfil your life's purpose.

"Life is lived forward, but only understood backward."
—Dharius Danials

Descriptive feedback serves as a powerful form of encouragement, enabling us to maintain a positive mindset, embrace growth, and fulfil our divine purpose, just as the Apostle Paul did. **Encouragement** instills in us a sense of optimism and confidence in our ability to succeed. In the context of the Bible, encouragement emphasizes the value of incremental progress and celebrating even the smallest victories. We build upon past triumphs and find joy in every step taken in the right direction. The Bible itself is a vast source of encouragement, with every book containing inspirational and uplifting verses through "I Am" and "In Him" statements. These profound insights provide us with strength and encouragement during our most challenging moments, when we may feel tempted to give up. They empower us to persevere and continue pressing forward towards the prize for which God has called us (Philippians 3:14). The Bible not only provides us with principles for successful living, but it also offers the encouragement we need to keep progressing. It is a comprehensive resource that equips us with both guidance and inspiration.

"It is unfortunate that some people cannot see Jesus functioning in the role of encourager; they can only envision Him as a critic."
—Tony Cooke[72]

Radiate such a positive energy that it repels negative individuals from wanting to be in your presence.

---

[72] Tonycooketcm. *Instagram post- what would Jesus say- Book.* Nov 17, 20

Happiness is a byproduct of encouragement and perspective. It is a choice that can be nurtured as a habit. While maintaining happiness or staying encouraged during challenging times may seem daunting, learning to manage your mindset and making it a consistent practice will strengthen your resilience and fortify your happiness. [73] The happiness of your life depends on the quality of your thoughts.

When your happiness is rooted in God's kingdom mindset, it becomes impervious to the enemy's tactics. Refrain from entertaining and believing statements such as, "I will be happy when I pay off my mortgage, get married, go on vacation," and so on. These are lies from the enemy that try to defer your happiness to a future time, rather than embracing happiness and contentment in the present. Happiness stems from appreciating what you currently have, rather than fixating on what you lack. It arises when you find contentment in your present position on the journey. Though you may not have reached your desired destination yet, remember that you have made progress and are no longer where you once were. Each day, you are moving forward, and this progress brings purpose, contentment, and happiness. You are a precious gift to the body of Christ, and your journey is a continual work in progress. Keep pressing on!

It is inconsequential who you once were; what holds significance is who you choose to be today. You are not defined by your mistakes, your past, your wounds, your job, or your possessions. Today, you have the power to adopt a different mindset. Each day presents a fresh opportunity to transform your thoughts and actions. Opt to focus on things that align with everything God declares about you.

> **"Optimism doesn't mean being happy all the time. Optimism means seeing roadblocks as temporary and something you have the power to overcome with time, patience, community support and self-compassion."**
>
> **—*Dr. Caroline Leaf***

Condemnation

According to the Oxford dictionary, condemnation is the act of expressing strong disapproval or censure. Condemnation originates from the enemy and is associated with a fixed mindset (Romans 8:1). It keeps us trapped in feelings of guilt, shame, and distance from God. At times, we judge and label ourselves with negative statements such as "I'm so stupid, clumsy, absent-minded, obsessive, ugly, fat, lazy, and

---

[73] https://bitr.ly/StayHappy2020

useless." <u>Embracing the lies of the enemy or maintaining a fixed mindset leads to self-deprecating thoughts and unhealthy work habits.</u>

An example of a negative outcome resulting from a fixed mindset is engaging in *self-destructive behaviours*. Some examples of self-destructive behaviours include alcoholism, drug addiction, promiscuity, overeating, gossiping, excessive work, overspending, obsessive-compulsive behaviours, and self-harm, among others. The more we hear something repeatedly, the more likely we are to believe it. When we internalize the lie that things will never change or that we will never meet others' expectations, we lose hope. As a result, we may stop making efforts and instead turn to self-destructive behaviours as a means to numb the pain of our seemingly hopeless situation.

<u>Excessive behaviour and a lack of self-restraint are indicators of a fixed mindset.</u> These behaviours stem from feelings of hopelessness and condemnation. However, God is a God of order and discipline (1 Corinthians 14:33). Our habits play a significant role in shaping who we are. When we lack self-control, we tend to develop harmful habits, while discipline helps us form healthy and positive habits. Impulsiveness is detrimental to our well-being, and addictions can be seen as amplified versions of these bad habits.

Moderation is essential, as both doctors and the Bible emphasize. Satan, on the other hand, wants us to go to extremes and indulge in things that harm us. He tempts us to fulfil our legitimate needs in inappropriate ways. His counterfeit means include gambling, alcohol and substance abuse, pornography, adultery, excessive shopping, and even resorting to plastic surgery. These actions represent misguided attempts to satisfy our legitimate needs.

In contrast, God is the only one who can truly fulfil our needs. He intentionally created a void within us that only He can fill (Psalm 139:14). God provides us with positive and uplifting ways to address this void. He fills us with purpose and guides us towards implementing positive habits that lead to victory in every aspect of our lives.

"Emotions are just information, guiding and directing us to do something. The goal isn't to get rid of your negative thoughts and feelings. The goal is to change your response to them."
—*Dr. Sasha Heinz*

<u>The most effective way to overcome condemnation is through encouragement.</u> Condemnation breeds negative habits, while encouragement fosters positive ones. However, change is not an easy process. It requires effort, motivation, and consistency. In my personal experience, I have attempted to rely on willpower and good intentions

to change my habits, but I achieved only limited results. The reason for this is that willpower can only take us so far. We cannot overcome temptations or break free from bad habits solely through our own strength. If it were possible, we would have accomplished it a long time ago.

This is why the Lord's Prayer includes the phrase *"lead us not into temptation but deliver us from evil."* I often find myself succumbing to temptation. For years, I've been struggling to lose the same ten pounds. The challenges of menopause have only made the struggle more difficult. Every New Year, I make resolutions to exercise more, eat healthier, and drink more water, but I never seem to stick to them. Why is that? It's because we need to seek God's help in changing our mindset to align with His, in order to successfully transform our habits. Relying solely on my own willpower is not enough; I need to incorporate His "why power" as well. <u>By shifting my mindset, I can tap into His stronger motivation.</u> Changing the narrative in my mind is the key to switching my mindset.

For example, to reshape my mindset regarding weight loss, I need to stop perceiving exercise as a form of punishment and instead embrace it as a valuable opportunity to enhance my well-being. By finding joy in physical activity, I will cultivate the lasting motivation needed to establish a new, healthy, and positive habit in my life. The "why power" is rooted in the understanding that God loves me and desires the best for me. His intention is for me to lead a happy, abundant life and fulfil my purpose, which includes maintaining good health (3 John 2). To regain control, I must consciously align my thoughts with the principles outlined in the word of God.

For instance, I can start intentionally thinking positive thoughts and saying motivating words such as, "Many individuals face health challenges that prevent them from exercising, but I am fortunate to be able to do so. I have the ability to make positive changes in my life. I can develop a healthy habit of regular exercise, leading to weight loss and reducing my risk factors for various diseases. I genuinely enjoy exercise, and I am grateful that I can engage in it. Each day, I am becoming healthier through my exercise and weight loss journey. I am becoming more toned and stronger. God desires my well-being, and taking care of myself is a way to honour Him. My body is a temple of God. Practicing self-love and self-care is an act of glorifying God."

<u>Holy Spirit's use of descriptive feedback can assist us in transforming the narrative within our minds.</u> As the One who knows our wants and needs, God is the source of their fulfilment. He encourages us to cultivate new, healthy habits aligned with His kingdom mindset, thereby replacing the old detrimental ones. <u>While good intentions are</u>

essential to begin the journey, they, along with mere willpower, have their limitations and tend to diminish over time. It is not our intention to overeat, yet it occurs because we have not changed our habits. Without altering our habits, we are destined to repeat them endlessly, as they have become ingrained in our brain's programming. How will I ever shed that weight if I fail to modify my habits? If I do not introduce positive changes, I will succumb to temptation as my willpower and intentions waver. Fortunately, I am not alone in this endeavour, and I am grateful for that. With God's grace we can form new healthy habits (1 Corinthians 10:13).

"Action always beats intention."
—*Terri Savelle Foy*

Learn to allow the Holy Spirit to provide you with ideas that can help you maintain control over your actions. Instead of indulging in binge-watching Netflix and mindlessly eating in front of the television, consider incorporating a workout session while enjoying an episode of your favourite series. You can also divert your attention by painting your nails or whitening your teeth, engaging in activities that are beneficial for you. Take advantage of your natural inclination for multitasking and use it to support your goals. These suggestions not only promote your well-being but also make it challenging to snack excessively or overeat. Remember that the Holy Spirit always has your best interests at heart, and His suggestions will consistently build you up and encourage positive changes. Try taking up a healthy hobby or a positive interest to counteract bad habits. Consider creative hobbies such as baking, jewelry-making, candle-making, and woodworking that allow you the benefits of a finished product. Intentionally carve out time by reserving 30 minutes to one hour a week and scheduling that time on your calendar. Hobbies can trigger happy and positive memories from our childhood allowing us to remember parts of ourselves that we have forgotten. Hobbies can empower you to overcome temptations by giving you something positive and healthy to do instead. I encourage you to give it a try. God wants you to break free from bad habits.

Positive habits will sustain you even when your willpower weakens. Willpower alone can only carry you so far. Having an accountability partner is also beneficial, and the **Holy Spirit can serve as your accountability partner.** He will regularly check in with you, help you shift your thinking, and empower you to overcome challenges. Positive habits keep you on the right path and enable you to prioritize important aspects such as pursuing your God-given goals and dreams. Remember, taking good care of yourself is essential so that you can run your race and emerge victorious. God is relying on you, and you will not disappoint Him.

"Day by day, what you do is who you become."
—Heraclitus

<u>Bad habits can originate from childhood,</u> as some of your current habits may have been ingrained in you since then, making them difficult to change. Perhaps you didn't receive sufficient encouragement and attention during your upbringing, which has impacted your self-confidence and self-worth. Maybe you felt unable to meet your parents' expectations and carry a sense of disappointment. As a result, you may feel unloved and unworthy, seeking affirmation through unhealthy relationships or numbing the pain through temporary highs. <u>Bad habits form when we attempt to fulfil legitimate needs in counterfeit ways. We've been looking for love and validation in all the wrong places. This can only come from God.</u>

Perhaps you have heard phrases like "Just wait until your Father gets home," which can instill a fear of the father figure in your life. This fear may also affect your relationship with your heavenly Father. You might become afraid of God and associate Him with punishment. However, this book aims to help you transform your relationship with your Heavenly Father. It emphasizes that you are completely accepted by your loving Papa God, who is your greatest supporter rather than your harshest critic. (1 John 4:9-10) You are precious to Him. Today, allow this message of encouragement to sweep away all condemning thoughts from your mind. Let God's acceptance and love empower you to cultivate new positive and healthy habits in your life.

Did you know that God has the ability to re-parent you if you open yourself to Him? He is not just any Father; He is the absolute best Father and the ultimate parent you could ever hope for. He is the Father you longed for but never had. He desires to fulfil every role you need in your life. **The Bible affirms that God is a Father to the fatherless (Psalm 68:5), a husband to the widow (Psalm 68:5), a friend who remains closer than a brother (Proverbs 18:24), and our soon-to-be bridegroom (Revelation 18:23).**

God's thoughts towards you are more numerous than the grains of sand (Psalm 139:17-18). Since grains of sand are innumerable, it means that God is constantly thinking about you. Isn't that amazing? God desires to fulfil all your needs (2 Chronicles 16:9). He serves as the parent you never had, the spouse you lost, and the best friend you always longed for. Through the Bible, God continuously speaks affirming words to us. His constant thoughts about us show that we always have His undivided attention. It's crucial for you to know that you are accepted, seen, and heard by God. He is ever-present for you (Psalm 46:1-3). Allow His affirming words to uplift and encourage you today. Your heavenly Father is your biggest cheerleader. While your earthly parents may not have provided adequate encouragement during your upbringing, your heavenly Father affirms you in the present moment. Let His affirmation and love replace any thoughts or feelings of unworthiness and low self-esteem. Your Father God sees you as incredibly remarkable; He dedicates all His thoughts to you. By embracing His kingdom mindset, allow Him to become the parent figure you never had.

Prolonged exposure to condemnation can lead to feelings of hopelessness, which can manifest as depression and mental illness. What we repeatedly hear eventually shapes our beliefs. It is my belief that the high prevalence of medication use in our society is a reflection of the lack of hope. There is currently a crisis of hope unfolding. Prozac is the most commonly prescribed antidepressant in North America, and even young people and school-aged children are being prescribed antidepressants. We are witnessing a rise in mental illnesses such as suicidal thoughts, opioid overdoses, depression, obsessive-compulsive disorders, anxiety, stress, and fear. The development of these conditions is influenced by various factors, including the food we consume, the level of exercise we engage in, the quality of our sleep, the thoughts we entertain, the toxins we are exposed to, the stress we experience, and the unresolved anger and unforgiveness we hold onto.

People in today's world often struggle to cope with the continuous barrage of negative messages from the news and social media. The recent pandemic has only exacerbated this issue. It's important to recognize that our bodies were not designed by God to handle excessive negativity, stress and anxiety. In His word, God encourages us to cast all our cares onto Him (1 Peter 5:7). He is the ultimate provider, just as He provided for Adam and Eve in the Garden of Eden. **Through His mindset, God is working to restore us to His original intention for us on Earth. Adam and Eve enjoyed authority and dominion, as well as a close relationship with God.** We were not created to have a fixed mindset or to dwell in negativity, fear, and hopelessness. By embracing God's mindset, we are brought back into alignment with Him. God instructed Adam and Eve to be fruitful, multiply, fill the earth, and subdue it (Genesis 1:28). They were given the role of ruling over all of God's creation—a position of royalty and power. With His kingdom mindset, God desires to restore us to our original position of power. The word "subdue" implies overcoming and gaining control. As God's children, we were created to rule and reign on this earth with His kingdom mindset, rather than succumbing to the enemy. Embracing God's kingdom mindset empowers us and enables us to exercise our authority, triumphing over the limiting thoughts and lies of the enemy (2 Corinthians 10:4-5). God expects us to reclaim our dominion and take control. We can stop allowing things to happen to us by resisting, praying, and speaking God's word over our lives. We can even challenge certain things in the courtroom of heaven. The enemy has been encroaching upon God's territory (which is you), and it is time for you to evict him. **Don't settle for a life below God's plans for you— remember, He has so much more in store.**

Constant exposure to negative messages takes a toll on our bodies, causing both mental (depression, fear, anxiety) and physical illness. Proverbs 17:22 A cheerful heart is good medicine, but a crushed spirit dries up the bones. Repeated negativity crushes our spirits. Negative thinking induces stress, which hinders our body's natural healing and coping abilities. "You cannot passively wait for happiness, health, and a positive thought life; you must actively choose to make it happen."[74]

The truth is, earthly experiences can never fully satisfy us because we were created for something greater (Ecclesiastes 3:9). While we may encounter moments of happiness in our lives, they pale in comparison to the magnificent plans God has in store for us in eternity.

<u>We can learn a lot about the kingdom mindset of God through the story of the Prodigal Son, found in the Gospel of Luke.</u> The story begins with the youngest son asking for his share of the inheritance, and the Father complies without any questions. After receiving his portion, the youngest son leaves home and squanders all his money on wild and reckless living. When his funds run out and he finds himself starving, he has a realization: "I will go back to my Father's house."

In the story, we see the Father looking out from His porch, indicating that He was eagerly anticipating his son's return. Likewise, God expects us to "come to our senses" and return home. What does this mean? It means we should stop trying to do things our own way, relying solely on our own strength. We need to abandon a fixed mindset and adopt His kingdom mindset. It's about letting go and letting God guide us and help us.

The Father in the story represents God, who is the King of Kings. Typically, kings do not run; they have servants to attend to their needs. Kings only need to give commands, and things are done. However, in this story, when the father sees his son returning from afar, he begins running towards him. <u>Reflect on this: God runs towards us when we choose to come back home.</u> This demonstrates tremendous love. The

---

Bible teaches that when we draw near to God, He moves towards us (James 4:8). The son was returning home, and the father ran towards him. Instead of walking, the father ran with reckless abandon. Although kings do not typically run, God the Father did in this parable, illustrating His immense joy at seeing His son return.

Today, we are faced with a choice. We can either choose to persist in doing things our own way, following the world's way and maintaining a fixed mindset, OR we can choose to do things in accordance with God's way. To embrace God's way, we need to adopt His kingdom mindset. It is essential to understand that only God's way is truly effective. All other paths will ultimately lead to failure. While they may seem to work temporarily, they are bound to falter in the long run.

We all make foolish mistakes, poor decisions, and sometimes follow misguided advice. We are all prone to making errors. The encouraging news is that we have the capacity to change and learn from our mistakes. Similar to the prodigal son, who had a moment of clarity while in the pigpen, we can turn towards God and adopt His mindset— the way He perceives and approaches things. You are not bound to remain trapped by foolish choices, selfishness, addictions, jealousy, offence, convenience, comfort, or complacency. God grants you the freedom to choose. Regardless of your current circumstances, the wise decision is to align your heart with a mindset that extends beyond yourself. It's about embracing Jesus, His love, and His kingdom mindset, as well as fulfilling the assignment He has for your life.[75] <u>The power of the pigpen is it can change our perspective.</u>

With God's assistance, we can exercise control over our thoughts and, as a result, our reactions and responses to life's events. The composition of our lives is predominantly shaped by what we think about. What we consistently see and hear eventually becomes ingrained in our minds and beliefs. Hence, our thoughts possess the power to transform our brains and even impact our genetics. Whatever occupies our thoughts the most will grow within our minds and manifest in our lives. Let us redirect our thinking towards what we desire instead of dwelling on our current circumstances. Shift your focus to envisioning your future and release the hold of the past. Rediscover the ability to dream once again. Cease dwelling on what has been lost and instead remember what you still possess. Begin visualizing how you desire your life to unfold. Rekindle your vision and restore your hope.

***

---

[75] Craig Hagin. *Don't Be Stupid-book.*

<u>The story of the Prodigal Son raises important aspects of a kingdom mindset that require attention, such as</u> **free will** <u>and</u> **failure.**

As leaders, educators, coaches, therapists, employers, friends, parents, guardians, and grandparents, we often struggle with allowing individuals to exercise their free will and make their own choices. Our overwhelming desire to assist them sometimes makes it difficult for us to witness their mistakes. However, let us observe the Father in the story who permitted his son to make his own decisions without trying to convince or stop him. They didn't seek family therapy or organize prayer meetings. Just as God has granted us free will, we should extend that same freedom to others. Surely, the father wasn't pleased when his son demanded his share of the inheritance and then departed. The son deviated from the path his father had envisioned for him. Undoubtedly, the father experienced grief over the loss of the life he had hoped to share with his son. Perhaps you, too, find yourself grieving at present? Your life hasn't unfolded as you envisioned, and you believed you would be further along by now. Does this resonate with you?

We all have diverse learning styles. Some individuals must learn the hard way and hit rock bottom before they are willing to change. However, in the end, the son in the story reached his destination by returning home. It's natural to feel discontented with the choices made by our loved ones. <u>It's crucial to avoid taking their decisions personally and internalizing them as our own failures.</u> Do not allow guilt to consume you, as failure is merely an event, not an inherent characteristic of who you are (as Zig Ziglar reminds us). Failure is something that happens to you, but it does not define your identity. Even if you have done everything right as a parent, your child may still go astray. Why? Because they possess free will. It is their life, and they ultimately make their own choices. **God is the perfect parent, yet He doesn't have a single child who wasn't a prodigal.** So, He knows better than anyone what you're going through.

Parents/Guardians with rebellious, wayward or even special needs children often carry a heavy burden of self-blame, feeling like failures in their role as parents. They blame themselves for the choices their children make, leading to overwhelming guilt and shame. However, it is crucial to remember that our children possess their own free will to make decisions about their lives. We will not understand all things on this side of eternity. We must resist succumbing to guilt, as it is a negative and unproductive emotion. <u>Guilt keeps us focused on the past, without offering any solution or remedy.</u>

Instead of spiralling into a negative guilt cycle, let us entrust our children to God through prayer. Prayer is an act of faith that propels us forward. It is an activating force. In the story of the Prodigal Son, I believe the father found peace because he surrendered his son to God in prayer (Philippians 4:7). He relied on God's promises and patiently waited for the fulfilment of his requests. He could wait without fretting and driving himself crazy because he reminded himself of *Isaiah 54:13 that says "all your sons will be taught by the Lord, and great will be their peace.* I am sure he quoted *Proverbs 22:6 too "Train up a child in the way he should go, and when he is old he will not depart from it".* I firmly believe that the father in the story had unwavering confidence in his son's eventual return. This is evident from his patient waiting and watchful stance on the porch. He had a steadfast expectation in God's faithfulness and His ability to fulfil His promises. *1 Peter 5:7, "Cast your cares on Him because He care for you."* What are your own expectations?

When we stand on the promises of God, we can experience peace even in the midst of challenging relationships with a wayward child, estranged spouse, family member, business associate, or friend. By surrendering control and entrusting them to God, we place our trust in His power to bring about positive change for their well-being and His glory. Letting go can be difficult, but it is indeed possible. As long as we insist on trying to manipulate the situation and change their minds, God's work is hindered. It's time to let go of the need to control everything! When we rest in faith and trust that is when God begins to actively work in the situation.

<u>God will never cease pursuing your prodigal.</u> He is willing to leave behind the many to seek after the one (Luke 15:3-7 & Matthew 18:12-14). Unlike us, God never gives up on a person. Never. Long after we have moved on, God remains present, stirring their conscience, kindling conviction, and orchestrating redemption. God is unwavering in His faithfulness. However, it is crucial for you to be completely convinced of God's goodness and faithfulness in order to trust Him fully with your beloved family members.

I have personally wrestled with accepting this truth as a mother, educator, Bible teacher, coach, and mentor. There have been numerous instances where I have felt responsible for someone else's thoughts or actions, and as a result, I have felt like a failure. I began questioning every word I spoke and every action I took, placing the blame on myself. This self-doubt even extended to questioning God. These incessant questions only fuelled my tendency to overthink and engage in toxic rumination. It's essential to recognize that toxic rumination is a tactic employed by the enemy, aiming to trap us in repetitive negative thoughts.

<u>Do not permit the shame of having a wayward child to undermine the calling that God has bestowed upon your life.</u> It is vital to liberate yourself from the clutches of guilt and shame, and instead,

151

wholeheartedly embrace the purpose and mission that God has entrusted to you.

"Make sure your worst enemy is not living between your own two ears."

—*Toby Mac*

I realized that I was expending more time and energy on grappling with these thoughts rather than actively seeking to assist the other person in a more fruitful manner. Instead of spending time beating myself up and feeling sorry for myself, I should have directed my focus towards prayer. Allowing such thinking patterns only intensified my self-centredness, leading to increased feelings of guilt, resentment, and frustration, thereby exacerbating the toxic spiral of negative thoughts. Guilt is a poisonous notion implanted by the enemy. If left unaddressed, it can profoundly impact our mood and interactions with others, particularly our family or those closest to us. Satan consistently endeavours to divert our attention away from others and onto ourselves. By distracting us with guilt, regret, shame, or toxic rumination, he seeks to diminish our effectiveness in any given situation.

Prayer, on the other hand, redirects our focus onto others and God. It enhances our effectiveness by enlisting supernatural assistance. Guilt, shame, and regret are the toxic triplets orchestrated by the enemy to keep us ensnared in the mistakes of our past. God does not desire for us to live tormented by the lies propagated by the enemy. Use the truth found in *Romans 10:11 "Anyone who believes upon Him will not be put to shame"* to resist and replace those toxic thoughts.

If you resonate with any of the above feelings, here are some things that can help.
1. Remember, you cannot control others. You can only control your own emotions, thoughts, actions, and reactions. Stop attempting to control others, especially your spouse and children. (James 1:14)
2. Approach everything with love. Ensure that all your actions, opinions, and advice stem from a place of love. Seek guidance from the Holy Spirit, asking for the right words to say. When you pray and ask the Holy Spirit to provide you with words and wisdom for a situation, you are doing the very best you can (Mark 13:11). The outcome lies in the hands of the Holy Spirit, not in your own. Release yourself from the burden of achieving specific results. Our role is to walk in love and pray, while the responsibility for producing results rests with the Holy Spirit (John 16:8).

3. <u>Recognize that you cannot be someone's Savior</u>; you can only be a supporter and encourager. Jesus alone is the Savior. Entrust them to God through prayer. Pray for God's will to be done in their lives. You cannot fix anyone, but through your prayers, God can and will bring about transformation.

4. <u>Acknowledge that making mistakes in your interactions and communications with others is inevitable</u>. It's a natural part of being human and cannot be completely avoided. Even if your intentions were good, they may unintentionally cause hurt. We all make errors. The key is to apologize and be open to learning from those mistakes. As parents, we don't have to strive for perfection at all times. As educators, it can be beneficial for our students to witness us making mistakes. By exemplifying the process of making mistakes, learning from them, and moving forward, we provide a valuable model for growth. It's crucial to consider the bigger picture and view things through the lens of God's eternal perspective. What are the primary lessons our children are learning from their experiences? In fact, when we make mistakes and apologize, it can be beneficial, as it demonstrates the reality of life, which is often messy.[76] God can even turn your mistakes into a golden ticket. He works all things out for out good when we adopt His kingdom mindset (Romans 8:28).

"Life is messy, it's full of sticky situations but God is able to clean them all up if we let Him. Something that seems like a gigantic mistake can become a golden ticket in the Master's hands."
—*Natalie Masucci*

A golden ticket is akin to a "pass-go" card in Monopoly, granting you passage without having to pay the price. On America's Got Talent, when a judge presses their golden buzzer, the contestant is propelled into the final round. God's forgiveness and mercy are our golden tickets. Receive God's mercy today (Psalm 23:6).

5. <u>Examine your identity.</u> If you feel like a failure, ask yourself what you are basing your identity and worth on. Do you only perceive yourself as valuable when you can "help" or "save" someone? Are you overly focused on solving other people's problems as a means of avoiding your own? We should derive our identity from God, not solely from our actions. If we base our identity and worth solely on our actions, we fall into the trap of a "works" mentality. **Our value**

---

[76] Dr. Tina Payne Bryson-*Cleaning up the mental mess with Dr. Caroline Leaf-Instagram*

does not come from what we do, but from whose we are (Ephesians 2:9). Feeling like a failure arises when we attempt to rely on our own strength. Never define yourself by failure or make it a part of your identity. Instead, view failure as valuable information and begin to question it. It didn't unfold as I had planned. What could I have done differently? Next time, I will... By questioning your thoughts and actions, you can avoid repeating harmful patterns.

6. <u>Seek support from others,</u> such as God, a trusted friend, mentor, pastor, priest, therapist, or coach, to gain perspective and clarity. Avoid suppressing your emotions. Allow yourself to feel uncomfortable and express these emotions so that you can address and resolve them, preventing the formation of toxic patterns in your mind.[77] You cannot suppress emotions indefinitely—I learned this the hard way. They will resurface at the most inconvenient times. I encourage you to sit with your emotions, experience them, and process them until their intensity subsides. <u>Remember, feelings are not facts; they are only your response to your perception of the situation.</u>

7. <u>It is possible to love your life and your child while also grieving the life that could have been.</u> These two things can coexist. The healing process is not always straightforward and linear.

Feelings of guilt, shame and regret are negative feelings that are not from God.

You are not a failure. People have the freedom to make choices, and unfortunately, they may make wrong or unfortunate decisions. Your worth and success are not determined by these choices because God never fails (Luke 1:37). When you rely on God and have faith in Him, you cannot be considered a failure. Remember that God resides within you, and by keeping His Word in your mouth and His thoughts in your mind, you will realize that God has the final say in every situation. He is the God of the impossible. While you may have experienced failure, God never will. Entrust the person or the problem to God and allow Him to work it out. He desires their salvation, healing, deliverance, and restoration even more than you do. Let go and let God take control. Trust in Him. Your identity is defined by the Word of God. You are not a failure. You are a blessing to your family, workplace, and community. You are the answer to someone's prayer. Don't let the shame and guilt associated with a wayward child hinder God's plan for your life.

---

[77] Dr. Caroline Leaf. *Instagram post*- Sept 26, 20

Having God's mindset means trusting Him and relying on His Word, standing firmly on His promises. Those who possess God's mindset never lose hope, even in the face of mistakes or challenges. Failure is not an option because their hope is deeply rooted in God. <u>Hope is a powerful aspect of God's mindset.</u> When we have His mindset, we can trust the next chapter of our lives because we know that the Author is in control. We hold onto hope, believing that things will improve, circumstances will change, and our prodigal will return home because God is actively working in the situation.

Perhaps you are the prodigal son? Your life has gone astray. God is not disappointed in you, and He's not mad at you. It's time to come home.

<u>Action Step:</u> On a separate page, write down any ways you feel that you let God down OR you were let down by God. Then bring them to God in prayer. It is important to resolve these feelings. Feelings are not truth.

Jesus told the story of the Prodigal Son to make a simple point: never mind what you've done; just come home. Luke 15:11-32

"It's better to explore life and make mistakes than to play it safe. Mistakes are part of the dues one pays for a full life."
—*Sophia Loren*

Positive Self Talk (Kingdom mindset) versus Criticism/Negative Self Talk (Fixed mindset)

How we speak to ourselves and about ourselves holds significant importance. It shapes our self-talk and mindset. God desires for us to transform our thoughts and the way we speak to ourselves. He wants us to reprogram our minds. To embrace God's kingdom mindset, it requires a shift in our vocabulary. Our self-talk reflects our mindset.

"Unfortunately, we have been programmed by the world to accept and feel insults and criticism more deeply than compliments; therefore, we have to rewire our minds to respond and embrace encouragement from God's word more." [78]

---

[78] Dr. Caroline Leaf. *Instagram post-* Sept 26, 20

Positive self-talk is characterized by kindness, support, and affirmation (in the form of compliments and praise). It sounds like statements such as "I'm making progress", or "I will keep trying." or "Today will be a great day!" or "It shall be as God has said," or "This is the day that the Lord has made, I will rejoice and be glad in it". It acknowledges that though you may not have reached your desired destination yet, you are not where you used to be. It recognizes that you are a work in progress. Engaging in positive self-talk enhances confidence and resilience, empowering you to achieve goals and navigate difficult circumstances.

<u>Positive self-talk goes beyond merely speaking positive words.</u> It involves viewing yourself through God's eyes and embracing His love for you. It encompasses maintaining an optimistic mindset that consistently focuses on the bright side. <u>It's like having an inner cheerleader who uplifts and encourages you.</u> Positive self-talk involves blessing your life by speaking God's Word over yourself. It includes expressing positive affirmations and declaring faith-filled statements concerning your life and circumstances. By aligning yourself with the truth found in God's Word, positive self-talk becomes your voice of faith.

Positive self-talk is one of the things that people with a growth mindset **do regularly.** It is a habit of the most successful people.

Everyday when you wake up, say to yourself "Today is going to be a great day!" You have to nudge your brain. You have a conscious mind and an unconscious mind and a self-image. Your subconscious mind is listening to the words that your conscious mind is saying. If you wake up and say "I don't want to get out of bed. Today is going to be a bad day" you are going to have a bad day because you just programmed your subconscious mind to do that. Every day when your feet hit the floor say to yourself "Today is going to be a great day!" I have been doing this for years and it's so helpful.

Positive self-talk is what God does all the time. An example is found in *Isaiah 45:21, in which God states, "There is none besides me."* God boldly declares who He is. He is not being prideful; this is just a statement of the facts. OR *Exodus 3:14 "I am who I am."* Or *Revelation 22:13 "I am the Alpha and the Omega, the First and the Last"*

We have the greatest influence over ourselves. We are the ultimate authority in our own lives. Our body and spirit respond primarily to our own voice amidst the multitude of voices we hear. What we repeatedly speak, we eventually internalize and believe. Therefore, it is crucial to be mindful of how we speak to and about ourselves. In Proverbs 13:3, it is emphasized that our words have the ability to bless or curse our lives. We should exercise wisdom and choose our words carefully. Just as God never utters a word in vain, we should follow His example and be intentional with our speech. God understands the power that lies within words. When we speak the Word of God, those words have the potential to bring life and build others up (Proverbs 18:21).

"What have you been saying about yourself lately? What you have been saying has gotten you what you presently have. If you don't like your present life and circumstances, then change what you say!"
—*Terri Savelle Foy*

Start saying what you want rather than what is.
Learn to align yourself with God by adopting His mindset and embracing His strategy of positive self-talk. This transformative approach will revolutionize your life. Satan seeks to attack your mind, and his arsenal consists of lies. Therefore, intentionally fill your mind with the Word of God, leaving no space for his deceitful narratives. If what you are saying doesn't line up with your dreams and goals then don't say it. Positive self-talk is saying what you want and what you are believing for rather than what is. It is like prophesying over your life. Positive self-talk speaks to the end result emulating what God does. Example: I am healed, I am rich. I have more than enough for every good work. I am a new homeowner. I am a New York Times best-selling author.

"You can't control other people's opinions of you, but you can control your opinion of you. Don't let others' opinions of you change your opinion of you."
—*Dr. Caroline Leaf*

The Power of YET (positive self-talk)

There is tremendous power in the word "yet." The way we speak about ourselves and to ourselves has a significant impact on our future. Our words shape our outcomes. Instead of using definitive statements like "I'm not good at controlling my reactions," incorporate "yet" into your self-talk: "I'm not good at controlling my reactions yet..." <u>This simple addition signals to your mind and brain that there is room for growth, learning, and transformation.</u>

"By reframing how you state your feelings, emotions, and mood, you can either create space for growth and exploration or close yourself off to healing and hope."[79]

God understands the importance of our self-talk and encourages us to foster a growth-oriented mindset. By incorporating words like **"yet"**

---

[79] Dr. C. Leaf. *Instagram post*

and **"next"** into our thoughts, we create space for personal growth and transformation. This shift in perception helps us break free from toxic thought patterns and negative self-talk, allowing for the development of new, healthy neural connections in our brains. Embracing God's Word through positive self-talk and declarations of faith contributes to the formation of healthy neural networks, promoting a healthy and constructive mindset.

God understands that our journey towards fulfilling our purpose is filled with ups and downs. We may make mistakes, face obstacles, and experience setbacks. However, God wants us to adopt His kingdom mindset and allow Him to guide us. He uses detours and challenges as opportunities for growth and protection. Through the Holy Spirit's guidance, God provides feedback to keep us focused and shield us from distractions. It's important to trust in His leading and believe in the best outcome as we pursue our purpose.

Incorporating words like **"Yet"** and **"Next"** in our self-talk allows room for growth and transformation in our thought processes. It's important to be compassionate towards yourself. Instead of being hard on yourself and saying things like "I'm so behind," shift your perspective and ask, "What progress have I made?" Rather than getting frustrated and saying, "Why can't I figure this out?" ask yourself, "What can I learn from this situation? What is it here to teach me?" and "What can I do differently next time?" Remember that you haven't cracked the code yet, but you're on the right track to do so soon. People often say things like

"I take one step forward then two steps back", which suggests that progress is often illusive. Try changing it to "Two steps forward, one step back" and celebrate every step in the right direction. Slow progress is better than no progress. Slow and steady wins the race.

Instead of declaring, "Life is such a battle," consider reframing it as, "How can I approach life as an adventure?" "How can I enjoy the journey?" Start viewing challenges as new opportunities for exploration. Embrace the adventure of adopting God's mindset and declare, "This battle is gaining new ground" and "I will reclaim what the devil has stolen from my life."

God invites us to allow the Holy Spirit to transform us from the inside out by taking control of our own words. <u>Transformation begins with our words.</u> It may sound simple, but it holds true. By changing our words, we can change our lives. Create space in your mind for growth, exploration, healing, and hope. When you do so, the possibilities become limitless!

"Are you taking matters into your own mouth?"
—*Jesse Duplantis*

Negative self-talk is unkind, critical, and distressing. It can manifest as thoughts such as "I am not worthy," "My opinion doesn't matter," or "No one will take me seriously." Negative self-talk has detrimental effects, including lowering self-esteem, damaging true friendships, impeding goal achievement, and increasing stress levels.[80]

Negative self-talk can take on the form of **regret.** Who told you that you were supposed to be in a certain place by now? You should have graduated? You should be married? You should have a family? Own your own place? Where did that thought originate? How does it make you feel? This is an example of negative self-talk. The enemy wants to fill us with regret. He wants us to believe "I should be married, my house should be paid off, I should have children by now etc.

"Just a reminder: You are not a failure for not being where you think or were told; you should be by now."
— Dr. Sasha Heinz

Sometimes the life we envision for ourselves may not align with God's plan. Examples like Moses, Joseph, David and Paul show us that unexpected circumstances can be part of God's greater purpose for us. Even though their paths were filled with challenges, God was shaping their character and preparing them for their future roles. Similarly, we may find ourselves in situations we didn't anticipate, but it could be part of God's plan to prepare us for something greater. It's important to change our perspective and make room for God to work in our lives. We should trust that we are where we are meant to be and remain open to His leading and promotion (Isaiah 49:46).

What will you do about your negative self-talk? Will you simply allow it to continue? Recognizing and challenging our negative self-talk and toxic or limiting thoughts are essential aspects of adopting God's mindset.

Don't allow that inner voice to hinder your progress. Are you sabotaging yourself? Do you constantly doubt your capabilities and fear a lifetime of struggle? Are you afraid of falling behind and never being able to catch up? Do you believe you'll always be comparing yourself to others?

We must recognize our worth and value as children of God in order to overcome the negative voices and thrive. We are far more valuable than we realize. If we truly understood our worth, our self-talk would be transformed. I am here to assist you in embracing this truth and to

---

80 *Biglifejournal*

encourage positive self-talk. When you are having a bad dad, say to yourself "You've got this!" and see how that works for you. This technique is a valuable tool to sustain your motivation and determination.

"If we realized that God was listening, I believe our self-talk would be very different."
—Natalie Masucci

"Outside of praying, your most important words are the words that you say to yourself."
—Dr. David Jeremiah

Life can be an adventure, a journey of learning and growth. When we make ourselves available to God, life becomes an exciting and fulfilling experience. The way we speak to ourselves and about ourselves is crucial. It shapes our self-talk and mindset. Speak kindly to yourself.

God desires for you to transform your self-perception and the way you communicate with yourself. He wants you to reprogram your thought patterns and adopt His kingdom mindset. To do this, you'll need to make changes to your vocabulary. <u>Replace the word "never" with "**yet**" or "**next.**" Instead of using "later" or "someday," embrace "now because faith is now (Hebrews 11:1)." Additionally, introduce the power of "**but**" into your thought processes.</u> Say, "But God". Your self-talk reflects your mindset, so it's essential to be intentional with your words.

"How you see yourself will determine how you see God."
—Pastor Lynette Farrier

God uses self-talk all the time. God is the author of positive self-talk.
Positive self-talk is a powerful strategy within God's kingdom mindset. It refers to the internal dialogue we have with ourselves, influenced by our thoughts, beliefs, questions, personality, and ideas. Self-talk can be either negative or positive. However, <u>God exclusively uses positive self-talk. He is eternally positive and committed to good news and prohibits any bad news in heaven. He promises to wipe away every tear and eliminate mourning, crying, and pain (Revelation 21:4).</u> His self-talk is uplifting and optimistic. Embracing God's positive and powerful word is a part of our self-talk as well.

Positive self-talk involves cultivating a more optimistic perspective on life. Numerous studies have demonstrated its health benefits, including stress reduction, improved performance, and a higher quality of life. God's instructions are always intended for our well-being. Engaging in positive self-talk helps develop mental skills that enable us to problem-solve, think differently, cope more effectively with challenges, and mitigate the negative impacts of stress and anxiety.

<u>Here are some examples of God's self-talk:</u>

In <u>Malachi 1:11,</u> *God gave us an example when He says, "From the rising of the Sun even unto the going down of the same my name shall be Great saith the Lord of hosts."* He is saying and declaring that His name will always be great.

In *Philippians 2:10-11 we see another example. "At the name of Jesus, every knee should bow in heaven and on earth and under the earth, and every tongue acknowledges that Jesus Christ is Lord."* God proclaims a positive truth even before it manifests. When God utters His words through Scripture, they often precede the actual events. By speaking these potent and positive words in advance, God shapes the atmosphere and prepares the stage for His desired outcomes. From the outset, God declares victory. As our ultimate role model, we should follow His example and speak words of triumph and positivity.

<u>Isaiah 46:8-10</u> *is a good example of God himself using positive self-talk. "I am God, and there is no other; I am God, and there is none like me."* God exudes unwavering confidence in the fulfilment of His words. His spoken command brings forth the creation of galaxies and planets while stars emerge from the very breath He exhales. When God speaks, countless molecules, particles, neurons, and living beings spring into existence, aligning with His divine purpose. <u>Similarly, as we utter our words, the molecules and neurons within our brains respond, forging new neural pathways and shaping our thoughts and actions.</u>

Another example of God's positive self-talk is found in *Isaiah 55:11 "So shall My word be that goes forth from My mouth; It shall not return to Me void, but it shall accomplish what I please, and it shall prosper in the thing for which I sent it."* <u>We are to be confident, too,</u> not just in our own abilities and resources but in God's. We are instructed to imitate our Father God and use positive self-talk.

We need to cultivate the confidence that speaking God's word over our lives and situations will bring about change. God's word carries an anointing of creative power. Hebrews 4:12 assures us that it has the ability to transform our circumstances. When we declare God's Word over our lives, it has a profound effect. It causes negative emotions such as offence, pride, shame, guilt, trauma, regret, unforgiveness, negative self-talk, and condemnation to diminish. Through God's positive self-talk, even the neurons in our brain are impacted, leading to the development of mental skills necessary for victory in every area of our lives.

"As we speak God's Word to ourselves, billions of neurons in our brain respond to what we say by increasing or decreasing, building pathways or tearing them down."

—*Natalie Masucci*

In the Bible, we see that God consistently uses positive self-talk. If God Himself employs positive self-talk, then it is essential for us to do the same. It is a powerful strategy that helps us stay on the right track as we speak God's Word and adopt His kingdom mindset. To improve your self-talk try reframing "I'm Bad at_____" to "I struggle with____" instead. This leaves room for improvement. Even better would be to say to yourself "I struggle with__but I am doing ____to improve. Be specific, give your brain the pathway you want it to take. Talk to yourself the way you would speak to someone you love (Proverbs 16:24). This is how Holy Spirit speaks to us through His descriptive feedback.

"Every time you rehearse the truth, you negate a little more of the lie."

—*Jesse DuPlantis*

God's positive self-talk is a means through which He releases blessings into our lives. It's remarkable to realize that when Father God blesses us, He does so by employing positive self-talk. He uses positive affirmations not only for Himself but also for us. For instance, in Romans 8:37, God declares us as more than conquerors through Jesus Christ even before we have won any battles. He proclaims our triumph even before we engage in the fight.

Another remarkable example can be found in Ephesians 1:4, where God refers to us as holy and blameless in Him before the foundation of the world. Even before we were born, God chose us and declared our righteousness.

We are commanded to follow God's example and use positive self-talk over our own lives and over those of our family members. **Positive self-talk is like a spoken blessing. It is prophesying over your life.** The Word of God is positive, edifying and restorative; therefore,_the Bible is the source of positive self-talk found in God's kingdom mindset. A spoken blessing is a positive, biblical statement that invokes the blessing of God in your life or the life of another. The power of spoken blessings comes from God who Himself *"hath blessed us with all spiritual blessings in heavenly places in Christ." (Ephesians 1:3)*

In Numbers 6:24-26 provides us with an excellent example of a Godly blessing.

Pray this blessing over yourself and your family.

May the Lord bless you and keep you. May the Lord shower you with His kindness and abundant mercy. May the Lord faithfully guard over you and grant you a deep sense of peace.

"Your brain is a supercomputer, and your self-talk is the program it will run."

—Jim Kwik

What program have you been running? Your brain is literally a super computer. It will follow the directions that you program it with. Your brain simply believes whatever you tell it most. What you repeatedly say to yourself matters. Whatever you repeatedly say you will eventually believe. This isn't science fiction this is science fact. Neuroplasticity. More specifically, Hebb's Law, neurons that fire together wire together. Your self -talk shapes your brain. Which shapes your beliefs, which drives your behaviour and creates your thoughts, feelings, experiences, which creates the totality of your reality. Your self-talk shapes your brain. The brain believes whatever you tell it the most. Whatever you tell it the most about yourself and your experience of time it will create, it has no choice. Whatever you repeatedly say to yourself matters. Your brain simply believes whatever you tell it the most. So remember, the brain believes whatever you tell it the most. It has no choice but guess who does? You do!

Your positive self-talk plays the role of an inner cheerleader, uplifting and encouraging you. On the other hand, <u>your negative self-talk takes the form of an inner critic,</u> undermining your confidence and self-worth. Ecclesiastes 5:2 God will hold us accountable for the words we say. Therefore, let's be intentional and use only positive self-talk.

"Your inner critic is your prophet of doom and gloom."
—Natalie Masucci

Which Self-Talk Are You Using? INNER CRITIC or INNER CHEERLEADER?

Your brain, body, and mindset are profoundly influenced by the quality of your self-talk. The words you speak about yourself and the beliefs you hold about your worth have a tremendous impact and possess immense power.

"God has hard-wired and soft-wired our brains exactly the way they are on purpose. He has made our brains unique for His cause."

—*Natalie Masucci*

Negative self-talk, or the inner critic, can serve as motivation to improve, but it should be silenced when it becomes overly harsh. Redirecting our focus to our accomplishments and practicing gratitude can help silence the inner critic and activate our inner cheerleader. This strategy aligns with adopting God's mindset and breaking free from toxic thoughts. Engaging in negative self-talk contradicts having God's spirit and mindset, as it aligns with the enemy's language. Overcoming this pattern is essential to avoid getting trapped in unproductive cycles.

"Your voice is your address in the realm of the Spirit." Acts 16; 25-26 Mark Hankins

Negative self-talk refers to the internal dialogue that undermines your belief in yourself and your capabilities, hindering your potential for growth. It encompasses thoughts that diminish your ability to bring about positive changes in your life and erode your confidence in your own capacity to do so.

Researchers estimate that we have approximately 50,000 to 70,000 thoughts per day, and a staggering 80% of those thoughts tend to be negative. This abundance of negative self-talk is truly concerning. We subject ourselves to significant pain and suffering by allowing these thoughts to freely roam within our minds. Examples of negative self-talk include statements such as "I'm not worthy," "It's pointless," "I can't do it," "I'll never follow through," "People won't like me," "Others are superior to me," "I am inadequate," "I must be perfect," "My opinion doesn't matter," and "I'll never change." [81] Never speak negative about yourself. Change "I'm bad at__" to "I struggle with__" instead leaving room for growth and improvement. Your self-talk reflects your mindset, so it's essential to be intentional with your words.

These negative thoughts stem from the enemy who seeks to undermine our confidence and faith, hindering our progress towards the goals that God has given us. <u>It's important to recognize that our minds tend to believe whatever we tell them.</u> Therefore, it is crucial to nourish our minds with positive self-talk.

---

[81] https://psychcentral.com/blog/nlp/2013/04/negative-self-talk Feb 21/21.

Inner Critic vs. Inner Cheerleader:
- ❖ I can't do this. I'm not able vs. It's ok if I don't get it right. I will try again. God says I am able (2 Corinthians 9:8)
- ❖ I always do the wrong thing. I don't know how vs. My mistakes help me learn and grow. I'll try my best.
- ❖ I'm falling behind everyone else. I'm not qualified vs. I don't compare myself to others. My journey is unique. I'm going to learn how.
- ❖ This is impossible vs. With God, all things are possible. (Matthew 19:26)
- ❖ We can't let any voice speak louder than God's voice in our lives (John 10:27).

Self-Talk Scriptures:
- ❖ The mouth of the righteous is a well of life. Proverbs 10:11
- ❖ The words of a man's mouth are deep waters. Proverbs 18:4
- ❖ A man has joy by the answer of his mouth. Proverbs 15:23
- ❖ Anxiety weighs down the heart, but a kind word cheers it up. Proverbs 12:25
- ❖ Pleasant words are as a honeycomb. Proverbs 16:24
- ❖ Life and death are in the power of the tongue, and those who love it will eat its fruit. Proverbs 18:21
- ❖ A word fitly spoken is like apples of gold in settings of silver. Proverbs 25:11

Our self-talk plays a significant role in shaping our self-image, which in turn influences our destiny. Our self-image is closely intertwined with our mindset and is formed through our self-talk. The way we perceive ourselves and the words we speak to ourselves greatly impact our behaviour. If we believe we are unintelligent, we may refrain from pursuing educational opportunities. Similarly, if we perceive ourselves as unattractive, we may neglect our appearance and grooming.

Satan seeks to steal our identity, acting as an identity thief. However, <u>Satan's power over our lives only emerges when we speak words of negativity (fixed mindset-gossip & excuses and complaints) and engage in negative self-talk, inadvertently granting him access.</u> It is crucial to cease opening doors for the enemy through our thoughts and self-perception. Our identity remains secure unless we unknowingly provide an entry point. If we fail to love, value, and respect ourselves, it becomes challenging for others to do so as well.

When we reach heaven, I firmly believe that we will perceive ourselves as God sees us (1 Corinthians 13:11-12). However, until that time comes, cultivating a kingdom mindset is the closest we can get. It entails perceiving ourselves as God sees us, whole and complete, lacking nothing (James 1:4). Embracing a kingdom mindset enables us to have unwavering faith in our abilities and gifts, knowing that we possess everything necessary for success and that with dedication and perseverance, we can develop them further. God's kingdom mindset involves consistently engaging in positive self-talk derived from His Word.

God's positive self-talk differs from the self-talk commonly discussed in mental health circles. It goes beyond simply speaking positive words about ourselves and focuses on affirming and uplifting ourselves with God's Word. God's Word carries supernatural creative power. Positive self-talk not only boosts confidence but also strengthens faith, resilience, gratitude, and perseverance. It helps create new neural pathways in our brains and releases chemicals that promote good health. Positive self-talk is beneficial and plays a crucial role in embracing God's kingdom mindset.

In the story of David and Goliath, found in the Book of Samuel, is an example of using **God's positive self-talk to erode the enemy's lies in our minds** and erode the enemy's confidence at the same time. David unnerved Goliath with his words. David said to the Philistine, *"You come against me with sword and spear and javelin, but I come against you in the name of the Lord Almighty, the God of the armies of Israel, whom you have defied. This day the Lord will hand you over to me, and I'll strike you down and cut off your head."(1 Samuel 17:45-46)* I believe that David demonstrated **kingdom resolve** when he faced Goliath, who was mocking God's people. David was not hesitant but fully confident in his authority. He saw himself as a representative of God in that battle, determined to put an end to Goliath's unlawful actions. Kingdom resolve stems from having a kingdom mindset. It means refusing to tolerate the enemy's illegal activities in our thoughts and lives anymore. With kingdom resolve, we can rise up, take our place, engage in battle, and reclaim territory for the kingdom of God. It begins by reclaiming territory in our minds and mindsets, which leads to victory in our lives. God is always victorious and has never lost a battle. With God's kingdom mindset, we can overcome every obstacle and conquer any challenge and take back what the devil has stolen in our lives (1 Samuel 30:8). God is encouraging us to pursue, "Pursue, for you shall surely overtake them and without fail recover all'.

God is profoundly intentional and deliberate in His speech, for His words carry extraordinary creative power. Every aspect of creation obediently responds to God's Word. The very existence of all things is a result of God's spoken command (Genesis 1:1). The intricate functioning of the entire universe is sustained by God's Word (Hebrews

1:3). God's laws govern the world, and not a single syllable He utters is without purpose. God is attentive and mindful of His words, and when He speaks, the forces of nature and the principles of science align themselves to His voice.[82] When we engage in God's positive self-talk, it brings about transformative change within us. It has the power to reshape our minds and hearts, fostering growth and renewal. By embracing God's affirming words, our self-confidence and faith are strengthened, while the deceptive lies of the enemy are diminished.

Even in the world of sports, we can find examples of positive self-talk. **Muhammad Ali,** one of the greatest heavyweight boxers of all time, used a song to boost his own confidence and intimidate his opponents. The song, known as "The Black Superman Song," proclaimed his agility and strength: "**Muhammad Ali**, he floats like a butterfly and stings like a bee, the black Superman says catch me if you can." By singing this song to his opponents before matches, **Ali** aimed to plant seeds of doubt in their minds and assert his dominance.

Positive self-talk not only boosts our confidence but also weakens the power of the enemy in our lives. It is an essential component of cultivating a Kingdom Mindset. By engaging in positive self-talk, we effectively dismantle the lies the enemy tries to plant in our minds. Numerous studies on athletes, as well as the example of boxer Muhammad Ali, demonstrate that <u>positive self-talk is a significant predictor of success.</u> Ex. You have to believe that you can win and declare that you will win before you will ever win. In other words, positive self-talk sings "We Are the Champions" song by Queen before the game not just afterward.

CRITICISM is a form of negative self-talk: The opposite of positive self-talk is criticism or having an Inner Critic. According to the Oxford English Dictionary, criticism is the expression of disapproval of someone or something based on perceived faults or mistakes. <u>Criticism is similar to negative self-talk as it diminishes your confidence and hinders your ability to make positive changes in your life. It is like having an INNER CRITIC whose excessive negativity brings us down.</u> Criticism can cause significant stress and impede your success. It manifests in various forms and, if left unchecked, can lead to depression and hopelessness. Examples of critical self-talk include statements like "I can never do anything right!" or "I'm such a klutz, I will surely break it", or "I got a C on this test; I guess I'm not good at math" or "I'll never be able to go to university" or "It's all my fault" or "That was a fluke or sheer luck." and "I should have known better" or " If I fail this exam, I

---

will never get the job I want." and "If this relationship doesn't work out, I will never find the right person." This type of thinking often leads to rigid opinions and judgements where individuals believe something is right or wrong, good or bad, without considering other alternatives or perspectives. <u>Criticism tends to exaggerate and fixate on worst-case scenarios in our minds.</u> Take a moment to reflect on your own self-talk patterns.

Before you can begin practicing more of God's positive self-talk, it is important to identify and address your negative thinking or negative self-talk. Your inner critic often falls into these four categories:

1. **Personalizing:** You tend to blame yourself for everything, even when it isn't your fault.
2. **Magnifying:** You excessively focus on the negative aspects of a situation, disregarding any positive aspects.
3. **Catastrophizing:** You have a tendency to expect the worst and are often resistant to logic, reason, or faith that may suggest otherwise.
4. **Polarizing:** You perceive the world in extremes, categorizing things as either black or white, good or bad, without acknowledging gray areas or middle ground for processing life events.

When you start to recognize the types of negative thinking mentioned above, you can work on transforming them into positive thinking. This process is achievable but requires practice and time. When you catch yourself engaging in negative self-talk or listening to your inner critic, you can learn to replace those thoughts with God's perspective.

<u>Positive self-talk takes practice because it is not our natural instinct.</u> Forming new habits requires time and effort. Over time, our inner dialogue can shift to become more encouraging, uplifting, and aligned with God's Word. This is what God desires for each of us.

New revelation: <u>God wants us to Catch our Critic and Challenge our critic.</u> In other words, God desires for us to become aware when we are listening to critical and negative thoughts and to begin stopping them by catching them and then challenging them. We do not have to agree with the criticism. We have a choice. We don't have to listen to our inner critic. It's important to remember that our thoughts and feelings don't always reflect reality. We can challenge our critic with the Word of God. Additionally, we can challenge our critic with our Inner Cheerleader. We should check if a thought or feeling aligns with the Word of God. If it doesn't, we should not agree with it.[83]

---

[83] *verywellmind.com - negative self-talk*

I will share some techniques that you can use to challenge your inner critic and change the narrative in your mind.

1. **Identify your triggers.** When are you most tempted to speak negatively about yourself or your life? What triggers those moments? Certain scenarios, such as work or family events, can be particularly challenging and increase self-doubt, leading to negative self-talk. Navigating holidays can also be tough. Here's a trick to change your self-talk: Identify the negative thought and behaviour, and then memorize a faith statement to speak instead. This way, whenever you're tempted to speak words of defeat, you can consciously choose words of victory.[84] For example, instead of using negative or profane language, try replacing it with positive and empowering statements aligned with God's word. For instance, rather than saying "sugar" as a substitute for a negative word, say "I am blessed and highly favoured." This shift in language is more positive and in line with God's teachings.

You can also try visualizing yourself covered in a suit of armour, where hurtful words are unable to penetrate the shield, reinforcing your resilience and protecting your self-esteem.

2. **Create a faith statement.** To combat negative self-talk, create a faith statement and carry it with you at all times. When the temptation to speak negatively arises, read the statement aloud to yourself. This practice can be repeated throughout the day as needed. Keeping the Word of God close to you is powerful, as seen in Deuteronomy 6:6-9 where God instructs His people to bind His words upon themselves and display them as reminders. Many believers sew the Word or promises of God into their clothing as a visual reminder. By consistently focusing on and believing in the Word of God, your life can be transformed in remarkable ways. God encourages us to keep our eyes focused on His teachings in Proverbs 4:21. For example, if you are feeling unqualified, say, "I can do all things through Christ who strengthens me. God has qualified me by making me a partaker of the inheritance of His holy people." (Philippians 4:13 & Colossians 1:12)

3. **Cast down every word that contradicts God's Word about you.** I have had the privilege of working with numerous individuals, both young and old, whose confidence has been undermined by the

---

[84] Keith Butler. *Instagram*

words of a teacher, coach, parent, spouse, or employer. These individuals were told that they would never amount to much or that they weren't good enough. Perhaps you have also heard such words growing up, and maybe they still echo in your mind, causing you to doubt yourself even now. I want you to understand that this is not God's will for you. 2 Corinthians 10:5 *We demolish arguments and every pretension that sets itself up against the knowledge of God, and we take captive every thought to make it obedient to Christ.*

Statements like "Who do you think you are?" or "You don't have what it takes", or "You'll never amount to anything" should not be accepted as truth. They are not the truth. Your feelings do not determine your truth. Your truth is found in the Word of God. Personally, I have had to turn to God in prayer <u>to nullify the negative words spoken over me by others (Isaiah 54:17).</u> These negative words do not have to manifest in your life. You do not need to internalize them and empower your inner critic. It is time to put a stop to the negative self-talk and the negative perceptions you hold about yourself. Embrace your unique qualities and learn to love who you are. Remember, you are a one-of-a-kind masterpiece. God's signature is on you!

Gossip is a negative word. Gossip is like junk food: Just because it's tasty doesn't mean it's nutritious.

4. <u>**Begin to speak what God says over yourself.**</u> Use the "<u>**I Am" statements provided in this book**</u>"
   Practice positive affirmations for yourself. Sometimes, simply seeing positive words or inspirational messages can redirect your thoughts in a positive direction. Consider placing small reminders in your office, home, and other places where you spend a significant amount of time. I personally like to use sticky notes and place them everywhere.

For example, you can write affirmations such as:
   - ❖ I am filled with focus.
   - ❖ All I need is within me right now.
   - ❖ I am powerful and capable.
   - ❖ I am constantly growing and evolving into a better person.
   - ❖ This, too, shall pass.
   - ❖ As long as I have breath in my lungs, God has a purpose for my life.
   - ❖ My best days are still before me.

During my school days, we used to create bulletin board displays titled "Today is a Good Day to..." where we would include phrases like:

- Be kind
- Dream big
- Shine
- Believe in yourself
- Work hard
- Smile
- Learn
- Be grateful
- Do great things
- Be creative
- Be amazing
- Be happy
- Be polite
- Be happy for others
- Give compliments

These positive affirmations and reminders can have a powerful impact on shifting your mindset and fostering a more positive self-talk. Students and teachers were encouraged to take the notes off the board as needed to act as visual reminders.

Surround yourself with positive words and positive people. Whether you realize it or not, the outlook and emotions of those around you can have an influence on your own mindset. Therefore, it's crucial to intentionally surround yourself with positive individuals. Pay attention to your inner circle and be selective about who you allow to speak into your life. Remember, not just anybody should have the privilege of influencing your thoughts and beliefs. Proverbs 13:20 Walk with the wise and become wise, for a companion of fools suffers harm.

> **"When you know God's acceptance, you can endure people's rejection."**
>
> *—Eric Petree*

Caution: Holy Bible. Engaging with the Bible can lead to habitual use. Regular reading may result in the reduction of anxiety, fear, and a diminished desire for impatience and anger. Common symptoms include heightened feelings of love, joy, peace, patience, kindness, goodness, faithfulness, gentleness, and self-control. If these symptoms persist, simply continue to Praise the Lord![85]

"Day one or one day? How you frame statements and situations can determine what you grow in your brain and your direction. How can you reframe a statement or situation?"
—Dr. Caroline Leaf

Positive Self-Talk in Children: (For parents, grandparents, coaches and educators)

When we consistently uplift our children and express our love and pride in them, it helps cultivate their self-confidence and positive self-image. Conversely, when we constantly criticize our kids, it doesn't make them stop loving us, but rather, it can cause them to lose love for themselves. Reflect on the significance of this statement.[86]

If speaking to plants helps them grow, imagine what speaking kind words will do for our children.

Our children can lose love for themselves due to our criticism. The Bible instructs us not to provoke our children to anger (Ephesians 6:4). As parents, we should avoid actions that irritate, frustrate, or discourage our children. We should not be excessively harsh, harass them, or make them feel inferior. Instead, we are called to raise them tenderly, providing guidance, discipline, counsel, and admonition according to the principles of the Lord.

Being an overbearing helicopter parent, constantly involved in every aspect of your child's life, can have negative effects. It involves constant criticism, nitpicking, and unrealistic expectations, which can erode your child's self-esteem and create insecurities. This behaviour promotes a fixed mindset and can hinder their growth and development. As parents, it's important to strive for the best for our children while fostering a healthy and supportive environment for their personal growth.

Instead of criticizing or finding faults, let's use positive affirmations to help our children and students rise higher and become who God created them to be. Focus on and praise something that they are good at. This could include character traits like kindness, manners, a sense of humour, or patience. For instance, you can say things like "You're so polite" or "What a gentleman you are." By building up their self-confidence in these areas, we can help them grow.

---

[85] Biblestrength. *Instagram post*- Dec 14, 20
[86] Mark Hankins

Instead of fixating on their weaknesses, it's beneficial to overlook those aspects and instead identify one or two things that individuals excel at and concentrate on those. In the context of education, the approach of "Pick your battles" suggests addressing one area of improvement at a time. For instance, if the objective is for a student to raise their hand before speaking, it is more effective to praise them whenever they successfully raise their hand and overlook the times they don't. <u>Constantly highlighting mistakes can be counterproductive. Focusing on strengths and areas of improvement in a positive and constructive manner fosters confidence and growth.</u>

We can encourage our children by praising their efforts and progress. Use phrases like "Good effort" or "Good try." Let them know that they are getting better with each attempt. Say things like "Good for you" or "I like the way you..." to acknowledge their achievements. For example, you can say, "I'm so proud of you! You remembered to raise your hand two times today. Let's try for three times tomorrow. I believe in you; you're such a quick learner."

<u>Remember to celebrate even the smallest of successes and build upon them</u>. By offering positive reinforcement and focusing on their strengths, we can help our children and students develop a strong sense of self-confidence and encourage them to reach their full potential.

As educators, we must acknowledge that certain children attend school not solely for academic purposes but rather to receive love and encouragement. Once they receive such affection and positive support and feel secure, we can subsequently focus on their academic development.

"Next time, you may consider exploring..." Providing loving and positive guidance on the next steps, along with areas for improvement and growth, is crucial for ongoing learning. The Bible emphasizes the power of words, capable of either bringing life or causing harm. The words we speak to our children are deeply received by their souls. Are you speaking words of life and blessings over your children and students or words that may discourage them? It is easier to nurture a child's development than to mend an adult's brokenness. Therefore, choose your words wisely. Let Holy Spirit's example guide you when offering descriptive feedback.

Every day, we make deposits into the memory banks of our children and students. The manner in which we communicate with them becomes their internal voice or self-talk. Their self-talk serves as a significant predictor of their success, mental well-being, and overall happiness.

I desire my children to possess confidence and embrace positive self-talk, don't you? It would be disheartening if their inner critic echoed the critical voice they hear from us. May the Lord forgive us. Let's educate our children about God's strategy for cultivating positive self-talk and exemplify it ourselves. Let's equip our children with the tools to combat the negative thoughts and battles within their minds. Instead of being their inner critic, let's become their inner cheerleader. <u>Even better, let's teach them to recognize and challenge their inner critic with the Word of God.</u> Challenging your critic involves replacing a lie from the devil with the truth from God's Word. This powerful strategy aligns with God's kingdom mindset and will benefit them throughout their lives.

We are commanded to guide our children in the right path, and the Bible assures us that when they grow old, they will not stray from it (Proverbs 22:6). By imparting knowledge of God's kingdom mindset, which encompasses positive self-talk, to our children, grandchildren, and students, we are equipping them with a valuable set of skills that they can utilize throughout their lives. The ability to recognize and challenge their inner critic is a skill that can be cultivated and will greatly benefit them. It will enable them to remain focused, maintain a positive outlook, and continually progress towards higher achievements in life.

Choose to confess a positive promise from the Word of God over your children instead of the circumstances you may be experiencing. Try these:

- ❖ **Isaiah 54:13** says that our children shall be taught by the Lord, and great will be their peace. Say "My child is peaceful" instead of "He's hyperactive, distracted, bad, and impulsive."
- ❖ **1 Corinthians 2:16** says that we have the mind of Christ. Say "My child has the mind of Christ. They can focus, and they can listen and learn at school."
- ❖ **Daniel 1:20** states that in every matter of wisdom and understanding about which the king consulted them, he found Daniel and his friends ten times better than all the learned and magi in his whole realm. Say "My child is ten times smarter than their peers" They can learn and will learn. They are the top of their class."

"Your thought life will lead you to destruction quicker than your mouth, and your actions will because thoughts always precede words and action."

—*Doug Jones*

Frequently, children are penalized for exhibiting normal human emotions. They are not permitted to have moments of grumpiness, off days, disrespectful tones, or negative attitudes. However, as adults, we experience these emotions regularly. None of us are flawless. It is crucial that we cease expecting our children to meet a standard of perfection that even we ourselves cannot achieve. [87]

Avoid living vicariously through your children. Cultivate your own life and allow your children to lead their own. It is possible to be an engaged parent without suffocating them. Grant your children some leeway. Just as God grants us grace every day, we should extend the same to our children.

Perhaps you have been heeding your inner critic, which has led you to feel down. Just like consuming unhealthy food affects your physical well-being, listening to your inner critic negatively impacts your mindset. Cease consuming the wrong mental "foods" that harm your mental health. You have the power to make a change starting today. Repent and turn away from destructive patterns. Remember, it is never too late with God. Refrain from listening to your inner critic and perpetuating its negative messages. Instead, choose to embrace God's positive self-talk strategy for yourself and your children. By doing so, you will enhance your mental well-being and happiness.

Positive self-talk is like having an INNER CHEERLEADER cheering you on and telling you who you are and all the things that you can do according to the Word of God.
When your inner critic relentlessly criticizes you for a mistake, your thinking can become negative and toxic. However, you have the ability to change the narrative. You do not have to be a passive victim of your own thoughts. Remind yourself that you are in control. You possess cognitive sovereignty and the power to shape your thinking. God has bestowed upon you the ability to govern your thoughts. Reclaim your power and evict your inner critic. Remember, God is the God of transformation and redemption. With God's kingdom mindset, you and God together have the authority to determine your thoughts and beliefs about yourself.

Definition: God's positive self-talk encompasses more than mere positive confession. It involves deliberately choosing to declare God's Word over our lives. It entails aligning ourselves with God, the creator of the universe, and embracing His principles, laws, and mindset (kingdom principles/success criteria). Additionally, it involves attuning

---

[87] Rebecca Eanes. *Instagram post-classful.offi,* Dec 31.20

ourselves to our inner cheerleader, which is the voice of the Holy Spirit residing within us.

Remember that parenting using God's kingdom mindset and success strategies is the goal.
It is important to avoid excessively criticizing yourself for parenting mistakes and instead see them as valuable lessons. Negative self-talk about your parenting abilities, such as believing you are a terrible parent or that others are doing better than you, is unproductive and can contribute to parental guilt. These toxic beliefs hinder effective parenting and rarely inspire positive change. Let go of shame and regret, as perfection is not the ultimate goal. The ultimate goal is to parent with God as your guide, aligning your mindset and success strategies with His principles. God does not engage in negative self-talk, and adopting a positive self-talk approach is encouraged in His kingdom mindset.

Stop paying attention to your inner critic and recognize yourself as a commendable parent. God specifically chose you among all individuals to parent your children, demonstrating His trust in you and equipping you with everything needed for this task. Despite any doubts or feelings of inadequacy, you are anointed for this role. The resources you require are already within you. You are the right person for the job, with seeds of greatness, hidden talents, and abilities instilled by God. By adopting a kingdom mindset, you can awaken and utilize these qualities. Embrace your inner cheerleader and remember that you are not alone in raising your children; God is by your side. He will assist you and show you how to access the patience and strength that already exist within you (2 Timothy 1:6).

Prayer: This is a prayer that I say over my children to this day.

Father, I express my gratitude to you for (insert child's/children's names here). They bring immense joy to my life each day. I am thankful for their obedience and respect. I appreciate their strength and good health. I acknowledge that your favour encompasses them like a protective shield. Your goodness and mercy accompany them wherever they go. I declare that no weapon formed against them shall prosper in the name of Jesus. I am grateful that they possess a kingdom mindset and practice positive self-talk.
Father, I am thankful that (child's name) is exceptionally intelligent, surpassing their peers. They are enriched with your knowledge and wisdom. An excellent spirit resides within them.

They are positioned to be leaders and not followers, to rise above and not be defeated, to lend and not borrow. My children are remarkable individuals, destined to make history and bring about positive change in the world. They attentively listen to you, their inner cheerleader, and are continuously growing, learning, and transforming into the individuals you have created them to be. They will live out their days in good health, peace, love, joy, and prosperity.
Father, I thank you that my children will fulfil their divine assignments, making a positive impact in the world, and bringing you great glory. Amen.

Click the link in the footnote to download a powerful children's decree I created. Pray it over your chlid/children every day.[88]

When we engage in positive self-talk, we are mirroring our Father God, who uplifts His Word above His name, and He remains steadfast in fulfilling it (Isaiah 55:11). Positive self-talk is an integral aspect of cultivating God's kingdom mindset. It boosts confidence and reinforces our sense of purpose. <u>By speaking the solution instead of dwelling on the problem, we align ourselves with God's Word. As we voice the answer, we present God's promises back to Him, and He faithfully brings them to pass. Positive self-talk is akin to expressing our faith through confession.</u>
The small steps you take each day will lead to greatness or ruin over time. We need to cultivate the good habit of positive self-talk in our lives.
—Natalie Masucci

Developing habits, maintaining <u>consistency,</u> and demonstrating dedication on a daily basis is crucial for unlocking our full potential. Consistency is vital for transforming our mindset and ensuring its sustainability. God desires our devoted practice and commitment in all areas of life.

<u>Your consistent actions shape your identity.</u> Engaging in cheating or lying consistently will label you as such while demonstrating punctuality and keeping your word earns you a reputation for reliability and trustworthiness. Faithfulness extends beyond good intentions and

---

[88] https://empoweredwordministries.ca/wp-content/uploads/2022/08/Children-Decree-min.pdf

can also be directed towards destructive patterns. It is effortless to fall into negative habits, but intentionally cultivating positive routines and patterns requires deliberate effort. The areas where you choose to invest your faithfulness reveal what you truly place your hope in. Your actions of faithfulness hold more weight than mere words. While words reflect aspirations, actions serve as proof of one's character.

Take a moment to consider what is your faith in? Is it in God? [89] Are you following His kingdom mindset? Think how many years of smoking before it caused cancer. Think of how many times you overdrank before becoming an alcoholic? Think of how many times you overate before you became obese. Think of how many times you went to the casino before you lost your home. Think of all the times you disrespected or took advantage of your spouse before your marriage fell apart. Think of all the times you slacked off at work before you lost your job? <u>Things build up over time, both good and bad.</u> With God's kingdom mindset, He wants us to build good habits in our lives. Start by practicing positive self-talk.

"The smallest deed is greater than the biggest intention."
—*John Maxwell*

<u>Intentions, no matter how good and sincere, do not accomplish anything.</u> What truly matters is consistent action. Are you consistently employing God's positive self-talk? "Old habits die hard" holds true for those with a fixed mindset. Statements like "I just can't seem to quit smoking" or "I just can't seem to lose weight" reflect this mindset. However, those with God's kingdom mindset understand that they can change their habits with God's assistance as He extends His grace to us.

At times, you need to say "no" to yourself in order to attain your true desires in life. <u>Short-term discomfort leads to long-term gain.</u> When faced with temptations that satisfy your flesh, you resist because you are focused on your mission. For instance, if your goal is to lose weight and improve your health, you must decline certain foods and snacks. The saying "Where there is a will, there is a way" resonates with this idea. The truth is that God can always pave a path for you, even in seemingly impossible situations (Isaiah 43:19). All you need to do is remain steadfast in His Word. The determination and capacity to tackle difficult tasks now, through dedicated practice in developing positive self-talk, will ultimately make things easier for your future self.

---

[89] thefarrellmama *Instagram*

"By adding in repetitive action, your brain will begin to relinquish any beliefs you have over what you can and cannot do."
—*Dr. Clifford Saunders, Ph.D.*

There is a prevalent issue in today's society, stemming from the well-intentioned actions of parents who have attempted to boost their children's self-esteem by constantly praising their intelligence and talents. We have followed the advice of experts, fearing that telling our children the truth might make them sad. However, it is important to understand that descriptive feedback differs from constant praise. Genuine praise should be uplifting and authentic, serving as a source of edification.

Constant and unwarranted praise can have detrimental effects on children, as they become reliant on receiving stickers or rewards for every action. Consequently, we now see adults who are in constant need of reassurance, validation, and struggle to handle criticism. This indicates a fixed mindset, wherein individuals exhibit weak self-confidence, fear making mistakes, are unable to accept any form of criticism (even constructive) and require constant affirmation and incentives to perform.[90]

"In all our seeking for validation, we forgot to look up."
—*Natalie Masucci*

Risk Versus Reward

If you were aware of the rewards that come with embracing new knowledge and facing challenges, you would likely be willing to pursue them. Did you know that God always compensates us for our obedience? Yes, He uses positive reinforcement of appropriate behaviour with us. Hebrews 11:6 confirms that God rewards those who diligently seek Him and follow His ways. As we strive to adopt a kingdom mindset and walk in alignment with God, we experience blessings and rewards in our lives. Our self-confidence and faith grow, empowering us to fearlessly embark on new endeavours. Additionally, we begin to view failure as an opportunity for personal growth and resilience. By taking risks and exercising faith, we are attracting blessings and new possibilities. God will reward our efforts, regardless of the outcome. God is more concerned with our obedience and ongoing learning than with the final result.

---

[90] *Dweck* P.136

To foster stress resilience in children, otherwise known as a kingdom mindset, minimize excessive micromanagement of their schedules and encourage them to explore and overcome boredom and fear through curiosity and experimentation. Children need to develop the ability to recognize when a situation has become difficult and choose a response that leads to growth. The author reflects on their own childhood, where parents were less involved, and highlights experiences of playing outdoors, resolving conflicts independently, and requesting sleepovers without much guidance. In contrast, today's parents are overly involved, scheduling play dates and controlling friendships, which is disheartening as they may be trying to fill a void that only God can satisfy.

Stress resilience isn't developed solely by constantly feeling good. It is nurtured through the process of becoming better at embracing, acknowledging, and resolving negative emotions. This cultivates mental endurance and toughness. [91]

When children experience conflicts with others, they may feel upset. Instead of immediately intervening to fix the issue, allow them to try working it out on their own. Resist the urge to take over or solve the problem for them. Only if they are unable to find a resolution should you step in with suggestions. Encourage them to try again independently, incorporating your suggestions. By resolving conflicts themselves, they build resilience and confidence.

Regrettably, many individuals tend to avoid problems rather than seeking solutions. However, God has not called us to evade problems; He has called us to be problem-solvers.[92] God desires us to develop resilience within ourselves and has designed us to be problem solvers in this world.

"Failure has terrific value. Failure goes along with success: you fail your way to success."

—John Maxwell

Confronting mistakes is essential for growth as we learn most from failures. Persistence and learning from mistakes are valuable, as reflected in the saying, "If at first you don't succeed, try, try, try again." However, there's a tendency to avoid mistakes, especially among perfection-seeking students, which hinders learning. Making excuses or seeking retests doesn't benefit children in the long run, as it teaches them to avoid effort and deadlines. Acknowledging failure, learning

---

[91] Dr. Leaf, *Instagram.* May 29/20
[92] Tony Cooke. *#kindlequotes*

from it, and adopting a growth mindset is key. Embracing God's kingdom mindset can guide this process.

It is important not to shield our children from negative emotions. By attempting to protect them from feelings such as sadness or anxiety, we inadvertently send them the wrong message. Rather than teaching them that these emotions are a natural part of life and helping them build resilience, we convey a lack of trust in their ability to handle challenging situations. **According to Dr. Tina Payne Bryson, this undermines children's self-image and sets them up for future failures.** It is crucial for them to learn how to navigate the trials of life. In both sports and life, there are winners and losers. Sometimes we win, and other times we lose. Losing a game does not make someone a loser, just as making a mistake does not define us as failures. <u>God uses both victories and mistakes to shape us into the individuals He intends us to be. Our children need to experience both too.</u>

"In sports, you must play by the rules in order to win. In life, you must operate according to God's laws to be victorious."
—Natalie Masucci

Chapter Four

Compliments-Positive Self-Talk

"In every seed, there is a potential of a great harvest. In every fish, there is potential for a school. In every bird, there is potential for a flock. In every man, there is potential for a nation."
—John Hagee

Compliments are a positive form of communication. A compliment is a courteous way to express praise or admiration towards someone. When we offer compliments, we not only make others feel good, but we also contribute to boosting their self-confidence and faith. In our society, many individuals experience a sense of invisibility or being unseen. Thus, people are often yearning for genuine compliments. Each time we extend a compliment to someone, it can open up a conversation and provide an opportunity to sow a seed and share about Jesus. Contrary to the narrative in the world today; you can disagree with someone, and still love them. You can have differing views, and still be kind.

On the other hand, insulting people erodes their confidence. Practices such as poking fun, making jokes, bullying, cyber-bullying, micro-managing, name-calling, criticizing, and gas-lighting have become commonplace and are all hurtful and destructive.

According to Ephesians 4:20, we are instructed to speak words of edification; otherwise, we grieve the Holy Spirit. Grieving the Holy Spirit leads to a loss of intimacy with Him. Criticizing others is a sin that hinders our intimacy with the Holy Spirit. As a result, He ceases to prompt and communicate with us because we fail to listen. Descriptive feedback is withheld, and we are left to our own devices. Hence, it is important to stop criticizing. Instead of merely pointing out someone's faults, focus on highlighting their strengths.

We often underestimate the power of our words. There is a story I once heard about a woman who had battled depression for years and had reached the point of contemplating suicide. However, on the day she had decided to go through with it, a colleague at work offered her a simple compliment. That single act of kindness caused her to reconsider her decision. It was as if the compliment helped her shift the negative script in her mind and halted her toxic rumination. That small act of kindness became the sign she needed to find hope and choose not to give up. A kind word had the power to alter the course of that woman's life.

"Kindness is one of the most sought after commodities in the world because it is so scarce. Make sure to stockpile kindness and share it with others who cannot afford any right now... they need it most."

- *Coach Monica Soares*

It is important to always be mindful of the impact our words can have. <u>They can be lifesavers</u>. Take a moment to reflect on that. Our words have the potential to save lives. I personally aspire to be a source of positivity and support. How about you? Let us strive to be kind always because we never truly know what battles others may be fighting. Kindness is shown by being respectful, giving compliments, positive affirmations and gratitude. A simple act of kindness, like offering a compliment, has the potential to make a profound difference in someone's life.

"People are often unreasonable and self-centered. Forgive them anyway. If you are kind, people may accuse you of ulterior motives. Be kind anyway. If you are honest, people may cheat you. Be honest anyway. If you find happiness, people may be jealous. Be happy anyway. The good you do today maybe forgotten tomorrow. Do good anyway. Give the world the best you have and it may never be enough. Give your best anyway. For you see, in the end, it is between you and God. It was never between you and them anyway."

- *Mother Teresa*

Compliments don't cost anything to give, yet they have the ability to profoundly affect the fabric of our brains. Not only do they make us feel good, but they also have a significant impact on memory, learning, motivation, and self-esteem. I challenge you to compliment your loved ones for 30 days straight and see the transformation that follows.

<u>God encourages us to go beyond the saying, "If you can't say something nice, then say nothing at all," and intentionally find something positive and encouraging to say.</u> Just as God is intentional with His words, He desires us to do the same (2 Thessalonians 1:11-12). Let's make a conscious decision to speak life and blessings into others each day, whether it's our loved ones, colleagues, employees and staff or strangers we interact with. Compliments trigger the release of

dopamine in our brains, which is associated with motivation and positivity. God wants us to choose to compliment others more often because He does the same for us. Complimenting others not only uplifts them but also brings joy to ourselves.

Embrace the practice of using positive affirmations and compliments for yourself and others. Take a moment to compliment yourself and acknowledge your achievements. Even simple phrases can make a difference. <u>As you uplift others, you'll experience God uplifting you in return.</u> Treat others as you would like to be treated, following the golden rule. Remember that what you sow, you will reap. So, let's sow compliments, kindness, positivity, and love instead of criticism and sow seeds that will bring forth fruitful and joyful outcomes.

Creating special rituals and affirming ourselves can positively impact our self-perception and confidence. The author shares a joyful experience of having a fashion show with their daughter, where they affirmed how great they looked while dancing to "You sexy Thing" by Hot Chocolate. This practice helped their daughter grow into a confident young woman. The names we call ourselves hold power and shape our reality. Being kind to ourselves and using positive affirmations grounded in the Word of God reinforces our true names and identities. What we repeatedly hear, we eventually believe.

<u>The kingdom mindset of God protects our mental health by creating a safe and nurturing environment where children are taught to appreciate and compliment both themselves and others.</u> Phrases like "Good try" or "I like the way you..." serve as examples of positive self-talk when we acknowledge and compliment ourselves. "I'm trying my best" "I'm doing a good job" "I am working towards my goals" "I am a work in progress" "I can't do it yet." In other words, positive self-talk is singing "we are the champions" song before the game.

"When you see something beautiful in a student, let them know. It may take a second to say, but for them it could last a lifetime."
—Robert John Meehan

My mission is to promote God's kingdom mindset in schools and positively transform the lives of children by equipping them with the necessary tools for success in life. God has unleashed the greatest rescue operation this world has ever seen. This generation belongs to God. Through God's kingdom mindset this generation will rise up and take back what the enemy has stolen.

The Bible contains valuable teachings about the power of compliments and affirming words.

"Gracious words are a honeycomb, sweet to the soul and healing to the bones." Proverbs 16:24 Can you believe it? Kind words or compliments have the potential to bring healing to your body! It's important to speak to your body with kindness and gratitude. For instance, you can say, "Body, thank you for functioning perfectly as God created you" or "My immune system is strong."

"A word aptly spoken, Compliments is like apples of gold in settings of silver." (Proverbs 25:11). Love sings the praises of it's beloved (Song of Songs 6:4-13)

"If speaking kindly to plants helps them grow, imagine what speaking kindly to humans can do?"

<u>Throughout the Bible, Jesus showers us with compliments through His "I Am" statements and "In Him" statements.</u> He constantly reminds us of our immeasurable value to Him. In Psalm 139:2, He refers to us as "Precious ones," and in Colossians 3:12 and 1 John 4:7-8, He calls us "Beloved."

Unfortunately, we often label ourselves incorrectly by believing the lies of the enemy. We may use derogatory terms such as stupid, ugly, fat, old, worthless, loser, addicted, incompetent, poor, weak, or sick. However, **God sees us as He created us, not as we perceive ourselves.** How God sees us reflects the truth because He recognizes the seeds of greatness He has planted within us. <u>When we use negative names to describe ourselves, we dishonour God, our creator</u>.

For example, God called **Gideon** a mighty man of God when he was hiding and afraid.

Similarly, Jesus calls us His **Beloved,** as mentioned in Song of Solomon 6:3, Romans 1:7, Romans 9:25, and Colossians 3:12. This is true even when we may feel unloved or struggle to fully grasp His love.

If you are fortunate to have a special someone in your life, make sure to express your compliments to them. If you have a mother or father figure in your life, consider yourself rich and never take them for granted. Let them know how much they mean to you and how much you love and appreciate them. <u>Love should never be left unspoken.</u>

Husbands, remember that your wives need to hear your compliments. Tell them that they are beautiful, great mothers, best friends, amazing cooks, and wonderful wives.

Wives, understand that your husbands need your approval and encouragement. Compliments not only make us feel good but also strengthen our self-esteem. I firmly believe that if you compliment and express gratitude to your husband for helping around the house, it will encourage him to do more. <u>We often become what people call us.</u>

Parents, bless your children with heartfelt words of love and pride, for your compliments hold immense value and become their inner cheerleader. Similarly, express to your best friends the significance of their friendship, as they may not always be there. <u>Just as Jesus compliments us, we should strive to compliment those in our lives.</u> Let's elevate it by expressing compliments back to Jesus through prayer, embracing the essential components of God's mindset.

Here is an example:
In adoration from your heart, tell Jesus that;

- ❖ He is the fairest of ten thousand
- ❖ He is altogether lovely
- ❖ His love is better than wine
- ❖ He is the Rose of Sharon & the Lily of the valley
- ❖ He is more precious than silver
- ❖ He is more costly than gold
- ❖ He is more beautiful than diamonds
- ❖ And nothing that you desire compares with Him
- ❖ He is perfect
- ❖ He is sweet as honey
- ❖ He is high and lifted up
- ❖ He is a good, good father
- ❖ And You see the future in His eyes

Human words are insufficient to describe the immense beauty of Jesus. According to the Bible, the roads in heaven are paved with gold and precious stones (Revelation 21:21). Interestingly, in heaven, these materials are considered less valuable than they are on Earth, and they are used as mere pavement. It's truly an awe-inspiring thought.

<u>Complimenting Jesus through prayer, worship, and adoration helps us shift our focus to His infinite love and beauty, aligning us with God's Word and cultivating a positive mindset.</u> Singing praises to God is an important aspect of adopting the kingdom mindset, as it opens the door for more blessings and gives us reasons to express gratitude. Similarly, complimenting and encouraging ourselves and others aligns with God's kingdom mindset. Holy Spirit utilizes affirming words and compliments to provide descriptive feedback, motivating and strengthening us. By following God's example, we can genuinely uplift those around us through compliments, counteracting insincerity, low self-confidence, poor self-image and negative self-talk.

The Power of NAMES: Encouragement/Compliments

The Bible serves as a vast source of encouragement. It contains our true names, and through its words, God expresses His faith in us, saying, *"I have faith in you"* and *"I believe that you can do it."* God would never assign us a task that we cannot accomplish. God is not like humans who are prone to lying (Numbers 23:19). The Bible assures us that He equips us with everything we need to succeed and overcome the devil (Hebrews 13:21 & 2 Peter 1:3). We were created to excel and have dominion in our spheres of influence, such as education, sports, entertainment, business, politics, and more. **Excel** means to reach the highest level of achievement and prosper. God's plan is for us to rule and reign as kings and priests through the redemptive work of Jesus (Revelation 5:10). Our purpose is to influence and restore authority in the world, bringing heaven on earth and restoring mankind to their original position of authority before the fall (Matthew 6:10).

God perceives our potential. He sees the seeds of greatness that He has planted within us. Those seeds require nourishment, love, and guidance from the Holy Spirit through descriptive feedback so that they may grow into saplings and eventually become fully-grown trees that bear fruit.[93]

God is the ultimate source of transformation in people's lives. He created us to embrace a kingdom mindset, and He supports, protects, and encourages us. God uplifts us by calling us by our true names. He refers to us as His "beloved," "victorious," and "overcomers."

As parents and educators, we have the opportunity to empower our children by teaching them about God's kingdom mindset and affirming their true names and identities. We can start by using positive names when addressing our children and spouses. For example, if we want our husband to take on the role of the spiritual head of the household, we can refer to him as a mighty man of God from the Bible and show him respect (Ephesians 5:23). By expressing our appreciation, love, and trust, we will empower them and in turn, we will witness positive changes in their behaviour. Offering a daily compliment can bring about transformative effects in our spouse and family life. Encouragement and support are vital for our loved ones to fulfil their God-given potential, and it is our responsibility to uplift and strengthen them rather than tear them down.

People greatly benefit from encouragement and reminders of their inherent worth and capabilities. It is essential to believe in others, affirm their bravery, intelligence, and their ability to achieve their

---

93 Bill Winston

dreams and more. Let us continually remind and uplift one another with these affirmations. Ephesians 5:19 tells us to "speak to yourselves in psalms and hymns and spiritual songs, singing and making melody in your heart to the Lord."

It is our responsibility to uplift and support our loved ones, providing encouragement for them to fulfil their God-given potential. I used this practice with my students by giving them nicknames like "Ace" and "Meglio" to encourage and motivate them. They absolutely loved their nicknames. I love the names that God calls me too. Names like beautiful, beloved, blessed, chosen, strong, free, and powerful, to name a few.

"We're called to have an impact for God on this world, and that impact should always be increasing."
—Kenneth Copeland

In stories like **David facing Goliath** and **Joshua and the walls of Jericho** falling, we see that while God grants strength and performs miracles, <u>human action is also required</u>. When we embrace God's kingdom mindset and take initiative with faith, supernatural occurrences can happen in our lives. It is a partnership where both God and we have a role to play. God has fulfilled His part, and now it is up to us to fulfil ours (Philippians 3:14).

In the examples of **Gideon, Sarah, Peter,** and **Moses** from the Bible, we see instances where they doubted themselves and resisted God's calling. They failed to recognize their true names and potential. If you have experienced similar doubts and questioned your abilities, remember that you are not alone.

Even though Gideon was hiding and filled with fear, God called him a brave and courageous man. God referred to him as a hero, a warrior, and a mighty man of courage, despite no outward evidence of such qualities. God speaks of things that are not as though they already were through faith (Romans 4:17).

Gideon asked God for a sign to confirm that it was truly Him speaking. He requested a fleece (Judges 6:36-40). We have all experienced fear at times and may have asked God for a sign. It's okay to seek a sign from God. He understands that fear can make it challenging to discern His voice, and we desire assurance of His will. Perhaps you are currently struggling with fear or awaiting a sign to move forward. It's possible that the message within this book is the sign you have been waiting for. What is it that God has called you to do? What names have you been answering to?

Gideon, by faith, embraced the names God called him and fulfilled his assignment of delivering the Israelites. You, too, can finish well by answering to your new names and facing your fears, just as Gideon did. You are capable of accomplishing it!

"The devil knows your name, but he calls you by your sins/weaknesses. God knows your sins, but He calls you by name."

God often turns fear to His advantage, using it as an opportunity to showcase His power and bring glory to Himself. In the story of **Gideon**, God instructed him to reduce the size of his army, ensuring that the victory would be credited to God and not human strength. Gideon overcame his fear and fulfilled his purpose by believing in God's calling. Gideon became the mighty man of valor that God called him. It's important to remember that courage is not the absence of fear but the triumph over it. We should not let fear dominate our lives but instead, trust in God's power. Through His kingdom mindset, God empowers ordinary individuals to accomplish extraordinary things. It's not about our abilities but about the greatness of our God. With faith, we can fulfil the calling and purpose that God has placed upon us.

God calls us by our true names, but we must be courageous and obedient enough to respond to them. Our level of self-confidence is not even a factor. Confidence is built through taking action despite fear, repeatedly doing the thing we are scared of. The truth is that successful people aren't necessarily the most confident but rather the most courageous. They take action despite their fears. It's time to gather the courage to do what God is asking of you or what the desires in your heart are leading you towards. "Be strong and courageous" is repeated several times in the bible. Joshua 1:9 "Have I not commanded you? Be strong and courageous. Do not be afraid; do not be discouraged, for the Lord your God will be with you wherever you go."

God is the inventor of the kingdom mindset because He calls us who we are; he sees our potential and talents to become what he planned for us to be from the very beginning. God has a purpose for our lives and a destiny for us to fulfil as we read in *Jeremiah 29:11. "For I know the plans I have for you' declares the Lord, plans to prosper you and not to harm you, plans to give you hope and a future."*

The story of Cephas, also known as Simon Peter, demonstrates the transformative power of names. Jesus called him out of his occupation as a fisherman and gave him a new name - Peter, symbolizing his role as a foundational stone in the Church (Matthew 16:18). Despite his initial impulsive nature and moments of failure, Peter grew into the man and leader that Jesus intended him to be. His journey highlights that personal growth is not always linear and that setbacks can be overcome.

Peter had to learn to believe and act upon Jesus' words, even when they seemed contradictory to the circumstances. In Luke 5, Jesus instructed Peter to let down the nets to catch fish. Initially, Peter objected because they had fished all night without success. Have you ever found yourself protesting when God asks you to do something too? Saying, "Lord, I'm too tired" or "I've already tried that before, and it didn't work."

Peter's obedience to Jesus' words led to a miraculous abundance of fish, highlighting the principle that obedience to God's Word brings abundant provision. Despite any initial doubts or perceived foolishness, Peter acted upon Jesus' instruction and witnessed astonishing results. This story emphasizes the importance of embracing the names and roles God assigns to us. Peter transformed into an unshakable leader, embodying God's mindset, who proceeded to change the world.

God has chosen a unique path for you to follow. Instead of complaining about the journey or protesting like **Peter,** embrace and enjoy the process. Trust that God will guide you to your ultimate destination. Names hold great power. The names we call ourselves and respond to have the ability to shape and transform us. In this book, you will uncover your true names, the names that God has designated for you. Allow God to bring about a name change in your life as well! You and I have the potential to become everything that God declares in His Word.

What is God calling you to be? A loving parent, a compassionate teacher, a successful businessperson, a talented author, an inspiring singer, a skilled doctor, a dedicated scientist, an adventurous astronaut, or even a wise leader? Within you lies the potential to fulfil the calling God has placed upon your life. Embrace your new name and let it extinguish any fear or doubt that may hinder your progress.

Changing people's names is a powerful strategy that God frequently employs in the Bible:
After Jacob wrestled with the angel, God changed his name to Israel (Genesis 32:28 & 35:10). Furthermore, Jacob, following God's example, changed his son's name from Benoni (meaning "son of my trouble/sorrow") to **Benjamin** (meaning "son of my right hand"). Jacob's wife Rachel initially named their son Benoni due to her pain, but Jacob renamed him Benjamin (Genesis 35:18). Jacob imitated what God had done with him by renaming his son, thereby implementing God's successful strategy. As God's children, we are called to imitate Him. It is God's desire that we do not repeat the same mistakes but instead follow His example. The names God gives us are always positive, uplifting, and life-giving.

When we encounter Christ, our old selves die and are buried, and we are reborn as new individuals (2 Corinthians 5:17). **Our Heavenly Father desires to change our names.** While God Himself remains unchanged, we are transformed. Our new names reflect our potential and surpass what has been buried. God wants us to focus on what is being birthed in our lives rather than dwelling on the past. <u>Direct your attention towards your name change,</u> not your previous experiences. What lies ahead of you is greater than what is behind.

God graciously assigns us meaningful names that reflect our true identity in Him (1 Corinthians 2:9 & Isaiah 43: 18-19). We are His cherished children, victorious conquerors, and recipients of power, healing, righteousness, and freedom. While you may not currently feel mighty or powerful, this book aims to expose the enemy's lies and help you embrace your untapped potential. Today can mark a transformative turning point as you let go of past hurts and failures, embracing God's kingdom mindset and fulfilling your divine purpose. Through God's empowering names, you will find encouragement, faith, and the courage to surrender control and let Him work in your life. Answering to our new names aligns us with God's kingdom mindset.

The Bible is not merely a source of motivation or cute quotes. While it is valuable to share Bible verses daily, they hold no significance if we fail to apply them to our lives. God's Word was written for us to live by. It possesses the power to transform, change lives, break curses, refresh souls, and cut through the flesh. Daily reading of the Bible can be a powerful tool for personal growth and spiritual development. [94]

"When you trust God, you don't know the outcome, but you are at peace because you know who has the outcome."
—*Susan Popoola*

As an example, of the power of names, let me share the story of one of my students, Dante Alessandro. In my first year of teaching back in the classroom after being a Special Education teacher, Dante was placed in my class due to his challenging experience in grade one. Children are at different stages developmentally, and not all children are ready for school at 4 or 5 years old. There were concerns that Dante might require early intervention and as a teacher with special education experience and qualifications, I was assigned to work with him.

When I first met **Dante Alessandro**, he appeared to be a kind, well-mannered boy, who had very low self-esteem. Even simple tasks like writing his name would make him cry. He would cry every day and

---

[94] Axisportjeff-#*dailybiblereading*

multiple times throughout the day at school. Although crying on the first day of school is common due to separation anxiety, it usually resolves itself quickly. I tried various strategies to help him, but nothing seemed to work. I felt anxious and frustrated as my efforts were ineffective. I started expressing my frustrations to my colleagues, family, and anyone who would listen. I adopted a mindset of self-pity, constantly thinking, "Woe is me this year." I even began doubting my own teaching abilities. I was trapped in a fixed mindset, losing hope that I could make a difference for Dante Alessandro.

I exhausted every teaching technique in my arsenal and sought advice from my colleagues and support staff. I was relying solely on my own strength and abilities, but still, nothing was yielding positive results. Both Dante and I were growing increasingly frustrated with the situation.

Finally, after a couple of weeks of desperation, I turned to prayer and asked God to help me reach Dante and put an end to his crying. I realized that prayer should have been my initial response, not my last resort. Seeking God's help is adopting His mindset, and I should have gone to Him first. It would have saved both Dante and me from much heartache and frustration.

Upon praying, God prompted me to have a conversation with Dante about his name. While Dante Alessandro already had a meaningful name, inspired by the renowned Italian writer Dante Alighieri, God had a deeper message in mind. I explained to Dante the significance of his last name, Meglio, which means "the best" in Italian. His reaction was one of curiosity and openness. From that moment on, I decided to address him as Meglio, believing in his potential to excel in the class and at school. I also encouraged him to refrain from crying, as the best among us do not shed tears.

Gradually, things began to change. Every time Dante Alessandro started crying, I would remind him of his name and express my belief in him, then offer him a tissue. I would assist him with the task, and he would wipe away his tears and continue. Each time he completed a task with less or no crying, I praised him and reminded him of his new name, saying, "Meglio, you're simply the best! Better than all the rest." "You can do it. I believe in you!" "I'm so proud of you!"

Dante's journey towards self-confidence and growth was fuelled by embracing his new name and the positive reinforcement he received. He took risks, explored new things, and made remarkable progress in his academics. The combination of name change, support, and a growth mindset led to a complete transformation in his life. Dante's continued success and thriving are a testament to the power of names. All credit goes to God, and there is great anticipation for the amazing achievements Dante will accomplish in the future. When God changes our names, it is to build our self-confidence and cause us to grow into the person He created us to be. Names are very powerful. Changing one's name has truly transformative power! God uses this strategy in Scripture many, many times.

Teaching is not just about the curriculum; it's about forming relationships with our students and making them feel valued. Similarly, God's kingdom mindset is about cultivating our relationship with Him and experiencing His empowering presence and love. <u>As seen in the Bible, real people embraced God's new names for them and received His promises.</u> God's mindset includes acknowledging our true names found in the bible. Stop answering to the wrong names.

God sees us according to our real names.

When others saw a barren woman in **Sarah,** God saw the mother of all nations. He changes her name from Sarai to Sarah and her husband's name from Abrim to Abraham when He announces the birth of their son Isaac (Genesis 17). These name changes reveal the Abrahamic covenant through which God not only blessed Abraham and Sarah but all their descendants, which include us!

When others saw a poor young shepherd in **David**, God saw a mighty king of Israel. When they saw a prisoner in **Joseph,** God saw a powerful Minister of Egypt. So, disregard what others perceive in you. Align yourself with what God sees in you and how He addresses you.

<u>Embracing God's kingdom mindset requires courage to break free from old thinking patterns and face the unfamiliar. Although it may bring fear, following God's ways leads to success. By adopting God's mindset, you'll be transformed and respond to your true names—those God calls you in His Word. The enemy's name-calling loses power when you embrace your true identity. God's names hold incredible power, revealing who you are and what you can achieve.</u> **They are visionary and prophetic tools that empower and guide us.** <u>Through His names, God declares our true identity, potential and possessions.</u>

"Fear motivates people to do and say things they'd never do if they weren't scared."
—*Jesse Duplantis*

"When your identity is found in Christ, your identity never changes. You are always a child of God."
—*Tim Tebow*

Fear

Fear is a tactic of the enemy that often obstructs our dreams and God-given assignments. Fear causes us to forget our true identities. It is tormenting. According to the Oxford Dictionary of English, fear is an unpleasant emotion triggered by the threat of danger, pain, or harm. It is the feeling of anxiety regarding the outcome of something or the safety of someone. <u>Before we can walk in what God has for us, we must conquer fear.</u> How do we do that? By confronting it directly. We overcome fear with the Word of God. For instance, when you lose your job, it's natural to feel afraid. Thoughts like these may flood your mind: "How will I pay my bills? What will people think of me? What if I can't find another job? What am I going to do? I'm too old to start over." Counter these thoughts with statements aligned with the Word of God, such as: "When one door closes, God opens a better one(Revelation 3:8). He has a better job for me. He is promoting me. This setback is a setup for something greater. Thank you, Father, for providing me with a new and better job—higher wages, better benefits, more vacation time, and closer to home." <u>Fear says, **"What if,"** but faith says, **"Even if."**</u> Even if I lose my job, I know that God is my provider. His name is Jehovah Jireh, and He will provide a new, better job for me.

<u>Fear not only creates unpleasant emotions but also labels us with negative names that attack our identity.</u> It speaks through destructive thoughts, toxic self-talk, and tormenting names like weak, coward, loser, and more. Fear aims to paralyze us, preventing us from fulfilling God's instructions and returning us to old patterns of thinking. It seeks to bring us back into bondage and undermine our progress(Galatians 5:1). Recognizing fear's tactics is essential to break free from its grip and embrace the mindset God has for us.

Which names have you been answering to?

I struggled for years with paralyzing fear in the form of anxiety and panic attacks, specifically related to checking rituals before leaving my house. The fear of something going wrong or my house burning down consumed me, leading to repeated checks and a sense of impending doom. This fear-controlled routine made it difficult for me to leave the house and caused distressing feelings.

❖ I was consumed by intense fear and anxiety, constantly worried about my house burning down even after reaching my destination. My mind was preoccupied with worst-case scenarios, trapping me in a cycle of rumination. I knew deep down that my fears were irrational, but the anxiety was overpowering. I resorted to extreme measures like calling my neighbor to check if I had unplugged appliances. The fear was tormenting and hindering me from fulfilling my purpose. However, I found freedom by turning to the Word of God and embracing the principles of God's kingdom mindset. I learned that fear is not my ally and discovered biblical truths about fear and anxiety.

- ❖ ***2 Timothy 1:7*** *"God has not given me a spirit of fear but of power, love and a sound mind."*
- ❖ ***Philippians 4:6-7*** *"Do not be anxious about anything, but in everything, by prayer and petition, with thanksgiving, present your requests to God. And the peace of God, which transcends all understanding, will guard your hearts and minds in Christ Jesus."*
- ❖ ***1 Peter 5:7*** *"be anxious for nothing but instead cast all your concerns and fears onto God for He cares for you."*

I copied out these scriptures on pieces of paper and read them out loud to myself over and over again when the fear would grip me. I kept a copy in my purse, in my car, another in the kitchen, another taped to my bathroom mirror. When a panic attack began, my heart would pound, I would begin to sweat, my eyes began to twitch, and I had a queasy feeling in my stomach. The feelings and symptoms were real. The enemy works through our five physical senses. I had to face my fears head-on. I had to recite the word of God out loud over myself while I was experiencing scary symptoms in my body.

"Maybe you're struggling from anxiety too? Do you have trouble breathing? Feel short of breath? Feel queasy? Feel nauseous? Feel dizzy?" **I found out a powerful truth that fear is a name, and it must bow to the name of Jesus** *(Philippians 2:9-10-) Therefore God exalted him(Jesus) to the highest place and gave him the name that is above every name, that at the name of Jesus every knee should bow, in heaven and on earth and under the earth."*

By reading and reciting verses about fear, <u>I realized that I had power.</u> As a child of God, as a citizen of God's kingdom, I have the authority to tell Fear to bow to the name of Jesus and leave me alone. This is exactly what I did.

This is an example of what I would say to myself:
"God has not given me a spirit of fear, but of power, love, and a sound mind. I have a sound mind. I have the mind of Christ. I refuse to fear. Fear, I resist you in Jesus' name. Fear, you must bow to the name of Jesus. I will be anxious for nothing, but instead, I will cast all my concerns and fears onto God, for He cares for me."

As I recited these scriptures, I could feel my body slowly calming down. <u>I also discovered that practices like deep breathing, listening to praise</u>

<u>and worship music, engaging in meditation, expressing gratitude, and praying were helpful to me.</u>

After some time, with the help of the Holy Spirit, I developed a new routine. God assisted me in creating a new positive habit aligned with His Word and more in line with my purpose. It required intentionality and consistency to transform the mental mess I was in. First, I would check that everything was turned off once and affirm out loud, "Stove off, check, I have checked, and everything is turned off." Then, I would recite the above-mentioned scriptures aloud, the ones I stood upon, and finally, I would pray. I would cover my home with the blood of Jesus and commission the mighty angels to guard my home and property, including all my appliances.

Here is the prayer I would say:
"Thank you, Father, for the blood of Jesus Christ. In the name of Jesus, I draw a bloodline around my life, property, and loved ones (say their names). I cover us and our properties (home and all appliances) with the blood of Jesus. I forbid you, Satan, from crossing that bloodline today. According to Matthew 16:19, I have the authority to bind you, so I bind you and all your demonic forces away from my life, health, job, marriage, my home, my family, and property (list anything else). You may not steal, kill, or destroy anything that I have or am. In the name of Jesus, you cannot bring any sickness, accident, or death to me or those from whom I have bound you away. No weapon formed against us will prosper today. In the name of Jesus, I bind your mouth and the mouths of your demons, and I forbid you to speak against us.
I am more than a conqueror through Jesus Christ over you, Satan, and over all of your kingdom. According to James 4:7, when I, as a believer, resist you, you must flee! So, Satan, I resist you, and now you must flee. I bind you away from every situation, and I forbid you to work or move against me.
Angels, I charge you to guard me, my family, and my property in all our ways today, according to Psalms 91 and Psalm 103.
I thank you, Lord Jesus, for the victory. I have all authority and power in Your name. I thank You for it." [95] [96]

After praying, I found the courage to leave my home with less fear. Through the deliberate practice of my new positive habit, I began to

---

[95] Mary Birt-*Victorious Living Ministries*
[96]https://empoweredwordministries.ca/wp-content/uploads/2022/08/No-Weapon-Formed-PDF-compressed.pdf

trust God over my fears. Each time I returned home to find it safe and untouched, my fear lost its validity. Gradually, I realized that my fear was neither valid nor beneficial, and I released it. I learned to rely on God and His angels to protect my home from any harm, including fire, and they have faithfully done so every time. Trusting in God is an assurance that He will never let us down. **Assessing the validity and usefulness of our fears helps us challenge and dismiss them.**

<u>**Remember**</u> <u>is repeated 253 times in Scripture.</u> God wants us to remember all the times He answered our prayers and protected us. This will build our faith and help us challenge our fears.

Renewing my mind with the Word of God was a process that took time and effort. I had to debunk the lies of the enemy that had taken up residence in my brain. It took deliberate, purposeful practice. I had to take those toxic and debilitating thoughts captive. Kylie Oats Gatewood shares how she fought thoughts of suicidal ideation. She would put her hand on her forehead and say the following to herself out loud:

"That's not my thought. I don't think that thought. I think thoughts of life, not death. I plead the blood of Jesus over my mind; I have the mind of Christ."

Eventually, I reached a point where I trusted God and His Word more than my feelings of fear and anxiety. I had fully embraced God's kingdom mindset and believed that I could overcome this fear through Christ, who strengthens me, and I did.

Now, I have complete trust in God. When I leave my house, I simply check that everything is turned off, pray, and go about my day without giving fear a second thought. I know that God has my back. He is faithful and true, and His word always proves to be effective. You can reach this place of freedom, too, by following the strategy listed above. God desires for us to be free from fear and anything else that is holding us back from becoming the person we were destined to be and fulfilling our life assignment.

"Anxiety attacks can come from living in the future. Depression can come from reliving an event in the past. But peace and sanity come from living in the present. Win today, and you will win the future."
—Patrick Bel-David

My battle with anxiety has become a source of strength, teaching me how to overcome my senses and the influence of my feelings. It allowed me to expose the lies planted by the enemy and dismantle them. Now, I have a powerful testimony that can inspire others to break free from their own fears and anxieties. Experiencing freedom is a remarkable feeling—light and unburdened. I never want to return to the bondage of fear that once held me captive, hindering me from fully enjoying life and causing constant worry and dread. The enemy's "What if" thoughts no longer have power over me.

"Sometimes the thing that is holding you back is all in your head."

No matter what fear or anxiety you may be facing today, I want to encourage you to follow the same pattern that I did and set yourself free. God desires your freedom. Freedom comes from God, while fear originates from the enemy (John 8:36). You have a choice to make: fear or freedom? Choose freedom and embrace God's kingdom mindset. Surrender to the process, and don't give up. Your current test can transform into a future testimony. <u>When fear presents its "what if" scenarios, God's mindset responds with "even if."</u> By learning to take toxic thoughts captive and embracing God's kingdom mindset, you are equipping yourself to handle difficult situations and setting yourself up for success.

Even if you lose your job, remember that God is still your provider. He has the ability to make a way even in seemingly impossible situations. Trust in His provision and have faith that He will open up supernatural doors for a new and better job for you (Philippians 4:19).

Even if you left the iron on, have confidence in God as your protector. He commands His angels to guard and safeguard your property from any damage or loss (Psalm 91 and Psalm 103).

Even if you experience the loss of a spouse, know that you are not alone. You may feel lonely, but God is still with you. He promises to be your spouse and never to leave or forsake you (Isaiah 54:5 and Deuteronomy 31:8). Find comfort in the presence and faithfulness of God in your time of grief and loss.

<u>Remember to respond to the enemy's "What if?" questions with an "Even if" statement to challenge fear. **Even better, change the narrative and ask yourself, "What if it turns out better than I could have ever imagined?" Shift your perspective and trust in God's ability to bring about amazing outcomes.**</u>

By embracing the "Even if" mindset and flipping the script on fear, you can overcome its grip and walk confidently in God's promises and plans for your life. Trust in His faithfulness and believe that He is working all things together for your good (Jude 24).

There are 7 fears that can hold people back. Identify which one(s) are affecting you:

1. <u>Fear of Change:</u> This fear can cause us to miss out on opportunities for growth and improvement.
2. <u>Fear of Loneliness:</u> This fear may discourage us from leaving unhealthy relationships, even if they are detrimental to our well-being.
3. <u>Fear of Failure:</u> This fear can prevent us from taking risks and trying new things, hindering our personal and professional development.
4. <u>Fear of Rejection:</u> This fear may prevent us from asking important questions or seeking help, limiting our learning and growth.
5. <u>Fear of Uncertainty:</u> This fear can keep us stuck in our comfort zones, preventing us from embracing new experiences and possibilities. One of the greatest prisons people live in is the fear of what other people think.
6. <u>Fear of Being Judged:</u> This fear can lead us to hide our true selves, wear a mask, or conform to societal expectations, hindering our authenticity.
7. <u>Fear of Losing Freedom:</u> This fear may cause us to avoid making commitments or taking on responsibilities, limiting our potential for growth and deep connections.
   Fears often show up as procrastination, indecisiveness, being pessimistic, complaining, living in the past, avoidance of learning and taking risks, impulsivity, excuses, and envy.[97]

Holy Spirit is the sharpener. We are the pencils. He is shaving away those things that would hinder us from making our mark on this world, such as fear and anxiety, negative self-talk and bad habits.

---

97 Inc.com -*The Top 10 Fears that Hold People Back in Life, according to a Psychotherapist.* Nov 4, 2019, by Amy Morin

"God is the author and editor of the book of our lives. Renewing our minds with the Word of God and adopting His kingdom mindset is submitting to His editing process. When He is finished, we will be His masterpiece. We will be His bestselling book."
—*Natalie Masucci*

It is important for us to effectively manage our fears and anxieties, distinguishing between helpful alerts and chronic worries. Satan aims to keep us trapped in constant stress, preventing us from embracing our true identities in God's Word. He tries to steal the power of God's Word from us, recognizing the significance of names within God's kingdom mindset. However, with the guidance of the Holy Spirit, we can shed our fears and anxieties, allowing God to transform our thought processes and remove toxic thoughts and false identities.

In the song "Hello, My Name Is" by Matthew West, he begins with the line, "Hello, my name is Regret, these are the voices in your head." However, he later turns it around and sings, "Hello, my name is Child of the One True King. I've been saved, changed, and set free. Amazing grace is the song that we sing." Let this become your new mantra! The descriptive feedback from the Holy Spirit will assist us in recognizing the false thoughts and names planted by the enemy.

"There is always something or someone trying to hold you back. Many times the someone is our own feelings of inadequacy and fears of failure."
—*Kylie Oaks Gatewood*

In the Bible are so many scriptures dealing with **anxiety.** God knew that we would encounter anxiety in this life, so He gave us kingdom practices to successfully deal with it. Anxiety is a by-product of fear. If left unchecked, anxiety becomes a hindrance, an obstacle in your life preventing you from moving forward and possessing all that God has for you.

Did you know that Jesus dealt with anxiety while He was on the earth? As a human, Jesus was anxious when the hour of his passion drew near. He told his disciples before he entered the garden, *"My soul is overwhelmed with sorrow to the point of death"* (Matthew 26:38). Once Jesus was by himself, he fell face to the ground and prayed: *"My Father! If it is possible, let this cup of suffering be taken away from me"* (Matthew 26:39) Jesus prayed this prayer not just once but three times. In His despair, Jesus petitioned the Father to see if there might be another way. But He finished His prayer with a declaration that had been true His entire life. He surrendered Himself to His Father: "Yet I want Your will to be done, not mine."

This "yes" was the climax of Jesus' life purpose.

In the Garden of Gethsemane, it is said that Jesus sweat drops of blood due to the intensity of His anxiety. He experienced the physical symptoms of anxiety in the form of sweating blood, a condition known as Hematidrosis. This occurs when an individual is under extreme levels of stress. Jesus had a choice, just as we have a choice. He could have saved Himself, but then He couldn't have saved you and me. Jesus never allowed fear or anxiety to hinder Him from fulfilling His purpose, and we shouldn't allow it to hinder us, either. Jesus chose God's will over His own. He chose the nails because He couldn't imagine eternity without you.

Throughout His life, Jesus continually sought direction from the Father through prayer and found the power to live according to the Father's will through the Holy Spirit. He said "yes" to God every day of His earthly life, even when He was anxious and scared, and we can do the same.

If we allow fear and anxiety to cause us to compromise our destiny, we will experience a life far below God's best for us. Succumbing to fear puts us in God's permissive will, which is not what God wants for us. Choosing not to change and grow will keep us trapped in a fixed mindset and prevent us from experiencing the abundant life God has for us. However, we can break free from the destructive thoughts of fear and anxiety that hold us back. We can rely on the power of the Holy Spirit, just as Jesus did.

We need to stay challenged to learn more and continue growing in grace to be more effective for the kingdom (2 Peter 3:18). Adopting God's kingdom mindset will enable us to live life in His divine will. I want to experience all that God has for me. How about you? I desire to live in God's divine will, so I will adopt His kingdom mindset, face my fears and anxieties, and say yes to the Father.

Wisdom is recognizing that life is short, and we must adopt God's kingdom mindset and remain focused on fulfilling our assignments. **The wisdom of God goes beyond common sense; it acknowledges that there are principles and laws that operate in the kingdom. When we align ourselves with these principles, we experience success and victory in every area of our lives.**

However, there is a price to be paid. This is not just a theory; it is the truth from the Word of God. To operate in God's kingdom mindset, we need to be rooted in His Word, the Bible. Being rooted means being firmly established and unshakable, like a mature tree with deep roots (Psalm 1:3). The Word of God must have authority over every thought, fear, anxiety, and situation in our lives. **God's Word possesses prevailing power**. <u>Meditating on God's Word is like equipping ourselves with powerful ammunition.</u> The Word must prove more potent than any circumstance we face. It is God's mindset, and it must prevail over everything: troubles, temptations, sickness, toxic thoughts, perceptions, assumptions, failures, setbacks, mistakes, fears, and anxiety.

We do have a spiritual enemy who desperately wants to distract, dissuade, and discourage us. However, we are responsible for our actions. The devil cannot force us to do things; he can only try to convince us. We still have the power of choice. No one falls into temptation; it is a decision we make. While we will make mistakes, it is essential that we accept accountability for them. The good news is that God doesn't expect us to be perfect or to do it alone.

"The Bible is a book that reveals the mind of God, the state of man, the way of salvation, the doom of sinners, and the happiness of believers. It's doctrines are holy, it's precepts binding, it's histories true, and it's decisions immutable. Read it to be wise, believe it to be saved, and practice it to be holy. "

—Anonymous

God's power resides in His Word. Scripture tells us that Jesus is the Word of God (John 1:1). Our power, authority, success principles, and kingdom mindset come from our faith in His Word, the Bible. Jesus has given us the authority to speak His Word in His name because of His shed blood. It is necessary to be willing to face resistance, such as tests, mistakes, failures, and fears, for the sake of our purpose. Will you quit? Will you back down? Will you let fear rule your life? No, I believe that you won't. I believe that you will adopt God's kingdom mindset and learn to step out in faith, even when afraid, knowing that God has your back. This choice and action will debunk the lies of the enemy in your life. In scientific terms, you are bringing your fears and anxieties into conscious awareness and utilizing neuroplasticity to your advantage. **<u>Neuroplasticity</u>** refers to the brain's ability to form and reorganize synaptic connections in response to learning, experience, or injury. <u>God's kingdom mindset empowers you to fight giants, starting in your mind and then in every other area of your life.</u>

The adult brain is much more changeable and modifiable than previously understood. There is now a significant amount of evidence showing that damaged neural brain circuitry resulting from adverse childhood experiences and trauma can be corrected, reshaping our brain anatomy and influencing our behaviours through appropriate therapeutic interventions. This is incredible news! <u>We now know that the structure of our brain continues to change throughout adulthood, and these changes can be directed towards highly beneficial outcomes.</u> Neuroplasticity has been proven to facilitate recovery from stroke, injuries, improve symptoms of autism, ADD and ADHD, learning disabilities, brain deficits, alleviate depression and addictions, and reverse obsessive-compulsive patterns.[98]

Indeed, the intersection of God's kingdom strategy and modern science is a fascinating area of exploration. When we confront our fears and step out in faith, despite feeling afraid, we activate a powerful process that aligns with the principles of <u>neuroplasticity</u>.

Neuroplasticity refers to the brain's remarkable ability to reorganize itself and form new neural connections throughout our lives. <u>It has been scientifically observed that when we intentionally challenge the validity and usefulness of our fears, we can initiate positive changes in the structure and function of our brains.</u>

By bringing our fears into conscious awareness and subjecting them to the truth of God's Word, we engage in a transformative process. The truths found in Scripture have the power to reshape our thought patterns and reorganize synaptic connections in our brains. This process leads to the reduction of fear and anxiety structures while simultaneously fostering the development of new, healthier structures, such as faith and confidence.

As we consistently apply God's truth to challenge our fears, we can experience a gradual shift in our behaviour and mindset. The power of God's Word combined with the brain's inherent plasticity enables us to overcome fear and anxiety, allowing us to live with greater freedom, courage, and faith.

It's remarkable to see how scientific findings align with the timeless wisdom found in the Bible. By embracing God's kingdom strategy to combat fear and leveraging the potential of neuroplasticity, we can embark on a transformative journey that leads to greater emotional well-being and a stronger faith in God's provision and guidance.

> **"God's Word is like power bullets that search out and destroy toxic thoughts in our minds."**
>
> **—*Natalie Masucci***

---

[98] Robertson, Ian. *"A Neuroplasticity Approach in the Treatment of Substance Abuse and Mental Health."* Laurier University, 2023.

Those power bullets attack and destroy toxic thoughts, such as fears and anxieties, in our brains. The Word of God is often referred to as the sword of the Spirit, capable of cutting off and breaking the power of negative influences in our minds (Hebrews 4:12).

"God says, if you have the faith to keep moving, I have the power to keep blessing."

—Pastor John Gray

Here are some of my favourite scriptures on anxiety:

- ❖ ***Matthew 6:25 AMP*** *is referred to as the cure for anxiety. "Therefore I tell you, <u>stop being worried or anxious (perpetually uneasy, distracted)</u> about your life, as to what you will eat or what you will drink, nor about your body, as to what you will wear. Is life not more than food and the body more than clothing?"*
- ❖ ***Psalm 37:7-*** *Be still before the Lord and wait patiently for him; <u>do not fret</u> when people succeed in their ways when they carry out their wicked schemes.*
- ❖ ***2 Corinthians 4:8-9-*** *We are hard pressed on every side, but not crushed; perplexed but not in despair, persecuted, but not abandoned; struck down but not destroyed.*
- ❖ ***Philippians 4:6-*** *<u>Do not be anxious about anything,</u> but in every situation, by prayer and petition with thanksgiving, present your requests to God.*

"The pain of uncertainty is temporary. The pain of staying stagnant is permanent."

—Dr. Caroline Leaf

Strategies to Managing Fear and Anxiety:

1. One strategy that I have found effective in managing anxiety is deliberately changing my focus. <u>Instead of dwelling on my weaknesses or fears, I choose to focus on God. I intentionally shift my attention to the greatness of God rather than the magnitude of the problem.</u> I meditate on how awesome God is and reflect on all that He has done for me. I strengthen my faith by recalling the prayers He has answered in the past and how He has consistently guided me through every situation. I constantly remind myself that God is faithful (1 Corinthians 10:13). This empowers me to overcome the anxieties that would otherwise paralyze me. **By keeping my mind fixed on God, I eliminate fear because fear**

cannot reside in a mind focused on Him. When we keep our eyes on God, there is no reason to fear anything because our strength and talents come from Him. <u>God assures us in His Word that He will fight on our behalf, and our role as believers is simply to believe ((Exodus14:14).</u> Embracing a kingdom mindset means wholeheartedly trusting in the truth of God's Word.

"The presence of anxiety is unavoidable, but the prison of anxiety is optional."

—Max Lucado

When the enemy comes with his lies, deceptions, distractions, anxieties, and temptations, we can learn to respond with a resounding "No, devil, not today!" We can refuse to engage in his tactics and declare that his days of tormenting us are over. Instead of submitting to fear, we choose to overcome it with faith. The key to doing this is by shifting our focus. We redirect our attention from our own abilities to God's abilities. We purposefully adopt His mindset and begin to see things from His perspective. Psalm 1:1 provides us with a strategy for success - meditating on the Word of God.

As we engage in this practice, our trust in God grows. <u>Through meditation on His Word, we surrender our fears to Him and decide to place our complete reliance on Him.</u> In John 8:30, Jesus says, *"If you abide/remain in My word, you are My disciples indeed. And you shall know the truth, and the truth shall make you free."* Those of us who consistently meditate on the Word of God will come to know the truth and experience freedom. Like any ongoing activity or deliberate practice, meditating on the Word requires continuous focus and commitment. It's not a one-time event. To truly focus on something, we need to keep looking at it. One-time reflection on a scripture won't make all our fears and anxieties disappear. <u>"Meditate" and "remain" are words that imply a prolonged and intentional mental focus.</u>

The Bible assures us that the truth will set us free. Embracing the truth of God's Word frees us from fear and empowers us to stand on His promises in faith. When our minds are fixed on God, He keeps us in perfect peace (Isaiah 26:3) and grants us a peace that surpasses human understanding (Philippians 4:7). We cannot be in a state of perfect peace and fear simultaneously. We must choose to believe what the Word of God says over what our senses, emotions, and circumstances may be telling us. No matter what is happening in our lives, God's Word remains true. The facts may be unfavourable, but God's favour is greater (Psalm 90:17). The Bible should be our standard of truth. We are called to measure everything against what the Bible says (1 Corinthians 11:1).

That is God's desire for us, to adopt His mindset. In the chaos and changes of life, God's Word becomes our constant anchor. I encourage you to anchor yourself to God's Word. It will keep you steady and unwavering during times of uncertainty and testing.

2. <u>You can develop a new, healthy habit to manage your anxiety and fears.</u> It is commonly believed that it takes 21 days to form a new habit, but this notion is actually incorrect. According to Dr. C. Leaf, it takes 21 days to build a long-term memory, but it requires 63 days to establish a habit and develop a new neural network to support it. Instead of succumbing to the enemy's anxiety spiral, God wants us to develop healthy habits instead. These habits will keep you healthy, strong, and well-equipped to fulfil your purpose. When you start experiencing symptoms of anxiety or fear, try engaging in activities such as going for a walk, exercising, deep breathing, singing along to praise and worship music, or praying. These practices can help alleviate anxiety.

    Examples of healthy habits to counter anxiety:

    a) Try <u>deep breathing.</u> "Breath" in the Bible also means "spirit'. As we breathe deeply and slowly, we remind ourselves that Holy Spirit is within us.

    b) <u>Meditate</u> or Pray for Peace. Use Psalm 94:18-19, John 14:25-27 & Philippians 4:4-7.

    c) <u>Listen to music.</u> Music can change your mood. In Ephesians, 5:18-20 Paul tells us to speak to one another in psalms, hymns and spiritual songs.

    d) <u>Recognize the source.</u> The enemy is the one making you anxious Ephesians 6:12. Therefore, resist anxious thoughts because they are not from God.

    e) <u>Practice Gratitude.</u> Write down three things you are thankful for. As you do this, it will change your outlook. Psalm 103:2-3

    f) <u>Think about Jesus.</u> Jesus felt fear and anxiety; therefore, he can empathize with us and help us (Hebrews 4:15).

    g) <u>Think about eternal life and heaven.</u> Paul tells us to set our minds on things above (Colossians 3:2). This helps us to shift our focus and alleviates our anxiety.

    h) <u>Go for a walk or exercise.</u> This releases feel-good endorphins and chemicals that can enhance your sense of well-being (1 Timothy 4:8).[99]

[99] Odhner, John, Rev. "Ten ways to beat anxiety during difficult times." newchurch.org, New Church, n.d. URL. Accessed 13 June 2023.

Sometimes it can be challenging to maintain a new habit for 63 consecutive days. To assist you on your journey towards healthier habits, here are some tips:

First, <u>find an accountability partner</u> who can check in on you and provide encouragement to persevere. Join a support group.

Second, <u>set reminders</u> on your phone or place sticky notes in visible areas to prompt you to recite your faith declarations. These declarations will strengthen your faith in your ability to overcome. "I can do all things through Christ who strengthens me! "(Philippians 4:13)

Third, <u>practice self-compassion</u>. If you make a mistake or experience setbacks, it's okay! Just pick yourself up and continue moving forward. Remember that God is on your side, not against you, and He will support you. "The Lord Himself will fight for me" (Exodus 14:14). You are well on your way to successfully managing your anxiety.[100]

The Other Serenity Prayer

"God, grant me the serenity to stop beating myself up for not doing things perfectly, the courage to forgive myself because I'm working on doing better, and the wisdom to know that you already love me just the way I am."

Adopting God's kingdom mindset involves replacing bad habits with good habits. It means exchanging toxic thinking with positive thinking that promotes optimal brain function. Research indicates that it takes a minimum of 63 days to develop the neural networks or habits that currently keep us trapped in fear and mental anguish. Therefore, it's important to be patient with ourselves as we undertake the work and time required to rewire our brains in a healthy direction. Change is a process that takes time, but how many of us are truly willing to invest the necessary time and effort? Unfortunately, many people give up after just a few days. However, God desires us to cultivate perseverance and provides success strategies within His kingdom mindset to keep us motivated.

3. <u>Focus on one day at a time.</u> Address one problem at a time. Fear often tempts us to view all of our problems simultaneously: those from yesterday, today, and tomorrow. Fear seeks to overwhelm us. John Maxwell wisely advises, "You only have to focus on today's problems because that's the only thing you have any control over." In the Scriptures, Jesus reminds us that each day has enough

---

[100] Dr. C. Leaf

trouble of its own, so we should not worry about tomorrow, as it will take care of itself (Matthew 6:34).

Individuals with a God's kingdom mindset learn to concentrate on one day at a time, preventing themselves from being overwhelmed. They confront their fears and continue moving forward, trusting in the effectiveness of God's kingdom mindset.

Shift your focus to how far you have come rather than how far you still have to go. Celebrate your victories rather than dwelling on your battles.

"One of our biggest misconceptions is that courage equals a lack of fear. In actuality, the opposite is true. By admitting our fear, we can then challenge its accuracy."

—John Maxwell

"Faith is a lifestyle, not a formula."

—Marilyn Hickey

Chapter Five

Be Careful <u>How</u> you Hear and <u>What</u> you Hear

The tradition of anointing with oil dates back thousands of years, originating with shepherds who would daily anoint their sheep's heads with oil to protect them from bugs that could enter their ears and cause harm. In Psalm 23:5, it is mentioned that God, the Good Shepherd, anoints our heads with oil. This carries great significance as our head is the most vital part of our body, housing our mind, brain, eyes, ears, nose, and mouth. Our head is also where our offensive weapons are located. The battle against the enemy takes place in our minds as he attacks us with harmful thoughts. God desires us to be aware of our thoughts so that we can resist those that do not align with His will. Our mindset, which is crucial, is also found in our heads. Therefore, we must learn to anoint our heads daily with God's Word to safeguard ourselves from the enemy's lies that seek to destroy us. <u>Our head contains entry points that require constant guarding and protection.</u>

Satan tempts us through various entry gates, including our eyes, ears, mouth, mind, spirit, flesh, and emotions. Most of these gates are located in our heads. This is why the symbolism of anointing our heads with the oil of the Holy Spirit is incredibly powerful. God's oil serves as a shield and protection against the lies and deceptions of the enemy.

EYES: Sight is an essential aspect emphasized in the Bible. According to Matthew 6:19-24, our eyes are compared to lamps that provide light for our bodies. Therefore, it is crucial to monitor what we see. When our eyes focus on positive and pure things, as instructed in the Word, our entire being becomes healthy and filled with light (Philippians 4:8).

The ability to see by faith is vital for God to work in our lives. Through meditating on God's Word, we develop the capacity to see beyond what the world perceives. We begin to see through the eyes of faith, gaining insight into the spiritual realm. Even before our prayers and dreams come to fruition, we can envision their fulfilment. Faith possesses both sight and speech—it sees and speaks.

When God promised Abraham the land, He told him that it would extend as far as his eyes could see (Genesis 13:15). <u>The extent of your vision determines your promised land</u>. Your success and blessings in life hinge on your spiritual sight. Do you see yourself as a failure or a success? How you perceive yourself impacts the outcome. If you see yourself as a success, your potential expands and improves.

God has bestowed upon each of us the gift of <u>imagination</u>, enabling us to venture into our future. Maintain a positive mindset and allow yourself to dream of a better life. God wants us to dream big and remove all limits. His Word affirms that if we can envision it, we can obtain it. Allow your <u>imagination</u> to paint the best future for yourself. What do you see through the eyes of faith and God's kingdom mindset? Is it starting a business, purchasing a new house or car, achieving academic qualifications, starting a family, pursuing creative endeavours, or attaining significant milestones? Envisioning your future with hope and expectation, guided by God's kingdom mindset, is essential. If you can see it, it will manifest in your life. This is the power of biblical vision (Proverbs 23:7).

<u>Vision boards for believers are what the world considers annual learning plans, which contain our yearly short-term goals as well as our long-term goals. Vision is very important to God. Proverbs 29:18 states that where there is no vision, the people perish.</u>

This practice is not synonymous with the manifestation concept found in the New Age movement. We are not merely indulging in positive thinking and hoping that our desires magically materialize. <u>Instead, we are utilizing our God-given imagination to envision the future that God intends for us—aligning our vision with His purpose and plan for our lives.</u> By partnering with God, we work towards creating the successful and abundant life that Jesus died to provide us.

If you envision yourself failing in school, losing your job, falling off the wagon, or ruining relationships, you are perceiving yourself as a failure and adopting the wrong mindset. Dr. Dharius Daniels introduces <u>the Principle of Perspective,</u> which states that where you are positioned determines what you see, and what you see influences your actions. According to the Bible, we are seated in heavenly places (Ephesians 2:6-9), safely positioned above all the tactics of the enemy. Can you visualize yourself seated with Jesus? Can you imagine yourself reigning over your problems and fears? Our eyes possess great power. Vision holds tremendous significance. <u>Through our eyes of faith, we perceive future possibilities, the realization of our prayers, and the fulfilment of our purpose.</u> (Proverbs 23:7)

In Joshua 1:3 God says, *"I will give you every place where you set your foot as I promised".* In **Deuteronomy 11:24** God says *"every place where you set your foot will be yours."* God desires to enlarge our territory, but He requires us to grasp the vision for it beforehand. He is about to expand the boundaries of our influence. God wants you to enter into your promised land, your place of blessing, with His kingdom mindset. His intention is for us to utilize our vision to exercise authority and make an impact within our continually expanding sphere of influence.

"Faith is to believe what we do not see, and the reward of this faith is to see what we believe."

—Augustine

The Bible says in ***Job 42:5,*** *"says my ears had heard of you, but now my eyes have seen you."* Job received a divine revelation from God. He had the privilege of encountering God's faithfulness in more magnificent and impactful ways than ever before. It is one thing to hear about God, but it is another to truly see Him. Seeing God involves recognizing His goodness and comprehending His mindset and the way He works. Can you envision God's presence in your future? Can you see yourself fulfilling your life's purpose? It is important to have a clear vision of it before you can attain it.

"Where you can't see, you can't go. What you can't see, God can't deliver."

—Bill Winston

Biblical vision is spiritual eyesight which is not dependent on circumstances.

Having biblical vision sounds like:

- ❖ "I can't see it in the natural, but I know it. God is working behind the scenes."
- ❖ "I didn't see that coming." "I see it now!"
- ❖ "I will own my own home!"
- ❖ "I am a New York Times Best-selling author!"

With our eyes, we have the ability to read the Bible, surf the internet, engage in gaming, or view pornography. It is often said that the journey of a lifetime begins with the turning of a page. <u>Reading is a powerful activity that we do with our eyes.</u> When we read the Bible, which is God's success criteria, we are immersing ourselves in the teachings of Jesus, who is the Word of God. The Bible, God's Word, serves as spiritual nourishment, providing us with answers and everything we need to succeed in life. It is like spiritual bread that sustains us (1 Peter 2:2 & 1 Corinthians 3:2).

Ears/Hearing

Our ears play a significant role as one of the entry gates through which we receive information. Positioned on both sides of our heads, our ears are not coincidentally given in pairs, unlike our mouths. This is because we are meant to listen more than we speak (James 1:19).

The metaphor of oil represents the Holy Spirit. It is only through the anointing or presence of the Holy Spirit in our lives that we can be protected from the lies and deceptions of the enemy, whose intentions are to steal, kill, and destroy (John 10:10). <u>The Holy Spirit's voice, conveyed through descriptive feedback, positive self-talk, and our inner cheerleader, helps us tune out the enemy's thoughts and lies.</u>

In our success manual, the Bible, we are cautioned to be mindful of what we listen to, as it profoundly affects our mindset. *Mark 4:24 "Consider carefully what you hear,"* and we are further instructed to be cautious about whom we listen to. Our ears are receptive to various voices, including our inner critic and inner cheerleader. It is important to be discerning about what we choose to listen to because what we consistently hear, we eventually believe.

The sounds going into our ears become words going through our brains.[101]

Who have you been listening to? Are they encouraging you or pulling you down?

Sound includes the entire world of vibrations, including our thoughts. <u>Our thoughts are audible to us, and they can, directly and indirectly, impact our cellular health.</u> When we embrace this responsibility and start thinking about our thinking, we will experience true transformation, breaking negative patterns in our minds through new neurochemical links and taking back control of our health.[102]

Our time is our most valuable asset. Our **time** is our treasure. The amount of time we have is the same for everyone. There are 24 hours in a day. **What we do with our time is what sets us apart.** In **Matthew 6:21** it says *"For where your treasure is, there will your heart be also. KJV"* If we treasure God's kingdom mindset, then we will spend the majority of our time in His Word-Reading, meditating, listening, reciting aloud, praying, decreeing, and declaring.

❖ Time is your life, if you are wasting your time, then you're wasting your life.

---

[101] *University of Maryland,* Nov. 29,2018

[102] Dr. Kulreet Chaudhary-*Cleaning up the Mental Mess* with Dr. C. Leaf-Instagram post

- ❖ What do you spend most of your time doing? <u>Watching</u>? Reading?
- ❖ What do you spend most of your time <u>thinking</u> about?
- ❖ What/Who do you spend most of your time <u>listening to</u>?
- ❖ The answers to these questions are indicators of your future success.
- ❖ The answers will show which <u>entry gates</u> in your life have been compromised. Once you recognize a breach, then you can shore it up. You may need to make some adjustments.

"Be very careful, then, how you live-not as unwise but as wise, making the most of every opportunity because the days are evil. Therefore, do not be foolish, but understand what the Lord's will is." **Ephesians 5:15-17**

"It is said that the secret to your success can be found in your daily routines. Take an inventory of how you have been spending your time."
—*Terri Savelle Foy*

God is not affected by time or space. Those with God's kingdom mindset understand that the greatest gift we can give to God is our time. We are only on this earth for a short time, and during that time, we have a purpose to fulfil. The good news is that God is able to redeem our time when we follow His purpose for our lives (Ephesians 5:16).

***

Parents and Guardians have a crucial role as the gatekeepers of their homes. They are responsible for protecting their children from the schemes of the enemy and raising them to know the Lord and His ways. This is accomplished through the exercise of their authority. God has granted us the right and privilege to pray for those within our personal spheres of influence, especially our families (Acts 16:31). We are called to pray for the protection of all the entry gates in our children's lives, shielding them from the enemy's deception. <u>It is important to recognize that both God and the enemy can enter our lives through the same gates.</u> Therefore, we must diligently guard what enters through our own entry gates as well as those of our children. This requires being mindful of what we regularly expose ourselves to. The entry gates include our eyes, ears, mouth, mind, spirit, flesh, and emotions, with the majority of them located in our heads. Hence, the symbolic act of anointing our heads with the oil of the Holy Spirit holds great significance. The Holy Spirit within us will assist in identifying any vulnerable entry points that need to be secured.

Proverbs 4:20-22- *My son, give attention to my words; <u>incline your ear to my sayings.</u> Do not let them <u>depart from your eyes;</u> keep them in the midst of your heart; for they are life to those who find them and health to all their flesh.*

With our ears, we have the capacity to listen to various things, such as music, news, negativity, gossip, complaints, and lies. On the other hand, we can also choose to listen to sermons, songs of worship, compliments, and positive affirmations.

- ✓ With our mouths, we have the power to speak words of either faith or fear.
- ✓ With our minds, we entertain thoughts, which can be both truths and deceptions.
- ✓ With our spirits, we can have faith or experience doubt and unbelief.
- ✓ With our flesh, we navigate issues related to our sexuality and our physical needs and desires, which may manifest as temptations and distractions.

With our **emotions,** we create our attitudes. We need to monitor our children's attitudes to ensure that they respect us. An example of an emotion is anger. In *Ephesians 4:26-27 it says to be angry but not sin. "Do not let the sun set upon your anger."* Take control over your anger; don't stew on it and go to bed with it." <u>If we remain in anger, it can lead to unforgiveness and bitterness, and it opens the door to slander, which can destroy our marriages, friendships, careers, and lives.</u> (Psalm 37:8 & Ephesians 4:26, 31) We must manage the gates in our lives with God's kingdom mindset and the authority He has given us (Matthew 16:18-19 - keys of the kingdom). Use your words in prayer to bind up the devil and tell him to stop assaulting you and your family through your ear entry gates. The gates we open in our lives determine who we are. Our future and success are determined by what we allow to enter through our gates. God wants us to feast on His powerful word through our entry gates. **God's word is supernatural in origin, eternal in duration, and inexpressible in value. It is infinite in scope, regenerative in power, infallible in authority, universal in interest, personal in application, and inspired in totality. Read it, listen to it, write it down, pray with it, and pass it on.** Therefore it is never too late with God. You can decide to change your life today. You have the power. You decide what you will spend your time on (Ephesians 5:14, 16-17).

<u>Parents and Guardians have a crucial role in modeling appropriate behaviour for their children.</u> For instance, they can demonstrate the importance of apologizing and letting go of anger. They can show their

children how to limit the consumption of news and excessive television content. They can also set an example by praying and being mindful of their screen time. Embracing God's kingdom mindset helps us manage the entry gates in our lives by being intentional about what we expose ourselves to. We are advised to restrict negative influences and instead feast on the positive and powerful word of God.

It all boils down to fixing our eyes on Jesus—looking at Him, reading about Him, and listening to Him. As we focus on Him, we experience a transformation, becoming more like Him each day (2 Corinthians 3:18 & Romans 8:29). Let's not overlook this powerful promise, my friend. Tuning our entry gates to Jesus results in Him bringing life and health to us. <u>There is a direct link between centring our attention on Jesus through every entry gate and our physical and mental well-being.</u> The blessing is inherent— the more we focus on Jesus (the Word of God), the happier, healthier, and stronger we become. His resurrection, life, and power infuse our mortal bodies, and His word empowers us (Proverbs 4:20-22).

Friends/Inner Circle

"Dimmi con chi vai e ti dico chi sei"
—*Maria Stefanutti*

This is a common saying, who you hang with determines who you are. My Mom, Maria, used to tell us kids to choose our friends wisely. This is scriptural because *1 Corinthians 15:33 says "Bad company corrupts us by corrupting our character."* Jesus recognized the impact that close friends and acquaintances can have on our success and mindset, which is why He was deliberate in choosing His inner circle. It is essential for us to be intentional about our own inner circle or close friends as well.

"Jesus loved everyone, spent time with everyone, including sinners, but He was very selective of his inner circle of 12 disciples. Interestingly, Jesus spent most of his time with only three of them; Peter, James and John. We need to learn from Jesus to spend time with people who encourage us and inspire us to grow. We need to be intentional and spend most of our time with people who encourage us towards our God-inspired goals. We should spend the most <u>time</u> with people with a growth mindset who we want to emulate."
—*Terri Savelle Foy*

In **Proverbs 13:20** *it says "If you walk with the wise you become wise, but a companion of fools suffers harm."* Scripture also states in **Proverbs 27:17** *that "as iron sharpens iron, so one person sharpens another."* We should consistently encourage, inspire, coach, and challenge each other in positive ways to elevate ourselves. God always encourages us to become the best versions of ourselves. The company we keep has a significant impact on our mindset. The people we spend most of our time with strongly influence our thoughts, beliefs, and behaviours. They can either uplift and propel us forward or hinder and destroy us. What we receive influences what we give. It might be time to reassess the relationships in your life and make some changes. <u>If someone has a negative impact on your life and you recognize it but choose to remain in that relationship, it may become your biggest regret.</u> God is warning you through this book. Do not allow someone to pull you away from God's will for your life by causing you to compromise and adopt a fixed mindset. No one is worth that. Decide today that negative and toxic individuals will not bring you down or distract you. Your mission is too important for that. God calls us to be wise and choose godly and encouraging friends. Select carefully who you allow to speak into your life. Surround yourself with people who fight for you even in your absence. In life, you will have many acquaintances but only a few true friends. <u>One's inner circle should be small, just as Jesus' was.</u>

"People who write you off when you fail know nothing about history and even less about life. No person ever fully succeeds until they fully fail."

—*Lance Wallnau*

Jesus didn't choose the most qualified or the smartest individuals to be His disciples; instead, He selected those who embodied a growth mindset with a passion for learning and the ability to overcome obstacles.[103] Similarly, God wants us to choose friends who possess a growth mindset. Don't settle for a fixed mindset. God has so much more in store for you.

Ask God to bring new godly friends into your life.

God doesn't play favourites (1 John 4:8). He wants to use all of us. He desires for each of us to experience success and victory in life. All we need to do is show Him our willingness, availability, and obedience. God employs ordinary people like you and me to accomplish extraordinary things. Allow the Holy Spirit to cultivate the seeds of greatness that God

---

[103] *Dweck*-p.141

has placed within you. Develop a kingdom mindset aligned with God's will. <u>Learn to see successful people as sources of inspiration, not competition.</u> Act. Be optimistic. Live in the present. Focus on the positive. Be a life-long learner. See obstacles as opportunities. Set long-term goals. Do not let failure define you or derail you. Be disciplined and focused on your goals and dreams. Put forth effort and perseverance towards renewing your mind and becoming the person God created you to be. Rely on God.

"Get around people who bring out the best in you, not the stress in you!"

—Paula Michelle White

Love

<u>An integral aspect of having a kingdom mindset is understanding God's profound love for us</u>. God's love possesses transformative power and empowers us. Through the guidance of the Holy Spirit, I have gained a unique interpretation of God's love that I would like to share. God desires us to perceive His love for us from a fresh perspective, with a renewed mindset. He wants us to comprehend the immense extent of His love and allow it to empower us in remarkable ways.

God's love for us is characterized by agape love. Agape love is the highest form of love, devoid of any sexual implications. It is a sacrificial love that wholeheartedly seeks the well-being of another, as exemplified in John 15:13, which states, "Greater love has no one than this: to lay down one's life for one's friends."

Agape love, also known as the God-kind of love, is unconditional. It surpasses human love, even the profound love of a mother for her child, remarkable as that may be. Agape love is a deliberate choice that requires commitment and sacrifice without expecting anything in return. It necessitates action. God demonstrated His agape love by sending Jesus to die for us while we were still sinners (John 3:16). An excellent description of agape love can be found in 1 Corinthians 13:4-13. I encourage you to read and meditate on it. God is willing to do anything and everything for us because of His agape love.

Agape love is referenced over 200 times in the Bible and is the most prominent type of love depicted within its pages.

The Bible says that "God is love" 1 John 4:7-21)

To truly understand love, we must acquaint ourselves with Jesus and His character, for He personifies love. <u>Every action Jesus undertook during His earthly ministry was driven by love.</u> His current role as our mediator of a better covenant is also motivated by love. And when He

217

returns, His actions will be motivated by love. **If Jesus is our example, then love must be the driving force behind everything we do in order to embrace God's kingdom mindset.**

Jesus desires us to perceive Him as our imminent Bridegroom. He invites us to accept His marriage proposal. As we read the Bible, we discover it as a magnificent love story that unfolds the courtship between Jesus and His Bride, the Church (which includes us). Jesus beckons us to make a commitment to Him, to embrace His way of doing things, His kingdom mindset, and His plan for our lives.

Jesus is our lover and Bridegroom. In Proverbs 18:22, a good wife is regarded as a prized blessing for her husband. Similarly, the Church is referred to as the Bride of Christ, and Jesus is our soon-coming Bridegroom. We are the Bride of Christ, His cherished prize. I want you to grasp the significance of this revelation: we are Jesus' prize. A prize is something eagerly sought after, and everyone desires to win a prize. Jesus eagerly awaits us. He yearns for us. We are His prize, His reward for sacrificing Himself on the cross. The entire world longs for our wedding day. All of creation eagerly awaits the manifestation of the sons of God and the joyous occasion of the marriage supper of the Lamb (Romans 8:19-22-23).

Jesus is the spotless Lamb of God, and we are the bride without spot or wrinkle. (Ephesians 5:27).

In order to become our Bridegroom, Jesus had to go to the cross and then rise again.

To become the Bride, we must undergo a transformative process. It entails changing our mindset, persevering through life's challenges, and fulfilling our life assignment. Embracing God's kingdom mindset is the path that leads us to the grand marriage ceremony, but it requires effort, perseverance, and resilience.

When we compare a girlfriend, a fiancée, and a bride, we see similarities in their love for the person. However, only the bride has made a public declaration to forsake all others and commit to a lifelong union. Similarly, Jesus tells us that if we boldly confess Him before others, He will acknowledge us before His Father (Matthew 10:32). Jesus openly declared His love for us through His death, and now He invites us to reciprocate by publicly declaring our love for Him.

Jesus made the ultimate sacrifice for us in a public manner. Let us not confine our devotion to Him within the confines of privacy. Live boldly and unashamedly for Him, declaring His love and lordship before the world.

The Bible is a magnificent love story. From beginning to end, God reveals and demonstrates His profound love for us. Out of His abundance of love, God created mankind to form a family. The Bible narrates the captivating tale of Jesus' love affair with us. Even before our existence, Jesus did everything for us, ultimately sacrificing His life. He willingly left the splendors of heaven and humbled Himself to become human. As a man, He endured a brutal death on the cross to atone for our sins, enabling our reconciliation with Him. Jesus desired nothing to come between us—no sin, no law, no enemy. His purpose was to protect us from Satan's destructive plans and reclaim us as His own (John 3:16 & John 10:10).

Jesus yearns for us with the intensity of a lover longing for their beloved (Song of Solomon). Just as a bridegroom eagerly awaits his bride, Jesus longs for our intimate connection. We are created in the image and likeness of God, designed to experience pleasure through intimacy. There is no comparable feeling to being embraced by one's beloved—feeling accepted, beautiful, respected, valued, protected, and loved. God desires us to experience these emotions in His presence continually. This is the ideal state that God desires for us, an intimate union with Him in the secret place (Psalm 91:1).

Recall the early days of meeting your partner—how your thoughts revolved around them constantly, how you yearned to spend every moment together, and how the mere thought of separation was unbearable. The Bible tells us that Jesus thinks of us in this way all the time. He loves us so deeply that He has engraved our names and images on His hands, signifying our significance and permanence in His life (Isaiah 49:15-16). Our lives, like blueprints, are continually before Him, and the story of our existence is inscribed in His book. Jesus consistently keeps us in His thoughts, watching over us and assessing our progress in fulfilling our life's purpose.

Jesus cannot bear to be apart from us. His love for us is immeasurable, unceasing, and everlasting.

Psalm 40:5 declares that Jesus' thoughts towards us are countless and immeasurable. His thoughts are constantly directed towards us. Jesus, the One who upholds the universe with His word, focuses His attention on us without ceasing. Reflect on the magnitude of this truth. <u>If Jesus' thoughts are continually fixed on us, then we should reciprocate by keeping our thoughts continually on Him and His Word.</u>

You are the centre of God's attention! He is always seeking ways to assist, protect, and bless us. I firmly believe that when we neglect to communicate with Him through prayer, it grieves His heart. 2 Chronicles 16:9 *The eyes of the Lord search the whole earth in order to strengthen those whose hearts are fully committed to him.*

You can ask the bridegroom anything on your wedding day, and his answer will be yes (2 Corinthians 1:20).

Jesus longs for a deep and meaningful relationship with us. He desires a connection that goes beyond casual or ordinary, one that is bound by blood and <u>marriage</u>. He doesn't settle for a common-law arrangement, compromises, or counterfeits. He desires to make a genuine and committed covenant with you.

Jesus yearns for a relationship with us to such an extent that He desires to fulfil every need we have in our lives. His love is passionate and extravagant. You are cherished and pursued!

- ✓ Jesus is the <u>husband.</u> **Isaiah 54:5**
- ✓ He is <u>Father to the orphan</u> and <u>husband</u> to the widow. **Psalm 68:5**
- ✓ He is the <u>Friend</u> that sticks closer than a brother. **Proverbs 18:24 & Psalm 119:63**
- ✓ He is the <u>lover.</u> **1 John 3:1 & Exodus 19:5**

Jesus' love for us is deeply intimate. To experience intimacy with someone, trust is essential, and we must allow them into our hearts. True intimacy requires vulnerability, letting go of our defenses and the walls we've built around our hearts. Jesus desires our relationship with Him to be so intimate that we can share everything with Him, even the deepest secrets that no one else knows. He is faithful to carry our secrets, and He wants to reveal secrets about our future as well. When we truly know Jesus as the lover of our souls (Psalm 23:3), we will not be afraid to be intimate with Him. As we grasp the depth of Jesus' love for us, we will eagerly run into His open arms (Deuteronomy 33:27). God's arms are always open to us because His love is unconditional. It is fear and religion that distort our perception of God's open arms as crossed. God is not angry with us but deeply and passionately in love with us!

<u>Understanding God's immense love for us dispels all fears and anxieties.</u> Perfect love drives out fear (1 John 4:18). God's love creates a safe and loving environment for us to examine our thoughts, mindsets, and feelings without fear of judgment. We can bring our thoughts to Him during our intimate times without fear or embarrassment, knowing that He will not criticize us or make us feel ashamed. Condemnation does not come from God. He already knows our hearts, but He desires us to come to Him and confide in Him. He wants us to seek His guidance and receive His help (Psalm 46:1).

<u>Jesus is a gentleman</u> (Revelation 3:20). He will never force Himself on us. Love is gentle and kind. God has granted us **free will**. He chose us

before the foundation of the world, and now He desires for us to choose Him and His ways. We have been chosen. We are wanted. We are loved. It is up to us to decide which mindset we will embrace.

Destiny is not a matter of chance; it is a matter of choice.
The Bible portrays Jesus' courtship of us. During this courtship, Jesus seeks to woo us, to establish an intimate relationship with us, and ultimately to marry us.

Courtship is a period in which a couple develops a romantic relationship before marriage. It is the action of endeavouring to win someone's love. This can be seen in the behaviour of male birds and animals as they strive to attract a mate.

Throughout the Bible, Jesus is actively pursuing us, seeking to win us over. He reveals all that He has done and provided for us: His unconditional love, His name, His family, His authority, His blood, His inheritance, His position, His home, His throne, and, most importantly, His kingdom mindset and principles by which we can live a victorious, abundant, and blessed life.

Jesus desires to hold first place in our lives. He doesn't want to share us with anyone or anything else. Anything that takes precedence over God in our minds and lives becomes an idol (1 John 5:21). In *Matthew 6:24* *it says that "no man can serve two masters."* You cannot love Jesus and the world at the same time. Jesus' exclusive love is a **jealous** love. In *Matthew 22:36-40* *"Love God with all your heart and mind."* Jesus is not jealous in an evil or unhealthy way but rather in an exclusive way. Loving God with our minds means adopting His kingdom mindset and allowing only His thoughts to occupy our minds. Jesus desires to hold first place in our lives. He doesn't want to share us with anyone or anything else. No idols.

In Song of Solomon 8:6-7 says **we are the object of Jesus' affection.** Jesus only has eyes for us. Jesus only has eyes for you!

Because of this, He wants us to love Him above all else and want to please Him above all others.

Agape Love wants to protect and warn their beloved
Love doesn't desire for their beloved to suffer. Jesus, through the Holy Spirit, is always communicating with us and guiding us. The Holy Spirit's intention is to protect us from making mistakes that could harm or endanger us. Moreover, the Holy Spirit continually provides us with descriptive feedback to help us stay on course and fulfil our assignments, ultimately joining Jesus in heaven. Jesus has assigned guardian angels to each of us for our protection (Psalm 103:20, Matthew 18:10).

Jesus has **given us Holy Spirit** to lead us and protect us (1 Corinthians 3:16).

Jesus has given us **His name, His authority, His blood** to protect us (Matthew 16:19 & Matthew 18:18).

Please note that you receive someone's name when you marry them, not before. However, Jesus calls us His bride by faith (Ephesians 5:27). He declares things that are not yet manifested as if they already are, using positive faith declarations towards us. Jesus has given us His name, the name above all names, the name at which every knee shall bow and every tongue confess that He is Lord. We have the privilege of using His powerful name!

Therefore, I am no longer just Natalie Masucci; my true name and identity are Natalie Masucci in Jesus Christ. I am in Christ, and this is my real name and identity. Jesus wants us to start calling ourselves by our new names, our true names, His name. Knowing and responding to our true names is part of God's kingdom mindset.

Jesus' love unites us and completes us. He makes us feel whole. When a man and woman marry, they become one flesh (Ephesians 5:27-32). Everyone desires to belong to something. When we accept Jesus, we become spiritually joined to Him, belonging to Him as part of His body. He is the head, and we are the body (Colossians 1:18, 1 Corinthians 12:12-27). Jesus places His Spirit within us, uniting us and sealing us (Ephesians 1:13). When we accept Jesus in our hearts, we become one with Him, just as a husband and wife become one in marriage. We become a part of His story in the Bible. God becomes the author of our life story.

Jesus provides us with a sense of belonging. Everyone desires to belong to something, and Jesus makes us part of His family. He adopts us as His very own children, allowing us to call Him Abba Father (Romans 8:15). We are no longer outsiders or beggars; we are His children. While you don't choose your biological children, God does choose them, and in the same way, He has chosen us. God has chosen you!

Our love for Jesus should inspire us to seek His approval and make Him proud. Just as we desire the approval and blessing of our human parents in our lives, we should strive to fulfil our mission and bring Jesus great joy and glory. We make our Father God proud when we operate in His kingdom mindset, take our rightful place, and fulfil our role in His story of love and redemption.

God's Love for us is unconditional

God has already determined that we are His prized possession and the pinnacle of His creation (Genesis 1:26-31). He has already redeemed us and positioned us to reign with Jesus forever.

Humans are the only beings that God personally fashioned with His own hands. While He spoke the worlds into existence, He created us from the dust, in His image, and then breathed His spirit into us. We were designed to function like our Father God.

There is nothing we can do to lose the love of God. No mistake, no sin can separate us from His love (Romans 8:38-39).

Likewise, there is nothing we can do to earn the love of God. It's not about our actions; it's about what He has done. God's love is a free and undeserved gift (Romans 5:15-18).

God will never change His mind about loving us (Romans 5:8). Let this truth empower you today.

Perhaps someone has hurt you by changing their mind about loving you, but I assure you that God never will. Maybe someone has let you down, betrayed you, or rejected you, but I promise you that God never will. If someone you loved made you believe that you are difficult to love, I am truly sorry. Remember, thoughts are not facts. **What is a fact is that you are loved by God. His love for you is unconditional and unfailing.** You haven't made too many mistakes, and it's never too late for you to accept His love, embrace His kingdom mindset, and transform your life.

Love never fails and love never ends

Jesus' love for us is eternal; it simply takes on another form when we expire. After death, our love affair with Jesus will continue, but in a different form in heaven for all eternity. Your love affair with Jesus will never come to an end (Romans 8:38-39). This understanding forms the basis of our eternal perspective, which is a part of God's kingdom mindset.

The Bible declares that the love of God is poured out in our hearts (Romans 5:5).

You may feel incapable of loving Jesus and others completely, but that is simply not true. We are capable of love because the agape love of God has been deposited within us through the Holy Spirit. We can love ourselves, Jesus, and others because we love with His love, not our own. Our human love is limited, hesitant, and easily offended. However, God's agape love dwelling within us enables us to endure and overcome challenges in our lives that we never thought possible. <u>God's love is a crucial element of His kingdom mindset. We press on and persevere because we love Him, and His love empowers us. God's love becomes our motivation and source of strength.</u>

"Love is the conduit on which faith works."

—Natalie Masucci

In God's kingdom mindset, our faith won't work without love.
In *James 2:14-26 it says "Faith without works of love is dead."* Love is both an action and a choice. Without corresponding actions, faith becomes fruitless and futile. Our prayers will go unanswered if we do not walk in love. Walking in love is essential for fulfilling our life's purpose. Faith is the currency of heaven. It pleases God and activates His intervention. Love gives birth to faith. Faith requires trust, and trust is built on love. God's immense love for us enables us to trust Him and take bold steps of faith. Each step brings us closer to our goals and dreams. Love must be our driving force, just as it was for Jesus.

God's love is submissive (Luke 22:42)

Jesus willingly submitted His life and will to the Father, and now He invites us to do the same. He desires our complete surrender and submission. Through His incredible love, He wants us to trust Him enough to let go of our own plans, knowing that His plans are the very best for us. Jesus' obedience to the Father changed the course of history. With a kingdom mindset, we will reclaim this generation for God!

God doesn't want us to strive or rely on our own strength and abilities; instead, He calls us to surrender to Him. He is the One who accomplishes the impossible. He takes responsibility for the outcomes. Our role is to allow the kingdom mindset of God to rule in our minds so that He can work with us and through us to fulfil His will and purposes on earth.

My Prayer

Father, I pray that the eyes of our understanding be opened. That we become rooted and established in God's love. That we might grasp how wide, how long, how tall and how deep is the love of Christ for us. I pray that we will know intimately this love that surpasses human knowledge. I pray that we will be filled with the agape love of God and live from that place of being loved.

224

(Ephesians 3:17-19)

Love is generous

Jesus has bestowed upon us all spiritual blessings in heavenly places (Ephesians 1:3). *John 3:16 tells us that "God loved the world so much that He gave His only begotten Son."* If God didn't withhold His most precious possession, He would also provide us with all things. He will give us everything we need to succeed in life and fulfil our purpose. There is no limit to God's generosity; He is a giver. To thrive in life, we must imitate our Heavenly Father and follow His principles of success. One of those principles is the Law of sowing and reaping (Galatians 6:7). Sow seeds towards your dreams and goals, and you will reap a bountiful harvest.

Love is precious (Psalms 39:4-13)

Human love is precious precisely because it is not everlasting. People pass away, and circumstances inevitably change. We must cherish the time we have and avoid any regrets.

True love does not take others for granted, nor is it abusive or manipulative. <u>Love is characterized by service, just as Jesus came to serve (Mark 10:41-45)</u>. It is important to value the individuals whom God has placed in our lives. Some may only be with us for a season, while others remain lifetime companions. Each person is strategically sent by God to assist, support, and collaborate with us in fulfilling our life's purpose.

Love trusts (Matthew 18:3)

In the Bible, Jesus assures us of His trustworthiness. He is the epitome of a good husband. Consider how babies exhibit blind faith, trusting their parents to provide for their every need and take care of them. This is the kind of childlike faith that Jesus desires from us – a faith that does not worry but believes wholeheartedly in His provision for all our needs.

God has designed us to embrace love and trust in Him. In Luke 18:8, Jesus poses a question: *"When the Son of Man comes, will he find faith on the earth?"* This prompts us to examine the depth of our trust in Him.

It is important to personally experience and comprehend God's love and faithfulness in order to become recipients of His true nature. As Habakkuk 2:4 states, *"the just shall live by faith."* Living by faith means living in His faithfulness. As we grasp the enormity of God's love for us, may we find rest in Him, regardless of our present circumstances, and entrust our lives to Him completely.[104]

F.A.I.T.H. = forsaking all I take Him

"What we love determines what we seek, what we seek determines what we think and do, what we think and do determines what we become."

—Uchtdorff

Jesus, the Bridegroom and lover of our souls, is knocking on the door of our hearts in this hour. Will we let Him in? Will you accept His marriage proposal? Now is the time to enter before the door closes (Luke 13:23-27). Don't wait. You can adopt His kingdom mindset and start living the life of your dreams today.

- ❖ Will we trust in His love enough to allow the Holy Spirit to perform open-heart surgery on us?
- ❖ Will we let Him remove any wrong mindsets, negative thought patterns, and hindrances (spot or wrinkle) from our lives (Ephesians 5:27)?
- ❖ Will we submit our will and life to Jesus?
- ❖ Will we let Jesus' love empower us enough to use His kingdom Mindset?
- ❖ If we do, I believe that we will get his blessing on the last day.
- ❖ "Well done, good and faithful servant" (Matthew 25:21).

It's imperative that we follow God's plan for our lives. Not everything that is good is of God. There are so many good initiatives and programs out there, but they may not be what God wants you to be involved in. The enemy tries to deceive us with many counterfeit opportunities to get us off track. If we do good works not led by God, Jesus will tell us that He never knew us (Matthew 7:21-23).

<u>Man may applaud you, but that doesn't mean that God has commissioned you.</u>

Prayer

Father, conform our will to your will. Teach us to love what you love and hate what you hate. Fill us with your agape love. We pray that when you return, you will find us busy with our Father's business. You

---

[104] Nancy Taylor Tate, *Parousia Ministries*-Elijah List email, April 2023

will find us busy doing things your way by following your kingdom mindset towards fulfilling our life assignment.

I believe that we are living in the last days. The era of revival, awakening, and a great harvest of souls is upon us. Now, we can better understand Jesus' urgent appeal for us to recommit ourselves to Him. The hour of decision has arrived. It's time for the Remnant to rise up! It's time for the Church worldwide to fulfil her assignment—the Great Commission (Matthew 28:16-20). Equipped with God's kingdom mindset, we are called to impact the world, making disciples of all nations and teaching them God's ways. The Lord has a purpose for us.

Nothing is wasted with God. He used the Covid-19 pandemic as an opportunity for His bride to refocus and cultivate intimacy with Him once again. God always turns what the enemy meant for evil into something good for us (Genesis 50:20). Satan's plans always backfire, while God's plans always succeed. If you embrace His kingdom mindset, the plan God has for your life will be successful. I decree that the plan of God for your life will succeed in Jesus' name!

Jesus laments that we have been lukewarm, neither fully committed nor completely indifferent. We have operated from a fixed mindset (Revelation 3:14-22), lacking passion and wholeheartedness.

Now is the time to make a decision. Jesus calls us to embrace His kingdom mindset and fully commit to Him. It's time to choose: either be passionately in love with Him or not, but no more sitting on the fence or settling for a casual relationship. Jesus desires for us to take our place as His bride. He longs for a deep and serious relationship with us—not merely as boyfriend and girlfriend, but as husband and wife.

God is disciplining us because He loves us. ***Hebrews 12:6-7-*** *"because the Lord disciplines the one he loves."* God's love for us is so great that He is actively working to transform us. Jesus is removing anything that hinders our relationship with Him, such as toxic thoughts and wrong mindsets. He calls us to offer our lives as a living sacrifice, just as He offered Himself to the Father (Romans 12:1-2). Jesus does not force us but desires for us to willingly choose Him.

Jesus, the bridegroom who will come soon, longs for an eternal union with us. Just as a bridegroom and bride dream of their life together, Jesus dreams of spending eternity with us. It is a matter of the heart.

Embracing God's eternal perspective, found in His kingdom mindset, helps us realize that this earthly life is a preparation for eternity. Pursuing our life assignment brings both blessings and victory in this life, as well as the accumulation of treasure in heaven (Matthew 6:19-21).

In this present hour, Jesus is knocking on the door of our hearts. Will we allow Him in? (Revelation 3:20) Will we let Him remove negative thought patterns and distorted self-images that hinder us? Do we trust in His love enough to allow the Holy Spirit to perform open-heart surgery on us? Will we trust Jesus enough to follow His guidance through the descriptive feedback of the Holy Spirit instead of relying on our own understanding and ways?

"Freedom is telling God what we desperately want. Trust is asking Him to change our want if gaining it would poison us."
—Beth Moore

Now that you have discovered Jesus' everlasting and unconditional love for you, what will you do with this knowledge? <u>Knowledge alone cannot bring improvement to your life; it is the actions you take based on that knowledge that make a difference</u>. **Allow the knowledge of God's love for you to transform your mindset. Embrace God's kingdom mindset today!**

Can you accept and believe what the Bible says about you? You were chosen, wanted, and desired. Can you accept Jesus as the lover of your soul? Can you acknowledge that you are valuable, you belong, and you are an integral part of God's redemptive plan for the world? This is the truth about you, regardless of how you may feel. These facts are grounded in the word of God. Remember, your feelings are not facts. Your emotions can change.

Those with a kingdom mindset do the opposite of what they feel. You feel like quitting, but you keep going by faith.

HOW do I adopt God's love and kingdom mindset?

To begin, you must have faith in accepting Jesus' love. You don't necessarily need to comprehend it fully; simply receive it as a gift from God. <u>The revelation of God's love for you brings the realization of your identity and the activation of your purpose.</u> Next, allow God's love within you to guide the way you live your life. Let Jesus' love for you serve as your anchor and ultimate authority. Learn to see all situations, circumstances, and people through the lens of Jesus' love. Embracing God's love within us and living from that place keeps us rooted in faith. With faith, all things become possible. God's Kingdom mindset encompasses His love, which is positive, hopeful, and empowering. It impacts our self-image, self-talk, and self-compassion. Viewing our lives and the world through the eyes of love represents having God's kingdom mindset. When we truly grasp the magnitude of God's love for us, it empowers us and gives us the courage to take risks and steps of faith, leading to continual growth and becoming the person God intended us to be.

"The blood of Jesus is the liquid love of God that flows from the heart of God and brings hope in all situations."
—Mark Hankins

Chapter Six

Identity Crisis

Have you observed the prevailing identity crisis in the world today? There is a significant amount of confusion, and many individuals are enduring sickness, suffering, and a sense of being lost and disillusioned. We are currently facing a global mental health pandemic, and the impact of the Covid-19 pandemic has only exacerbated the situation. In fact, having a mental health condition like depression can intensify the likelihood of experiencing an identity crisis.

In times like these, a shift in mindset becomes imperative. What we truly need is a revolution of our mindset!

"The devil knows that if he can challenge your identity, he will hinder your destiny."

—*Mark Hankins*

Satan has consistently targeted mankind in the realm of identity, and it has proven to be one of his most effective tactics. Satan himself was expelled from heaven because he audaciously claimed to be God (Isaiah 14:14). Similarly, in the Garden of Eden, Satan challenged Eve's identity. He deceived her by suggesting that God was withholding the fruit from the tree of knowledge because it would grant her godlike knowledge of good and evil (Genesis 3:1-6).

Satan even tempted Jesus in this area of identity. In Matthew 4, during the Temptation of Christ, Satan asked Jesus twice *"If you are the Son of God then tell these stones to become bread", "If you are the Son of God then throw yourself down for it is written that He will command his angels concerning you."* This was a genuine temptation for Jesus because, despite being God incarnate, He humbled Himself, took on the form of a servant, and became a man. The human aspect of Jesus was susceptible to doubting His identity; otherwise, the enemy would not have used that approach. Satan repeatedly employs this tactic, as evidenced by his attempt to cast doubt on Jesus' identity. Understanding our true identity in Christ is a fundamental aspect of God's kingdom mindset. It is crucial for us to have unwavering knowledge of who we are and to whom we belong. God, as the creator of all things, has the ability to speak things into existence. God said *"Let there be Light"* and the sun, moon and stars were created. God said *"Let the land produce living creatures according to their kinds"* and all animals were created (Genesis 1:3-25). Man is the only creation of God that He fashioned with His own hands. **You are handmade by God!** The Bible states that God formed man from the dust of the ground, making him in His likeness and image. <u>God designed us to resemble Him and to exhibit His qualities.</u> Furthermore, God entrusted man with the authority to rule over the entire earth. Man was given dominion over all creation. God blessed man and commanded him to be fruitful and to subdue the earth (Genesis 1:28). According to the Oxford Dictionary of English, "subdue" means to overcome or bring under control by force.

On my darkest days, when I feel inadequate, unloved, and unworthy, I remember <u>whose</u> Child I am, and I straighten my crown.
I identify as a child of God.
—*Natalie Masucci*

If you are doubting who you are or your identity, this is normal. Remember that Jesus was tempted with the same doubts, and he overcame them. **Hebrews 4:15** reveals that Jesus *"was in all points tempted like as we are, yet without sin"*. You and I possess the same ability. The power to overcome resides within you! With a kingdom mindset, we gain clarity about our authentic identity and can conquer thoughts of doubt, confusion, insecurity, and fear.

"God has planned for us to have a strong mind with the ability to control every thought, imagination, desire and emotion."
—*Morris Cerullo*

It is of utmost importance that we teach our children and that we, ourselves, understand our true identity according to the Word of God, otherwise, the enemy will come to confuse us and derail us from fulfilling our purpose. We must provide children with a clear and captivating understanding of God's grand narrative and their role within it. We all desire to be part of a great story, evident by the lines forming at attractions like Star Wars Land and Harry Potter Land. <u>Our longing to find ourselves in a significant story is precisely why God gave us the Bible. It reveals that we are part of a remarkable story, and each of us has a crucial part to play</u>. This eternal perspective is at the core of God's mindset. We need to improve in involving our children in the entirety of the Bible's story so they can discover their place in it, just as

Jesus did.[105] The revelation of identity brings the realization of opportunity.

"It's 11 o'clock, do you know where your children are?"
—Natalie Masucci

Jesus discovered his purpose and destiny in the scriptures, and we, too, must find ourselves in the Book. There is nothing more fulfilling than knowing that we are part of the Lord's Great Commission, sharing the gospel (good news) with our children, families, co-workers, and everyone within our sphere of influence (Matthew 28:18). While we each have a unique kingdom assignment to fulfil, we also share the same commission to spread the love of God to a lost world.

"Amber Alert: God has missing children, they have been abducted by their phones."
—Beth Moore

Jesus asked the disciples many times, *"who do people say that I am?"* He wanted to know who they thought he was. Jesus found his identity in the bible. From a young boy, he was always in the temple, hearing and learning the Word of God. Jesus found himself in the scriptures. **He found himself in the Book**. Jesus found his identity and purpose in the Bible. In Luke 4:18-21 Jesus recites a scripture from Isaiah 61:1 about himself and finishes by saying *"Today this scripture is fulfilled in your hearing"*.

We also need to discover ourselves within the pages of the Bible. We can identify with various bible characters and share their motivations. You may be an Esther or Deborah, a Joshua or David. I believe that Jesus carried the verse above with Him wherever He went and read it in various places to inspire belief in Him. Jesus repeatedly read the Word to reinforce His identity, finding solace in the truth it proclaimed. Likewise, when we recite "I Am" statements, we are engaging in the same practice. Speaking positively about ourselves affirms our true identity. The Bible provides us with our identity. We are children of God, co-heirs with Christ.

Our authentic identity and purpose can only be unearthed in the Bible. John 17:4 exemplifies finding ourselves within its pages. Just like Jesus, we aspire to say to the Father one day, "I have brought You glory on earth by completing the work You gave me to do." By fulfilling our

---

105 Seven Questions with Phil Vischer of VeggieTales Dec 29, 2019 interviewed by Fazal Karim Jr. Metrovoicenews.com

life's assignment, we bring glory to God. <u>The Bible illuminates our purpose.</u>

As we discover ourselves within the scriptures, we adopt a kingdom mindset, mirroring that of our Heavenly Father. We begin to see ourselves through His eyes from a position of victory. Following Jesus' example, we must also continually affirm our identity by declaring the truths about ourselves that the Bible reveals, encapsulated in empowering "I Am" statements and positive declarations of faith.

Satan is a skilled deceiver who spreads lies about our identity, abilities, and circumstances. Consider this: a thief targets valuable possessions, not worthless items. When was the last time a burglar stole worthless junk from a house? They seek valuable items like jewelry, electronics, artwork, and money. <u>Similarly, we are precious to God, which is why the enemy attempts to steal our identity and purpose.</u> Matthew 24:4 *"Watch out that no one deceives you."* God desires for us to be free from deception and to have the correct identity and mindset. He does not want Satan to steal from us.

What holds the greatest significance in life is not what others say about us, but what God says. When we have a kingdom mindset, we see ourselves as God sees us. Our identity and value come from God, not from our actions, possessions, achievements, or circumstances (Galatians 2:20).

Our validation should come from God, not from our actions, possessions, culture, or social media. <u>We must not let our identity be attached to temporary social agendas but to God and His eternal kingdom assignments.</u>

One way to gain insight into our true identity is by practicing a weekly <u>"Internet Sabbath,"</u> as recommended by entrepreneur William Power. This involves intentionally disconnecting from devices for specific periods during the day or week. For example, taking off the Fit Bit or Health App on Saturdays and focusing on the surroundings and thoughts that truly matter rather than solely on step counts or calories burned. This allows us to create space where we are not consumed by email or measuring ourselves by the number of messages responded to but instead contemplate our long-term goals and dreams. Placing excessive emphasis on incremental measurements can cause people to disregard research, sound reasoning, and the Word of God in favour of short-term gains. Our society often prioritizes short-term gains, with companies and shareholders being held accountable for quarterly results rather than long-term impact. However, God can help us in this regard, as He possesses an eternal perspective. When we start thinking of ourselves as descendants of Jesus, it connects us to a greater past and a future that surpasses our own.[106] By taking an <u>Internet Sabbath</u>, we ground ourselves and gain a perspective aligned with God's eternal view. Having an eternal perspective is part of God's mindset. Being a descendant of Jesus makes us part of His story.

The Bible meticulously traces the genealogy of Jesus, revealing that He was a descendant of Adam (Matthew 1:2-16 & Luke 3:23-38). This knowledge assures us that **we, too, are descendants of Jesus**. We are all interconnected, stemming from a lineage of strong, courageous, and victorious individuals. Let this truth empower you today. When we adopt an eternal perspective, we break down our life assignments into manageable short-term goals with the assistance of the Holy Spirit, all while keeping our focus on the ultimate outcome.

While we may be replaceable in our work roles, we are irreplaceable in the lives of our loved ones. God has intentionally placed us within our specific families to serve as reflections of His light. Regardless of what the current culture teaches, the roles of a mother and a father are vital and cannot be substituted. You are a capable and loving parent.

Let's strive to maintain our priorities in proper order. Taking a Sabbath or rest allows us to realign and rejuvenate ourselves. When we become excessively fatigued, we become more susceptible to the toxic thoughts of the enemy. Our families need us to be the person God has called us to be. Are you aware that they are eagerly waiting for you? **You possess something unique to impart to your children that no one else can provide.** It is part of your assignment. You are an essential part of Jesus' story and an integral component of His plan of redemption. Take a moment to pause and reflect. Observing a Sabbath grants us the opportunity for self-reflection, which aids in keeping our priorities in proper alignment in life. Our job is to expose our kids to God. We do our best parenting on our knees, praying. God fills in the blanks and does the rest.

> **"At work, you're replaceable...but as a parent, you're irreplaceable."**
>
> *—Maria Shriver*

20 years from now, the only people that will remember you worked late or checked emails on weekends will be your kids.... <u>Names hold significant power. They are intricately tied to our identity. The names we respond to and the labels we embrace have a profound impact on the trajectory of our lives. Throughout the Bible, we see God changing the</u>

---

names of many individuals, guiding them to shift their focus, transform their mindset, and fulfil their purpose. A name carries great power because it is intricately linked to one's sense of identity.

God's Word in the Bible is eternal, unchanging, and firmly established in heaven (Psalm 119:89). We cannot alter what God has called us, but we have the power to mislabel ourselves. We can adopt wrong names and identities, as pointed out by Steven Furtick. It would be foolish to base our sense of self on the ever-changing voice of culture and society. God's Word remains constant, and He is the Almighty One who can transform our identity. He can change our name from defeat to victory, from being seen as damaged goods to being a new creation. He can take us from feeling like worthless garbage to recognizing our value as a precious jewel.

If you have ever engaged in a Bible study focused on the names of God, you were probably blessed to uncover the profound ways our Lord is described throughout the Old and New Testaments. The names of God are filled with significance, not only revealing His true nature but also providing us with a vivid understanding of His past, present, and future actions. There is nothing that escapes His sovereignty. We can trust Him in all things.

1. God is "The Rock" who will always help you stand.
2. God is "The Lion of the Tribe of Judah" who is fighting your battles for you.
3. God is *"The Bright and Morning Star"* who will lead the way for you.
4. God is *"The Alpha and Omega, the beginning and the end." He will complete the transformation that He began in you.*

By delving into the names of Jesus as presented in the Bible, we can deepen our understanding of His character and nature. The study of His names has the power to strengthen our faith, ignite our love for Him, and activate our purpose. Furthermore, reciting and praying the names of God serves as a beautiful means of honouring and worshiping Him. It is through the very mention of His name that we nourish our minds with wholesome thoughts and fortify our identity, hope, and faith.

The Names of Jesus throughout the Bible:

- **GENESIS** –Seed of the Woman, Abel's sacrifice, Noah's Rainbow, Abraham's ram, Isaac's well, Jacob's ladder, Issachar's Burdens, Judah's sceptre,
- **EXODUS** –Passover Lamb & Moses' Rod
- **LEVITICUS-** High Priest
- **NUMBERS** –Star of Jacob & Pillar of cloud by day and pillar of fire by night & Balaam's Shiloh
- **DEUTERONOMY** –Great Rock & Prophet unto Moses
- **JOSHUA** -Captain of the Lord's Host/Captain of our salvation
- **JUDGES** -Sword of Gideon & Our Judge and Lawgiver & Gideon's Fleece

- **RUTH** -Kinsman Redeemer
- **1 & 2 SAMUEL** -Seed of David & Our Trusted Prophet & David's Slingshot & Samuel's Horn of Oil
- **1 & 2 KINGS** -Lord God of Israel-Our Reigning King & Elijah's Mantle & Elisha's Staff & Isaiah's Fig Poultice & Hezekiah's Sun Dial
- **CHRONICLES** -God of our Fathers
- **EZRA** –Lord of Heaven and Earth & Our Faithful Scribe
- **NEHEMIAH** -Rebuilder of Broken Walls
- **ESTHER** -God of Providence & Our Mordecai
- **JOB** –Ever-Living Redeemer
- **PSALMS** -Good Shepherd, King of Glory, Husband to the Widow & Father to the Orphan & Honey in the Rock
- **PROVERBS & Ecclesiastes** -Wisdom of God
- **SONG OF SOLOMON** -Altogether Lovely & The Lover and Bridegroom& Rose of Sharon and the Lily of the Valley
- **ISAIAH** -Wonderful, Counsellor, Mighty God, Everlasting Father, Prince of Peace & Rock in a weary land and Staff of Life
- **JEREMIAH** -Lord Our Righteousness- The Righteous Branch
- **LAMENTATIONS** -Weeping Prophet, Compassionate God
- **EZEKIEL** -Wheel in the Wheel & The Four-Faced Man
- **DANIEL** -Fourth Man in the Fiery Furnace
- **HOSEA** -King of the Resurrection
- **JOEL** -Baptizer in the Holy Ghost and Fire
- **AMOS** –Plumb line & Burden Bearer
- **OBADIAH** –Destroyer of the Proud & Mighty to Save
- **JONAH** -God of the Second Chance & Great Foreign Missionary
- **MICAH** -God of Jacob & Messenger of beautiful feet
- **NAHUM** -Avenging God-The Avenger of God's Elect
- **HABAKKUK** -Everlasting Glorious God-God's Evangelist
- **ZEPHANIAH** -King of Israel –Our Saviour
- **HAGGAI** –Desire of all Nations & The Restorer of God's lost heritage
- **ZECHARIAH** -Pierced in the House of his Friends & The Fountain
- **MALACHI** -Lord of Remembrance & The Son of Righteousness rising with healing in His wings
- **MATTHEW** -King of the Jews & Messiah & Pearl of Great Price
- **MARK** -Suffering Servant & Wonder Worker
- **LUKE** –Son of Man
- **JOHN** –Eternal God & Son of God
- **ACTS** -Ascended Lord & Holy Ghost & Paul's handkerchiefs and aprons & Stephen's signs and wonders, Peter's shadow
- **ROMANS** -Lord our Righteousness & Our Justifier
- **CORINTHIANS** –Resurrection & Our Sanctifier

- **GALATIANS** -Redeemer from the Law
- **EPHESIANS** -Head of the Church & The Christ of Unsearchable riches
- **PHILIPPIANS** -Supplier of Every Need
- **COLOSSIANS** -Fullness of the Godhead
- **1 & 2 THESSALONIANS**- Our soon-coming Christ
- **1 & 2** TIMOTHY -Mediator between God and Man
- **TITUS**- Great God and Saviour & Our Faithful Pastor
- **HEBREWS**- Heir of all Things & The Blood of the Everlasting Covenant,
- Better than the Prophets and Angels, Captain of our Salvation, Merciful and Faithful High Priest, Great Intercessor, Mediator of the New Covenant
- **JAMES** -Great Physician
- **1 & 2 PETER** -Unblemished Lamb & Chief Shepherd who soon will appear with a crown of unfading glory
- **JOHN**- Advocate, Propitiation & Love
- **JUDE** -Lord that cometh with 10,000 Saints
- **REVELATION** -Alpha and Omega, Lion of Judah, Slain Lamb, King of Kings and Lord of Lords, Bright and Morning Star, John's Pearly White City [107]

Jesus has a multitude of names representing various aspects of His divine nature. He is both the Lion of the Tribe of Judah and the Passover Lamb, showcasing His strength and sacrificial love. Just as Jesus embodies multiple roles, we, too, have the capacity for different mindsets. While we may still harbor remnants of a fixed mindset in certain areas, we can gradually shift towards adopting God's kingdom mindset in all areas as we navigate through life.

The names attributed to God serve as a means to comprehend His character fully. They reveal that He can fulfil every need we have. When we require the provision, we can call upon Jehovah Jireh. Jesus stands alone as the worthy, exalted, and Great One. He possesses the power to heal our hearts and make us whole (Psalm 147:3). It is through Him that our true identity is revealed. Our names are transformed from orphan to adopted child, from failure to triumph, from lost to found, from victim to victor, from weak to strong, and from blindness to clarity. The names of God carry incredible power. Take a moment to read and reflect on

---

[107]https://www.sermoncentral.com/sermons/jesus-in-every-book-of-the-bible-robert-simmons-sermon-on-miracles-of-jesus-43656
https://www.youtube.com/watch?reload=9&v=Uk8ZPye2jBM
https://youtu.be/Uk8ZPye2jBM

each name, for within them, God unveils profound truths. <u>It is through the names He calls us that our identities are shaped. The names that God calls us reveal our character, talents and potential.</u> When we meditate on and fully embrace our true names, it transforms us. I am a completely different person now. The revelation of being God's "Beloved" set me on a course of healing and restoration. I went from being a fearful victim to a confident warrior princess. I went from being broken to mended and then made whole. Mended means being healed. Made whole means it's as if it never happened. God always does a complete work ((John 19:30). God wants to change the names that you call yourself and answer to as well. If He did it for me, then He'll do it for you. There is nothing broken or missing in you (Isaiah 26:3-4). You are perfect, a masterpiece!

Chapter Seven

God Embraces a Kingdom Mindset with Us

God views us through the lens of His kingdom perspective, and He desires us to adopt the same mindset.

Consider how you perceive the world and the circumstances in your life. Do you see through the eyes of love or fear? Viewing through the eyes of love reflects a kingdom mindset while seeing through the lens of fear denotes a misguided mindset. Fear is a component of a fixed mindset.

When we pray, God hears our petitions and already perceives them as answered (1 John 5:15). <u>He sees us as victorious and considers the work accomplished through Christ Jesus on the cross of Calvary.</u> God sees things as already accomplished and has a clear vision of the future. He resides in our future and possesses a forward-thinking mindset regarding us. He is aware of all our days, which are recorded in His book (Psalm 139:16). God expects us to grow, persevere, change, and mature. He does not want us to be swayed off course by unfavourable circumstances, inconveniences, or even tragedies. <u>He recognizes our potential and the seeds of greatness that He has instilled within us.</u> He is the potter, and we are the clay. Throughout our lives, God molds us into the individuals He has designed us to be. He desires us to rely less on our own efforts (fixed mindset) and to place more trust in Him (kingdom mindset). God always anticipates our engagement and expects us to be proactive and resilient. Embracing a kingdom mindset prompts us to continuously express our beliefs, take action, and make a difference. With God, we are constantly on the potter's wheel, evolving, learning, and maturing (Isaiah 64:8).

Resilience is something that develops when we adopt God's kingdom mindset. Resilience encompasses various strategies that support one's mental health during challenging times. These strategies involve problem-solving, self-awareness, coping with difficulties, change of perspective, seeing the positive and finding new opportunities.

According to the Oxford English Dictionary, **resilience** is the ability to recover quickly from difficulties, displaying toughness or a thick skin, and the capacity to bounce back into shape. As a teacher, I have personally had to cultivate a thick skin and learn to let things roll off my back over the years; otherwise, I would have been tempted to give up. Developing resilience helps us to persevere (Romans 5:3-5). As a society, we lack resilience.

God desires us to be resilient like elastic bands. Although life's circumstances may stretch us, **we have the ability to bend without breaking** and spring back into shape. It's important to remember that delay does not equate to denial when it comes to God. Those who possess a kingdom mindset grounded in faith are flexible and resilient (Ephesians 6:13-16-having done all, stand). Delay can be many things. Learn to flip the script in your mind. Delay can be preparation, protection, or promotion.

Example: When we pray for healing or any other blessing, God sees that we already possess it. Healing was part of Jesus' sacrifice on the cross and His resurrection. It is often referred to as the "children's bread" because it belongs to us (Matthew 15:26). Healing has already been purchased and paid for. It is a gift from God that we simply need to appropriate by faith. When sickness comes into our lives, we must understand that healing has already been provided for us. We don't beg for something we already have; instead, we pray, stand on the promises of God, and expect to be healed and restored to wellness.

To stand on the promises of God, start by finding scriptures in the Bible that speak to healing like 1 Peter 2:24 and Psalm 41:3. Then, bring these promises before God in prayer. Confess with faith that the healing is yours. Declare, "I have it now by faith. I am the healed one. I walk in divine health. With long life, God will satisfy me and show me His salvation. I will see His goodness in the land of the living."

Finally, remember to praise God for answering your prayer request. God wants us to celebrate the successes of others and continue praying for them while we await our own breakthrough. Though sickness may bend us, it will not break us in the name of Jesus. It was when Job prayed for his friends that He was healed and restored (Job 42:10).

A kingdom mindset looks ahead with hope and anticipation. It envisions the answer of our prayers and the successful fulfilment of our dreams and goals. Revelation 12:11 "And they overcame him by the blood of the Lamb and by the word of their testimony."

God's what if? Versus Satan's what if?

God's kingdom mindset includes a questioning strategy that prompts you to ask yourself important questions. Questions like "What if?" can shift your perspective and reveal new possibilities. God didn't bring you this far so that you could fail now. Perhaps He closed a door to open a better one? Maybe this isn't the end, but rather a new beginning?

When you have a kingdom mindset, you approach the enemy's doubts and questions differently. Instead of succumbing to them, you challenge them with your own "What if?" questions. What if it's not over yet? What if your best days are still ahead of you? What if the Devil is a liar and his words hold no power over you? What if everything you have been through can be used for a greater purpose? What if your battle is breaking generational curses? What if God has brought you to this place because He is the God of turnarounds, second chances, new beginnings, and beautiful endings?

These "What if?" questions, shared by Steven Furtick in an Instagram post, remind us that God's kingdom mindset encourages us to embrace hope, trust, and the belief that God is working all things together for our good.

Those with a God's kingdom mindset understand the power of their thoughts and take control of their mental health by being mindful of their thinking patterns and asking themselves important questions. They embrace the positive use of the question "What if?" as encouraged by God.

While the enemy may try to prompt negative "What if?" questions to torment us, God wants us to approach them in a different light. What if God has something better in store for me? What if He is using this situation to teach me something and strengthen my faith? What if He is positioning me for a breakthrough or promotion? What if the answer I need is just around the corner, and I shouldn't give up?

On the other hand, Satan wants to exploit our vulnerabilities and tempt us with negative "What if?" questions. He may try to fill our minds with doubts and fear, such as "What if they find out what you said?" or "What if they discover what you did?" "What if it doesn't work out?" However, it's essential to reject these negative thoughts and use God's kingdom mindset to view your problems from His perspective. Flip the script in your brain and begin to challenge the enemy's "what if" questions with God's "what if" questions. Things aren't falling apart, they are falling into place. What if it works out better than planned?

Why not let God rewrite the story of your life? You are part of His story, you have an essential part to play.

Toxic **thoughts** are part of having a fixed mindset. All toxic thoughts stem from fear. Fear is the root cause of most toxic thoughts. Fear causes worry, stress, anxiety, panic, unforgiveness, victim mentality, negativity, confusion, doubt, complaining and excuses.

> **"Fear is one of the most dangerous parasites you can allow in your life. When you allow fear to stay in your mind and heart, you will eventually panic. When you panic, your heart pounds, your hands sweat, your chest hurts, and your body wants to dictate your actions fully."**
>
> *—Keith Butler*

When we allow the frenzy and negativity of the world to infiltrate our lives, toxic thoughts begin to take root. The problem is that many people aren't even aware of their negative thinking patterns. These thoughts have become so ingrained that they seem normal. Merely listening to the news or engaging in gossip can trigger negative thoughts in our minds.

Examples of toxic thoughts include thinking that you're not good enough or that you cannot change. Failing to address these toxic thoughts leads to unforgiveness, a victim mentality, stress, anxiety, complaints, and even depression. Failing to address toxic thoughts puts us at risk of falling into a cycle of overthinking, leading to **toxic rumination. Toxic rumination** involves excessively dwelling on and analyzing specific thoughts or life events. It stems from a desire for control. Research has shown that toxic rumination is associated with various negative consequences, such as depression, anxiety, post-traumatic stress disorder, binge-drinking, and binge-eating.

> **"Unchecked toxic thoughts cause toxic rumination which changes the structure of our brains wiring us for defeat."**
>
> *—Dr. C. Leaf-Instagram*

Toxic rumination is the result of relying on our own intelligence, knowledge, strength and ability to figure things out. It stems from a need for control. However, <u>God's mindset is designed to lead us to victory as we learn to depend on His strength and abilities instead of our own (John 12:32).</u> It is God's responsibility to navigate and resolve the challenges we face in fulfilling our assignments, allowing our minds to find rest in trusting Him (Exodus 33:12-14).

God's kingdom mindset equips us for success by incorporating the concept of **Emotional Intelligence (EI)**, which involves how we process thoughts and emotions. EI refers to our ability to understand, utilize, and manage our own emotions in positive ways, enabling us to alleviate stress and overcome challenges effectively. **Emotional intelligence** directly influences our self-perception and how we express ourselves to others. It impacts our relationships, decision-making, and our ability to handle stress with resilience. Examples of EI are being flexible, listening actively, taking on challenges and responding positively to new initiatives.

NEVER THOUGHTS: These are part of a fixed mindset that originates from the enemy. These thoughts attempt to steal all hope from you, making you believe that things will never change. They are rooted in fear. **The best way to refute Satan's never thoughts is with God's forever thoughts.**

> **"Learning to remain calm when you're disrespected is a superpower."**
>
> *@Sunkissedclw*

FOREVER THOUGHTS: These are part of God's Kingdom mindset. They aim to empower you to keep moving forward by instilling hope and faith within you. <u>Forever thoughts are based on God's Word and love for us, giving us a hopeful outlook for the future.</u>

For example, God tells us, **"I love you forever.** I loved you before you were born, and I will love you for always (Psalm 136:1-9)." God's thoughts towards us are everlasting. He is constant and unchanging—yesterday, today, and tomorrow (Malachi 3:6). The Bible assures us that nothing, not even death, can separate us from God's love (Romans 8:31-39). He will never alter what He calls us, His beloved. <u>God's love is a forever thought that will sustain us throughout life.</u> Understanding God's immense love for us is an essential aspect of His mindset that motivates and empowers us.

Another forever promise is "you are forgiven (Psalm 103:1-5)". God has chosen to forgive us. God doesn't change His mind. If you repent and ask God to forgive you He will (1 John 1:8-9). We must acknowledge and receive God's forgiveness. The enemy attacks us with thoughts of un-forgiveness. Un-forgiveness is a toxic thought process that stems from a fixed mindset. Thoughts like "I will never forgive them" and "I will never forget what they did to me" perpetuate the belief that you are incapable of forgiveness and that things will never change. <u>Let go of the word "never" from your vocabulary!</u> God would not ask us to do something that we are unable to do (1 Corinthians 10:13). If God asks us to forgive, it means we have the capacity to forgive if we choose to do so. Forgiveness is a choice and a decision. It is not based on feelings. You may never feel like forgiving someone who has hurt or wronged you. Your flesh or carnal nature will resist you at every step. You must learn to practice forgiveness as a conscious choice. <u>God has forgiven us, and He expects us to forgive others in return (Matthew 6:12-14).</u> Ask God to help you forgive.

When we rely solely on our own willpower, we attempt to do better and forgive, but willpower alone will never be enough. Operating in our own strength reflects a fixed mindset. Don't be too hard on yourself. You had the best intentions. <u>Those with God's mindset rely on His grace, not their own willpower.</u> Willpower can only take you so far. We recognize that God's grace within us is sufficient, and we actively rely on His grace (2 Corinthians 12:9). Philippians 2:13 says, "For it is God who works in you to will and to act in order to fulfil his good pleasure." It is God working in us through His mindset. We can forgive by His grace. <u>We lean on His limitless grace rather than our limited willpower.</u> When we do so, we will accomplish amazing things!

Furthermore, God will reward us for following His ways and forgiving others. God is even able to help us forget after we forgive. Imagine having all the painful memories erased! Did you know that you can ask God for supernatural amnesia in prayer? There is a "sea of forgetfulness" in heaven (Micah 7:19). God can do that for you when you choose to forgive. He will cast your hurtful memories into the sea of forgetfulness, and they will never torment you again. Once again, we notice how God blesses us when we do things His way!

<u>Instead of using the word "never," why not use "yet"? For instance, "I haven't forgiven yet, but I am working on it with God's help."</u> In our own human strength, we may never be able to forgive a wrong or injustice. We need to learn to tap into God's mindset to assist us. The Word of God states that His love is poured into our hearts (Romans 5:5). Therefore, I can choose to forgive using God's love within me. **God's mindset will empower us to do things we never thought we could.** He is skilled at His work! However, we must yield to Him and the process of change in our lives. Altering our thought patterns and choosing forgiveness are integral aspects of God's mindset.

<u>The enemy often uses the word "never" when he lies to us.</u> For example, "You'll never get out of debt," "You'll never get married," "You'll never overcome this addiction," "You'll never recover," "You'll never lose the weight," and so on. **Remove the word "never" from your vocabulary.**

Fixed Mindset:

- "That's just the way I am"
- "That person just irks me"
- "Every day it's the same garbage"
- "I will never forgive them for what they did to me"
- "I just can't do this"
- "I won't get the promotion."

- ▪ "We'll never afford that kind of vacation."
- ▪ "I could never go to that school."

Kingdom Mindset:

- ✓ "I can't do this <u>yet</u> but with God's help I can and I will"
- ✓ "Forgive me"
- ✓ "Thank you, Father, that you're working in me"
- ✓ "What is this teaching me?"
- ✓ "Today is a new day, a new opportunity"
- ✓ "I choose to forgive them by faith."

"Sometimes the hardest words we hear come from our own minds. Remember the One who is really in charge. If the winds and waves obey Him, your thoughts can too!"
—Tim Tebow

"Whenever you start getting 'never thoughts' circling in your mind, be alerted that those are from the enemy and resist them as soon as possible."
—Natalie Masucci

Don't allow these toxic thoughts to linger. Don't give the enemy any room, or he will invade your life. Close every door and don't give him a crack to enter (Ephesians 4:27-29). **Un-forgiveness is a stumbling block created by the enemy.** It is a spiritual weight (emotional baggage) that we carry, making us weaker over time and more vulnerable to the enemy's schemes. <u>Un-forgiveness delivers a double blow, draining our energy and stealing our peace.</u> Satan will ensure that you constantly replay your emotional baggage, trapping you in a toxic cycle of negative thoughts. <u>We must learn to forgive; it is vital for us to pursue God's plan for our lives</u>. Forgiveness is not easy, but it is necessary.

Un-forgiveness is like an unhealed wound that, if not treated through the Word of God and prayer, festers into anger, then resentment, and ultimately bitterness, which can destroy us. The enemy wants you to keep dwelling on your past and remain trapped in unforgiveness because he doesn't want you to see the bright future that God has for you. He wants to keep you fixated on the rearview mirror instead of looking ahead to the road before you.

<u>Un-forgiveness causes you to look in the wrong direction,</u> focusing on the past, which veers you off course and blinds you to the enemy's

schemes (Luke 17:32). Have you ever tried walking backward? You cannot see where you're going. That's exactly what the enemy wants—to catch you off guard with his deceptions.[108]

Have you ever heard the saying, "When it rains, it pours," or "If it's not one thing, it's another," or "Bad things always happen in threes"? This is how the enemy works. He bombards us in an attempt to weaken our resolve, and when we become vulnerable, he strikes. Satan desires your possessions, but above all, he wants your commitment to God. If he can make you give up your commitment to God, he will destroy you. However, your commitment to God's mindset will empower and equip you to fulfil your purpose and keep the enemy at bay. God's mindset keeps us focused on moving forward. He wants us to step out in faith, one foot in front of the other.

Gossip is a secret place for Satan. In that place you abide under the shadow of unforgiveness. Prophet Charlie Shamp

Forgiveness doesn't make what they did to you or what happened to you okay, but it sets you free (John 8:36). It frees you from carrying the baggage of past hurts and mistakes. It allows you to pursue the dreams and goals that God has placed in your heart. The enemy wants to keep you stagnant, trapped in the past, and constantly reliving those traumatic experiences to paralyze you and prevent you from fulfilling your God-given assignment. Satan will torment you with thoughts of regret, guilt, and shame. <u>If you don't take control of your thoughts, he will.</u>

Forgiveness is not cheap. It cost God His only begotten Son (John 3:16). The blood of Jesus is the only thing that can atone for our sins from the beginning of time until the end. Since God has forgiven us, He expects us to forgive ourselves and others. <u>This is not a suggestion but a command </u>(Ephesians 4:32 & Matthew 5:23). We cannot fulfil our life assignment if we harbour unforgiveness because it will negatively affect our prayers and perspective. You must forgive.

Here's the greatest lesson you'll ever learn about forgiveness: No one has ever died from a snakebite. <u>It's the venom that kills, not the bite itself. </u>Similarly, if someone has hurt you, that's the bite. It's the resentment, bitterness, anger, and hatred that you hold within yourself that becomes the venom, slowly consuming you from the inside out. The Bible warns us about bitterness on numerous occasions, and medicine confirms that bitterness makes the heart grow sicker, directly linked to cardiovascular disease (Hebrews 12:15).

---

[108] Terri Savelle Foy

Forgiveness doesn't mean that we disregard people's actions or continue to welcome them into our lives. Rather, it's a recognition that what others do to you is beyond your control and not your responsibility. You can only control yourself—how you react to the hurt and how you heal from it is your responsibility. It takes spiritual maturity and **emotional intelligence** to come to this understanding. If you're harboring revenge, resentment, Offence, contempt, bitterness, hatred, or anger towards someone, it's time to release that venom and forgive.

Holding onto unforgiveness is like drinking poison and expecting the other person to die. Forgiveness is the only answer. Let it go. Remember that God loves you, and He wasn't behind the touch of evil in your life. You can receive God's healing, freedom, and grace today.

The consequences of unforgiveness:
1. It will keep you imprisoned in your past. How long is long enough? How long are you going to beat yourself up? 5 years, 10 years, 20 years,? When will your self-imposed prison sentence be up? God has already forgiven you so now it's time for you to forgive yourself. That mistake, that tragedy doesn't have to ruin the rest of your life.
2. It never lets that wound heal. You go through life reminding yourself of what was done to you OR what you did, stirring up that pain and making yourself progressively angrier/guiltier. Every memory is like picking off the scab and making the wound continuously bleed. Unforgiveness causes you to bleed on people who didn't cut you. It hurts those around you. "Hurting people hurt people".
3. You go through life accumulating bad feelings about yourself and others.
4. Holding onto unforgiveness can hinder the plan that God has for your life. Why? Because unforgiveness breeds anger, resentment, and bitterness. These negative emotions are detrimental to your physical health and mental well-being. It has been medically proven that bitterness kills. It negatively affects your cardiovascular health and leads to depression. Another name for bitterness is blame. "It's not me. It's you." Stop being a victim in life. Stop blaming others for your problems, your reactions, and your bad mood.

Say this confession out loud:

With Jesus, I can walk over every obstacle, every toxic thought and every weakness. With God's kingdom mindset, I can control the thoughts I allow to stay in my mind. I can forgive, and I will forgive in Jesus's name. I choose by faith to forgive myself and those who have hurt me. I accept God's forgiveness and let go of all anger, regret, guilt and shame. I am leaving my past mistakes and moving forward into the new things that God has for me.

The benefits of forgiveness:

1. Forgiveness is for you, not for them. Forgiveness doesn't make what they did to you right, forgiveness sets you free. Free to move forward in your life and fulfill your purpose.
2. When you choose to forgive, you take your power back. You stop letting the person who hurt you have power over your life and emotions any longer.
3. Forgiveness removes all emotional baggage-weights from your life that were draining you and it gives you your energy back.
4. You develop better and healthier relationships because healed people, heal people.
5. It promotes better communication skills because you no longer feel the need to retaliate and make others pay for what they did to you. You can communicate from a place of love and respect.

Victim Mentality

Choosing to be a victim is another toxic thought. You can't be a victim and a victor at the same time. You have to choose one or the other. One is positive, and the other is negative. One is having a Kingdom mindset, while the other is having a fixed mindset. One is operating in faith, while the other is operating in doubt, fear, and unbelief. Remember, you're not a victim, so stop blaming others or your circumstances for your problems. Adopting a victim mentality is an obstacle to success. Realize that you, and only you, are responsible for your destiny.[109]

God has never failed, and He wants to share His success with us. You cannot be a victim if you are victorious through Christ. *"But thanks be to God! He gives us the victory through our Lord Jesus Christ."* (1 Corinthians 15:57)

---

[109] Carol Morgan. *12 Toxic Thoughts You Need to Drop for a Better Life-*Lifehack.org

When we say things like "poor me," "you don't know what I've been through," "if you knew what's going on," "I'm ruined," "I'm broken by life," "I'm a failure," "I'm a loser," etc., we sound like victims. <u>When we whine, cry, and complain, we sound like wounded animals, like prey. The devil, who goes around like a roaring lion seeking whom he may devour, hears us and comes in for the kill! (1 Peter 5:8)</u>

Being a victim with a fixed mindset opens the door to the enemy in your life. With a fixed mindset, you always see yourself as a victim of external forces, never taking responsibility for your actions. You make excuses and fail to take charge of your life or learn from your mistakes. Thankfully, we have the ability to change our mindset and shut the door on the enemy. We can transform our thoughts and words. Stop inviting the enemy into your life through negative words. **God's mindset will remove the victim mentality from your voice and replace it with the roar of victory.** You have the Lion of the Tribe of Judah within you, and you can boldly declare victory over the lies of the enemy. A kingdom mindset will change your victim's wimper to a lion's roar. Let us make positive confessions of faith and victory instead. When tempted to complain or wallow in self-pity try saying "This problem may have come but it's not going to stay in Jesus' name!", "It will be as God has said." "This situation has an expiration date!"

"When the angels hear our positive confessions, it gives them something to work with, and the heavens open, bringing divine help our way."
—Mark Hankins

Satan wants to instill a victim mentality in you. He wants you to feel sorry for yourself and give up on your dreams and goals. His goal is to hinder you from taking action and to keep you wallowing in <u>self-pity.</u> However, God never intends for you to feel sorry for yourself because He has equipped you with everything you need to overcome the enemy in every situation. Self-pity is a tactic used by the enemy, and if you indulge in it, you will remain a victim instead of becoming a victor in life. Personally, I desire affirmations from God rather than pity from people. No more pity-parties for me. How about you?

Remember, it is not just information that affects your mindset but revelation from the Word of God that impacts your heart and transforms your voice. Allow the revelation of God's mindset to change your perspective and shift your voice from that of a victim to that of a victor. (Ephesians 1:6-23)

"Action is the foundational key to success."
—John Hagee

<u>Depression</u> has become a prevalent toxic thought in today's society. It is characterized by feelings of severe despondency and dejection, as defined by the Oxford Dictionary. Depression deceives you by making you believe that you will always feel this way. However, the good news is that God's power is greater than the weight of depression. Depression is a name, and it must bow to the name of Jesus. (2 Corinthians 10:5).

<u>Depression</u> is often a silent killer, as many people suffer in silence with this mental illness. Satan's tactic is to isolate individuals and then torment them with toxic **"never thoughts"**. It is disheartening to see the increasing prevalence of depression, isolation, and self-harm among students in our school systems. Our society is facing a crisis of hope, evident in the rising rates of antidepressant use, suicide, divorce, and opioid overdoses.

<u>Depression is another "never lie".</u> It affects even Christians because they may place their faith in people, employment, self-help formulas, or the world system instead of God. This misplaced trust leads to a sense of hopelessness because everyone and everything ultimately lets us down. The only one who will never disappoint us is God (Deuteronomy 31:8). It is important to anchor our faith in Him and rely on His unwavering love and support.

"Most things are too good to be true except for God's kingdom mindset which is better than advertised."
—Natalie Masucci

We experience a loss of hope and fall into depression when we struggle to believe or envision a change or improvement in our circumstances. Depression stems from a fixed mindset that relies on our own abilities and the advice of the world rather than trusting in God. As a result, we often turn to medication to numb the pain and disappointment we feel. Antidepressants like Prozac and Lorazepam have become widely prescribed, as it seems that everyone is seeking some form of medication to cope with the negativity and hopelessness of the world.

During times when it appears that things are not changing, we can easily slip into doubt or cynicism. Depression distorts our perception of the world and causes us to view our lives through a negative and fearful lens. We isolate ourselves and entertain thoughts of self-harm or even suicide. Depression is a toxic thought planted by the enemy. Individuals with a fixed mindset believe that things will never change, leaving them with limited or no options. They may choose to medicate their pain or

250

even contemplate ending their pain altogether. When depression takes hold, it convinces us that our situation is hopeless and that we are powerless to change it.

The remedy for depression lies in embracing God's mindset. God's kingdom mindset offers hope because God Himself is the embodiment of hope (Romans 15:13). Without hope, life loses its meaning, and love becomes impossible. Hope enables us to persevere in love and fuels our aspirations, whether it's going on a dream trip, landing a new job, finding a life partner, or reaching retirement. God grants us more than just a superficial hope; He gives us an anchor for our souls (Hebrews 6:19). God's hope is pure gold.

In Matthew 19:28-29, Jesus makes a promise that He will renew all things and restore Eden for us. We will receive glorified bodies and live not just in heaven but on the new earth. It's not merely a new heaven but a new earth that awaits us. Isaiah 51:11 and Isaiah 65:17-19 describe our future hope, stating that the former things will be forgotten and no longer come to mind. This restoration includes our thoughts and minds. We will rejoice and find eternal gladness, and there will be no more tears. What an incredible hope! This unbreakable hope allows us to run our race in this life with an eternal perspective.

As believers, our hope begins when we realize that nothing is lost or wasted with God. He will restore all things—the earth, ourselves, and all the aspects that make life rich, such as art, music, food, and laughter. The hope we long for, the paradise Adam and Eve once knew, is coming to us. God is restoring us to our original position. This restoration begins in this life as we adopt God's kingdom mindset and continues in the glorious future that awaits us. Now this is a blessed hope! Jesus will restore the earth and us to our original condition (Acts 3:19-21). This hope stems from an eternal perspective that recognizes this life as a dress rehearsal for eternity. What lies ahead is far greater than what is behind us.

Jesus Himself, through His resurrection, provides us with an example of the promised restoration. After rising from the dead, Jesus met with His friends multiple times, even sharing meals together. God is not only a rewarder but also the ultimate reward for His people. The reward for faithfully running our race and fulfilling our life assignment is the privilege of spending eternity with God. Our present and future employment involves ruling and reigning with Jesus in the new earth (2 Timothy 2:12). The assurance of heaven, a new earth, and the restoration of everything we hold dear is clearly promised to us in God's Word. In Revelation 21:5 Jesus says *"I am making all things new."* Oh what a great hope we have!

"If you're worthless, why is the devil fighting you so hard? You're a valuable instrument. There's breakthrough with your name on it."

—Steven Furtick

We have an awesome hope and a bright future in store. Let this reality, this biblical truth, help you fight off the toxic thoughts of depression. You are never hopeless, and you are never helpless when you have God's mindset. Your future is bright.

The key thing about life on earth is change. Cars rust. Paper yellows. Technology dates. Caterpillars become butterflies. Nights morph into days. Problems resolve. Depression lifts.

<u>Depression often arises when we are faced with making decisions.</u> Those with a fixed mindset tend to struggle with decision-making due to fear of making mistakes. Do you find it difficult to make decisions? Are you plagued by indecision? **We are presented with a choice: either accept what God says about us in His Word and believe it or accept the lies of the enemy.** The lies of the enemy manifest as toxic thoughts that, when believed, can result in mental and physical ailments such as stress, anxiety, digestive issues, sleep problems, panic attacks, excessive worry, depression and OCD, among others. Depression stems from beliefs that contradict the Word of God. It arises from a fixed mindset that believes things will never improve, leaving no space for God to work and move in our lives. Depression takes hold when we entertain and ultimately embrace these debilitating lies.

The Word says that we have the mind of Christ and can operate according to God's kingdom principles (1 Corinthians 2:16). **Exciting new research on stem cells and depression has been conducted by Dr. Avery Jackson.**

Science has proven that our thoughts have a direct impact on our health. Stem cells are a built-in healing mechanism that God has placed within our bodies to assist us when we are sick. For example, when we sustain a cut, stem cells prompt the wound to scab and heal. Consider the fact that the skin is the body's largest organ, and stem cells have the ability to regenerate it. These remarkable cells can also differentiate into more specialized cells. God has equipped us with stem cells so that we can call upon them for healing when needed. Yes, you can speak to your body and command your stem cells to replicate and commence their divine function! The power of life and death is in our mouths (Proverbs 18:21)!

In his book, "The God Prescription: Our Heavenly Father's Plan for Spiritual, Mental, and Physical Health," <u>Dr. Avery explains that laughter is a remedy for depression.</u> Depression affects stem cells and weakens the immune system, leading to the depletion of stem cells present in bone marrow. Depression literally saps the life from our bones. In Proverbs 17:22 we're told *"A cheerful heart is good medicine, but a crushed spirit dries up the bones". "Light in a messenger's eyes brings joy to the heart, and good news gives health to the bones"* (Proverbs 15:30).

Science, medicine, and the Bible are in perfect alignment because they all stem from the Word of God. Let's consider an example: the law of gravity. Hebrews 1:3 states that Christ upholds all things by the word of His power, which includes the law of gravity. Furthermore, when Jesus walked on water (Matthew 14:22-33), He demonstrated His direct authority over the laws of nature.

6-year-olds laugh an average of 300 times a day. Adults only laugh 15-100 times a day. Be like a child again! Laughter is good for us.

Science helps us understand the physical laws that govern the Earth and our bodies, all of which were created by God. Medicine, on the other hand, provides us with the knowledge and framework to comprehend the intricate functioning of our physical bodies. In my belief, God not only desires to bring healing into your life, but He also intends to resurrect any dormant dreams and goals, just as depicted in the story of the dry bones in Ezekiel 37:1-10. God's kingdom plan encompasses both physical healing and the revitalization of our aspirations.

Depression can lead you to a point of giving up. I remember being in a deep and dark place when I was battling with depression. It felt as if I was trapped in a deep well, unable to reach the top where the light was shining. I didn't know how to escape. Perhaps you're feeling the same way right now? Maybe you believe that life is an overwhelming struggle and that things will never change, leading you to feel like everything is hopeless. I want to encourage you to shift the narrative in your mind. Remember the words of Christine Caine, **"Sometimes when you're in a dark place, you think you've been buried, but you've actually been planted."**

When a train goes through a tunnel, and it gets dark, you don't throw away the ticket and jump off; you sit still and trust the engineer (God). Trust God, no matter how dark your situation, God says, "You're coming out!"

Did you know that laughter, regardless of whether you feel like it or not, triggers the same positive reactions in your body? Laughing releases endorphins and reduces the levels of chemicals that contribute to cancer, autoimmune disorders, and stomach problems. When you make a conscious decision to laugh, it engages your reasoning frontal lobe and has a cascading effect on your master gland, the hypothalamus. From there, the impact reaches all 50 trillion cells in your body. It's truly remarkable how God designed this process. As Dr. Jackson explains, "Doctors don't heal. A neurosurgeon can remove a bullet and stitch up a wound, but true healing comes only from Jesus. He secured our healing through His stripes on Calvary."[110]

Laughter is God's remedy for depression. It is a precious gift from God and an excellent way to stay encouraged. When you laugh, endorphins are released, acting as natural painkillers in your brain. Laughter also reduces stress and brings about a sense of pleasure. So, when you start feeling depressed, try to make yourself laugh. Watch some comedy, find humour in the situations around you, and laugh at the enemy who is trying to impose depression on you. Laugh and rejoice because now you understand that you have power and authority over your mind. Through laughter, you can even stimulate the production of stem cells that will promote healing throughout your body from the inside out.

"You are as happy as you decide to be. To rejoice is a choice. Rejoice in the Lord."

—John Hagee

"Happiness is a decision you make. It's how you arrange your mind. Circumstances have nothing to do with it. It's a decision you make every morning when you wake up. You have a choice; you can go down the path of looking at what you don't have instead of seeing all that you do have."

—Natalie Masucci

Example: **Carl *D.* Tuyl** a WW2 war veteran shared in his book entitled Stories and Sermons of Survival of how he survived German concentration camps by finding humour in his situation. Holy Spirit helped him to find the moonlight bouncing off their bald heads as funny. This saved his life by stopping him from succumbing to the hopelessness of his situation. Laughter literally saved his life.

You have a choice each day: you can either dwell on the difficulties you face with the parts of your body that no longer function properly, or you can get out of bed and express gratitude for the ones that still do. Every day is a precious gift. As long as you wake up, make the decision to focus on the new day filled with opportunities. Choose to focus on the happy

---

memories you are creating and the positive impact you are making in your own life and the lives of others.

Breaking free from toxic thought patterns requires time and effort, but it is possible. Often, breaking these patterns requires persistent prayer. There is no need to become discouraged and fall into depression. If you don't see immediate changes or improvements in your life, don't give up and surrender to despair. Continue to trust in God, maintain your faith, and stay positive. In 1 Kings 17:21-22, the prophet Elijah had to pray three times before the boy was brought back to life. The persistent widow in the Bible also prayed repeatedly. Jesus himself prayed continually. Refuse to be discouraged. Even if the answer to your prayers seems delayed, keep standing firm in faith. If you stumble, simply rise again and try once more. Be resilient. Remember, God is on your side, and He desires your success and freedom. There is a purpose for the waiting period you may be experiencing. Delay does not mean denial. God is working behind the scenes on your behalf. While depression may have entered your life, it will not linger. In the name of Jesus, it will be overcome!

"The first place we lose the battle is in our own thinking. If you think it's permanent, then it's permanent. If you think you've reached your limits, then you have. If you think you'll never get well, then you won't. You have to change your thinking. You need to see everything that's holding you back, every obstacle, and every limitation as only temporary."

—Joel Osteen

The Bible affirms that God is our source of hope, as stated in Romans 15:13 and Proverbs 10:28. When we derive our hope from God, it becomes unshakeable and cannot be taken away by anyone or anything. Those with a kingdom mindset always possess hope, which is rooted in the Word of God and His principles of success. If you are currently feeling hopeless, I encourage you to adopt God's mindset and allow Him to be your hope today. Let God have the final say in your life, not the enemy. You are not helpless, and your situation is not without hope. Through the power of God's Word, every situation can be transformed. In God's mindset, we anchor our hope in His promises and blessings that are available for us to claim. God is the one who remains steadfast and will never let us down. When our hope is anchored in God, no one can snatch it away. It is not bestowed by the world, and the world cannot take it away. We place our hope on the solid rock of God's faithfulness, not on shifting circumstances or people. When we put our trust in the Lord, we will not be disappointed or put to shame, as stated in Romans

10:11. God promises that if we trust in Him and align ourselves with His mindset, we will experience promotion instead of demotion. He will turn things around in our lives. He assures us of a hopeful and promising future, as stated in Jeremiah 29:11. This is truly good news!

"It's very important that you expect God to move in your life. Expectation is faith. Get into God's word. Read the verses that specifically deal with blessings. Meditate on them, memorize them, confess them verbally, and act upon them."
—Marilyn Hickey

"Obstacles don't have to stop you. If you run into a wall, don't turn around and give up. Figure out how to climb it, go through it, or work around it."
—Michael Jordan

Superpower versus Achilles Heel

When we accept Christ as our personal Savior and Lord, we receive His supernatural power within us, transforming us from mere humans into superhumans (1 Corinthians 3:16). We now possess the power from another world dwelling inside us: the Holy Spirit, who is the third person in the Godhead. The Holy Spirit is the power component, the one who brought forth light when God spoke the Word. His power now resides within us. Instead of focusing on fictional superheroes from Marvel, we can recognize that we ourselves are superheroes. His supernatural power combines with our humanity, making us superhumans. **What's your superpower?**[111] Have you discovered it yet? What are you passionate about: Science, mathematics, languages, arts, music? These are clues to your purpose. God's will is that you excel in the area you are passionate about. With practice and effort, you can become super.

"I will no longer use the excuse, I'm only human because God's divine power is at work in me."
—Morris Cerrullo

Those with a kingdom mindset understand that greatness or excellence in a specific area can be achieved through hard work and perseverance. They recognize that God has placed potential within them, and they

---

[111] *Innovators Mindset- p231-237*

strive to become exceptional in their designated area, excelling in the way God has designed them. They focus on developing the talents and interests that God has instilled within them.

God expects us to utilize deliberate practice to develop the talents and potential He has placed within us. Fulfilling your assignment may require sacrifice and effort, but the rewards are well worth it. It may demand your time, effort, and focused thoughts. In my experience with Weight Watchers, they used to tell us, "Nothing tastes as good as skinny feels," to encourage us to persevere on our weight loss journey. Similarly, I say to you, "Nothing in this world compares to the fulfilment and joy of walking in your divine destiny."

The "gift" (talents and abilities) that you have been carrying within you needs to be unleashed upon the world. Do not overlook or underestimate what has been entrusted to you. God has granted you the authority to speak over this gift and shape it with your words (Romans 11:29). Refrain from dishonouring this gift by speaking contrary to God's Word, and avoid uttering anything that would diminish or devalue it. Instead of casting doubt and unbelief, choose to speak life into the precious gift that God has placed within you. Make declarations and affirmations that will activate its potential and purpose. Say "This is going to be a good day, great week, awesome month and wonderful year! This is my year to walk in the fulfilment of everything that God has for me! I will fulfil 100% of God's calling on my life and no less. God's plan will not be stopped in my life (John 17:4). I do not doubt God's purpose, but I am confidently walking it out day by day. I know God's plan for my life, and I have clarity of the plan. I know what God has for me!"

Deliberate practice can often outweigh natural talent. Numerous research studies have shown that individuals who engage in ten years of daily practice can surpass those with inherent talent in various domains such as chess, sports, music, and the visual arts. Furthermore, after twenty years of dedicated practice, individuals without natural talent can even achieve world-class proficiency. Deliberate practice can stir up the gifts within us (2 Timothy 1:6). However, it is common for us to believe that if we were not born with a particular gift, we will never be able to develop enough talent to attain success. This belief can lead to giving up prematurely without giving ourselves the opportunity to nurture the skills required for achievement. [112]

Example of deliberate practice-David:
The Lord has already equipped you with everything you need to overcome any obstacle that comes your way. As stated in 2 Peter 1:3-4, we have been given everything necessary for life and godliness. Let us strive to emulate David and confront the giants in our lives (1 Samuel 17). <u>David employed deliberate practice to develop his skills, as evidenced by his victory over a lion and a bear before facing the giant Goliath.</u> This practice sharpened David's abilities and bolstered his self-confidence. Although he only needed one stone to defeat Goliath, David collected five. He was prepared and confident. With a mindset aligned with God's, we will have the ability to conquer any hindrance that stands between us and the fulfilment of our God-given dreams and goals. 1 Corinthians 15:58; *"Therefore, my beloved brothers and sisters, be steadfast, immovable, always abounding in the work of the Lord, knowing that your labour is not in vain in the Lord."*

With God's Kingdom mindset, we can become Giant Slayers like David. God wants us to fearlessly step into our authority, equip ourselves for battle, and declare His Word, then watch giants fall!

Stress vs. Sabbath Rest

Stress comes from a fixed mindset because you cannot see how things can change, so you ruminate over them. You become anxious and overthink.
We were designed by God to have a day of rest and regularly observe a Sabbath (Exodus 20:8-11). God set the example by resting on the seventh day from all His work of creation (Genesis 2:2). As we are made in His image and likeness, we function best when we honour a weekly Sabbath. The Jewish Sabbath, observed on the seventh day of the week (Saturday), means "to rest." <u>However, it is not about the specific day but rather about using a designated day for rest and rejuvenation</u> (Romans 14:5 – "One person esteems one day above another; another esteems every day alike. Let each be fully convinced in his own mind").

Humans were not created to work non-stop, seven days a week. The widespread use of smartphones for both home and work has only intensified the problem. We are constantly "on," reachable day and night, on weekdays and weekends. God wants us to prioritize rest and release stress and worry. Taking a day of rest each week allows us to calm our minds and soothe our spirits.[113]

---

[113] Fazal Karim Jr. - Mission 2020 article. *The Christian Herold*

"What is without periods of rest will not endure."

—OVID

There is an underappreciation of rest in today's society. Despite the proven benefits of rest, intentionally setting aside regular time for rest has become undervalued in our culture. Many of us have become overworked, overstressed, overwhelmed, and exhausted. The practice of taking a Sabbath has become less common and is fading away. Several factors in our modern society work against the concept of rest:

1. Rest has been misconstrued as laziness.
2. The desire for money has become insatiable, leading to a constant pursuit of work and productivity.
3. Success is often measured incorrectly, focusing solely on achievements rather than overall well-being.
4. We live in a world that is always "on," with constant access to information and the expectation of immediate responses.
5. A false sense of urgency surrounds us, making it difficult to distinguish between important and unimportant matters.
6. Our minds crave distraction and have become addicted to stimulation and validation, making it challenging to disconnect from technology and social media.
7. Rest cannot be rushed, but our society is accustomed to shortcuts and multitasking. We seek quick fixes and instant results.
8. There is a misunderstanding that rest is purely physical when, in reality, it encompasses the physical, mental, emotional, and spiritual aspects of our well-being.

To truly experience the benefits of rest, we need to challenge these societal norms and prioritize rest as an essential part of our lives.[114]

Some days are meant to be restful, and that is perfectly okay. It is during these restful days that we slow down and appreciate what truly matters, such as being together with family and enjoying a meal or simply taking in the beauty of a sunset. On these Sabbath days, we find joy in the simple pleasures of life. This is how God designed it to be. By following God's ways and regularly observing a Sabbath, we can avoid succumbing to stress and anxiety. God, as our creator, knows how to optimize the functioning of our bodies.

Stress comes from trying to do it all on our own. Rest comes from putting it all in God's hands.

---

[114] Joshua Becker-Becomingminimalist website. *The Under-appreciation of Rest in Today's Society*

During the global pandemic of Covid-19, the world was forced to slow down and take a Sabbath rest. Quarantine and self-isolation were imposed, and in some ways, it turned out to be the best thing that could have happened. It caused people to pause the hectic race of life and find rest. This gave us an opportunity to press the "reset" button on our lives and reassess what truly matters. It brought many people to a place of surrender and repentance, where they let go of their own agendas and embraced God's agenda for their lives. This forced Sabbath rest proved to be beneficial for many individuals.

We often hear and believe the cliché "Just go with the flow," accepting whatever life throws at us. This leads to overwork, stress, depression, anxiety, and a fixed mindset. However, this is not in alignment with scripture. In reality, we are called to create the "flow" in our lives through our thoughts, words, and mindsets. We are to resist thoughts that contradict the Word of God and replace them with thoughts that align with God's kingdom mindset.

<u>The only time as believers that we should "go with the flow" is when we surrender to the leading of the Holy Spirit, who is the true "flow."</u> When we give our lives and agendas to God, He takes charge of the "flow" in our lives. The Holy Spirit guides us through descriptive feedback, and as we follow His directions, we move toward success and the fulfilment of our purpose.

Descriptive feedback is the work of Holy Spirit-it includes our inner cheerleader, as well as catching and challenging our critic.

"I'm not where I need to be, but thank God I'm not where I used to be."

—Joyce Meyer

We can observe the principle of rest in the Old Testament as well. In Leviticus 25, God provides instructions to His people on how to properly treat the Promised Land so that the soil continues to be fruitful. They were to work the land for six years, but on the seventh year, there was to be a Sabbath of rest for the land. This practice of working the land for six years and allowing it to rest on the seventh year is still followed today because it makes sense and allows the land to replenish. God, as the creator of the entire physical universe and the world we live in, knows how to be a steward of the earth and its resources. Taking a day of rest each week allows our bodies and minds to function optimally, just as God designed them to. In the Bible, the number seven symbolizes completeness and perfection, both in the physical and spiritual sense. There are seven days in a week, and God's

Sabbath falls on the seventh day. Similarly, the land is meant to rest on the seventh-year

Anxiety and stress come in various forms. It is not just being worried. It can show up as irritability, obsessive behaviours, over-scheduling, overworking, overindulgence, dizziness or numbness, sleepiness or insomnia, lack of concentration and avoidance behaviours.[115]

Notice how everything that is "over" or too much becomes **detrimental.** God is a god of order and moderation (1 Corinthians 14:33). Satan causes excess in our lives in an attempt to weaken us and destroy us by making us vulnerable to disease and, toxic thoughts and temptations.

Remember that you are not your thoughts. You have power over your thoughts. Worry cycles and self-pity spirals are not from God. The best way to deal with a worry cycle is to acknowledge, evaluate and resolve it so you build that thinking process into your brain. Pretending that everything is okay doesn't work. Ignoring thoughts doesn't work, either. Ignoring them doesn't make them go away. I know because I tried that for many years. Unresolved thinking processes tend to repeat over and over again in our lives. This creates a cycle of torment. First, acknowledge the thought. Second, evaluate the thought. **Who is the sender?** Is it beneficial or harmful? Third, resolve the thought by either accepting it or rejecting it (James 4:7). Over time, this will become a good habit affecting how you deal with future worry.[116]

God's kingdom mindset teaches us how to align our minds with His design and replace negative habits with positive ones. It's important to develop a new habit of regularly examining our thoughts and discerning their source. This is something we have control over, and it is part of the authority given to us. God has made us the CEOs of our own minds. If we don't take control of our minds, someone else will.

Just as we can wire thoughts into our brains through our minds, we can also wire thoughts out of our brains with our minds. Instead of allowing worry to consume us, we have the choice to redirect our thoughts and engage in prayer and gratitude. We have the power to choose our thoughts and shape our mindsets. Establishing a regular Sabbath practice can greatly assist in dealing with stress and worry in more positive and constructive ways.

Stress causes cortisol to be released in our bodies. Cortisol is good in balanced amounts as it helps us get up in the morning, maintain a healthy circadian rhythm and is anti-inflammatory. Cortisol is one of the

---

[115] Dr. C. Leaf-*Instagram*
[116] Dr. C. Leaf-*Instagram*

hormones released in the fight or flight response that occurs when there is a perceived harmful event or attack. Our bodies were not created to handle large and continuous amounts of stress, whether real or perceived. Our bodies consider stress as dangerous and react accordingly. If we are constantly stressed, we produce too much cortisol, which leads to an imbalance in our hormones and affects our neuroendocrine system. This, in turn, affects our mental and physical health, making us anxious, forgetful, overweight and potentially insulin-resistant.[117]

<u>God provides a remedy for stress through the practice of Sabbath rest.</u> By taking time to observe a Sabbath, we can realign our lives with what truly matters. This intentional pause allows us to find internal peace as we place our trust in God to fulfil all our needs.

"Too many priorities paralyze us."

—*John Maxwell*

Satan's goal is to overwhelm us with an excessive number of things and cause us to experience stress. He understands that an excess of cortisol can be harmful to us. <u>Even something good can become harmful when it becomes excessive. The enemy's signature move is to push things to the extreme or overload.</u>

Have you ever wondered why animal tamers always carry a four-legged chair at the circus? They carry the chair with its legs facing outwards because the lion tries to focus on all four legs at once, which overwhelms him. When the lion attempts to focus on the four legs coming at him, it paralyzes or tames him. He becomes docile or weak because his attention is fragmented, ultimately disabling him. Similarly, too much stress has the same effect on us. The same principle applies. Satan wants to tame, weaken, and disable us by overwhelming us with excessive thoughts and priorities.[118]

God never intended for us to spend our lives worrying about money and trying to figure out ways to meet our own needs. He never intended for us to constantly worry about our health and seek ways to heal ourselves. God desires to provide all of these things for us. In His word, He has already given us His promises, which serve as His success criteria. It is through toxic thoughts that our well-being is compromised, weakening our immunity and our body's ability to heal itself. However, <u>laughter has the power to boost our immune system.</u> So, the next time you feel stressed, try watching a comedy show, listening to a comedian,

---

[117] Dr. Anna Cabeca-*Instagram*
[118] Terri Savelle Foy. *Dream it Pin it Live It*

or intentionally making yourself laugh. Utilize God's success strategies to your advantage because He wants you to thrive.

"Worry only subtracts time you could have spent trusting God." With God's help, we need to learn to say no to certain things or people in order to maintain our focus on our purpose. Boundaries are a good thing, not a bad thing. The Holy Spirit is there to assist us in staying focused and setting priorities. It is perfectly fine and beneficial to postpone responding to a text or email until we are in the right mindset. The Holy Spirit guides us in maintaining a kingdom mindset, which allows us to continue growing and improving ourselves.

<u>When we believe Satan's lies, we become compromised as we let go of God's promises. Satan can only attack us when we are compromised (1 Peter 5:8).</u> The same principle applies to the Coronavirus, which preys on the most vulnerable individuals in our society, particularly the elderly and those with compromised immune systems. Toxic thoughts have a profound impact on us, affecting us not only emotionally but also physiologically.

"Garbage in, garbage out." That's not just a cliché, but it's what the Bible teaches (Proverbs 23:7).

It's time for us to refuse the influence of toxic thoughts from the enemy! Let's no longer allow garbage or junk food into our minds but instead feed on the healthy nourishment from the Word of God. Although the Coronavirus and toxic thoughts may be contagious, so is the presence of God. God's presence is always with us, manifested through His mindset.

While we cannot prevent thoughts from entering our minds, we can choose not to dwell on them. By training our minds to stay focused on the things of God, we gain victory in softening our hearts. If we refrain from speaking every thought that comes to mind, we prevent those thoughts from taking root in our hearts. <u>Remember, you don't have to verbalize every thought. Don't give it attention; simply allow it to fade away.</u>

With God's mindset, we learn how to make positive thought choices that shape our inner monologue or self-talk. Our inner monologue has a powerful impact and can become a self-fulfilling prophecy, so it's crucial to carefully monitor what we allow in and what we discard. The choice is ours: We can either worry ourselves sick or trust in God and experience wellness in every sense of the word.

"1 minute of anger weakens your immune system for 4-5 hours. 1 minute of laughter boosts your immune system for 24 hours."

—Dr. C. Leaf

Stress and anxiety are just as contagious as COVID-19.[119] In today's world of social media, people's thoughts and emotions can easily "sneeze on your brain" from all corners of the globe. Here are some tips to help you maintain a sense of calm.

1. **Get Curious**: You can't simply think your way out of an emotion. If that were the case, we would always be happy. However, you can observe your anxiety-related "habit loops" that lead to behaviours like lashing out, stress-eating, or worrying. Reflect on the trigger, your behaviour, and the outcome. There's a perceived reward hidden in those patterns; for instance, worrying might make you feel like you're taking action. Utilize the curiosity that God has given you to identify and examine these "habit loops" by exploring your thoughts and emotions. Ask yourself questions. Worrying is like a rocking chair; it gives you something to do, but it gets you nowhere. Asking questions gives you information, which is power.

2. **Label it:** Give a name to your feelings. Recognize and acknowledge guilt, worry, shame, regret, grief, anger, or any other emotions you experience. By doing this, you engage your prefrontal cortex or your "thinking mind" again. It's important to allow yourself to truly feel these emotions. As Jud Brewer explains, the more you try to suppress intense emotions, the more they'll persist and cause distress. Identify your feelings and name them. Give yourself permission to experience them. Sit with them until they begin to dissipate.

3. **Hack the System:** Challenge yourself by asking, "Is this really helpful?" If you find yourself worrying excessively or reaching for yet another cookie, chances are it's not beneficial. Allowing this realization to sink in can help "hack your reward system" because your brain will recognize that its coping mechanism isn't truly rewarding. By questioning the effectiveness of your actions, you can find healthier alternatives.

4. **Stay present:** God designed our brains to plan for the future and have a forward-thinking mindset. However, it requires information to do so effectively. During a crisis or difficult situation, you may not have enough information to make accurate predictions. Instead of getting caught up in a loop of "what-ifs," ask yourself, "Do I have enough information to make a decision? Is worrying helping me right now?" If the answer is no, shift your focus to the present moment. Ask yourself, "What can I do in this hour? In this minute?"

---

119 Dr. Judson Brewer. *Impact*-Brown Alumni Magazine-article

and take action accordingly. Choose to pray or praise in the present moment rather than endlessly ruminating about the future.

5. **Defuse Anger**: When we're stressed, we tend to default to negative emotions. Jud Brewer poses a question: <u>"How can we train ourselves to default to kindness instead of meanness?"</u> The answer lies in choosing the more rewarding option. Take note of how it feels to experience kindness from others and cultivate a habit of silently wishing people well. This is a conscious decision to walk in love and follow the golden rule. Kindness brings greater satisfaction than meanness.

6. **Take Five:** Take deep breaths, even up to ten, to calm your parasympathetic nervous system. One technique is called "five-finger breathing." Using the index finger of one hand, trace along the fingers of the other hand. Inhale slowly as you trace up one finger, and exhale as you trace down the other side. Repeat this process for all five fingers. By engaging your senses of touch, sight, and breath, this exercise occupies a significant portion of your brain's resources, potentially displacing worrying thoughts. Choose to focus on positive aspects found in the Word of God, such as promises, and imagine that you already possess them. This practice will push out anxiety and worry from your mind. Our thoughts occupy valuable space in our brains, which is why it's crucial to control them. As Psalm 119:37 states, "Turn my eyes from worthless things."

7. **Ground Yourself:** Jud Brewer's suggestion to "Feel your feet" is meant quite literally. Take 30 seconds to focus on the sensations in your feet. Count slowly to 30 to ensure you don't rush through it. Alternatively, perform a body scan, mentally going through each body part (starting with the big toe, ankle, calf, and so on) while attentively observing any sensations you may feel. Feeling your feet serves as a way to ground yourself, much like finding stability on the rock of God's Word.

8. **Plug In:** Make connections a priority in your life. Stay in touch with loved ones, give your kids or spouse a hug, spend time cuddling with a pet, or simply wrap your own arms around your shoulders and give yourself a tight squeeze. Say "Way to go me!" By engaging in these acts of connection, you are fostering positive emotional bonds. Remember, the new infection to spread is one of meaningful connections.

When you are feeling discouraged, tell yourself the following things, for they will help you stay in God's mindset.

1. This is tough, <u>but</u> so am I
2. I haven't figured this out <u>Yet</u>
3. This challenge is here to teach me something
4. All I need to do now is take one step forward and breathe
5. I did my best today, and that is good enough
6. Tomorrow is another day and another opportunity
7. My thoughts and feelings are temporary
8. These circumstances are subject to change
9. I cannot control events, people, or circumstances, but I can control how I respond. [120]

"God wants us to think like He thinks and not be victims of toxic thoughts such as un-forgiveness, victim mentality, stress, or depression. What you are not changing, you are choosing. We don't break habits, we replace them...we edit out thinking."
—*Jessi Jean-certified eating psychology coach*

The Bible says that we have the mind of God within us in Philippians 2:5 & 1 Corinthians 2:16. How do we operate with the mindset of Christ? What does God do? Do the opposite of what you feel.

"When you are tempted to worry, laugh by faith. Decide to use the strength that God gave you to have patience with joy. Many Christians fail to understand the importance and power of thanksgiving and joy."
—*Keith Butler*

God calls those things that are not as though they already were (Romans 4:17). God speaks by faith. He speaks what He wants rather than what is. Therefore, when you are tempted to stress, declare "I am relaxed in Jesus' name!" "I will not stress or worry because my God's got this!" "I will rest and receive!"

<u>God's success criteria include praise, gratitude, love, and prayer.</u>
<u>God uses praise as a weapon:</u> In Zephaniah 3:17 it says *"The Lord your God is among you; He is mighty to save, he will rejoice over thee with joy; he will quiet you with His love, He will rejoice over you with singing."*

---

[120] Dr. C Leaf. -Instagram post

Praise is a mighty offensive weapon in the hand of our God and in the hands of His children.

God uses gratitude as a boomerang: Gratitude comes right back to us. The more we thank God for what He has done for us and given us, the more things He sends us to be grateful for.

God uses prayer as an activation device: To activate the blessings in our lives. God takes what the enemy meant for evil and turns it for our good (Genesis 50:20). He turns things around. Your turnaround is coming!! God is the God of the Turnaround!

Praise: According to the dictionary, praise means to extol in words or song, to magnify, to glorify on account of perfections or excellent works, to honour and display excellence when applied to God. The word "Hosanna" also means praise. Praise is not just a feeling; it is a choice. It requires taking action and stepping out in faith, even when you don't feel like it. Praise is an attitude that you carry regardless of your circumstances. It is not merely getting emotional during a song because you identify with it; it is a spiritual expression that comes from your human spirit. Praise is a powerful offensive strategy in God's mindset. You can choose to have a pity party or a praise party, and the choice reflects whether you have a fixed mindset or a Kingdom mindset.

Joy, gratitude, and love are also success criteria that require choice and action. When it comes to our relationship with God, choice and action are always required. There is a part that God plays, and there is also our part in receiving the blessings and promises of God. Effort is always required in God's Kingdom mindset.

Praise is considered the highest form of prayer because it expresses gratitude to God in advance for the answers to our petitions. It is a weapon of spiritual warfare. The Bible instructs us to make the sacrifice of praise, which means praising God even in the midst of difficult situations when we may be struggling and weary (Hebrews 13:15). It can be challenging to give God praise when we may be tempted to blame Him. That's why it is called the sacrifice of praise. When we go against what our mind and circumstances are telling us and choose to obey God's Word and His ways, we are making the sacrifice of praise. Psalm 34:1 teaches us to praise the Lord at all times, whether in good times or bad times, when we feel like it and when we don't feel like it.

How can we praise God in troubled times? Our ability to praise is not dependent on our circumstances or feelings. Instead, our praise is rooted in the goodness and greatness of God, and it is based on His names and His character.

In the song "Surrounded" by Michael W. Smith it talks about putting on the garment of praise to dispel the spirit of heaviness and to fight our battles. Toxic thoughts can weigh us down spiritually, but praise acts as a garment that we can choose to put on (Isaiah 61:3). Therefore, praising God is a choice that we make, just like putting on a piece of clothing. The lyrics of the song say, "It may look like I am surrounded, but I'm surrounded by You. This is how I fight my battles." We fight our battles by praising God. Praise is an act of faith that moves the hand of God in our lives. When we praise, we magnify God and His abilities and goodness rather than focusing on our problems, doubts, and unbelief. Through our praise, we declare positive outcomes in the midst of life's storms. When we praise and shout, the enemy flees. Praise allows us to see into the spiritual realm with our eyes of faith. Through faith, we realize that we are actually surrounded by God's angelic forces, not by the enemy. Those who are for us are greater than those who are against us (2 Kings 6:16). If God is for us, then no one can stand against us. (Romans 8:31)

In the story of Jehoshaphat in 2 Chronicles 20:22, the Lord instructed them to put the praise singers in front of the army, and they sang their way to the battlefield. When they arrived, they didn't even have to fight because the Lord had already won the victory. Who sends singers first into battle? Only our God. His ways are not our ways, but His ways are better. <u>Trumpets and praise signify that we are already triumphant before the battle even begins.</u> We don't have to wait until the battle is over to praise God. We can praise Him in the midst of the battle or the storm because we know that we are victorious. God is a winner, and He never fails. We can praise God at the beginning of a battle by faith. Praise is a form of celebration where we anticipate and celebrate the goodness of God.

Trumpets have significant meaning in the context of war. In Numbers 10:8-10, God miraculously defeated the enemy by setting ambushes against them. The Lord Himself orchestrated the defeat of their enemies. Similarly, when we blow the trumpet in praise, the Lord will also remove our enemies. God fights our battles on our behalf when we engage in praise. The same God who helped Israel is the same God who will help us today. He instructs us to continue blowing the trumpets as a memorial to Him. God desires us to put on the garment of praise, blow the trumpets, and be joyful and glad because He is still God, and He reigns on His throne. The battle belongs to the Lord, and we know the outcome already—we are victorious! (2 Chronicles 20:15).

Personally, I want God to fight my battles, so I choose to offer Him the sacrifice of praise in the midst of my storms. I encourage you to shake off any heaviness and discouragement. If you feel like you have lost your praise due to disappointments in life, remember that putting on the garment of praise is a choice and an action. Blowing a trumpet or shofar may seem strange to the world, but it is a powerful weapon in God's arsenal. If we desire to obtain God's results, we must follow His ways of doing things. Those with a Kingdom mindset utilize the strategy of praise to dispel toxic thoughts, which are the lies of the enemy, from their lives and minds.

Psalm 22:3 states that God dwells in the praises of His people. When we praise, God's presence descends upon us. During praise, chains are broken, prison walls crumble, failures vanish, heaven invades the earth, and mighty miracles occur. Pursuing praise is, in fact, pursuing God because He dwells in the midst of His praises. Trumpets announce victory and royalty (1 Thessalonians 4:16-17) *As we blow trumpets during praise, it is announcing the arrival of God's presence among us."*

In the song "Raise a Hallelujah" by Jonathan and Melissa Helser, the lyrics say "I raise a Hallelujah, in the presence of my enemies, my doubt and unbelief. **My weapon is a melody.** Heaven comes to fight for me." Only God has the power to utilize a song as a weapon. What seems like foolishness to the world is a powerful tool for our God. Praise originates from deep within us, emanating from our spirit. It aligns with God's Word and stems from having His mindset. Praise is rooted in the understanding that Jesus has already overcome every circumstance. We offer praise to God because the battle has already been fought, and victory has already been achieved. It is through praise that we navigate our way out of every battle.

When we engage in praise, we are imitating our Father God, who continuously sings songs of deliverance, healing, and blessing over us. It is astounding to consider that the Creator of heaven and earth rejoices over us! (Zephaniah 3:17) God desires us to act in the same manner.

Within each of us, there is a unique song waiting to be sung. There is a shout that only you can unleash. When we make the choice to sing instead of cry, indulge in self-pity, or complain, it becomes a potent weapon in the spiritual realm. Opting to sing instead of succumbing to fear unleashes the angelic forces of heaven to fight on our behalf. Choosing praise over complaints aligns us with God's mindset while complaining reflects a fixed mindset. Complaints and excuses often go hand in hand. Praise empowers us to persevere and not give up. It realigns our priorities and strengthens us. There is a shout and a roar that only we can release. I challenge you to begin shouting and praising God like never before and witness the transformative impact it has on the circumstances of your life! A new frequency from heaven is being unleashed—a new sound. A kingdom sound is being released in this hour as God's children rise up equipped with His kingdom mindset and take the world by storm! A new kingdom sound for a new kingdom movement! It's time to release your roar!

"When we pray, we enter God's presence. When we praise, God enters into ours."

—Bishop David Oyedepo

<u>Praise emanates from a place of love.</u> It arises from a heart filled with gratitude. Praise stems from trust and a sense of safety, knowing that God knows us, loves us, and accepts us just as we are. There is no need to hide or fear because God already knows the depths of our hearts (Luke 16:15). We praise God because He first loved us. He chose us. He desires us. We are wanted and valuable in the eyes of the Creator of the Universe. Therefore, we offer our praise from a place of love. <u>We do not praise Him to earn His love but because He already loves us.</u> We do not praise God to manipulate Him into doing something for us but in response to what He has already done for us.

<u>Praise keeps our focus on God.</u> It directs our attention to the right perspective. Praise enables us to view our problems through an eternal lens or through MPA. Praising God allows us to fix our gaze on His greatness rather than the magnitude of our problems. Praise grants us insight into God's heart for us and brings clarity to His plans for our lives. In my personal experience, I have often heard from the Holy Spirit most profoundly when I am engaged in praising God, even more so than when I pray. If you desire to hear from God, start by praising Him! He dwells within the praises of His people. Through praising God, we have genuine encounters with Him (1 Timothy 6:17).

<u>God delights in receiving praise.</u> Praise is one of the few things that God desires from us. Throughout eternity, we will continually sing His praises—that is our destiny. The Bible declares that all the earth will resound with God's praises (Psalm 66:4). Praise is one of our inherent purposes. (Isaiah 43:21) Praise brings forth numerous physical, emotional, and spiritual benefits. We were created to fulfil our God-given assignments and to bring Him great glory.

The Bible reveals that God loves us so deeply and values us so greatly that He has inscribed our names and faces on the palms of His hands, so we are ever before Him (Isaiah 49:16). Despite having the entire universe and galaxies to behold, He chooses to keep us continually in His thoughts. Now, that is love! <u>As we begin to grasp the magnitude of God's love for us and comprehend all that He has provided through Jesus Christ, we will be compelled to offer unending praise.</u> I believe that the more we praise God, the more He showers us with reasons to give Him praise. This aligns with the Law of Attraction—like attracts like. What we think about and focus on is what we attract. Expressing our gratitude for God's goodness and acknowledging Him as a good Father motivates Him to do even more for us. God provides us with more opportunities to give thanks and praise.

All of creation continuously praises God. By observing the wonders of creation, His magnificent handiwork, one cannot help but be filled with awe. The mountains bow down in reverence, the oceans rise and fall at His command, resonating with the thunderous declaration of His greatness. The wind moves according to His direction, and all of creation trembles at His voice (Psalm 148:1-4). Jesus Himself proclaimed that if we were to cease praising Him, the very stones would cry out in response (Luke 19:40). If everything in existence praises God, then so should we. Even the angels offer praise to God. There is undeniable power in praise! As part of God's creation, we were designed to continually praise Him. Praise serves as a pillar of God's kingdom mindset.

Praise is not silent. It encompasses singing, dancing, shouts, and the use of musical instruments. "Zamar" praise denotes a musical expression of praise. It involves plucking the strings of an instrument, singing, and praising. It is a musical term extensively used in the Old Testament, appearing 26 times.

Psalm 150 says "Praise the Lord. Praise God in his sanctuary; praise him in his mighty heavens. Praise him with the sounding of the trumpet, praise him with the harp and lyre. Praise him with timbrel and dancing, praise him with the strings and pipe. Praise him with the clash of cymbals, praise him with resounding cymbals. Let everything that has breath praise the Lord."

That sounds like a band to me, maybe a concert. Heaven is a pretty noisy place filled with praise. Praise is an outward expression of a heart desiring to magnify God. I believe that we haven't truly praised God as we should. We have been hesitant to raise our hands and clap unto the Lord. Religious traditions that encourage quietness and solemnity are not necessarily aligned with Scripture. If we can scream and clap at a sports event for our favourite team or player, we should be wholeheartedly shouting and clapping praises to our Father God.

In our attempts to praise God, we have often relied on our intellect rather than our hearts and spirits. John 4:23 "the true worshippers will worship the Father in the Spirit and in truth, for they are the kind of worshippers the Father seeks." When we genuinely praise God and enter into His presence, we no longer care about who is watching or what we may look like, because praise is not about us—it's about God.

He desires our freedom. He wants us to be unrestricted in how we praise Him, following the guidance of the Holy Spirit. If you feel like dancing, then dance unto the Lord. If you are led to run, then run. If you feel compelled to bow down, do so. If you sense the urge to kneel in reverence, to cry, to laugh, to clap, or to raise your hands—do it all. If God Himself dances over us, then we should dance before Him as well. David danced unto the Lord, and the Bible says that he was a man after God's own heart (1 Samuel 13:14). 2 Corinthians 3:17 states "Where the spirit of the Lord is, there is freedom."

Heaven is described as a place filled with praises. *In Revelation 4:10, "the twenty-four elders fall down before him who sits on the throne and worship him. They lay their crowns before the throne and say. You are worthy, our Lord and God, to receive glory and honour and power, for you created all things, and by your will <u>they were created and have their being."</u>*

"Heaven will be like the best concert you've ever attended, only better."

—*Natalie Masucci*

When we praise God, we experience freedom. Our troubles and problems fade away. <u>Praise is not just a mere physical action; it has a spiritual activation connected to it. It is one of the most powerful weapons in our arsenal for cultivating a Kingdom mindset.</u> Through praise, we can let go, forgive, and experience true freedom.

For example, in the Book of Joshua, chapter 6:1-27, we read about the battle of Jericho and how Israel conquered Canaan. God instructed the Israelites to march around the city once for six days and then seven times on the seventh day. He commanded them to send the worshipers and priests ahead of the army. According to the Bible, on the seventh day, when they blew their trumpets and shouted, the stone walls of Jericho fell. Their obedience to God's instructions and their praises brought down the enemy's defenses. If we, too, obey God by adopting His kingdom mindset and strategy of praise, who knows what plans of the enemy we could disarm in our own lives? Next time you come up against something in your life, I encourage you to give God the sacrifice of praise rather than to despair. I believe that it will change the outcome in a positive way. By doing this, you are giving God permission to intervene on your behalf. Say "God I don't know what I'm going to do, but I know that you are already on it. You promise that no weapon formed against me or my family will prosper. You are so faithful and good. Thank you for making a way where there seems to be no way."

It is noteworthy that God often precedes a battle with praise. This is not what people typically do. God's ways are opposite the world's ways. (1 Corinthians 1:25).

Another example is found in Acts, chapter 16:25-26, where we encounter Paul and Silas imprisoned and chained after being arrested. Instead of having a pity party, they chose to praise God. Their praises were heard throughout the jail at midnight. Their praises caused an earthquake that not only brought down the prison walls but also set them free.

In both of these examples, we witness the incredible power of our praises. Praise is a choice and an action that demonstrates our faith. When we praise God in advance for the victory, it releases the forces of heaven and angelic beings to fight on our behalf. Praise disarms and confuses the enemy. There is a sound of praise, a kingdom sound that precedes a move of God, as exemplified in these two instances. God desires for us to adopt His kingdom mindset and release our kingdom sound in this hour.

"Ever slay a dragon? It's not farfetched at all in the spirit realm."
—Daniel Kolenda

God sings praises and dances over us. In Zephaniah 3:17, it says that He surrounds us with a song. Let that sink in: God is always cheering us on! He is our heavenly cheerleader, telling us to keep going, not to give up, and that we can do it. There is nothing that God won't do for us. Not only does God cheer us on, but the Bible also tells us that there is a great cloud of witnesses cheering us onward (Hebrews 12:1). God uses praise as a weapon in His arsenal and as a means to encourage us. Praise is a form of spiritual protection, like a garment, in the spiritual realm. As God sings over us, His words create what He is saying. Praise creates a hedge of protection around us. (Isaiah 60:18).

The Bible describes God's love for us as reckless because He will leave the 99 to go after the one who has gone astray (Luke 15:4 and Matthew 18:12). God is still able to calm the waves and the wind, so we can confidently sing that it is well with our soul in any and every circumstance (Psalm 46:1-3). God's love for us is like a mighty rushing wave, unstoppable. Our praise is not conditional to our circumstances; it comes from our kingdom mindset and knowing who we are. Our praise should be as unstoppable as God's love for us. When we constantly have God's praise on our lips, we won't have time to have a pity party, make excuses, or complain. Therefore, praise releases us from the clutches of the enemy's mindset. Praise helps us pray as it ushers us into the throne room and God's presence. Praise keeps us in

God's mindset mode and produces perseverance, persistence, and power.

Praise comes from an understanding of God's love. God's love is uncontainable, unexplainable, and never-ending. The Bible says that nothing can separate us from the love of God (Romans 8:38-39). We don't deserve it, and we did nothing to earn it, but God desires to have fellowship with us. He wants us to be part of His family. We have been adopted into God's family (Ephesians 1:5). God chose us, and He wants us to depend on Him for everything. When we realize how much we are loved and that God is our provision, we adopt God's kingdom mindset. Having God's mindset causes us to praise and thank Him for everything He has done, is doing, and will do in our lives. Praise reminds us of all the things God has done for us. It helps us have a good memory (Proverbs 10:7) and remember the right things, such as when God answered our prayers in the past. We are the body of Christ on the earth. We are God's voice, hands, and feet. He desires to do great things through us. This is why it is so important to adopt God's Kingdom mindset. We all have an important assignment to fulfil, and we need God's help. Our time on earth is limited, and praise is a success criterion given to us by God to help us have maximum impact. God created music and designed us in a special way so that we can use music to draw closer to Him and glorify His name (Psalm 47:6). The enemy has corrupted music and uses it as a means to deceive people. Be careful what types of music you listen to. Music engages our whole being, concentrating our soul (mind) on God as we are stirred by the lyrics, melodies, and harmonies of the songs. There are many different types of praise in the Bible, and they all require action and sound, just like the rest of God's kingdom mindset. Action is required!

1. Yadah is to worship with extended hands.
2. Tehillah is to sing and to laud.
3. Barak is to kneel or bow.
4. Halal is to make a show, to boast and to celebrate.
5. Towdah is agreeing with what has been done or will be done.
6. Zamar is to sing with instruments.
7. Shabach is to shout.[121]

Praise is not only therapeutic, it is a defense mechanism: In Psalm 8:2 it says that *"praise creates a hedge of protection in our minds."* Praising and worshipping God creates a positive stronghold in our minds, reminding us of the goodness of God and blocking negative

---

[121] *Tehillahword.com*

thoughts from entering. As Psalm 8:2 says, "Through the praise of children and infants you have established a stronghold against your enemies, to silence the foe and the avenger." Praise has the power to silence the enemy, which is incredibly powerful!

There are numerous benefits of praise. Praise gives us hope. It lifts our spirits and puts us in a good mood. Praise dispels fear and unbelief. It reaffirms our identity as children of God and demolishes the lies of the enemy that we may have believed. Praise relieves stress and alleviates depression. It is empowering because it serves as a potent weapon in the spiritual realm, ushering in supernatural assistance. Praise reminds us of the almighty nature of God, prompting us to recognize our dependency on Him. We acknowledge that we are not in control, but He is. Praise has the ability to heal broken hearts and draws us closer to God. It is a pillar of God's Kingdom mindset. It is demonstrated through positive self-talk (praising oneself), compliments (praising others) and gratitude (praising God).

In addition, research conducted by the Mor's Music and Memory project at Brown University has shown that listening to a personalized music playlist reduces behavioural symptoms in Alzheimer's patients and decreases the need for antipsychotic medications.[122] Once again, science is demonstrating the truth of scripture. Praise not only has emotional and physical benefits but can also have an impact on a genetic level. It is worth considering whether negative emotions and toxic thoughts, such as fear, depression, victim mentality, excuses, stress, and unforgiveness, could lead to excessive strain on certain areas of the brain. Could these toxic thoughts be damaging? Scientists are investigating the effects of a continuous onslaught of negative emotions and their potential role in causing **neuro-inflammation** and the accumulation of plaques over time. There is a link between Alzheimer's disease and pronounced neuro-inflammation.[123] This research is indeed exciting. Praise has the power to bring about peace and is beneficial for both our bodies and brains. It serves as God's antidote to neuro-inflammation, which is a precursor to many diseases. This is why God created us to praise Him at all times, as it is ultimately good for us (Psalm 34:1). Everything that God asks us to do is for our good.

In Colossians 3:2, we are instructed to set our minds on things above rather than earthly things. Setting our minds on things above means focusing on God and His goodness instead of the chaotic world we live in. If you've been keeping up with the news, you'll know that there are numerous distressing events happening around the globe—

---

[122] Brown University- *Impact Magazine* 2020, p.25
[123] *Impact Magazine 2020*, p.27

deadly viruses, shortages, shutdowns, economic instability, and more. The news often instills fear in people, as it is a part of earthly matters and the world system. It's important for us to be mindful of our exposure to the news and limit it accordingly. While it's crucial to stay informed, excessively consuming news can lead to depression and feelings of despair. We should use praise as a form of medicine for our minds and bodies, enabling them to function optimally as God intended. Praise can counteract the impact of toxic thoughts in our lives. Our bodies respond positively to the praises of God as our cells are awakened, aligning with the physiology that was designed for a regular lifestyle of praising God. Ultimately, praise uplifts our spirits and makes us feel good.

"Don't copy the behaviour and customs of this world, but let God transform you into a new person by changing the way you think." Romans 12:2

Action Plan to combat toxic thoughts and patterns:

1. Monitor your intake. Watch less television, reduce news consumption, and limit time spent on social media.
2. Increase reading habits, focusing on uplifting and inspirational material. Read your Bible.
3. Listen to uplifting and motivational content such as podcasts, audiobooks, and CDs. Engage in listening to praise and worship music, being cautious about the type of music you choose.
4. Speak positive declarations aligned with God's Word, using "I AM" statements.
5. Practice meditation on God's Word, focusing on one scripture at a time. Scripture encourages us to meditate on God's Word in Psalm 1:2-3 and Philippians 4:8. Meditation involves contemplating and pondering the scripture repeatedly, similar to how a cow chews its cud. It is an ongoing process that helps internalize the Word, allowing it to transform our mindset. As it takes root in our hearts, it will naturally manifest in our speech and circumstances.
6. Increase prayer time, communicating with God more frequently and earnestly. Create a prayer closet or war room.
7. Keep a gratitude journal to record prayers, dreams, and how God has answered those prayers, cultivating an attitude of gratitude.
8. Develop a lifestyle of praise. Always look for the good or positive in every situation. When you are tempted to complain or swear or shout, choose to shout praises, sing, give

compliments and positive reinforcement instead. Praise your efforts, praise those in your life, praise God for all His blessings, guidance and protection.

Praise scriptures:

- ✔ Psalm 67:5-5
- ✔ Psalm 150 all
- ✔ Psalm 35: 18 & 28
- ✔ Psalm 95:2-3 Let's come before Him with thanksgiving
- ✔ Psalm 113;3
- ✔ Psalm 34:1.
- ✔ Isaiah 61:3 the garment of praise
- ✔ Psalm 148:1-4.
- ✔ Zephaniah 3:17
- ✔ Acts chapter16: 25-26 Paul & Silas
- ✔ Joshua chapter 6:1-27 Battle of Jericho
- ✔ Revelation 4:10 -24 elders
- ✔ John 4:23

Praise Recap:

- ✔ Praise is part of God's kingdom mindset.
- ✔ Praise is a mighty spiritual weapon.
- ✔ Praise reminds us that only God is Almighty. He is able. He has no rival and no equal.
- ✔ Praise gets our focus off ourselves and our problems and back on God.
- ✔ Praise brings us to a place of humility, repentance and surrender.
- ✔ Praise makes the enemy flee.
- ✔ Praise leaves no room for complaining and negativity or a fixed mindset.
- ✔ Praise makes room for God's blessings over our lives.
- ✔ Praise ushers in the presence of God and causes us to want to know Him more (1 Peter 2:9).
- ✔ Praise causes our spirits to be refreshed and renewed in His presence (Psalm 16:11).
- ✔ Praise paves the way for God's power to be displayed in our lives.

✓ Praise causes miracles to happen because praise is an act of great faith. [124]

You may be just one praise away from experiencing a breakthrough, deliverance, or healing! Offer God a heartfelt and exuberant praise, and observe what unfolds. Praise holds incredible power!

Praise is an integral aspect of God's mindset, inspiring and propelling us forward as we strive to fulfil our divine purpose. It serves as a <u>constant motivation to press on</u> until we reach the finish line.

"If Jesus is coming, let's act like it, and talk like it, and live like it and be like it."

Gratitude: Gratitude is a Boomerang

<u>Gratitude is a vital element of the success criteria outlined in the Word of God, encompassing God's kingdom mindset.</u> The Holy Spirit has revealed to me that gratitude is not just an occasional feeling but an attitude, a way of life, and a mindset. The word "gratitude" originates from the Latin word *"gratus,"* which means both thankful and pleasing. When we experience gratitude, we are not only thankful for what someone has done for us but also pleased with the results. Gratitude is a virtue that influences not only our thoughts and emotions but also our actions and behaviour. It is an essential component of a growth mindset. Gratitude is a way of life for those who are blessed and successful, and especially for God's children. Moreover, gratitude stands as one of God's most powerful tools to enhance our mood, mind, and mental well-being. Despite its simplicity, it is often overlooked and underutilized because many people are unaware of its numerous benefits.

"Gratitude is an attitude, a lifestyle and a mindset of the world's most successful people."

—*Natalie Masucci*

God commands us to have a lifestyle of gratitude. God created us, and He knows how our minds and bodies work best. In 1 Thessalonians 5:18, he says *"Give thanks in all circumstances; for this is God's will for you in Christ Jesus."* We are told to always give thanks. Even when we don't feel like it. Even when we haven't received our answered prayers.

Not sure what to thank God for? Not in the habit of expressing gratitude to God? Start with something small. Thank Him for waking you up this morning and giving you breath in your lungs. Thank Him for

---

[124] Debbie McDaniel. *What the Power of Praise can Do: 8 Reminders from His Word*-Crosswalk.com

providing food on your table, a roof over your head, and clothes to wear. Give thanks for the sacrifice of Jesus and the ministry of the Holy Spirit. Recognize that you are still here and persevering by the grace of God. Thank Him for the new day filled with possibilities and for the gift of second chances. Express gratitude for His attentiveness to your prayers.

Individuals with a Kingdom mindset develop a habit of gratitude and are able to praise and thank God in advance by faith. They take God at His Word and trust that He will bring about growth and improvement, change circumstances, open doors, and bring the prodigals back home. Gratitude brings a sense of fulfilment, relief from stress, an atmosphere of peace, the presence of God, the manifestation of blessings, and the realization of dreams. <u>Gratitude serves as God's free anti-depressant.</u> If your mind has been racing lately, God understands your needs. Are you caught in a cycle of worry or overthinking? Stop the spinning and worrying about what God is already working on. Instead, worship and thank Him for His faithfulness and provision. By consistently practicing thankfulness, negative thought patterns will gradually weaken and diminish in your mind.

The highest demonstration of your faith is expressing gratitude to God in advance for what He is about to do in your life. It takes faith to look forward and believe that God will make a way even when you cannot see one.

"Thanking God after He answers a prayer is gratitude. Thanking God in advance is faith."
—*Terri Savelle Foy*

According to scientific research, expressing gratitude offers numerous benefits. Science continually reinforces the truth of God's Word. Firstly, gratitude acts as a free antidepressant. Secondly, it functions as a natural pain reducer. Thirdly, it improves the quality of sleep. Fourthly, it aids in stress regulation. Lastly, it builds and enhances relationships.

1. <u>Gratitude serves as God's free antidepressant.</u> When we express gratitude and receive it from others, our brain releases dopamine and serotonin, essential neurotransmitters responsible for our emotions. These chemicals generate a sense of well-being and happiness, instantly improving our mood. [125]

2. <u>Gratitude acts as God's free and natural pain reducer</u>. A study conducted in 2003 called "Counting Blessings vs. Burdens" examined the impact of gratitude on physical well-being. The study revealed that 16% of patients who kept a gratitude

---

[125] Dr. C. Leaf - Instagram post, Nov. 2020

journal reported reduced pain symptoms and displayed greater willingness to cooperate with their treatment protocol. Further analysis discovered that gratitude regulates dopamine levels, increasing vitality and reducing subjective feelings of pain. If you don't have a gratitude journal, I highly recommend starting one. It can positively transform you in many ways. Instead of seeking temporary relief, try expressing gratitude the next time you experience pain. Thanksgiving and gratitude have transformative effects, redirecting our minds from worry and aligning our spirits with God's Word.[126] Gratitude helps our brains flip the script from pain to praise. This flip releases hormones which promotes feelings of well-being.

3. <u>Gratitude serves as God's natural sleeping aid.</u> Studies on gratitude and stress have shown that experiencing and displaying simple acts of kindness activate the hypothalamus, regulating various bodily functions, including sleep. When we acknowledge that God is working behind the scenes in our lives through gratitude, we can enjoy restful sleep. Proverbs 3:24 states, "When you lie down, you will not be afraid; when you lie down, your sleep will be sweet."

4. <u>Gratitude acts as God's stress reliever.</u> Expressing gratitude helps regulate stress. In a study by McCraty and colleagues (1998) on gratitude and appreciation, participants who felt grateful exhibited a significant reduction in cortisol, the stress hormone. They also demonstrated improved cardiac functioning and greater resilience to emotional setbacks and negative experiences. Gratitude strengthens our resilience against the enemy's toxic thoughts and schemes (Philippians 4:6-7).

5. <u>Gratitude serves as God's relationship builder.</u> Gratitude aids in building and improving relationships. A 2014 study published in Emotion found that expressing appreciation to a new acquaintance increased the likelihood of developing an ongoing relationship. Proverbs 18:24 confirms this saying that if you want friends, show yourself friendly.

Gratitude consists of our words. It requires faith to say thank you before receiving; therefore, gratitude provides God with something to work with. Your words and your faith can bring about a turnaround in your circumstances. God is the God of the Turn Around! **When we practice gratitude, we attract more things to be grateful for.** The Law of

---

126 Keith Butler - Instagram post

Attraction, as found in Proverbs 23:7, states that like attracts like. Everyone, including God, appreciates being acknowledged, so develop a habit of thanking God every day. The more we express gratitude to God, the more blessings He will bestow upon us. James 3:10 reminds us that blessings and curses come from the same mouth. Thankfulness and gratitude invite blessings into our lives. Psalm 100:4 encourages us to be thankful and openly express it.

> **"A grateful heart is a magnet for miracles."**
> —*Terri Savelle Foy*

Gratitude serves as a reminder of our past victories and triumphs with God. It strengthens our faith by recalling answered prayers, instilling confidence that God will work in our favour once again. Gratitude keeps us humble as we acknowledge that it was God, not ourselves, who helped us conquer the giants in our lives. A heart filled with gratitude resists pride, as we recognize that credit belongs to God for what He has done. Always remember to acknowledge God's goodness in your life. Every good and perfect gift is from above, coming down from the Father of the heavenly lights, who does not change like shifting shadows (James 1:17).

Practicing gratitude can save us from sorrow and depression. When we closely examine our lives, we can always find something to be grateful for. The song "Count Your Blessings" encourages us to name and appreciate the many things the Lord has done. So go ahead, express gratitude for something today and push away toxic thoughts from your mind (1 Thessalonians 5:18).

It's important to understand that Thanksgiving extends beyond a single day on the calendar. When thankfulness becomes a way of life rather than an isolated event, we open the door to God's blessings. The more gratitude we express, the greater abundance we experience. Don't we all desire to enjoy more blessings in our lives? Gratitude is like a boomerang that comes back to you.

Make gratitude a positive habit in your life by consciously replacing complaints and excuses with gratitude and praise. This is what God asks of you as part of His mindset. Have you expressed thanks today?

For example, when faced with a fender bender accident, you have a choice in how you react. You can complain, saying, "This is the last thing I needed today. My day has gone from bad to worse." Alternatively, you can choose gratitude, saying, "Thank God it was only a fender bender; it could have been much worse. I'm grateful that no one was injured or killed. This is why having insurance is important. Thank you, Father for protecting me."

"It is always possible to be thankful for what is given rather than to complain about what is not given. One or the other becomes a habit of life."

–Elisabeth Elliot

Some of us may struggle with gratitude because we tend to compare ourselves to others instead of looking within. However, gratitude prompts us to engage in self-reflection and introspection, which is encouraged by God. This psychological exercise helps us question our thoughts, develop our minds, and find value in our mistakes. Gratitude involves refocusing our minds on the positive aspects of our lives. Research shows that we have more than 50,000 thoughts per day, with over half of them being negative and more than 90% being repetitive from the previous day. Practicing introspection enhances our understanding of ourselves and enables us to shift our focus from the distractions of our fast-paced lives to a sense of fulfilment.[127]

"A person who feels appreciated will always do more than what is expected." The benefits of using the success criteria of Gratitude and Praise in the workplace are improved staff morale, increased productivity and effective communication. People who feel recognized and appreciated will always do more than what is expected of them. Things that cost nothing to implement can bring huge returns.

When I taught kindergarten, I would give each student a reward certificate every Friday as a form of positive reinforcement. Each week, I indicated something positive that I witnessed during the week. I intentionally focused on the good and encouraged growth. For example, I would say, 'I like the way you shared with your classmates' or 'I love the way you put away your toys. You are becoming a good tidy-upper!' I would also say, 'Way to go! You remembered to print your name on your work!' or 'I like the way you got along better with your classmates this week.'

Years later, a former student named **Tyler James Holgate** contacted me. He wanted to visit me and give me a copy of the children's book he wrote entitled 'Follow That Monkey.' During the visit, he pulled out a piece of paper from his wallet. It was one of the reward certificates he had received in kindergarten. He went on to tell me how much those rewards meant to him and how they had inspired him to become an author, regardless of his disability. This experience showed me the

---

[127] Wood. *What is Introspection*-Positivepsychology.com 2013

power of praise and compliments, otherwise known as positive reinforcement. We have no idea of the effect that our actions have on others.

"I alone cannot change the world, but I can cast a stone across the waters to create many ripples."
—Mother Teresa

It's important to recognize that the enemy wants us to compare ourselves to others. If we're still waiting for our prayers to be answered while witnessing others receiving answers, it can be challenging to feel grateful. However, we must resist the temptation to compare our lives with theirs. The enemy wants us to believe that others have a better life, but this is a lie. What people portray on social media is often an illusion with little truth behind it. Instead, we should look within ourselves. Regardless of our circumstances, God's goodness and mercy never leave us (Psalm 23:6). He prepares blessings for us even in the midst of difficult seasons and in the presence of our enemies. <u>The grass is not greener on the other side of the fence. The grass is greener where you water it.</u> Gratitude helps us redirect our focus to the only One who can turn our problems around for His glory and our benefit. Each of us has our own race to run, and as the body of Christ, we are interconnected. We are called to work together collaboratively to fulfil God's plans and purposes on earth. The spirit of division comes from the enemy, so let's concentrate on our own lives and recognize how good God has been to us.

"Today (and everyday!) Don't count calories, carbs, or steps. Count your blessings, achievements, hurdles overcome, and people you love. Build those healthy positive brain structures! This is the foundation of mental toughness and resilience."
—Dr. C. Leaf

Gratitude scriptures:
- ✓ **1 Chronicles 16:34** -Give thanks to the Lord, for He is good; His love endures forever.
- ✓ **Philippians 4:6-** Do not be anxious about anything, but in everything by prayer and petition, with thanksgiving, present your requests to God.
- ✓ **Psalm 118:24** -This is the day the Lord has made. Let us rejoice and be glad in it.
- ✓ **Psalm 107:21**-Let them give thanks to the Lord for his steadfast love, for his wondrous works.

- ✓ **Ephesians 5:20-**always giving thanks to God the father for everything, in the name of our Lord Jesus Christ.
- ✓ **Psalm 95:1-2-**Come, let us sing for joy to the Lord; let us shout aloud to the Rock of our salvation. Let us come before him with thanksgiving and extol him with music and song.
- ✓ **Psalm 100:4-**Enter His gates with thanksgiving and His courts with praise.
- ✓ **1 Thessalonians 5:16-18-**Rejoice always, pray continually, give thanks in all circumstances; for this is God's will for you in Christ Jesus.

"Prayer is an activation device in the spirit realm."
—Natalie Masucci

The next success criterion we will discuss is prayer.
Prayer is the foundation for everything that God has called us to do. According to the Oxford Dictionary of English, prayer is a solemn request for help or an expression of thanks addressed to God. It is an earnest hope or wish. Jesus himself spent a significant amount of time praying while He was on Earth, indicating its great importance. He would often separate himself from His disciples to pray alone.

It is often said "A prayerless life is a powerless life." Prayer is our way of communicating with God the Father and receiving His direction, and appropriating what He has already given us through Jesus. <u>It's important to note that we don't pray for victory; rather, we pray from a position of victory (1 Corinthians 15:57).</u>

"Prayer is the connector with us and God."
—Pastor Lynette Farrier

Prayer is founded on God's Word. When we approach God the Father, we come with His Word in the name of Jesus (John 16:23). We bring the answer, the promises found in Scripture. In prayer, we remind God of His Word. It is essential to use the right scriptures for the situation at hand. Through our covenant with Him, we have a legal right to approach God in prayer (Hebrews 8:6). The Word of God represents His contract with us, which is why we can boldly come before Him, aligning our prayers with what He has said. We declare, "Father, Your Word declares..." Jesus is our advocate (1 John 2:1-2).

Prayer should be the key of the day and the lock of the night.
God sees us through the lens of what Jesus accomplished on the cross. We are recognized by the Father because of the blood of Jesus.

God sees us "IN HIM".. Prayer is not an attempt to persuade God to act because He has already done everything. It is not an effort to get God's attention because He sees all. We don't need to beg God; instead, we simply remind Him of His promises, knowing that He loves us and has already provided for us. When we approach the throne of God, we do not leave empty-handed because we come as heirs of the inheritance (Romans 8:17). We depart from the throne room with the answer, praising God. We act as though it is already done, for we will receive the fulfilment of the prayers we have prayed (1 John 5:15).

Prayer brings about change in us and in our circumstances. Prayer does not change God because He is unchanging (Hebrews 13:8). The Word of God is alive because Jesus is alive, and it remains the same yesterday, today, and forever. We can stand on it with confidence. While doctor's reports, stock markets, and circumstances may fluctuate, God's Word remains steadfast and settled in heaven. It is an unchanging promise upon which we can rely when we pray in faith. God and His Word are inseparable. He exalts His Word above His name (Psalm 138:2). His Word is always available and ready, waiting for someone to believe it and apply it in faith during prayer. God's Word becomes his thoughts given to us in our prayer life.

In prayer, we seek God's supernatural assistance in our lives. Prayer moves the hand of God and grants Him permission to intervene on our behalf. It is an acknowledgment that we cannot accomplish things on our own. Prayer is an act of surrender.

Seven days without prayer make one W.E.A.K.

"If it's big enough to worry about, it's big enough to pray about."
—Jentezen

Some of my favourite scriptures on prayer.

1. **Philippians 4:6:** "Do not be anxious about anything, but in everything by prayer and supplication with thanksgiving let your requests be made known to God."
2. **James 5:16:** "The prayer of a righteous person has great power as it is working."
3. 1 **Thessalonians** 5:16-18: "Rejoice always, pray without ceasing, give thanks in all circumstances; for this is the will of God in Christ Jesus for you."
4. Ephesians 6:17-18, Mark 11:23-25, 2 Corinthians 10:4-5, 1 John 5:14-15, Romans 10:8 and Matthew 21:21-22.

See more scriptures in my eBook Prayer 101 available on website @ Empoweredwordministries.ca

When we pray, we are to stand immovable on the promises in the Word of God. We confidently stand on God's success criteria. No one can change God's Word, so we can have confidence in standing on it.

Prayer is so important and powerful, yet many people don't know how to pray. Pray this over yourself today.

Lord, You are mighty in me. You made me. You put every cell together and came up with me. You are the Lord of my life, and You are the Lord of my mind. Lord, I have believed things that are not true, and I'm sorry for that. Please forgive me. Lord, because You are good, would You let the ways I used to think die off and then would You blaze a new trail in my mind? Would You stop connections in my brain that are tied to my old way of thinking and form new neural pathways with Your good truth? Thank You, Lord, for Your forgiveness and for the miraculous way You made me. Please remake my mind to be more like Yours. [128]

God has a kingdom mindset. In **Revelation 12:11**, at the end of the Bible, God declared ahead of time that we would win! Look closely at this verse as we have a part to play. "We conquer the enemy with the blood of the lamb Jesus and by the word of our testimony. Our testimony is what we say or declare, which comes from what we believe in our hearts." We believe what we think about most. Kingdom mindset or fixed mindset? **What you repeatedly hear, you will eventually believe. We believe what we say above all others.**

Let's not waste our lives with a fixed mindset and fail to fulfil the plan and purpose God has for us. Instead, let's adopt a kingdom mindset that believes in the potential for our abilities to grow. We need to keep moving forward and embrace difficult situations as opportunities for growth. The death of a loved one, the end of a marriage, an illness, or the loss of a job do not have to define us or hold us back. They can be moments that propel us to new levels or seasons with God. It's all about perspective. Don't give up, keep pushing forward. If flying is not an option, then run; if running is not possible, then walk; and if walking seems impossible, then crawl. The important thing is to keep moving forward with God. Do what you can.

---

[128] Morgan Hayley. Daily Devotionals email "*Preach to Yourself*"-Copyright Hayley Morgan.

Satan wants us to remain stagnant, trapped in fear and bondage with a fixed mindset. However, Jesus came to set us free from toxic thought patterns and wrong mindsets. He expects us to keep growing and maintain a kingdom mindset. We must continue progressing towards fulfilling our assignment in life.

Our life is a continuous journey of growth and maturity. Each day, every interaction and every experience contributes to our expansion and transformation. Over time, these cumulative changes lead us to make different choices that become our new normal. <u>Additionally, our cells are constantly regenerating, making us physically different from who we were in the past (Galatians 2:20).</u> Changing our mindset takes time, but the effort is worthwhile. It has the power to transform our lives, leading us to success and victory.[129] God never said that the journey would be easy but that the destination would be worthwhile.

---

[129] Despault, Michelle. "*Add-Cultivating A Growth Mindset.*" Catholic Teacher Magazine, Feb./Mar. 2020, pp. 16-17.

Chapter Eight

Cultivating a Kingdom Mindset

Life is a journey of discovery. First and foremost, it's about discovering how much God loves us and allowing His love to transform us by adopting His Kingdom mindset. Secondly, it's about discovering our God-given potential and talents and using them to fulfil our divine purpose. God has given us the Bible, His Word, as our success criteria, containing everything we need for our journey. God provides us with His mindset, which includes success criteria, descriptive feedback, and positive self-talk, serving as His formula for success. As we have seen, God uses these strategies Himself. He would never ask us to do something He wouldn't do. Our Father embodies a kingdom mindset.
It is essential to make time in our schedules to read the Word of God, understand how these strategies work, and apply them in our lives.

The good news is that we have the power to choose our mindset. We can shift from a fixed mindset to a kingdom mindset, opening the door for new and different perspectives in our lives. Obstacles can turn into opportunities, and failures can become learning experiences when we adopt God's mindset. God expects us to change our mindset by continually renewing our minds with the Word of God and following His kingdom principles.

According to researcher Dr. Carol Dweck, we all have a mixture of fixed and growth mindsets, and this mixture continually evolves as we do. The parts of our lives and hearts that we haven't surrendered to God yet are examples of a fixed mindset. Some common examples include beliefs such as "I am not good at math," "I am not a morning person," "I'm accident-prone," "I could never run a marathon," "I'll never lose the weight," "I'm not good with people," and "I will never fit back into my wedding dress." The problem with having fixed mindsets is that they can hold us back from achieving the things we want and fully pursuing our goals. They leave no room for reinterpretation and, thus, no opportunity for growth. For instance, if you believe you are not smart enough, you're unlikely to invest more time studying because you don't see the point. If you believe you can never lose weight, you probably won't integrate exercise and a healthy diet into your routine because you don't see the point. It is important to identify our areas of weakness and address them. Dealing with our weaknesses means allowing God into our hearts and letting Him heal us. God desires to heal us wherever we are hurting. He doesn't want us to simply cover up our weaknesses with Band-Aids, masks, or counterfeit coping strategies. He wants to heal us and make us whole so that we can move forward in our lives. Ignoring our weaknesses won't make them disappear. God doesn't want us to bury our heads in the sand and pretend that everything is okay. We need to face our weaknesses with God's help. We can choose to view them as obstacles or opportunities, depending on our mindset. We will all encounter obstacles in life, and our current hindrances and weaknesses may turn out to be our greatest opportunities in the future. When we maintain the right mindset and recognize that the obstacles we face are actually opportunities, God will make a way for us.

"Don't play with what tempts you, or you risk opening a door the devil will barge through."
—*KCM Canada*

A kingdom mindset recognizes that our talents can be developed through hard work and input from the Holy Spirit, which comes in the form of descriptive feedback. This perspective allows for a different outcome. <u>When you believe that something can change, you will take action accordingly</u>. With a growth mindset, a student who fails a test acknowledges the need to study harder for a better grade. An athlete who misses an opportunity understands the importance of more practice. Once you start considering the possibility of change in your circumstances, your mindset begins to shift from fixed to growth. There is hope in this mindset.[130] Our mindset continues to change and evolve throughout our lives. <u>A kingdom mindset is superior because it is a partnership with God.</u> You are not relying on your own strength, knowledge or abilities but on God's. As long as you're still breathing, it means that God isn't done with you yet. He still has a purpose for your life. With God, there is always hope. Don't let limited thinking hinder you from fulfilling your destiny. You have the power to change your thoughts and mindset, thereby altering your circumstances and the outcome of your life.

Take a moment to reflect on areas where you may have a fixed mindset, and ask yourself, "Is this the truth?" Consider the origin of this mindset. Did it come from God or the enemy/world? Mastering your

---

[130] "Catholic Teacher Magazine-OECTA." Feb/March 2020.

mindset involves uncovering the lies that we have accepted as truths in our lives. Growing your mindset means renewing your mind with the Word of God, which reminds us that our circumstances are subject to change. 2 Corinthians 4:18 says to *"fix our eyes not on what is seen but on what is unseen since what is seen is temporary, but what is unseen is eternal."* God has the ultimate authority in our lives. As the creator who knows us better than we know ourselves, why not place our trust in Him for our lives and our mindset?

Instead of striving to be the perfect someone, whether it's a teacher, parent, employee, boss or any other role, let's shift our focus to becoming better than we were yesterday. Keep moving forward, embracing the journey of growth. It's important for people to witness your struggles, failures, and mistakes. By being transparent about your humanity, they will learn that success is not about perfection but about persistence and maintaining God's positive mindset.

***

What do you want people to say about you in your eulogy/obituary?

When I was in Bible College, one of the first exercises we were asked to do was to write our own obituary. At first, I found it to be a peculiar request. However, the purpose behind it became clear: it serves as a guideline for how we want to be remembered. What do we want people to say about us at our funeral? It made me reflect deeply.

Do we want our obituary to focus on how we were never able to overcome trauma or abuse? How did the loss of a loved one consume and derail our lives? How do we succumb to bad habits, addiction and let it define us? How did our divorce shattered us, leading us into a spiral of depression and wasted years? Absolutely not!

Instead, our obituary can serve as a mission statement for our lives. It can guide us towards long-term goals and dreams, giving us a clear sense of purpose. It's a reminder to live a life of significance, overcome challenges, and make a positive impact on others. God desires for us to grasp these lessons and continue moving forward so that we may live a life without regrets.

Our obituary should reflect the legacy we want to leave behind, the impact we want to have, and the change we want to create, thus inspiring others to do the same. Your legacy is not something to be thought about towards the end of your life because it's already begun by the choices and decisions you make today. The good news is that you can start following God's success criteria that will positively influence generations. Let us be able to say, "I gave it my all for the things I valued." I gave my utmost effort to fulfil the assignment that God gave me.[131]

"She was a force to be reckoned with."

—Mayor Hazel McCallion

Fixed/God's mindset:

Fixed: I just want to quit.
God's: I made you and I will carry you Isaiah 46:4

Fixed: It's impossible.
God's: All things are possible through Me. Luke18:27

Fixed: I am so alone.
God's: Behold, I am with you always. Matthew 28:20

Fixed: I'm so exhausted.
God's: Come to me and I will give you rest. Matthew 11:28

Fixed: I'm so screwed up.
God's: Though you may stumble, you will not fall. Psalm 37:24

Fixed: I can't do it anymore.
God's: I will carry and save. Isaiah 46:4

Fixed: I don't deserve to be loved.
God's: I love you more than you will ever know. 1 John 4:7 [132]

Fixed Mindset versus Kingdom Mindset:

1. Addictive spirit versus God of moderation and order- virtue of self-control/discipline. (Proverbs 25:28)
2. Worry versus Trust-God will provide/cast all your care on the Lord (1 Peter 5:7).
3. Glass half full/glass half empty; looking at the problem rather than at God-Psalmist says my glass is overflowing (my cup runneth over) (Psalm 23:5).
4. Hopeless situation/ Nothing is impossible with God (Luke 1:37).

---

[131] *Dweck*-p.44
[132] Gotestmonio-*Instagram*

5. I can't do it/I can't do it **yet** but I will keep trying until I can or I can do all things through Christ who strengthens me (Philippians 4:11-13).
6. I'm a failure vs. God's the author and finisher of my faith (Hebrews 12:2).
7. I'm broken vs. He's my healer (Isaiah 26:3-4).
8. I'm a sinner vs. He's my saviour so I'm forgiven (Like 6:37).

When we make the decision to accept Jesus as our personal Savior and Lord, the Bible tells us that we become entirely new beings. (2 Corinthians 5:17) Our old self ceases to exist. It is as though we have been reborn into a new creation that reflects the image of God Himself. This transformation initiates our journey toward embracing God's Kingdom mindset, which involves renewing our minds through the study and application of His Word. As we grow in our faith, our lives should increasingly reflect the character of Jesus Christ, so that when others look at us, they see glimpses of His love, compassion, and righteousness. **We literally become the mouth, hands and feet of Jesus in the world.**

"God may take you through some things to bring you to something new."

—*Natalie Masucci*

Nothing is ever wasted in God's economy. Even the times of preparation are not in vain, for God's timing is always perfect (2 Peter 3:8). It is never too late to pursue your purpose and fulfil God's plan for your life, regardless of your age or circumstances. <u>Your mindset is one of the few things that you have control over. Focus on the aspects of life that you can control, such as your thoughts, words, actions, reactions, decisions, efforts, emotions, and self-care.</u>

In the realm of research, there are exciting developments taking place at Brown University, such as the BrainGate project. BrainGate is a brain-computer interface that enables individuals who have lost their ability to move and communicate to translate their thoughts into action. Additionally, inspiring research in psychiatry at Brown University has shown that targeted electrical stimulation in specific areas of the brain can alleviate symptoms of obsessive-compulsive disorder. These advancements remind us that what once seemed unimaginable is now becoming a reality, and it challenges us to reconsider what might be possible in the future.[133] Nothing is impossible with God (Luke 1:37).

---

[133] *Impact 2018*, p.29

Science is proving the biblical connection between our thoughts and the world around us. Our thoughts are powerful; they create the world we live in. As we have learned, how we think positive or negative determines our mindset and our outcome in life.

God is the master of using faith to give substance to things. This is how He created the entire universe. He spoke it into *"being so that things which are seen were not made of things which do appear"* (Hebrews 11:3). Now, God has graciously given us His Word so that we can utilize it just as He does. <u>When we store God's Word in our hearts and speak it out, it becomes more than mere words. It takes on substance and carries creative power. It has the ability to transform us and bring about changes in our circumstances.</u>

It is crucial that we actively listen to and follow God's instructions, adopting His kingdom mindset in every aspect of our lives. We bear the responsibility for the outcomes we experience. Ultimately, when we stand before God, we will be held accountable (Matthew 12:36). We will give an account of how we responded to Jesus, our words, and what we did with the teachings found within the bible. Did we embrace and apply them, allowing them to reshape our mindset and lead us towards the successful life that God has planned for us? Or did we delay or neglect their application? Did we compromise and live a life less than what God planned for us? In Psalm 32:8, God tells us *"I will instruct you and teach you in the way which you should go; I will counsel you with my eye upon you."* God's mindset is His proven success strategy.

> **"If you desire to make a difference in the world, you must be different from the world."**
> *—Elaine S. Dalton*

Are there dreams that God has placed in your heart, dreams that you may have buried and given up on? I want to encourage you to stir them back up. You have the power to awaken those dreams through your words and your mindset. Embrace God's Kingdom mindset and speak to those dreams in faith. In the book of Ezekiel in the Old Testament, God instructed the prophet Ezekiel to speak to the dry bones, representing dead dreams, using the Word of God. Ezekiel obeyed, and God brought those bones to life, forming a vast army. I encourage you to speak to the dry bones or dead areas in your own life, using the Word of God. This can be done by declaring positive faith statements aligned with God's Word. When you do so, I firmly believe that God will also bring life to the areas that seem dead in your life. Just as Jesus left the grave behind and rose from the dead, He can resurrect your dead dreams. He can restore your marriage, revive your business, provide the house you desire, bless you with the child you've always longed for, or grant you the education you seek. God is capable of resurrecting your dormant dreams. If He did it for Ezekiel, He will do it for you and me as well.

When we embrace God's Kingdom mindset, the possibilities become endless! Jesus willingly chose surrender. He surrendered His own plans and agenda to embrace God's will. <u>Our choices play a significant role in this process. I encourage you to use your free will to choose God's will for your life.</u>

I believe that I am speaking to individuals who are destined to solve problems, create new innovations, break records, make history, and change the world. It is not by chance that you have come across this book. It has always been part of God's plan for you. He wants to encourage you not to give up. God desires for you to keep moving forward, to continue trusting Him, and to strive for growth and learning. Your best days are still ahead of you (Job 8:7). It is never too late, and you are never too old. You haven't made too many mistakes or wasted too much time. God specializes in the impossible. The impossible is His norm. God can redeem the time you feel you've lost (Ephesians 5:16). He is not limited by stock markets, medical reports, or the world economy. Take the lessons you've learned from this book and reignite the fire of your dreams. I prophesy that a fire will be ignited within you, a fire that comes from God and cannot be extinguished (Exodus 24:17 & Luke 3:16). You will embrace a renewed identity, faith, and confidence. This fire, ignited by God, will propel you to fulfil your God-given destiny and bring glory to the Father. <u>This has always been His plan from the very beginning.</u> God has revealed His mindset to you and me to assist us and empower us on this journey.

Today could mark the beginning of a new chapter in your life. Will you see it as just another day, or will you see it as the start of a new journey? Today could be the day when you embrace God's agenda for your life by adopting His Kingdom mindset. It's time to discard the distorted perspective of a fixed mindset and view your life through the lens of God's plan. God desires for you and me to experience a better and abundant life, the very best life He has designed for us. While we may not always understand how God's plan will unfold, we can have unwavering confidence that He is orchestrating everything for our good. God initiated this journey of discovery in our lives, and He has a steadfast plan to bring it to completion. God is a faithful finisher (Philippians 1:6). With His strength and empowerment, we are capable of accomplishing all that He has called us to do. He equips us to fulfil His purpose for our lives.

> **"If we walk with God by using His Kingdom mindset, we will always reach our intended destination which is the successful fulfilment of our life assignment."**
>
> *—Natalie Masucci*

Ant Colony Analogy

One morning, during my prayer time, the Holy Spirit gave me an analogy comparing our brains to an ant colony. Ant colonies are highly organized, with each member having a specific role. Similarly, our minds function in an orderly manner. Depending on the species, ant colonies can consist of thousands or even millions of ants. Within a colony, there are three types of ants: the queen, the female workers, and the males. The queen and males have wings, while the workers do not. The queen is the only ant capable of laying eggs, and her primary responsibility is to ensure the colony's propagation. She holds complete control over the entire colony. By secreting a chemical, she inhibits wing growth and ovary development in the female larvae, resulting in the production of numerous workers. The queen resides within the settlement at all times, protected and cared for by her workers. The only way for a queen to die is through intervention by the worker ants or external factors. When the queen dies, the colony perishes. Ants do not abandon their territory if the queen dies; they remain until their own demise due to old age or external circumstances. The males' role is to mate, after which they typically die shortly thereafter. Worker ants, on the other hand, are female ants responsible for foraging food, constructing the nest, tending to the eggs, larvae, and pupae, as well as feeding and cleaning the queen. Their primary purpose is to protect the queen and the nest from danger. With all these organized chambers and workers within the colony, the queen ant is untouchable. The queen represents the root cause of our deception or dysfunction. <u>The only way to eradicate the root cause of our fixed mindset is through intentional action on our part.</u> This ant analogy helps us understand the importance of finding the root cause (queen) of our fixed mindset and the need for the ongoing renewing of our mind to eliminate the persistent toxic thoughts (worker ants).

In this analogy, the queen represents the fundamental deception or lie that we have believed. It serves as the underlying cause of our weaknesses and limitations in life. The worker ants symbolize the toxic and tormenting thoughts that persistently plague us. They tirelessly carry out their tasks of bombarding our minds, affecting our thinking, actions, and well-being.

"Ants are creatures of little strength, yet they store up their food in the summer." Proverbs 30:24-25[134]

Holy Spirit revealed to me that as we meditate on God's Word and allow it to penetrate our minds and sink into our hearts, thousands of lies and deceptions from Satan, both conscious and unconscious, begin to scatter. It's like ants scrambling out of a colony when it comes under attack. The Word of God confronts and challenges the enemy's lies that have held us back from becoming the individuals God created us to be and from fulfilling our purpose.

We must persist in renewing our minds with the Word of God until we reach the core belief or "Queen Ant" of our deception. Just as the queen ant in an ant colony is larger than the worker ants and possesses great power, the root deception/core belief in our minds, protected by various chambers, also holds significant influence. Core beliefs lead to negative self-talk. They are responsible for reproducing toxic and limiting thoughts continuously. This root cause is concealed behind walls and shielded from discovery, as the enemy does not want us to find it.

We are thankful that the Word of God is sharper than any two-edged sword, capable of penetrating through the walls of lies and exposing the root cause of our fixed mindset (Hebrews 4:12). By removing the root, you will remove the fruit. The root is the deception, the trauma, the maladaptive and negative thoughts that cause the fruit which is negative words, bad habits, wrong choices, etc. Once the root cause is uncovered, destroyed and removed, God can bring healing to our hearts and minds, making us whole again (Psalm 147:3).

Destroying an ant colony can be a challenging task. I have personally experienced an ant problem in Nobleton, where I reside. The number of ants was overwhelming. Even when using ant bomb products and directing them into the heart of an anthill, it did not destroy the colony. The worker ants simply relocated the queen a few feet away and started rebuilding. My son, Thomas, tried various methods to eradicate the anthills on our property, including pouring hot boiling water, gasoline, bleach, ant spray, and ant bombs. However, none of these efforts proved successful. The ants would just move a short distance away and rebuild the colony. It became clear that a single blast or bomb would not work. Continuous and ongoing action was necessary to destroy the colony, as the ants tenaciously held on for dear life. Newton's first law of motion states that an object in motion will continue to move unless acted upon by an external force. Similarly, if we allow our minds to be filled with false beliefs in the form of toxic

---

[134] *Proverbs 30:24-25*-NIV

thoughts, we are likely to continue believing them. It requires effort and energy to halt these false beliefs in their tracks. This is why the ongoing process of renewing our minds is crucial (Romans 12:2).

"I trained 4 whole years to run 9 seconds. Some people don't see results in 2 months and give up."
—Usian Bolt

Our failure to destroy the ant colony stemmed from attempting to destroy the entire colony when all we needed to do was flush out and eliminate the queen.

The root cause of emotional dysfunction may be early childhood trauma, child neglect, traumatic brain injury, fear, and unforgiveness. The persistent worker ants in the colony symbolize the tormenting and toxic thoughts that plague us. Renewing our minds is a gradual process that requires ongoing effort in order to eradicate the root cause of our fixed mindset, destructive habits, and automatic negative thoughts. Even after addressing the root cause, residual toxic thoughts may remain. <u>By changing our thoughts or "worker ants" and challenging their validity and alignment with the Word of God, we can ultimately destroy the root cause or queen.</u> Once the queen is eliminated, it is important to replace the deception or lie with the truth found in God's Word. This transformation will bring about a change in our internal self-image.

It is essential to understand that reading this book alone or reciting positive self-talk declarations a few times will not instantly reverse years of ingrained thinking patterns. It requires effort and persistence to renew our minds and adopt God's kingdom mindset. While God promises to assist us, we must also play our part. We are not powerless or helpless. When we speak the Word of God, we have the backing of heaven's power (Hebrews 6:18-20). Endurance is what will carry us through to the end of our race and lead us to receive our reward from God.

Let's recall how the brain functions. It consists of billions of neurons that fire with each thought we have. These neurons form connections and patterns over time. At this point, you may have become entrenched in patterns of thought that need to be changed in order to transform your life.

Within your brain, there is a small, seahorse-shaped structure known as the hippocampus. This region of the brain plays a role in regulating emotions and motivation. The hippocampus contains abundant granule cells, which are among the few types of neurons that the brain can generate more of. The formation of new neurons is referred to as **Neurogenesis.** Neuroplasticity describes how these neurons connect with each other, forming new pathways. Despite its small size, the hippocampus is a bustling hub of activity.

In January 2017, researchers at the University of Alabama at Birmingham made a significant discovery. They found that the brain has the ability to generate fresh neurons that integrate themselves into existing neural circuits, resulting in stronger and more robust synaptic connections. As these new connections are formed, the old neurons eventually die off. This finding, as referenced by Christopher Bergland, highlights the fact that relying solely on the passage of time is insufficient for breaking down established connections in the brain. Active effort is required to retrain the mind and establish new connections. This process is known as renewing the mind, and it is an ongoing endeavour.

In this realization, we discover a source of great hope. To progress and embark on something new and different, to move forward in life, we must engage in the continual renewal of our minds. This renewal involves embracing God's kingdom mindset.[135]

God's Word or His success criteria is the method God uses to change us. Through God's mindset, we learn how to make those new healthy connections by identifying our thought patterns and resisting and replacing those not of God.

This book has provided you with the knowledge and tools to rewire your mind and transition to God's kingdom mindset. Within each of us, there exists an invisible switch in the brain that can eliminate low self-esteem, toxic thoughts, destructive habits, identity issues, and a fixed mindset. Through a form of neuro-coaching that involves controlling your thoughts and renewing your mind with the Word of God, you can successfully adopt and operate in God's kingdom mindset.

When you become aware of a toxic thought or habit, the physical structure in your brain that holds the associated memory, thought, or habit weakens and becomes more adaptable. Once it enters your conscious awareness, you can begin to break it down and build a new, healthy network through directed neuroplasticity; this process takes approximately 63 days.[136]

As an educator, I can attest to the fact that it takes a long time to build new positive habits and modify student behaviour. As a wife, I have been trying to get my husband Nino to put his clothes away for years.

---

[135] Bergland, Christopher. *"How Do Neuroplasticity and Neurogenesis Rewire Your Brain."*-Psychology Today, 6 Feb. 2017.
[136] Dr. C. Leaf-*Instagram post.* October 10.

The key to living a successful life with God is not achieving perfection at all times. Instead, it involves having His mindset and being quick to repent, change, forgive ourselves and others, and continue moving forward. The secret lies in endurance through faith rather than striving for perfection.

"Winning means you're willing to go longer, work harder, and give more than anyone else."
—Vince Lombardi

In Romans 12:2, the apostle Paul writes, "*Do not conform to the pattern of this world, but be transformed by the renewing of your mind.*"
You participate in the process of renewal, but it is God who brings about transformation. <u>It is a partnership between you and God.</u> When we talk about being "transformed," it means that there is an external force at work changing us from within. While it is your responsibility to take captive your thoughts, ultimately, it is only God who can truly change our minds. He has the power to turn our "I can't do this" into "I can do all things through Christ who strengthens me" (Philippians 4:13). As we faithfully renew our minds using God's success strategies, such as positive self-talk, thought exchange, word therapy, positive faith declarations, and praise, among others...

God, in turn, remains faithful to transform our minds to resemble that of Jesus more and more (2 Corinthians 3:18). We begin to adopt His kingdom mindset and principles, and we operate the way we were originally designed to.

None of us truly knows our full potential until we step out and try. You are capable of achieving more than you may think. So, go ahead and take action! You will discover that you'll be glad you did.[137]

Through this book, I believe that God is gently nudging you forward with love. He desires and needs you to step outside of yourself, utilizing the strategies presented in His mindset, and assess whether unhealthy habits and toxic thoughts have taken root in your life. <u>God wants to work in partnership with you.</u>

Stress, the pandemic, life's burdens, past traumas, insecurities, negative influences and unforgiveness can lead us to engage in excessive eating, drinking, watching, scrolling, working, indulging, and reacting. As we have witnessed, these are tactics employed by the

---

[137] Bergland, Christopher. *"How Do Neuroplasticity and Neurogenesis Rewire Your Brain."*-Psychology Today, 6 Feb. 2017.

enemy to distract us, steal from us and ultimately destroy us. The enemy's agenda is to prevent you from fulfilling your purpose. While we cannot eliminate thoughts, temptations, anxiety, tests, and trials in life, <u>we can change our response to them.</u>

In order to live a life of maximum impact and fulfil your purpose, it becomes necessary for you to step outside of yourself, using MPA (or God's eternal perspective), and identify the unhealthy habits and toxic thought patterns that have taken root in your life. Once identified, you must be resolute and committed to intentionally removing them. However, as we have learned, mere suppression or removal is insufficient. Toxic thoughts and bad habits must be replaced with God's positive faith declarations and positive habits based on His success criteria (the Bible). It requires effort and deliberate ongoing practice to ensure success. **God wants you to regain control of your mind, which He created in His image and likeness.** We possess the mind of Christ. We regain control by renewing our minds with the Word of God and adopting God's Kingdom mindset, which allows us to function as God intended. We are empowered to overcome every obstacle and expose every scheme or deception on our journey to fulfil our life's assignment.

God's kingdom mindset encompasses renewing our minds and creating new positive habits that will empower us to pursue our purpose. Breaking bad habits is a process. The best way to overcome bad habits is to replace them with good ones. Take up a healthy hobby or a positive interest. Try gardening, reading, photography, cooking, music, art, dance, lego, models, puzzles, knitting, sewing, exercising etc. Hobbies for adults are a powerful method to replace bad habits and even addictions because they keep your mind and hands occupied with constructive and positive things. Then when you feel tempted to succumb to a bad habit do your hobby instead. There are many benefits of adult hobbies. They can anchor us back to our most positive childhood memories. They remind us that life doesn't always have to be so serious. Hobbies promote mental relaxation. They can divert your focus away from negative thoughts. Hobbies can reduce our blood pressure and improve our mental health. Hobbies allow us to feel successful and competent in a world that can feel very much outside our control.[138]

<u>God's mindset reminds us that we are valuable, loved, and never alone.</u> It assures us that each day is precious, presenting us with the gift and opportunity to make the most of the day ahead and be our best selves. Do not waste any more time with the wrong mindset and toxic

---

[138] 5 Reasons why you should revisit your childhood hobby as an adult by: L'Oreal Thompson Paynton Feb 25, 2023 Fortune Well-<u>fortune.com</u>

thoughts that are holding you back. Embracing God's mindset will propel you to excel and take you to heights you never imagined possible.

"What I learned is that God is good, He is faithful, and if you trust Him, He will set a place for you at a table you never dreamed possible."
—Dr. Monica V. Masucci

You only get one life to live. Don't live it to please other people. Don't sacrifice what you believe in and want. Don't compromise or make excuses. Chase your dreams. Face your fears. Take risks and adventures. Spend time with people you love and those who inspire you. Live your life for God. Choose God's mindset and accomplish your God-given purpose. <u>When you let God be the author of your life's story, you are always in for a happy ending.</u>

Your victorious and bright future begins today! Adopt God's Kingdom mindset and start running your race with Him.

Reading this book is a pivotal moment in your life. It marks a moment of destiny. What you think, say, and do following this moment will shape your future. God desires your success. He wants you to embrace His mindset and criteria for success, enabling you to fulfil your life's purpose and live a blessed and victorious life. God longs for you to run this race called life with His mindset and emerge as the victor. Today, make a decision that aligns with your destiny. Apply the lessons you have learned, fulfil your purpose, make this world a better place and bring honour to the Father.

"Life is like a camera, focus on the good, develop from the negative, and if things don't work out, take another shot."
— Natalie Masucci

Adopt a Kingdom mindset, take back your position of royalty and authority to be part of a kingdom movement in the world. You and I were born for such a time as this. Be empowered by God's kingdom mindset to chase after the dreams and goals that He placed in your heart. The world is waiting for us to rise up (Romans 8:19)!

If not you, then who? If not now, then when? (2 Corinthians 6:2). I leave you with the words of Jesus the Master Teacher: 'Very truly I tell you, whoever believes in me will do the works I have been doing, and they will do even greater things than these because I am going to the Father. And I will do whatever you ask in my name, so that the Father may be glorified in the Son' (John 14:12-14).

<u>Here are some highlights of a Kingdom mindset:</u>
1. **Embrace Your Royalty:** Recognize that as a child of God, you are part of a royal priesthood (1 Peter 2:9). Embrace your position of authority and dignity.
2. **Divine Purpose:** Understand that you were created for a specific purpose and that your dreams and goals are God-given. Seek to fulfill that purpose with passion and dedication.
3. **Heavenly Perspective:** Shift your focus from worldly success to heavenly impact. A Kingdom mindset values eternal rewards over temporary gains.
4. **Unity and Collaboration:** Recognize that the Kingdom of God is not a solo endeavor. Collaborate with fellow believers to advance the common mission of spreading love, grace, and the message of salvation.
5. **Faith and Boldness:** Trust in God's promises and have the boldness to step out in faith. A Kingdom mindset involves taking risks and believing that God is with you.
6. **Prayer and Seeking God's Will:** Regularly seek God's guidance through prayer and meditation on His Word. Let His wisdom guide your decisions and actions.
7. **Hope and Endurance:** Embrace hope, even in challenging times. Understand that God's Kingdom is unshakable, and your perseverance in faith will lead to victory.

Bibliography

"Catholic Teacher Magazine-OECTA." Feb/March 2020.

"The Believers' Voice of Victory Magazine." Kenneth Copeland Ministries.

Ackerley, Sarah and Deak, M JoAnn. *Your Fantastic Elastic Brain: Stretch It, Shape It.* Scholastic, 2017.

Anderson, Neil. T. *The Bondage Breaker.* Harvest House, 2020/2019.

Bergland, Christopher. *How Do Neuroplasticity and Neurogenesis Rewire Your Brain.* Psychology Today, Feb 6, 2017.

Bible-Scripture References

Brown Alumni Magazine-IMPACT. Brown 2018 & 2020 Edition.

Couros, George. *The Innovator's Mindset.* Dave Burgess Consulting Inc., 2015.

Despault, Michelle. "Cultivating a Growth Mindset Article p16-17." *Catholic Teacher Magazine* (2020): 16-17.

Devotionals Daily newsletter@e.faithgateway.com (mailto:[newsletter@e.faithgateway.com])

Dweck, Carol S. *Mindset: The New Psychology of Success: How We Can Learn to Fulfil Our Potential.* Ballantine Books, 2008.

Hagin, Craig W. *"Don't Be Stupid: A Prodigal Story."* 2016, Faith Library Publications.

James W. Goll. *"Declare a 'No Competition Zone'.* The Elijah List email, February 5, 2023.

Leaf, Caroline. *Switch on Your Brain.* Baker Books, 2013.

Morin, A. (2020, January 28). *Top 10 Fears That Hold People Back in Life.* Retrieved from Psychology Today; https://www.psychologytoday.com/intl/blog/what-mentally-strong-people-dont-do/202001/top-10-fears-hold-people-back-in-life

Payton, L'Oreal Thompson. "Health Habits of Hobbies | Fortune Well." *Fortune Well*, Fortune, 25 Feb. 2023, https://fortune.com/well/2023/02/25/health-benefits-of-hobbies/.

Savelle, Terri Foy. *Dream it. Pin it. Live it.: Make Vision Boards Work for You.* Terri Savelle Foy Ministries, 2015.

The Word of Faith Magazine. Hagin, Kenneth Ministries.

About The Author

Natalie is the founder of **EmPowered Word Ministries.** She is an author, teacher, a conference speaker and empowerment coach to many.

Natalie's mission is to equip and empower all people (young and old) to remove any hindrances standing in the way of them fulfilling their life assignment, and living the abundant and victorious life God has for them.

Natalie and her husband Nino have been married since 1986 and are the proud parents of their son Thomas and daughter Monica. They live in Nobleton, Ontario, Canada.

Follow Us On

Instagram
@empoweredwordministries

Facebook
Empowered Word Ministries

Linkedin
Natalina (Natalie) Masucci
Empowered Word Ministries

Visit our website!

www.empoweredwordministries.ca
for prayer requests and to download powerful resources designed to help you advance in every area of your life!

PROVERBS 29:25
"I will not allow the opinions of man to bring me to a place of anxiety, fear, or depression. My faith is in the Lord, my trust is in the Lord. He will not fail me, or put me to shame."

KINGDOM MINDSET